D0771034

THE
HONORED
DEAD

The Honor Series
by Robert N. Macomber

At the Edge of Honor
Point of Honor
Honorable Mention
A Dishonorable Few
An Affair of Honor
A Different Kind of Honor

THE
HONORED
DEAD

A Novel of
Lt. Cmdr. Peter Wake, U.S.N.
in French Indochina, 1883
(seventh in the Honor Series)

Robert N. Macomber

Pineapple Press, Inc.
Sarasota, Florida

Inquiries should be addressed to:

Pineapple Press, Inc.
P.O. Box 3889
Sarasota, Florida 34230
www.pineapplepress.com

Library of Congress Cataloging-in-Publication Data

Macomber, Robert N., 1953-
The honored dead : a novel of Lt. Cmdr. Peter Wake, U.S.N. in French
Indochina, 1883 / Robert N. Macomber. -- 1st ed.
    p. cm. -- (The honor series)
ISBN 978-1-56164-438-4 (alk. paper)
1. Wake, Peter (Fictitious character)--Fiction. 2. United States. Navy--
Officers--Fiction. 3. United States--History, Naval--19th century--Fiction. 4.
Americans--Indochina--Fiction. I. Title.
PS3613.A28H67 2009
813'.6--dc22
                                                          2008033713

First Edition
10 9 8 7 6 5 4 3 2 1

Design by Shé Hicks
Printed in the United States of America

This novel is dedicated
to the folks who got me there in one piece—

Captain Marco San Giacomo
of the
M/V *Silver Cloud*

through two cyclones,
the fabled lands of Indonesia, Malaysia, and Singapore,
then across the South China Sea
into Vietnam . . .

Purser Neville Joseph
of the riverboat
Tonle Pandaw

up the River of Nine Dragons,
into the heart of Cambodia . . .

Prologue

An extraordinary turn of events has recently occurred with the Honor Series, one I am pleased to report should intrigue both longtime and newer readers of Peter Wake's adventurous life. It happened seventeen months ago, on a sweltering August afternoon in Key West, when the executor of a will was cataloguing the possessions of one Agnes Whitehall, who had died a month earlier at the considerable age of ninety-seven.

Up in the attic of Agnes' old home on Peacon Lane, the executor discovered a scarred seaman's trunk. The huge thing was stoutly built of a strange, amber-colored wood, framed by heavy iron straps ornately engraved with flourishes and secured by an ancient-looking iron padlock. A barely legible name stenciled in white paint was centered on the gouged and rust-stained lid.

SEAN WAKE
Rear Admiral
United States Navy

The executor, Tom Doherty, a twenty-something neighbor who had befriended Ms. Whitehall the previous year, debated what to do. Should he open the trunk, even though Agnes' name wasn't on it? He'd never heard her mention the name Sean Wake. There was no key. He'd have to smash the lock open with a hammer. Or should he just drag the damn thing down to the ground floor and put it with her other worn-out stuff in the trash pile? Agnes had no relatives left. The decision was Tom's.

The trunk was heavy when he tried to shove it. Clearly, it wasn't worth the hassle of moving, or even trying to open. Tom sat down on the trunk for a moment, pondering whether he should just leave it there and let the future buyer of the place deal with it. He decided to hell with it—he would. It was precisely at that point that one of those odd twists of fate intervened, an outwardly inconsequential act that engendered a significant outcome. Tom walked toward the attic ladder, but glanced back at his nemesis. What he saw made him return and examine the trunk far more carefully.

It seems the place where he'd been sitting had smeared away layers of grime, exposing a strange Oriental motif. He quickly brushed away the rest of the filth and discovered a design covering the entire lid. It was an undulating yellow dragon with large claws and wicked-looking fangs. Just beyond the tail was a ship, an old warship. On the aft mast of the ship was a flag with large vertical bars of blue, white, and red, which reminded Tom of a picture he'd seen in his high school history book. A French flag. There was another banner near the dragon's head—a yellow square with three Chinese symbols in red, the whole thing fringed with blue. He'd never seen anything like that flag. Next to it were Chinese characters forming a message of some sort, as if they came out of the dragon's mouth. A greeting? A warning?

Well, my friends, human nature is such that even the cynical Tom Dohertys of our world occasionally succumb to curiosity. He went next door to his house and returned with a large hammer. Upon smashing the lock and opening the lid, Tom found at least ten cardstock boxes inside, their seams split open by time. Laid atop them was a tarnished silver and gold ceremonial sword, attached to a fancy sash belt.

On the hilt of the sword was an engraving.

> *To Rear Admiral Peter Wake, U.S.N.,*
> *With the greatest appreciation,*
> *from President Theodore Roosevelt, 1907*

Well, *that* certainly got his attention. Tom carefully examined the uppermost of the fragile boxes. There was only a single line of words across the center of the top page, which was yellowed and brittle. The words were in a peculiar kind of font— uneven, with some letters missing their curlicues. A typewriter had printed it, he realized.

This was 2007, and Tom had never seen a typewriter, but he remembered his father talking about them. The faded ink was still readable enough to understand, and what it said made him forget the sweat soaking his shirt and dripping down his face. He felt a rush of adrenaline—the words were frightening and beckoning at the same time.

~The Honored Dead~

At the bottom of the page was another line. Tom read it aloud, questioning its connection with the name on the lid and the sword. Brother, son, father?

by
Commander Peter Wake, U.S.N.
26 June 1890

By then, of course, Tom Doherty was completely hooked. For the next two days he called in sick from work and read through that first pile of papers, spellbound by the story within—a mission to Southeast Asia in 1883. On the third day, he went to the Key West Public Library over on Fleming Street and showed them the pile of papers. Forty-eight hours later, a naval historian in Washington, D.C., was notified.

Things began to happen quickly, for what Tom Doherty had discovered was nothing less than Peter Wake's personal account of an inimitable life in the shadowy world of naval intelligence, with an insider's view of momentous events. But it was more than just a view, for Wake had *influenced* history during those decades when America transformed from a continental nation into a global power. But there was more.

Loose in the bottom of the trunk was a handwritten note from Wake, dated June 26, 1908, the year following his retirement from the navy, explaining that then-Commander Wake had decided in 1890 to begin recording his exploits for his son and future descendants. He did this because the nature of his naval intelligence work from 1881 onward was secretive and few knew of his efforts. Wake wanted his son, Sean, who had just graduated from the U.S. Naval Academy in 1890, and others to know what he had done in his life—not just through the boring and often obscure official language of a bureaucratic report hidden away in some archive, but from the special private insights of a participant in history.

He was certainly successful in that endeavor. Peter Wake's account had a novelist's engaging view of the people, places, and events he encountered in Asia. And we are fortunate this was not his only story. There were several boxes of yellowed pages. The others were written throughout the 1890s and early 1900s.

The dates on the letter and the pile of papers are noteworthy also. Peter Wake completed that first story, *The Honored Dead,* on his fifty-first birthday in 1890, ironically, the same day his son graduated from the Naval Academy. The handwritten letter was written on his sixty-ninth birthday in 1908, after he finished all the stories and retired from his naval career.

What of the sword? Both the date and the donor are very interesting. It was right after President Roosevelt was awarded the Nobel Peace Prize for ending the war between Russia and Japan—something Peter Wake had a lot to do with. One of the other boxes in the trunk held the explanation of how it really happened—but that's another story.

I've speculated about Agnes Whitehall, several questions rising in my mind. Who was she? How did she end up with the trunk? What was her relationship to Peter Wake's son, Sean? Or to Peter Wake himself? She was born in 1910, when Sean was forty-three and Peter was seventy-one. Sean didn't make rear admiral (his rank on the trunk) until 1919. Did Agnes even know the contents of that trunk? I hope someday to know the answers to these questions. Rest assured that I'm searching for them.

And the message in Chinese letters on the trunk's lid? Photographs were taken of the design and characters and sent to the university at Hué, the old imperial capital of Vietnam, where they were examined by historians. The translation into English that came back only added to the mystery surrounding Wake and his time in French Indochina.

For my friend Peter, who saw the
future and warned me, without success.
Hiep Hoa,
Celestial King, Son of Heaven, and Emperor of Annam,
Tonkin, and
Cochin. Sixth of the Nguyen Dynasty. Year of
the Middle Kingdom, 4519

The university experts explained that the imperial court of Vietnam used the Confucian calendar of imperial China—hence the year 4519 in the inscription, which meant nothing to me. Then they translated the text into the commonly used Gregorian calendar for me. It ended up being October 1883. That was a date of great consequence once I'd read about Peter Wake's mission to Indochina.

Worthy of note are the maps he included in the story. I do not know how Wake became acquainted with the well-known French geographer and anarchist Élisée Reclus, but they evidently met sometime in the 1880s. It is possible, if not probable, that Reclus was part of Wake's motley assortment of sources around the world that he relied upon for his intelligence work. At any rate, he must have used some of Reclus' brilliant maps of Condore, Touran, and Hué as the basis for his personal sketch maps found in this tale.

I have kept Peter Wake's chronicle as untouched as possible, including misspellings of people and places. Please be aware that Wake was a product of his time and some of his descriptions would be politically incorrect now. But still, his narrative shows a remarkable tolerance and empathy for the various cultures of the world with whom he came into contact. His political and naval opinions, and predictions, show considerable perceptive ability, quite a useful asset in the field of naval intelligence.

Also, students of Asian languages will notice the absence of the official *Quôc Ngü* diacritical accent marks for the Vietnamese words in this book. Peter Wake did not use them and I have echoed that decision in order to make the words more understandable for the average Western reader.

At the end of this book, I've included some notes on information gleaned while researching this project. These notes are arranged by chapter to assist the reader in understanding the people, places, and events Wake saw as his mission unfolded in bizarre ways.

So, after six previous novels about Wake have already garnered awards and captivated readers around the world, you will learn of his 1883 journey into the heart of French Indochina directly from the man himself, in what novelists call "first person."

Like Tom Doherty on that sweltering day down in Key West, I think you too will be fascinated by this rare tale of an American overcoming adversity in far-away Southeast Asia—eighty years before it became a vivid, and tragic, part of our own history. I wish certain people in Washington had read it in 1963.

—Robert N. Macomber
Serenity Bungalow
Matlacha Island
Florida

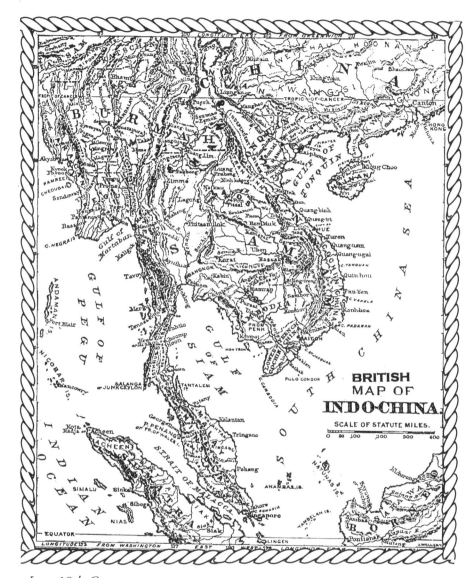

Late 19th Century

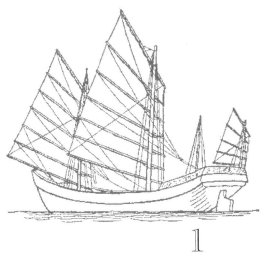

1

The Riverboat

Sunday, the 22nd day of April, 1883

Latitude 10 Degrees, Twenty Minutes, North
Longitude 106 Degrees, Thirty Minutes, East

on the Song Cuu Long—
River of the Nine Dragons
(known in the West as the Mekong River)
downstream of Mytho, Cochin
French Indo-China

When I finally reached the steamboat on the Mekong River, the first words I heard weren't in some exotic Oriental tongue, but rapid-fire French, afterward repeated in very good English.

"We are honored by your august presence, sir, and humbly request you grant us the considerable favor of knowing how we may honorably address you." This came from an impeccably uni-formed Asian of advanced age who stood on the main deck. Unlike me, he was apparently not encumbered the least bit by the afternoon's mind-numbing heat and humidity.

Naturally—this being Indo-China—the penalty for a wrong answer would be my death.

Oh yes, I realize my reaction seems exaggerated to Western sensibilities. You, my dear and gentle reader, studying this narra-tive from the comfort of modern, late nineteenth-century America, might be excused for thinking the man's question a romantic gesture of genuine hospitality. I, however, knew the man wasn't being romantic or hospitable.

The revolver held at the ready behind his back dispelled *that* notion.

No, this was something far different from one of the Alexandre Dumas novels that are so popular these days. There is no romance on the Mekong River. It is a tepid watercourse, wind-ing its way through a dense green morass, throughout which the Orientals live and die in slow-motion inevitability. The whole place is permeated by cloying indolence—the very opposite of America and Europe.

After a month of traveling in the region just to get to that fetid brown mess of a stream, I understood quite well that the man's little speech was a demand for me to explain *exactly* who the hell I was and why the hell I was getting on his vessel—all softly couched in the polite style of the East, of course. The tim-ing and style of my immediate reply was crucial.

If I hesitated, or answered incorrectly, and was judged to be a ne'er-do-well, that pistol would be discharged into my face. No further discussion. There were pirates on this river. My skin color and dress were no guarantee of innocence—some of the worst of them were French renegades.

Suddenly, I realized how I must appear, which was, in fact, pretty much like a French renegade. Disheveled after the hot, wet, and muddy two-day cart journey from Saigon to Mytho, then soaked during the final five-hundred-yard row to the steamer in a small dugout sampan, I felt anything but "august" as I hauled myself up the ladder and boarded the *Tonle Queen*. Actually, I felt pretty damn exhausted and short-tempered. But one's image had to be kept up in Asia, especially when facing a flinty-eyed man holding a pistol, a man who looked like he'd used it before. So I stood as tall and professional as I could before calmly replying.

"I am Lieutenant Commander Peter Wake of the United States Navy. The priest ashore said he sent a man to reserve passage for both myself and my assistant. And who, sir, might you be?"

"Ah, yes, our esteemed *American* guest. I am Hau, the chief steward. We have been expecting you, Commander," he said, allowing a short pause for additional scrutiny of this most unusual passenger—Americans were little known or seen on the river. Presumably I passed muster, for he smiled and went on. "Your cabin is ready, sir. My staff and I will be privileged to make your journey upriver as comfortable for you as possible."

Now that he was certain of my identity and purpose, the diminutive Hau, resplendent in the garnet and gold livery of the Indo-China Steamship Company, positively glowed in welcome as I peeled off my dripping blue uniform half-coat and squeezed out a pint of the Mekong. The pistol, one of those little Belgian contrivances, useless for anything past fifteen feet but accurate enough when within three feet of *my face*, was stealthily slipped into a pocket under his tunic. Both hands folded together as he bowed in respect to me.

Down in the sampan, the ancient who rowed me to the steamer handed up my seabag and valise, both of them half submerged in the tiny boat's filthy bilge water. I shook them vigorously, trying to shed the slimy coating, then finally noticed that Hau was still bowing repeatedly, looking expectant. Evidently more was needed on my part, so I used the few words in Cochinese I knew to say thank you, referring to the man as an older brother, a sign of friendship and respect.

"Cam on, anh."

Well, that certainly did the trick for cementing our friendship. I was rewarded with a huge beaming grin and three more bows, followed by a magnificent swirling flourish of the hand. This from a man who seconds earlier was about to kill me. Such is the Orient.

"You speak our language very well, Commander! I see that you are a philosopher as well as a warrior. I am now doubly honored to have you as our guest."

I absentmindedly offered another *"Cam on,"* which elicited another round of bowing and profuse compliments. Hau ended them with "Captain MacTaggert has requested the honor of your attendance at his table this evening, Commander, and would be greatly pleased if you would accept."

I thought that might happen—visiting naval officers are expected to pay respects to the ship's captain by sitting at his table and tolerating his ego, but after my trek and the attendant difficulties, I just wasn't in the proper frame of mind to endure that tribulation. Shrugging my shoulders with exaggerated sadness, I said. "Why yes, it would indeed be an honor to dine with Captain MacTaggert. I would like to accept, but as you can see, my clothing is in terrible condition. So I fear I must decline. My appearance is just not suitable for dining with the captain. Perhaps another time."

Hau made a tsk-tsking sound, pulled out an enormous gold-plated pocket watch, then waved a hand dismissively. "Not to worry, Commander! It is now one o'clock in the day. I will personally ensure that a hot bath is drawn for your refreshment, and that your uniforms are laundered, pressed, and ready by thirty minutes after five o'clock in the day. Drinks are at six o'clock in the evening in the bar salon, and dinner is at seven in the evening in the dining room. Plenty of time, sir. My people and I are here to help you. Your every want shall be answered."

The only thing I wanted at that point was six hours of uninterrupted sleep in a real bed, but any further excuse would've been quite bad form. And in that part of the world, form was everything. "I am overwhelmed, Hau, by your generosity and efficiency. Please inform Captain MacTaggert that I will be delighted to see him for drinks at six."

"Very good, sir." Hau stopped abruptly, then frowned. "You will dine with the captain at seven o'clock in the evening, but shall not see him beforehand. That is for you to meet the other passengers. The captain never enters the bar salon before dinner."

His tone shifted to pleasant again. "And now, you will be shown to your cabin, Commander. One of our very best. It is on this deck and has windows facing the bow and the side—good breeze. Thank you, sir, and again, welcome aboard the *Tonle Queen*."

Hau's face crinkled into a smile once more and he gave an unintelligible order to a passing steward, a junior type not nearly as tricked out as his chief, who immediately took up my things and trotted down the steamer's narrow side passageway. At the forward-most cabin on the port side of the main deck, the steward opened the door and stepped inside, flinging aside curtains and unlatching windows to allow light and air into the dark mahogany-paneled room. It contained two bunk bed beds with real mattresses built into the bulkheads, a desk between them, a woven-cane chair, an ink drawing of a Mekong village scene above the desk, and a corner locker for stowage.

I was impressed—it was twice as large as any officer's cabin I'd ever inhabited aboard a warship. The steward displayed the washbasin and towels, the night-bowl under the bunk, and mumbled something in pidgin French—*bain thung go*—about a bathtub being brought in soon. Then he silently padded out, leaving me dripping on a finely varnished teak deck.

Marveling at how my luck had changed for the better in the last five minutes, I allowed myself the first smile in a week. For I'd gone from wandering about a jungle river delta, looking without success for transport upriver to Cambodia, to being installed in new surroundings that were nothing short of luxurious. Yes indeed, it was starting to look like I was not only going to complete the mission I'd been given ten thousand miles earlier, but would do it in some semblance of style as well. Now all I had to do was get my petty officer aide-de-camp out of a feverish sick bed ashore and safely aboard. Once that was accomplished, our assignment could continue. It was a simple mission—deliver a confidential message, check the political lay of the land, and leave. We'd be in and out, then homeward-bound again, in two weeks.

It wasn't long before my meager possessions were unpacked and laid on the bunk for disposition. A week's worth of my dirty laundry lent a noticeable change to the air in the cabin, and I was just about to call for the steward when a faint knocking sounded outside. I opened the door to find two pretty local girls out on the side deck lugging an empty copper bathtub. Inside was a large sponge and jar of powder, evidently soap. Clad in the *ao dai,* the form-fitting beige dress I'd seen on women all over Cochin— which a Frenchman in Saigon had described to me as "revealing nothing but displaying everything"—they cast their eyes downward and gestured that the tub was to be brought inside.

The cabin steward came up behind them, carrying two huge buckets of steaming water suspended on leather thongs from a bamboo pole slung across his shoulders. Being the senior of the group, he made an announcement in some sort of lingo far beyond my powers of comprehension. Then it struck me he was trying to speak French, the assumed language of all Westerners in Indo-China. The words were lost on me, but not the intent. It was time for the bath.

I beckoned the whole entourage to enter. They set up the tub with a practiced minimum of movement, then took away my clothes that needed washing. The trio returned with more hot water, the steward filling the tub, the girls smiling demurely as they sprinkled purple frangipani and white jasmine flowers into the soapy bathwater. The whole effect was quite enchanting, particularly when the girls stifled a giggle as I stretched and sighed aloud in anticipation of soaking away my accumulated stresses and strains. At last, when all was ready to their satisfaction, the steward and girls departed the cabin, bowing and softly uttering, *"Au revoir, Monsieur."*

It took only seconds for the uniform to be shed and for my aching body to submerge into the suds, the muscles reacting with tingling sensations at first, then relaxing into almost dead weight. It was, as I would learn that the Hindus say, *nirvana*—absolutely heavenly. Asia does some things very, very well. Another knock came at the door and the steward's arm reached around, snatching the disheveled uniform and shoes off the chair and away for washing and polishing.

While surveying this grand domain, I thought of my ailing petty officer aide-de-camp and longtime friend, Sean Rork. Calling out in the general direction of Mytho, where he lay in a hospital bed, I said, "Rork, you big Irish rogue. Just wait till you see all this. You'll be able to convalesce quite nicely in *these* surroundings. Yep, quite nicely, indeed."

My smile spread out into a grin.

Hau was true to his word. My uniform underwent a miraculous transformation. I still don't know how he did it, but my rig looked better than it had for the last six months. Before meeting my fellow passengers for drinks, the chief steward and I took a walk around the vessel. Hau explained the various parts of the ship.

The *Tonle Queen* had four decks. The lower deck was a suffocatingly hot dungeon below the waterline inside the black-painted iron hull. It was devoted to the engine, boiler, and coal rooms, along with berthing spaces for the crew and steerage-class passengers. The crew was mainly from Cochin and Cambodia, with a few Burmese working as clerks, stewards, and as the carpenter. The steerage class passengers were mainly Cochinese and

Cambodian as well—middle-class merchants—with a few French drifters stuck down in the hellhole also. Steerage passengers, Asian and European alike, ate their meals and lived through their passage down in that stifling nightmare. In the ensuing days, I would never see them ascending to the upper decks even for air or exercise. Only occasionally did they come up to the main deck. *Tonle Queen* was a European-owned ship, and European class expectations prohibited that sort of thing.

From the main deck up, the steamer was constructed of beautifully crafted teak, ebony, and mahogany. On that main deck were the second-class cabins, of which mine was most definitely the best, since it had both a side window and a forward one that overlooked the small working/cargo area on the foredeck. The dining room for the use of first- and second-class passengers was amidship on the main deck, with large paneled sliding doors on the sides that opened up to provide cross ventilation and panoramic views for the diners. The galley I never did find, assuming it was below, on the cramped lower deck. Another cargo area was at the stern of the main deck, just ahead of the great stern paddle wheel.

Topside, the upper deck was the accommodation area for first-class passengers and the ship's officers. Hau told me apologetically that I, as a distinguished naval officer, would of course normally be in one of the upper-deck cabins, but very unfortunately they were completely booked up by other passengers. Then he leaned over and whispered, "Besides, sir, your cabin is the only one aboard with ventilation from a window overlooking the bow. Better than the captain's!"

At the forward end of the upper deck—above my cabin—was the bar salon, for first- and second-class passengers and ship's officers only. It was filling with people in dinner dress, the conversation buzzing already in French and English. I noted the location and continued the tour by going up to the promenade deck, which lorded it over the whole ship.

This third deck was built apparently as an afterthought,

being erected upon a teak framework two feet above the sloping roof of the upper deck. It stretched from fifty feet aft of the bow to within fifty feet of the great stern wheels. The riverboat's wheelhouse was at the promenade's forward end, after which came an awning-covered area with folding chairs—the French call them *chaises longues*—that leaned back, complete with silk cushions. Two tables holding pastries and juices were stationed at either end to accommodate the passengers' wants. This delightful piazza was the domain of the first class only, but Hau assured me that I was considered one of the elite as well and had *entrée* at anytime.

Overall, the theme of the ship was French colonial elegance, but Hau enlightened me with the fact that even though the *Tonle Queen* and her sister ships plied the waters of the French empire, the Indo-China Shipping Company was in fact owned by Scottish interests. Most of their riverboats were in Burma; this was their first on the Mekong.

"*Très bons entrepreneurs,* the Scots," Hau said in serious awe as he turned to go back to his duties. "The company is to make as much money as possible. Very successful company." Another side comment: "No monkey business allowed, *whatsoever.*"

I, with my regrettably jaded mind, instantly wondered what the company might consider "monkey business." But instead of making some facetious quip, I controlled my humor and merely said, "Thank you," then *"Chao,"* to Hau.

By saying the Cochin word for goodbye—and hello—I received bows, smiles, and handshakes from Hau, who again complimented me on my linguistic ability. Before he left, Hau added quietly, "Europeans usually do not take time to be polite in our language. However, the few Americans I have met are different. You, too, were once colonials under the dominion of a European country. Now you are the country with the most freedom in the world. No other power dominates or intimidates you. We in Asia appreciate that, sir, very much."

There was something in the way he said that which alerted

me. Hau, colonial subject of the French and employee of the British, showed more than just a touch of resentment in the way he pronounced the word "Europeans," most of whom were French in that region of the Orient.

Well, well, I thought. Obviously, not everyone is happy with the political arrangements in Indo-China. The French Revolution's grand concept of fraternity, equality, and liberty among the people came to my mind. It seemed that in the case of the colony of Cochin, those lofty ideals were solely for the French themselves, and not extended to those unfortunate enough to be dominated by them. Listening to Hau, I figured it probably wouldn't be long before the kettle blew.

I am sorry to report that time would prove me sadly right on both accounts.

The conversation over pre-dinner drinks in the rattan, mahogany, and bamboo bar salon was pleasant—to a point. By the light of swaying lanterns, giving off nauseating wisps of oily smoke, I received confirmation that the riverboat was staying at anchor another day in order to load more cargo. I asked Sandingham, the first officer, if a boat could be sent to the French Catholic hospital at Mytho to pick up Sean Rork and bring him to the steamer. Sandingham initially said, "Yes, of course." Then Wallace the engineer gave him a warning look and he backtracked clumsily, explaining that only the captain could authorize that sort of thing.

Sandingham switched subjects by presenting some of my fellow passengers who had also boarded that day. He started with the lone American already aboard, whom Hau, curiously, had never mentioned to me. I say American, but it had been a very long time since Archie Ford had been back home to his native South—thirty-one years to be exact—and he preferred the designation "gentleman of the world." With a dapper style and eyes that missed nothing, Ford was a self-professed former riverboat *bon vivant*—I surmised that meant gambler—who said he'd plied the Mississippi in the forties, then decided that he'd better immediately see what the other side of the world looked like. He didn't elaborate why the sudden departure and, out of civility, I didn't press.

Evidently, Ford usually stayed in the casinos of Hong Kong and Singapore, but currently was bound for Cai Be, just upriver, where he said a plantation man owed him money. The little fellow wasn't an imposing figure, but those eyes looked very dangerous and I formed the immediate resolution to stay out of his way.

Next came the Brits, a diverse selection of imperial backwater types, the men introduced by last name only. Rockford, an elderly gentleman originally from London, suffering from vacant eyes and a slight drool, mumbled a hello in mid-sentence while demanding a whisky from the bar man —"A Scotch whisky with no bloody 'e' in the name. Bloody Frogs get it wrong all the time!" Sandingham described Rockford as a rubber planter from Malacca, bound upriver to visit a planter friend.

The only Western woman was Miss Olivia Marston, evidently a famous Liverpudlian opera diva. I'd never heard of her, but that meant nothing since I wasn't an aficionado of the performing fine arts. Few sailors were. We tended toward more base entertainment, I'm sorry to admit.

Marston was a woman of an indeterminate upper middle age, whose ample girth was corseted into a positively painful-looking hour-glass figure. My back hurt just to see it. She was dressed in blue satin right up to her neck, with a bustle that inadequately balanced an inordinately large bosom. Above a glittering diamond choker and matching earrings—I would assume false due to their size—she had long, blonde hair done up in a black, silk-netted bun that appeared, like her corset, about to burst. Upon the introduction, she held out her hand with disdainful nonchalance for me to kiss. I complied, feeling ridiculous at the time. It all felt a bit like some stage production. I was tempted to bring her down a notch or two by asking why an opera diva was in the middle of nowhere in Indo-China, then thought better of it. No reason to be impolite. Later, I wished I had.

The third and final Briton to whom I was introduced was immediately recognizable from across the salon as a military man, even though clothed in civilian attire. With flamboyantly long, wavy, gray hair, a ramrod-straight back, and a head that swiveled about as if he were still barking out orders on the parade ground, he was every inch a man used to being in charge. Colonel Tredegar Fountjoy, V.C., was twenty years older than me, which put him in his early sixties, and clearly enjoyed showing off his virility. Even in civilian garb he looked able to give a good account of himself in any physical altercation. His eyes were pale blue and large, seldom blinked, and burned into the targeted person. Bombastic side-whiskers and a walrus mustache completed the face, flaring outrageously when he spoke, and giving him the aspect of an enraged—and with those eyes, slightly perplexed—old bull.

Fountjoy brusquely nodded acknowledgment of my presence, inspected my naval uniform, and spun on his heel in a perfect about-face without a further word, heading for Miss Marston's substantial company by way of the bar. Upon his arrival there, the barman had two glasses ready, one of Scotch whisky and the other of arrack rice wine. Fountjoy continued his march toward Marston without loss of step, executing a left-oblique while sipping out of both glasses. Not a drop was lost.

I knew that variety of military man well—the kind that loves a parade ground, as long as the parade is for him. Every navy and army has them. I found myself wondering if he'd gotten that Victoria Cross for being anywhere near shooting. There were no visible scars. Probably got it for killing spear-tossing natives someplace, I decided uncharitably.

As the first officer steered me to some others in the salon, I thought it interesting that not one of the Brits inquired as to *my* reason for being in the middle of French Indo-China, where the

United States had very little contact and no influence. Then I realized that they were fish out of water as well, so to speak. Why were *British* here, in a distant French colony? Traveling through? Settling down? Was there some inter-European competition for colonial gain going on? Singapore and Hong Kong weren't that far away; neither was British-influenced Siam and British-led Sarawak, on Borneo.

Those questions, along with Mr. Hau's candid assessment of the Gallic empire in the East, might have intriguing answers useful to my superiors, and I resolved to try and find out the explanations later. Curiosity is an asset in my line of work, as long as it is controlled and has something to do with national interests. Occasionally mine is. So, leaving the Anglo-Saxon corner of the bar salon, I concentrated on Sandingham's introductions of the other passengers.

All were French except for Señor Paolo Altamonte, a middle-aged, bespectacled Spanish trade representative bound upriver to Cambodia's King Norodom, for a talk about tariffs on silks bound for Manila in the Spanish East Indies. Altamonte constantly glanced around at the French passengers, nervous, as if he were surrounded by an enemy. I realized in a way he was, since he was a foreign government official interloping openly through a French colony, bound for a French protectorate. Actually, I was too, but Europe knew the United States had no designs on Asia. We were traders, not colonizers.

And what of the Spanish? The Spanish Philippines were but a plundered shadow of their past imperial grandeur. There was no real Spanish military power in the area. Were they seeking to build influence, or even real dominance? I wondered for a moment—was the Cambodian king playing the Europeans off against each other in an effort to stay at least nominally independent? And since I was bound upriver to see him as well, was I part of that design? Probably so. It was an old trick the British had mastered against local potentates in the darker reaches of their empire—divide and conquer. Perhaps the natives had learned that lesson as well. During my briefing in Washington, that possibility had come up, but no one there knew the answer for certain.

The French aboard were mostly tired-looking planters and traders, with a few government functionaries mixed in. Maurice Blundell was one of the latter, an economic adviser to King Norodom. Lean, with jet-black hair and a thin moustache, he had the air of ambition about him. I thought the man more than merely a financial hack for the France's puppet-in-charge in Phnom Penh. No, he wasn't some mindless bureaucrat, not with the way he studied the others in the salon, especially the Spaniard. Whatever his true occupation, Blundell was a man worth watching, especially since we were heading for the same place. And the same man.

Meanwhile, amidst the sham frivolity in the room, an international conflict of sorts was brewing at the bar. Rockford, using a condescending tone, was agitating a French planter with a narration of British gutta percha rubber growing, citing an 1877 issue of *The Living Age* magazine and droning on about his own experience as definitive proof that the plantations of British Malaya were producing the very finest quality of rubber in the world. Then he added casually that all of the submarine telegraph cables around the world used it for insulation.

The Frenchman was having none of that and countered in a loud impassioned voice, his accented English making the words sound comical. He exclaimed the fact that the French plantations growing India rubber in Cochin and Annam cultivated a product giving a much greater quantity, as documented in *Manufacturer and Builder* magazine! He raised his finger in the air, said something in French that sounded off-color, and stamped off muttering. Rockford just stood there, staring at his drink, while the onlookers went back to their previous conversations. Just another spat between the masters over who was a better farmer. I found it amusing that they both referred to American magazines to bolster their points.

Meanwhile, near the starboard salon door, Altamonte was engaged in a comparison of Spanish and German wines with a French trader from Saigon. Both agreed that by the time any Continental wine got out to the Far East it was past its prime, if not turned into vinegar completely. That agreement evolved into a general lament about the lack of any local wines, concluding that it was a clear indication of the cultural deficit of the Oriental mind. Oh well, you could only educate them so far.

I saw that Blundell wasn't part of all this inane jabbering. He had moved to the far corner and was sitting in a rattan wingback chair, pensively watching the various discourses while sipping a glass of sherry. Near me, a half-dozen Frenchmen jammed around a low bamboo table and held an intense discussion about lack of work ethic among the locals, congratulating themselves for carrying the white man's burden and bringing the natives into the modern world of agricultural export. Meanwhile, Hau glided in amongst everyone, quietly ignoring the insults about his people, asking if all was well, and departing just as silently minutes later.

All in all, it was a scene of desperation, I thought—Europeans far from their mother countries, engaging in a sad illusion of security in a part of the world where Christians had been slaughtered not so long before. I'd seen it played out in other, less-dangerous areas, with Europeans in the Caribbean, Americans in Panama. A gloomy sight, no matter where it is found.

But the focal point of noise soon shifted to the forward corner of the salon, where Miss Marston was holding court before an entourage consisting of Colonel Fountjoy, Sandingham, and Wallace. Someone there told a joke evidently, and the lady's refined high-pitched laughter and Fountjoy's hearty guffaws counter-pointed into the dominant sounds in the room. Others at the bar turned and watched while Fountjoy slapped Wallace on the back as Sandingham politely chuckled, while in the far corner Blundell's face showed just a touch of sneer in reaction to his English shipmates' humor. Altamonte looked startled at all the commotion, but I was beginning to get the impression he startled easily.

Surveying my fellow passengers, it appeared that the journey upriver to King Norodom's palace at Phnom Penh was going to be an excruciatingly long two weeks. And an insufferable bore. A few minutes later, rum drink in my hand, I was reduced to conversing with a French planter about life on a rubber plantation along the upper river, on the Cambodian border. My French isn't that good, but I learned far more than I needed about the ravages of ants and worms, with the man beginning to warm up for a discourse on horticultural grafting. Just as I was trying to decipher the man's description of tree cutting—his pantomime indicated something else—my evening became decidedly disagreeable.

I was struck hard on the back of the shoulder and turned to see Fountjoy, who announced in a booming voice that "The Yankee, being the junior man in the room by reason of his recent arrival in Indo-China, should stand the drinks for everyone!"

That comment managed to unify the countries represented, eliciting a mild cheer by everyone present. I felt my face go red and stammered something about my low pay regretfully not being equal to the task, which was embarrassingly true.

Fountjoy, leaning toward me, followed up with another quip, his smile constrained, his breath reeking of arrack. "What's this, then? A *lieutenant commander* not able to hold his own in a bar full of gentlemen? I realize the former colonials are rather poor, Commander, but really—one must be able to walk the walk as well as talk the talk, eh? If one wants *respect,* that is."

That got a round of laughter from the assembled dolts, who turned their eyes to me for some kind of witty rebuttal. Was it a regular game at the expense of the new arrivals or directed particularly at me? Or perhaps at my country? Well, I just wasn't clever enough for a witty rebuttal at that moment in time. In fact, my mind unfortunately took the low road and I began imagining how pleasant it would be to wipe that arrogance right off of Fountjoy's face.

Later, when I analyzed it in my bunk, I couldn't come up with a good reason why I let the pompous ass anger me. Pompous asses are a dime a dozen in the world and not worth the trouble of raising one's pulse. Maybe it was my concern over Rork, or my ingrained dislike and distrust of snobs. In any event, at that instant I'd exhausted my limited supply of patience and wasn't in the mood for bullying by anyone.

As the now silent crowd gazed at the two of us, I stepped close to the colonel, smiling for the others, but uttering in a low tone that only Fountjoy could hear, "You know what, Colonel? I'm not one of your Limey underlings that'll put up with dung like that from pretentious fools like you. So I think it's time you regrouped and started over—*right now.*"

Then, to the crowd, I declared, "Well, you certainly have me there, Colonel."

The others chuckled, but Fountjoy didn't take the hint. With his mouth pursed up in a smirk, he said, "Touchy little bugger, aren't you?"

"Bugger" is not a term of endearment among Britons. Particularly when used in his tone of voice. It put me beyond restraint. "Colonel, call me bugger one more time and you'll see just how touchy I can be."

The last was said a bit louder than I had intended. A collective gasp went through the guests. The colonel and I stood there facing each other, neither backing away, waiting for the other to move first. Out of the corner of his eye, I noticed Hau standing by the port side door, looking horrified and ready to bolt for help. Blundell, on the other hand, sat forward in his chair sipping his aperitif, enjoying the show and plainly hoping for it to escalate.

At that point two things happened. First, a Cambodian steward entered the salon and struck a small gong, announcing that dinner would be served in five minutes. And second, Sandingham proclaimed that he, as the first officer, would buy a round of drinks for everyone as a gesture of welcome to Lieutenant Commander Wake.

That broke the impasse. Fountjoy harrumphed, executed a parade ground left-wheel, and strutted over to the lady of the salon, who tittered an idiotic comment about cheeky upstarts not knowing anything of social manners. Among the French, conversation quickly included the phrase *"l'Anglais soûl et l'Americain barbare."* I caught that plainly—the drunken Englishman and barbaric American.

I felt my face flush with embarrassment. Blundell's eyes met mine. He smiled and nodded, a noncommittal gesture. More of a register of the event. One more line in his notebook, I imagined. King Norodom would certainly hear of this. So would the French governor general in Saigon and the leadership in Paris.

As everyone was exiting the salon to descend to the dining room, Sandingham edged over to me, slight grin crossing his face.

"Nicely done, Commander. That lout must've been absolutely unbearable to serve under in the army. Too bad he didn't give you the excuse to deck him, good and proper." He sighed. "Oh, well—can't have everything, can we? But your reputation will be solid for quite a while. Fountjoy's widely regarded as a fool's fool, and within an hour of our next shore stop, this entertaining little moment will be known up and down the river. You'll be able to dine out on it for at least a month, I'd wager. By the way, you owe me for this round of drinks that I just stood for."

He was laughing, but I wasn't seeing the humor in what had happened, or especially in the consequences of it. The situation had nearly gotten completely out of hand, and all because of personal pride. So much for the low-profile entry into the area I'd hoped for. I'd have to be far more careful in the future. As it was, I'd made an enemy. And in that part of the world, as I was to find out only too well, one didn't make an effort to acquire too many of those. There were already enough to go around.

I shrugged at the first officer. "Well, I must thank you for your gesture, and also for the excellent timing, Mr. Sandingham. I shouldn't have let him get to me and yes, I am in your debt."

2
Memories

Sunday, 22 April 1883
On the Mekong River

I knew instantly that Captain Ezekial MacTaggert was not a gentle soul when I saw the tall, square-shouldered, taffy-haired captain berate one of the stewards for being late with his coffee during the first course of the dinner. The man's flaccid face grew redder and his yellowed eyes bulged even larger as the invective went on. That face didn't go with the teetotaler image suggested by Hau earlier. Neither did the tirade.

The temperance side of the *Tonle Queen*'s master might have been an incorrect impression on my part, but there was no denying the man's size, which he used aggressively to his own advantage. Within five minutes of sitting down at dinner I saw that MacTaggert's bulk obviously intimidated not only the Cochinese and Cambodian servants, but Wallace and Sandingham as well.

Over the initial fish soup course, I rethought my pleasant assessment of the riverboat. It appeared that *Tonle Queen* was not a happy ship—made starkly clear once everyone had gathered at the dining salon in the presence of the captain. It was morosely quiet, with only the occasional clink of silverware or glass as the officers and passengers dug into the food.

I was positioned at MacTaggert's table, along with Colonel Fountjoy, Miss Marston, Rockford, two Frenchmen, and Altamonte. Evidently seated according to perceived rank, I was halfway down the table from the captain's end, after Fountjoy and Rockford, and nearer than the Frenchmen and Spaniard. Sandingham headed a separate table, as did Wallace and Blundell. It was a long ten minutes before someone spoke, then MacTaggert's Scots accent was as thick as his meaty forearm as it boomed out, startling me so much I almost dropped my spoon.

"So, Commander Wake, what brings ye to a vessel like *Tonle Queen* in this forsaken corner o' the world!"

"Courier from my government to the royal court of Cambodia, sir."

"A courier! Must be a message o' great importance to send a naval officer on a post clerk's mission—but why anyone wi' any sense would send any message to a puppet like Norodom, I cannae' fathom." He turned to Fountjoy. "I had no idea the Yankee government had such money to waste."

"They won't for long at that rate, eh? Not that they had that much to start with," retorted the colonel, giving me a haughty glance.

They were baiting me to get me to blurt out more information, I surmised, promising myself that it wasn't going to work. Instead, thinking that if I was in for a penny I might as well go for a pound, I offered as kindly as I could to Fountjoy, "Well, you have far more experience with government waste than I, Colonel, so I will yield to your opinion—formed, I believe, by four decades of familiarity in that profession."

That got a laugh from the table and a huge rolling belly laugh from MacTaggert, who slammed a hand on the table in his mirth. The whole room watched as he pounded the table again, making the glass and silverware jump. "By God in heaven, you've been hoisted upon your own petard, Colonel. Aye, an' by a Yankee sailorman here on the far side o' the world! Well done, Commander."

I dared not gloat, but looked Fountjoy in the eye while I said as innocently as I could muster, "I, of course, meant no personal disrespect, Colonel. As I'm sure you know."

The colonel wasn't buying that, but said, "Of course, Commander."

I then judged the timing propitious for a segue to the matter uppermost in my mind. "Captain, as a ship's master I know you'll understand when I ask a favor for my aide-de-camp, a bosun who lies in the church hospital at Mytho. Can a boat take me there in the morning to retrieve him so he can accompany me upriver? I'll need him along and he is past the worst of it—a recurrence of malaria."

Fountjoy interrupted, "An aide-de-camp from the enlisted ranks? What's this, more American egalitarianism?"

I had to put it in terms the colonel would understand. "Bosun Sean Rork has been my servant for many years on assignments around the world. I'll not leave him."

But I wasn't ready for the response. "Rork, that sounds Irish—is he a Gaelic papist?"

"Is he Catholic? Yes. But that makes no difference."

"I think it does, young man. They are frequently disgruntled and occasionally anarchist."

Before I could reply, MacTaggert, who'd been watching the exchange with a grin, laid a hand on Fountjoy's arm. "Oh, I like Commander Wake's loyalty to his man, Colonel. An' I'm o' the belief ye'll be safe enough from the sick old bosun. He's already found his freedom in America, an' probably cares not for an Englishman's blood nae more. Besides, there's some in England that say even we Scots are anarchists an' anti-English. But nae on that, 'tis jes' a vicious rumor. *Right,* Colonel?"

As Fountjoy sputtered, the captain said to me, "Yes, Commander, our boat will take you to the hospital early in the morn. But, is there room in the steerage, I'm wondering? I think 'tis nae."

"Not a problem, sir. He'll stay in my cabin."

Fountjoy gasped in horror as MacTaggert pounded the table again in mirth. "Aye, that's the thing, Commander! Ye Yankee ways'll be the death o' this old colonel here, yet. Fountjoy, my fine English friend, let it go an' enjoy the dinner."

Yelling the eight feet to Sandingham, he continued, "Make it so in the morn, Number One."

"Aye, aye, sir," answered the first officer. "A boat will be ready at eight bells in the middle watch, Commander. You should have your bosun back aboard by sunrise. Then we'll load the last of the cargo, weigh anchor, and proceed upstream."

"Thank you, Captain, and Mr. Sandingham. I very much appreciate the assistance."

The rest of the meal consisted of quiet polite comments by the guests regarding the food, which consisted of curry spiced and boiled bully beef, stale bread, and anemic-looking vegetables, followed by a dried-out pudding affair. For my part, I thought it all in sad contrast to the nice surroundings, but saw that each of the British blandly complimented the cook's abilities, almost by rote, as if it might make the food taste better. The French withheld their culinary opinions. The captain, however, said nothing further, for he had settled into a glum silence, periodically grunting some sort of acknowledgment to himself.

What a bizarre, melancholy group to have signed on with, I decided, looking around the room. Then I caught sight of Blundell on the other side of the room looking at me. The Frenchman nodded slightly while evaluating the odd American who had suddenly arrived amongst them. Seeing Blundell's cold expression, I felt like a new butterfly specimen, pinned among an old collection, on my way to a quaint museum.

I remembered a similar expression on a man in northwestern Africa nine years earlier. The memory conjured up an instant vision in my mind of the episode that had ended with a bullet in my chest. I hoped no one noticed me flinch as I remembered the searing pain.

The after-dinner coffee was bitter chicory, but the cognac was decent—real French cognac. I've never enjoyed cigars, so decided to forgo the smokers in the salon and stayed outside, alone up on the promenade deck, sipping cognac and sitting in one of those folding chairs in the fading twilight.

My thoughts turned to Linda, my dear Linda, whom I missed so much it hurt. She'd died of cancer in Washington, D.C., two years earlier, at the young age of thirty-eight. We'd been married for sixteen years, through war and turmoil and separation. The separation had been the worst to endure, even to the end. I'd been away at sea on the coast of Peru in the South American war, not knowing she was even seriously ill, arriving home after the funeral, feeling I'd abandoned her.

Since that time I'd stayed at a desk in naval headquarters. My off-duty time was fully occupied taking care of my teenage daughter, Useppa, named after the island where Linda had found refuge during the War between the States, and my young son, Sean, named after Sean Rork. Two years of mourning, of slow day-to-day recovery, of throwing myself into my work, of letting time dull the sharpness of my heartache.

Now the children were staying with dear friends and I was back on assignment, this time in an area few Americans had visited. It was a straightforward mission, nothing too dangerous, but one that kept me busy mentally and physically, and I plunged into it. Putting the past behind me, I'd traveled with Rork all the way around the world to French Indo-China. During that time I'd kept focused, not allowing myself to become self-pitying anymore.

But right then, sitting by a dim lantern shedding a feeble glow over the jungle river, my mind drifted back in time to Linda. I missed her, missed everything about her, terribly. Especially with the

sultry moonlight, knowing how much she, born and raised in tropical Key West, would've enjoyed the vista around me.

The smoky haze of the day was gone. An easy breeze had
cleared the night sky and cooled the ship. Stretching away the
tension from dinner, I sat back and listened to the soft sounds of
chimes and drums wafting from a village nearby. In the dark distance, a three-hundred-foot line of small floats, spaced twenty
feet apart and each topped with a tiny yellow rice paper lantern,
marked the curve of a fishing net. Night-blooming jasmine scent-
ed the air from a huge ceramic jar on the deck close by. Jasmine
was Linda's favorite scent. She wore it on special occasions, and
no matter where I was in the world, it always reminded me of her.

Sighing at her memory, I felt the tears coming.

"Les mémoires de la nuit?"

Blundell stood ten feet away, waiting politely.

"Oui, Monsieur Blundell," I admitted, willing the tears to go
away. "Memories in the night—of a similar place, on the other
side of the world, in far happier times."

"And with a beautiful woman, no doubt," he continued in
English. "You are not alone in that sentiment, my friend. Many
of us here have those memories. They emerge at moments like
this. They are sweet and yet they are bitter. But at least we have
them. I know men who have never had them. They have hearts
made of stone. I think that is the saddest condition of all."

He was right. I'd known men like that. "I agree."

"May I join you? It is peaceful, *tranquille,* on this deck
tonight. I do not intend to intrude on your private thoughts,
Commander, but that salon is full of smoke and loud words,
fueled by drink. Everyone talking and no one listening. It is the
same every night in this Oriental land among the exiles that man
the European empires, no matter if on shore or on a boat. It
becomes tiresome for me. But you—you are from the New
World. An American. With young spirit, *avec élan pour la vie.*
Not like the old men in there."

Blundell was perhaps fifty, while I was forty-three and not

used to being described as a young spirit. I pointed to a lounge chair. "Yes, you are welcome to relax here, Monsieur Blundell. Please take a chair."

"*Merci.* Would you do me the further honor of using my given name, as a friend? It is Maurice." Blundell held out his hand, which I shook while trying to discern his motives. The other French had been distantly polite. Why was this one being friendly?

"*Oui, Maurice, et mon nom c'est Peter. Excusé-moi mon francais. C'est mal.*"

We clinked snifters as Blundell politely ignored my bad French and toasted. *"Peter, mon ami nouveau, bonne chance avec le travail et l' amour en l'Orient."*

He spoke slowly enough for me to mentally translate—*Peter, my new friend, good luck with work and love in the Orient.* Well, I'll certainly need the former, I thought, but it was far too late in my life for the latter. That part of my heart died with Linda.

Faint strands of mist rose from the river as the night cooled—just enough to form a gauzy filter that made everything seem even more mystical, distorting depth perception, hazing outlines. Now there was no more black, no more silvery white, the shades blending together, blurring reality and imagination.

For a long time both of us silently gazed out over the Mekong, watching the fishermen haul in the long net line, one dim lantern at a time extinguishing to show their progress. Periodically the Frenchman would extract a flask from an inside coat pocket and refill my glass. I felt myself relax, the muscles untense themselves, as the river flowed by, burbling along the hull below us and carrying away my apprehensions about Blundell. In an act of decadence unheard of aboard a warship, I stretched out my legs and put my feet up on the lower railing. At that moment I didn't care if anyone saw and thought less of me.

After a while Blundell broke the silence, his tone gentle, paternal—as smooth as the water drifting by us in the mist.

"And so, Peter, why are you *really* here?"

3

Under Way

Sunday, 22 April 1883
On the Mekong River

That jolted me out of any indulgent reverie. I scrutinized Blundell in the faint light, but he maintained his insouciance, just a friend asking an innocent question. Trying to remember if Blundell had filled his own glass from the flask, I couldn't recall. I felt groggy, slow-witted. *My God, did this man drug me?* Anything was possible. I had to be more vigilant.

"I am just a courier, Maurice—as I said before. And no, I do not know the message, except it's something about the piracy on the Cambodian coast. A protest of some sort, I imagine. They attacked some American merchant ships last year. But what about you? What is it you really do here?"

Blundell gave me that generic slight Gallic shrug that conveys that nothing is important, everything is possible, and some things are difficult to understand.

"Peter, I try to advise a man who does not want any advice, never follows my advice, but who always makes a show of listening to it." Another shrug. "It is what I do—my place in life. I think that maybe you have been in that place too, giving advice that is ignored by one's seniors who make the important decisions. It can be frustrating for us, yes?"

It was a shrewd answer, one without overt meaning but that reached out for confirmation of his skepticism about me. Usually a lieutenant commander is not a high enough rank to be in a position to advise anyone in real decision-making office. But I wasn't in a usual position for a mere lieutenant commander—I routinely briefed the president of the United States.

I tried to quickly assess the man next to me. Did Blundell know what I did for a living? Why I was really here? How could he? And if he did, what would he do?

It was time for nebulous talk. "Yes, Maurice. All gentlemen in uniform around the world can sympathize with that problem."

He smiled knowingly and nodded. I instantly knew I'd given the wrong reply. The vagueness of my answer probably confirmed the Frenchman's suspicions—I should've complained about a specific incidence with a low-level superior. Oh well, too late for that. He can have his suspicions, but he can't have my information.

Over the stern, to the southeast, the moon was rising. Pointedly changing the subject, Blundell aimed a finger toward it.

"Look, there is something wrong with the moon tonight. It should be full."

The moon was bright, but the lower left quadrant was missing, forming an unusual shape. We watched it for a while and I realized the missing part was growing larger.

"It is being eaten," he said sadly. "A bad omen."

"No, it's only a lunar eclipse, Maurice."

"Not in Asia, Peter. *Everything* has meaning here and nothing is logical. That the beautiful moon is being eaten as we watch is an omen—a bad omen."

The moon was higher now, the Earth's shadow on it diminishing. It would be only a partial eclipse. In half an hour the moon would be restored completely. To the right, Omega Centauri was rising. Soon the Southern Cross would come into sight.

I thought it time to lighten our dispositions. "Well, it appears like it'll only be a small bite, Maurice. I wouldn't worry about it much."

He looked at me oddly, shaking his head. "You should, Peter. In Indo-China, even a small bite can become infected and eventually kill you."

Blundell rose abruptly. "Well, I am very tired and imagine you must be also. I will bid you a goodnight, Peter. *Merci pour la conversation, et bonne nuit, mon ami.*"

The Catholic hospital at Mytho was built to handle twenty-two patients. That morning, forty-nine were jammed into every space available inside; several more were under canvas awnings outside. Dengue fever was rampaging through the delta—uncommon for that early in the year, before the monsoon had set in. The moaning and wailing of the ill as the fever wracked their brains could be heard from several blocks away as I approached in the early morning mist.

Located just behind a church displaying an enormous steeple with oriental trim on the gables, the hospital was run by nuns acting as the nurses and the parish priest acting as the doctor. Local girls did the menial work as training to be nurses. Sean Rork, as a European—all non-Asians were thought of as European, a moniker that made the bosun cringe—was privileged to have a bed inside, even though he had insisted on being outside, in the somewhat fresh air. Rork had first contracted malaria fifteen years earlier in China and was recuperating from a recurrence of the fever, something that happened every few years, especially when he returned to the tropics. I managed to get the damned stuff on a survey expedition in Panama in 1870 and occasionally suffered a return of the fevers myself. Not unusual. Many naval men ended up with it at some point in their careers. Most survived, but the recurrences could be hell to endure.

As I watched, the servant girl touched Rork's shoulder to rouse him from his sleep. The bosun had almost thirty-five years in the navy after emigrating from Wexford, Ireland, and was a tough old tar. But he started out that day with a moan, ignoring me as he looked dreamily into the girl's eyes, stroking her hand.

"Oooh, Lord, me sees the day arrivin' with a gentle bird caressin' these old bones—but I spy a buzzard in the offin'! Aye, that I surely do." A reluctant nod in my direction. "Good morn, Commander, an' welcome to me abode, humble that it is."

Even on a sick bed, Rork could make me laugh. "Good morning, Sean, you Irish dog. I see the girls're taking good care of you—but lollygagging time is over, my friend. Fever's gone, I see, and it's time to go back to work. And, by the way, I've arranged some pretty classy transport for us. I think you'll be pleased."

"Back to work an' away from these dainty creatures? Oh, me God above, 'tis a hard life for an ol' sailorman. A hard one indeed, Commander. Sometimes me heart wonders why me mind makes me do it."

The girl, clad in a gossamer-thin, ankle-length tunic, backed away from the patient, bringing forth another sad moan from Rork as he gazed at her walking away. The next second the rascal bounced up out of bed, already dressed in his uniform. He stretched to his full six-foot-three-inch height, an errant lock of brown hair springing down over his forehead. I was impressed by his revival, even after all the surprises he'd pulled on me over the years. Last time I'd seen him, two days earlier, the man had been delirious with fever, lamenting his long dead mother and sister back in Wexford, and desperate for cool water.

"Your recovery has been nothing short of phenomenal, Rork. Either the care or the medicine has done wonders for you."

"Well, both, actually. An' I was thinkin' you'd be 'round early.

this morn, so I got me rig ready ahead o' time. So now it's upriver, is it, sir?"

"Yes. We get under way at sunrise."

"Aye, sir, then lead on an' I'll follow. Can't be gettin' too soft now, can we?" He glanced quickly at the servant girl in the hallway. "Though 'tis a temptin' thought indeed to allow meself to stay here with the angels. Maybe one more day?"

"No, Rork. Time to go."

"Ah, yes—duty. 'Tis a gruelin' master, indeed."

As the eastern horizon began to lighten, the whole staff on duty lined up and shook Rork's hand, wishing him well. There was a certain glint in my friend's eye as he said goodbye to that servant girl, a look I knew the meaning of and didn't always appreciate. The bosun could be trouble at times. Serious trouble.

"Rork, can I come back here in nine months' time and be welcomed?"

He puffed up his chest. "Why, Commander, I am shocked, sir. Shocked an' possibly appalled at such a suggestion! A veteran petty officer in me sainted Uncle Sam's United States Navy I am, an' as close to a real gentleman as service regulations permit. Not an idea has formed in me head why we would not be welcomed back at any time by these lovely ladies o' the East."

His act didn't convince me. "Hmm. Yes, well, I still think it's good we're leaving now and hope when we come back downriver there won't be a lynching party led by an outraged priest here."

A sly grin flashed across Rork's face. "Oh, sir—a man o' God would never do such a thing as *that*."

Rork liked our accommodations, deeming them "ritzier than the bishop o' Derry's palace," though he was embarrassed to be sharing them with an officer. Said it just wasn't proper. I said it was the only choice. He resolved the matter by staying around the crew's petty officers most of the day, including at meals, but sleeping in our cabin at night. He explained, "That way we'll be knowin' what's really goin' on aboard this vessel, not just what the officers *think* might be goin' on."

Upon a moment's reflection, I thought that an eminently good point and bade him good luck. I'd been on many a vessel where the officers had not a clue as to the real condition of the ship and crew. I wondered what kind of food the crew ate. They seemed to be all Asians. Oh well, Rork'd always had a cast-iron stomach, he could handle it. And as for gathering intelligence, it was, after all, our profession.

For, you see, I was not just a courier delivering a diplomatic message protesting the lack of Cambodian sanctions against the piracy along their coast. That was a well-known, longtime problem in the area. No, I was there for other reasons. Reasons that it would not do well for the French, nor anyone other than King Norodom himself, to know.

Yes, I was carrying an official piracy protest message from my government, but the real message was not on the stationery of the secretary of state. That message was carried in my head, committed to memory—a personal reply to King Norodom of Cambodia from Chester Alan Arthur, the president of the United States of America. And should anyone else other than the intended recipient learn of the contents, there would be serious repercussions in Washington, Paris, and London. Even Rork, the man I trusted most on this earth, wasn't privy to it.

Our journey had taken us from the Navy Department in Washington by train to Charleston, thence by steamer to Panama. Crossing the Isthmus from Colón to Panama City on the Pacific side, we checked on the progress of the French canal builders. They were industrious men who had already altered history by constructing the Suez Canal thirteen years earlier. Their leader, Ferdinand de Lesseps, had organized a huge financial and operational effort, the largest construction undertaking the world had ever seen.

I'd met him four years earlier when he first arrived in Panama and had answered his questions about the place. Obviously, he'd expected the same fawning others had given him, but that's not what he got from me. He listened indifferently, bristling at some of my answers, the ones he didn't like. Having been there many times, including the Selfridge Surveying Expedition of 1870, I was well versed on the subject of Panama—he, a new arrival, just *thought* he was. So the outcome was that de Lesseps didn't like me, or what I told him. And, of course, he ignored what I had warned him about.

As Rork and I traveled across the jungle by wagon—the train tracks had buckled yet again—we saw the consequences of arrogance in an environment hostile to human endeavors. All the modern steam machines the French had brought in were rusting away and/or bogged down in the swamps. The laborers brought in from the Caribbean islands were too few and frequently outnumbered by the Europeans standing around supervising them. All of them, white and black, were getting sick from malaria, dengue fever, yellow fever, and dysentery, not to mention the snake and insect bites and the punishing heat and humidity. Medical facilities, crucial to handling the horrific diseases endemic to the region, were few and far between, and the workers' housing we saw was abysmal. The Panamanian interior is by far the worst jungle in the world I've ever known. And I've seen most of them.

Local workers were no fools and stayed out of the jungle for the most part—leaving the deadliest areas to the foreigners. The Indians simply faded back into the vast green carpet of thick foliage and waited until the tropical forest would inevitably scare away or kill these latest invaders. The French, with European efficiency, had surveyed out the route and started the work on the coastal sections, but were nowhere near to tackling the tough part—the interior. Rork looked at me as we traversed the Chagres River and shook his head. No words were needed. The final depressing intelligence learned in Panama City was that my friend Gaston Blanchet, one of the project's chief engineers and a newlywed, was dead of yellow fever.

From Panama City I telegraphed headquarters an innocuous missive—everyone and their uncle read telegram traffic in Latin America—advising our progress on the journey. More detailed impressions of the French canal were contained in a report deposited with the diplomatic mail pouch from the U.S. consulate office. I was curious what headquarters would make of my report, and how it might differ from what they were hearing from the consular people, who were known for their information being less than objective. Most of them were in business with the people they were reporting about.

It was a relief to set sail away from the sad chaos of Panama and be aboard a packet steamer bound for Samoa, halfway across the Pacific. Once there, we boarded a British sailing barkentine bound for Sydney, then a steamer around Australia to Singapore. From that crossroads we headed north on a French steamer, disembarking in Saigon, a bustling French colony for the last twenty-five years.

Rork had been feeling ill since Singapore. We both knew what it was from experience, and we both knew the disease could kill even a strong man unless he received medical care. By the time we'd gone across the Mekong delta country and ended up in Mytho, I was worried. Rork was out of his mind, burning with fever one hour, shivering the next. The wagon driver told us to seek help at the church in the town, that the priest was a doctor of sorts. I was glad he gave us that advice. The priest took one look at Rork and set events into action—dosing him with quinine and opium, getting him into bed, and assigning one of the servant girls to bring cool water or blankets, whichever was needed to make my friend comfortable. And now, two days later, he looked fine. Malaria is a strange, malevolent, and unfathomable disease.

Two hours after I brought Rork aboard, the *Tonle Queen* hauled her anchor and finally got under way, bound to our first port of call, Cai Be, two days upriver through the maze of streams and villages that make up the massive delta of the Mekong.

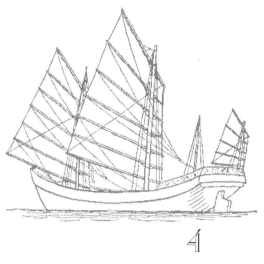

4

Lunacy at Cai Be

Wednesday, 25 April 1883
On the Mekong River

Late on his first night aboard the riverboat, Rork had asked me for a briefing on the geography of our route. In most navies, enlisted men do not normally make such requests of officers and would be rebuked upon exhibiting that sort of familiarity. It is usually thought that if the enlisted people needed to know something, their officer would tell them—that the lower ranks are there to *do*, not think. That's part of the stupid old European notion that only commissioned officers can understand complicated concepts. Feudalism at sea, really.

But our relationship was not the norm—there was too much shared blood, sweat, and tears for that kind of nonsense. And I respected Rork's ability to discern potential problems ahead of us. We had saved each other's lives on three continents so far, and realized we might well have to on this one. So, when Rork wants to be educated about a particular topic I count it an honor to oblige. And in this specific instance, I was unusually well armed with knowledge, courtesy of an unforeseen and very unique source.

A week earlier, while in Saigon, I had received a brief but rather thorough indoctrination on the colony of Cochin and the river system of the Mekong. I met my benefactor while having lunch with the American consul for Indo-China. The consul was a forgettable sort, but not the man he introduced me to that day. Professor Petrusky was a linguistics scholar at the College des Intreprètes in Saigon. Rork had been ill at the time and my visit with Petrusky had been solo, which was too bad, for Rork would have delighted in the man's company.

Petrusky was a devout Catholic who was part French and part Cochinese, and seemingly all brain. Small in stature, somewhere in his sixties in age, the bespectacled professor immediately impressed me with his fluency in English, then furthered my awe with flawless French, Italian, Latin, and Spanish. Indeed, when I arrived at his office the man was engaged in a theological discussion in Latin with a French priest on canonical law. But I found that his efforts went beyond conversation. After years of labor, he had written *A Comparative Analysis of the Languages of the World,* which included several Asian tongues, which he had, of course, mastered. I spent two hours with Petrusky that afternoon, then had dinner with him the following night. He was quite formal—I never did learn his first name—but friendly nonetheless. By the time I bid my farewell from Saigon, we were friends and had promised to assist each other in any way needed in the near future.

Thus filled with Petrusky's wisdom, by the light of our cabin lamp I explained to Rork that the Laotians, hundreds of miles upriver, call the great waterway of Indo-China the Mekong, meaning the Mother of all Rivers, but where we were in the delta country of Cochin, south of Saigon, it was known as Song Cuu Long—the River of the Nine Dragons. The number referred to the river's nine mouths that enter the South China Sea. The dragon part referred to the treacherous conditions caused by current, wind, and tidal confluences at their mouths. These mouths form a delta of small rivers for one hundred miles along the coastline.

Rork listened intently and asked questions a sailor would—the same I'd asked Petrusky. What were the depths? Were there government channel marks? Any ports? What was the bottom type? Any bridges? Amount of river traffic? Military defenses? I answered each briefly, then he asked where exactly the smaller rivers met upstream. I pointed to the newly finished Elisée Reclus map of the delta that Petrusky had loaned me—it seemed he knew Reclus personally—then told Rork that about sixty miles inland the nine rivers met their source of water, the two main streams of the Mekong.

These two great rivers were called by the Cochin people the Hau Giang, known to the French as the Bassac, to the south; and the Tien Giang, known to the French as the Mekong proper, to the north. They ran parallel each other—separated by perhaps twenty miles—all the way up to the Cambodian capital at Phnom Penh, two hundred miles away to the northwest. At that place they joined forces, along with a third river, the Tonle, for which the riverboat was named. Halfway to Phnom Penh there was the sole deep-water crossover stream between the two main rivers, near a village called Cho Moi.

He'd asked exactly where we were at that point. I put my finger on the map, tracing the line of the Tien Giang, the main Mekong River, then pointed at Mytho.

"That's where we're at, Rork. Just upriver from Mytho. Tomorrow evening we should be pulling into Cai Be."

He studied the map. "So we'll stay on this river all the way to the Cambodian king's palace at Phnom Penh, sir?"

"That's the plan."

Rork said, "Aye, sir," then laughed quietly and shook his head.

He looked as if he had something to say. "What?"

"Well, sir, it all reminds me o' what me dear ol' uncle Seamus used to say—'Sean, me boyo, if ye want to see if God's really got a sense o' mirth, jes' let him hear o' your plans an' then see what happens!' You know, sir, I've heard there's bandits up this river."

"Yep, I heard that too. Up by the border. But the French have supposedly ended most of that sort of thing. Why?"

He groaned and rubbed his knee. "Oh, you know how it goes with me, sir. I get these feelin's in me bones sometimes. An' right now me bones're tellin' me them piratical types'll get to meet a real Irishman pretty soon."

Oh, I wished I hadn't heard *that*. After twenty years of being in danger afloat and ashore with the man, it always bothered me when Rork's Gaelic intuition, and that damned right knee, would give him those premonitions. The big rascal was usually right.

Cai Be was reached a little ahead of time because the river flow against us was down—the monsoon rains wouldn't start for another month or two. The steamboat pulled up close to shore and blew her whistle, alerting the area she was in town. We turned up a side canal that led into the center of the town and edged in toward a rickety dock jutting out from a government building. A French tricolor drooped from its balcony.

Cai Be wasn't much to look at, just a few substantial buildings in the French manner, merchants mostly, and a profusion of crude shacks built adjoining and atop each other. It looked to me like a giant mistake of a town, with no rhyme or reason to its layout.

The captain did a good job of using the current to crab her sideways toward the jetty, stopping her way just as the lines were put over. Moments later we heard the engine room bells signaling to shut down the machinery, the stack bled off the excess steam, the constant thumping of the massive pistons stopped, and it got quiet. But seconds later the horde waiting at the head of the dock swarmed out and over the ship.

Worried-looking rice sellers, sharp-eyed merchandise buyers, painted prostitutes in Western dresses, bent-over coolies, dressed-up affluent native passengers, uniformed French authorities, sweat-stained European passengers—within seconds they were all aboard, jostling for space on the decks, lugging boxes, bales, and suitcases. Standing at the promenade deck rail overlooking the scene below me, I concluded that I'd never seen any such chaos on any ship in my life. And above it all stood MacTaggert up at the wheelhouse, looking out at the pandemonium with a satisfied air. Evidently, it was just another day at a port town on the Mekong.

There was a church in Cai Be too, a big one, with tall twin spires, located up the street from the dock. Rork pointed out a procession departing the main doors of the church, heading our way. Two priests in robes were striding along, followed by several nuns in outsized habits and four local men straining under a mound of baggage. One frail bespectacled Asian dressed in Western clothing brought up the rear. I looked again. Yes, it was Petrusky.

As the religious parade reached the head of the dock, Rork shook his head. "Uh oh, methinks this is not good. Not good at all, sir. Trouble's a'coming."

My friend was speaking of the age-old sailor's superstition against carrying clergymen aboard a ship. Rork knew all the old tales and seemed to select the ones he chose to follow.

Petrusky saw me at the railing and waved. I waved back, wondering why he hadn't told me he was going upriver when we'd talked the previous week in Saigon. The priest, nuns, Petrusky, and the overloaded coolies all pushed their way aboard and were met by Sandingham on the main deck. I couldn't hear above all the ambient racket of the crowd, but their manner of conversation indicated the guests were unexpected, though I did know that at least two of the French traders, and Ford the gambler, were due to go off at Cai Be, so there might be some room available aboard.

I looked at the railing by the wheelhouse and saw

MacTaggert's satisfied look change to one of consternation as he studied the situation. Then Sandingham glanced up at his captain and shrugged. MacTaggert pounded the rail and went back in the wheelhouse, while down below, the whole entourage disappeared into the dining room. Since the show was over, Rork headed below decks. I prepared to recline on one of those French deck chairs that I was beginning to appreciate.

I was sitting there, still trying to figure out Petrusky's presence aboard, when the steam whistle blew again and I felt the engines turn over. The *Tonle Queen* was getting ready to leave, but it seemed early to me—they were still loading. Obviously the move surprised everyone else, because the reaction of the crowd was immediate. Shrieks and curses in several languages erupted as the mob of humanity rushed to depart and the riverboat listed ever more seriously to starboard.

Already, MacTaggert had the crew bringing in the lines and I heard the engine room bells sound. We were getting under way even as people were leaping across the widening divide between dock and deck. It didn't make sense to me. Something was wrong here. I went to the rail to see for myself. There was total confusion on the main deck and the dock as they began to separate away from each other. People were throwing items across the water to their friends, all the while screaming invectives toward the wheelhouse.

MacTaggert stood at the rail, a slight grin creasing that red face as he gazed down at what he was causing. There was a splash, then another as people fell in. The *Tonle Queen's* huge paddle wheel thrashed the water—it would be instant death for anyone struck by it. I looked aft and down. Yes, there were several forms struggling in the water. The people on the dock screamed, pointing toward the paddle wheel.

The ship had way on, moving faster now, and was about to run over the swimmers. There was no time to lose with manners. I yelled to MacTaggert, standing forty feet forward of me.

"Captain—*stop engines!* You've got people in the water!"

"Ay, them silly slit-eyes should'a been more orderly an' left when I gave the signal. But oh nae, they Orientals were as they always are, just a lazy lot, coddled by a bunch o' lazy priests who think they run the place. Well, them clergy buggers doan' own or run me, by God in thunder! That'll teach 'em to get the bloody hell off my ship when I tell 'em to. Damned slopeheads cloggin' my ship . . ." His voice trailed off in a slur.

The man was hopelessly, stupidly drunk.

I rushed past him into the wheelhouse and roared for the Cochinese helmsman to stop engines. He was clearly frightened of his captain, but I was in uniform and pretty frightening myself at that point. The man leaped to the bell rope and pulled it five times—the signal for emergency stop—just as MacTaggert entered and put a beefy paw on my shoulder, spinning me around. His eyes were bulged in rage and he cocked back his right hand.

I ducked and managed to get away to my right, not easy in that confined space as MacTaggert's paw rammed past my head into the bulkhead. He stood there, turning toward my new position as I said, "You're drunk, Captain. Have Mr. Sandingham take over right now."

That's when I heard the high-pitched shriek rising above the rest and dashed out to the railing. I'd been too late. The engine had stopped but the wheel was still turning. Three of the four people in the water were smashed down by the boards of the paddlewheel, a red stain coming up aft in our wake, blooming across the canal. No bodies could be seen. The fourth person in the water, a child, was being dragged aboard by a crewman.

Then a low wail, a visceral sound of wounding, ascended from the dock, filling the air. The crowd was past the moment of shock and dismay—now they were angry, pointing at the wheelhouse, shouting curses. Someone threw something at the ship, then another. In seconds, anything on the dock that could be thrown was raining down on the *Tonle Queen*.

Sandingham, out of breath and clearly scared, bounded up the ladder to the promenade deck and forward to the wheelhouse.

"We just ran over several people in the water, sir! The crowd is throwing things through our starboard side windows and now we're drifting with the current back down on the dock. Sweet Jesus, Captain—they'll swarm aboard and kill us all! Put the engine in gear so we can get away!"

MacTaggert leaned back against the window sill and sneered. "Well now, I dunno 'bout that. Nae indeed, the Yank navy here says we should make nice-nice to them slopeheads. I think he actually *likes* the squinty bastards. Mayhaps he should get his arse down to the main deck an' be friendly to 'em."

I just stood there, dumbfounded at the insanity of it all. Then I heard Rork's voice booming out, down on the foredeck, "Shove off with those sounding poles!"

A missile of some sort crashed the window near me. From below I heard Rork again. "That's it—put your backs into it, lads!" Sandingham and I dashed to the rail and looked over the side to the foredeck. Rork was on the starboard bow, putting his own back into it with a sounding pole. Next to him were a dozen Cochinese and Cambodian crewmen, half his size, doing the same with three other poles. Each pole was bent until it looked as if it would snap, but each one held and together they slowed the bow from drifting to the right, toward the dock. The crowd could smell blood by then. The wailing was over, now they were chanting, low and menacing tones. I didn't understand the words, but understood that sound—it was the sound of impending doom, like a mob calling for an execution.

The bow stopped its fatal turn, then slowly swung the other way, into the middle of the canal. A growl swept over the dockside horde as they realized they weren't going to get us the easy way. Then some of the more vociferous pointed at the small boats moored further up the dock. Sandingham translated for me, saying the ringleaders were calling for the fishermen to take the mob out to the steamer so they could kill the *barang*—the foreigners. Already several were jumping into the boats. The mass, frenzied by the constant screaming of the agitators, followed suit. There must have been several hundred, but it seemed like thousands.

I tried to sound calm, but inside I knew we only had seconds remaining before the ship was overwhelmed. "Mr. Sandingham, get the engine in gear immediately—ahead slow. There should be enough steam left to engage the shaft and get some steerageway and speed."

The first officer was mesmerized by the sight of that terrible horde, but he finally broke his gaze away and looked at me. "Ah . . . yes, sir. Aye, aye, sir."

MacTaggert stood at the rail forward of us, chuckling at the scene below as Sandingham rushed past him into the wheelhouse. An instant later, as if nothing untoward had just happened, the captain called after him, his voice as nice as you please. "I suppose you may place the engine in gear an' get under way now, Mr. Sandingham. Kindly take her out into the main river an' proceed upstream to our next port."

Then the lunatic turned to me, his tone lowered into a growl. "I give the orders aboard this ship, you bloody Yank pip. Nae you, nor none o' your fancy friggin' navy ilk, hae power 'round here. Only *my* word goes."

And after saying that, he calmly walked aft, ignoring a rock crashing on the deck close by, and went down the ladder toward his cabin. Incredibly, MacTaggert was smiling benignly at the scene around him as his head dipped out of sight.

The rumble of the engine vibrated up through the decks as the gears engaged and the riverboat gradually increased the distance from the dock. I still heard threatening sounds from the boats that were now alongside us, but between the wind and what little propulsion we had, the *Tonle Queen* began to move faster than the sampans could row.

Rork came up the ladder onto the deck, his face a question mark. I anticipated his comment. "I don't know, Rork. The captain's crazy. He did all that on purpose. Something in him snapped. Damn good work with the poles, by the way. I think you saved our lives."

"Ah, well, sir, I'll tell you—'twas the lads that did most o' the shovin.' Me own part was to just set 'em about it an' holler a bit o' encouragement. So the old man's crazy, eh? I wonder what set him off?"

"It was the priests and nuns who came aboard and demanded passage," said Sandingham. "The captain hates them and the way they run the country around here. He did all that—killed those people—just to show everyone that *he* makes the decisions on this ship."

My thoughts escaped aloud. "The man's certifiably mad."

I instantly regretted it as a serious breach of discipline, but Sandingham didn't appear surprised or offended by my maritime blasphemy against a ship's captain. Instead, he looked out toward the cluster of boats behind us. The water in between was being pelted with chewed betel nuts, sticks, stones, any missile that was available to them.

"Yes, I suppose he is," Sandingham quietly said. "Sooner or later we all get a little bit that way out here . . ."

Rork glanced at me for a reaction. I didn't say a word, just shook my head slightly, sending him a signal to let it go. I thought of the priests and nuns, then of Petrusky, wondering again why he was aboard. Without another word, Sandingham strolled into the wheelhouse, leaving Rork and I staring aft at the bedlam *Tonle Queen* had left behind.

Rork turned to go, then paused. "Well now, Commander, it's surely lookin' like a right loony ship we've landed aboard, don't it? An' ta think ye were gettin' vexed at imagined troubles that *me* an' that wee little lass mighta' cooked up ashore. Yep, I'm a guessin' that compared to our fearless captain, me ownself don't look quite so bad right about now. . . ."

Seeing his mock innocent air, I said, "Rork, I must admit you do have a way of putting everything in perspective."

His face went from innocent to roguish. "Aye, well, ya know 'tis not just me, sir. Nay, it's a gift from God above to all o' us Irish down below, sir."

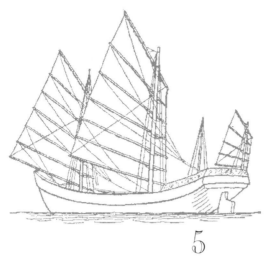

5

Friends of Friends

Wednesday, 25 April 1883
On the Mekong River, upriver from Cai Be

As the *Tonle Queen* chugged upstream at eight knots, Captain MacTaggert wasn't in the dining room that evening, but the new additions to the passenger list were in attendance in all their religious garb. Ensconced on rattan sofas around a bamboo table, they were sipping wine quietly, ignored by everyone except the first officer. That worthy was discussing the water levels of the river and when the monsoon would come to bring them up again.

"... For you see, navigation much beyond Phnom Penh on either the Mekong or the Tonle Rivers will be difficult, the water will be too low."

Sandingham caught sight of me entering the bar and immediately looked relieved. "Oh, look here, it's Commander Wake, our American passenger! Commander, please let me introduce our new passengers to you."

I dutifully bowed to the two priests and four nuns, giving

them my best wholesome American smile.

"Ladies, gentlemen," said Sandingham, "this is Lieutenant Commander Peter Wake, of the United States Navy, bound upriver to Phnom Penh also. Commander, may I have the honor of introducing you to Father Blanc and Father Lorraine, of the diocese of Saigon under the care of Bishop Galibert, both of whom are members of the famous Society of Foreign Missions of Paris. And our lady guests are Mother Chirac, Sister Moreau, Sister Bonnet, and Sister Roux, all of the Sisters of Providence of Portieux. They've come out from France and the fathers are escorting the ladies to their new mission house in Phnom Penh that was established last year. And we are doubly fortunate, Commander—our charming new guests also speak English."

The two priests appeared out of sorts, anything but "charming," possibly because the senior lady in question was a dour-faced biddy that looked like she hadn't smiled in decades. The young nuns under her command were just plain scared, their eyes wide at the nightly antics going on in the corner with Miss Marston and the colonel and that whole entourage. Probably the scene at the dock that afternoon hadn't improved their outlook much either, I realized, wondering if they knew our bizarre captain had done it because of their pushing aboard. On top of all that, the ladies were heading into a jungle country about as different from their native France as one could find. I felt sorry for them.

I decided to stick with English and not try my mangled French—they'd already been through too much. "An honor for me, indeed, ladies, and gentlemen."

Then, the very picture of an ignorant American abroad, I managed to ignite a moral fire. "Say, I thought I saw an acquaintance, Professor Petrusky, come aboard today with you, but I don't see him tonight. He did come aboard, didn't he? Is he coming to dinner tonight? I'd like to talk with him."

The first officer winced. There was an uncomfortable silence among everyone for a moment, broken by Father Blanc, who regarded Sandingham reproachfully as he spoke. "My friend Monsieur Petrusky, respected professor of languages and noted author, friend of the bishop of Saigon, is not allowed in this room, nor in the dining room, nor even on this deck, evidently. He is consigned to the dungeon of the ship."

Sandingham cleared his throat nervously. "A company policy, Father. Non-Europeans are not allowed to socialize here. Mr. Petrusky is dining with the third-class passengers. And we have no dungeon, sir."

Father Blanc, his face a study in ingenuousness but his voice pure steel, countered, "Really? How very interesting. Commander Wake here, as good a man as he obviously appears to be, is also not a European. And yet he is allowed."

Much as I liked Blanc's *touché*, I didn't quite appreciate being used as an American example of the folly of British social mores in French Indo-China. This kind of international incident I didn't need. I was about to try to defuse the situation with some good old American wit when Sandingham deftly put a foot squarely in his mouth with the next comment.

"We make an exception for Americans, sir."

Blanc's companions were silently watching all this, clearly on the side of their leader and against the perfidious British, and also clearly assuming I would side with them too. I glanced around, most of the French were giving their attention to our chat. Most of the British were still in the corner, raptly following Miss Marston's heaving bosom as she humorously described a post-performance cocktail gathering in Singapore. Blanc attacked the hapless Sandingham yet again.

"Oh yes, my son—I will admit Americans are exceptional in the world. They have managed to end codified racism, although it sadly took a war to do it. Perhaps the British who own this riverboat company, and the Europeans in this room, would do well to follow their example for changing social racism."

Oh no, I thought. Not only was he wrong—in the previous four years the Democrats in Congress had forced the legal end of most liberties gained for black freedmen since the war, fighting the Republicans on every related issue—but now I was being set up to make a statement that was sure to be turned around and used against me and my country.

Blanc smiled again, going for the *coup de grâce*.

"But no, I suppose the British would not want to change their behavior in that regard, for I seem to remember they backed the side in America's civil war that perpetuated racial slavery. Is that not so, Commander Wake?"

Time for me to stop this.

"Excuse me, gentlemen. This is a fascinating debate, but politics and social morals are not my bailiwick. They are far too elevated for my simple martial mind. So please let me egress from this discussion with a reiteration of my country's salient, and pretty successful so far, theme of foreign policy for the last hundred years—internationally polite to everyone, entangling foreign alliances with no one."

I let that sink in for a fleeting second, then lied through my teeth. "And now I must beg your leave, for I think my friend Colonel Fountjoy was just signaling he wanted to speak with me. It has been an honor to meet all of you."

Poor slow-witted Sandingham did a double take on that, while I used the pause to withdraw gracefully. I had backed two steps away when Blanc rose to shake my hand. "Very nicely done, Commander. Professor Petrusky was right, you are an intriguing man. We will converse again on this journey, with our mutual friend present."

"It would be a pleasure, sir." And with that I completed my retreat and walked to the bar to get my usual evening rum drink and have a moment of respite from the woes of Indo-China. That was not to be, however, for Chief Steward Hau arrived and palmed me a note from Rork, down below with his friends in the crew. In my friend's fashion it was concise:

Meet P on the foredeck after your dinner. Rork

Hau gave me an inquiring look, to which I said thank you

and that there was no reply needed. Allowing no reaction beyond bowing slightly, he then nodded to a Cambodian steward who hit a gong and announced to the assembled guests that dinner was served.

I sat at the captain's table, which was rather nicely subdued compared to the evening before. Interestingly, I heard no one in the bar salon or at dinner mention the incident at Cai Be, or our leader's conspicuous absence—the chair sat ominously unoccupied. Whether it was from shame or shock I don't know, but the subjects were studiously avoided.

Instead, the conversation at my table centered around the Cham people of the river ahead of us. I learned that there were Muslim villages in the delta, something I did not know previously. Unlike some of their warlike brethren I had met—and damned near been killed by—in Africa, these followers of Mohammed were known for their gentle ways as fishermen and farmers. It was a pleasant chat and good meal, and after a while the memories of the day's carnage faded. By the time the cognac had appeared, everyone had relaxed their grim faces and laughter could be heard around the room.

Amidst this scene, I presented my regrets for an early departure and made my way to the darkened foredeck, fortuitously just forward of my cabin. There I found Rork, who gestured to a figure sitting on the Sampson-post. No one else was around and I wondered where the usual bow lookout was. Rork saw me peering about and whispered that he had taken the man's watch for two hours.

Petrusky turned and saw me. In the starlight I could barely make out his facial features. He was smiling as he stood to shake my hand.

"Commander, how good of you to come. I regret taking you away from the genial company of the diners, but I needed to speak with you."

"I'd much rather be here, Professor Petrusky."

"Please, call me Petrusky. I would tell you my first name, but you would have difficulty in pronouncing it, so please do as my close friends do and omit the title."

"As you wish, my friend. Please call me Peter. I saw you come aboard and was sorry to have not had the opportunity before now to meet with you. But, of course, it was a bit of a hectic time there and . . ."

He waved a hand. "Yes, and that is an understatement. I heard how you saved the life of one of the people in the water this afternoon by getting the engine turned off, and also how you were dragged into a discussion of my passenger status this evening. I am grateful for the former and sorry for the latter. Indo-China is, unfortunately, very complicated in every way."

"And that is *your* understatement, my friend. I have a lot to learn about this place."

"That is why I wanted to speak with you. In fact, Peter, that is precisely why I am aboard the *Tonle Queen*. To educate you."

Petrusky saw my reaction and smiled. "I was sent here to go upriver with you."

"Sent here? By whom?"

"Friends of friends of yours. *Les Missions Étrangères de Paris*, or the MEP as they are commonly called. In English it is translated as the Society of Foriegn Missions of Paris. Father Blanc and Father Lorraine are members of the MEP. They have arranged a leave of absence from my position at the college—the Church supports it—in order to accompany you and Sean Rork. I am to educate and protect you."

"*You* are supposed to protect *me?* And some priests in Cochin have an interest in me? I'm not understanding any of this, Petrusky. I don't even know any priests here."

"But you have high-level connections in the Church. The very highest level. I do not even know who they are, but they must be very important, for when those connections found out you were here, they requested the MEP to assist you. The MEP assigned me to that task."

"I'm still lost on this—" Then, as I spoke I suddenly understood, though it was hard to imagine. "*Florence?*"

"Yes, Peter. And Rome."

"How did they even know I'm here?"

"Telegraph cable message. We are connected with Europe now. The cable leaves Saigon and goes to Singapore, from there to India and thence to Egypt and Europe. Bishop Galibert of Saigon keeps the regional archbishop informed of new events in the diocese. Your arrival was deemed an unusual event—we haven't seen an American naval officer in Indo-China in fifteen years and have never seen one on the Mekong. It would seem the archbishop thought that important enough to go to Rome, where it was copied to the Jesuit Curia Generalizia in Florence. Obviously, Rome took notice of it and directed that the Catholic Church in this area assist you."

"I'm not even Catholic. I'm Methodist."

"Nevertheless, you have powerful friends in the Church, Peter, both Jesuit and in The Holy See. The Superior General of the Society of Jesus, Jan Beckx himself, took an interest in this. It appears the Church feels honor-bound to you. I presume you have done some service to engender that unusual amount of loyalty to a non-Catholic from them."

He was right, but it wasn't widely known. I did have powerful friends in the Church. And yes, I had done a service to the Church. The whole thing had started nine years earlier, when a Jesuit priest provided an escape route from some very irate people bent on killing me in Sevilla, Spain, during the Carlist War. Several months after that, a Jesuit bishop in Italy had given some timely assistance to me regarding a delicate matter involving a lady's honor. And only two years previously, the Jesuit bishop of Panama had warned me of a Chilean plot to kill me during the War of the Pacific in South America.

But it was a two-way street. Six months after that warning in Panama, and still during the war, the relationship came full circle and the Church called in their markers with me through the bishop of Lima, Peru—also a Jesuit. The end result was that I led the escape of one hundred and seven Catholic Chinese-Peruvian refugee children through Lima's Catacombs of the Dead and out to sea to freedom in Panama. All during a chaotic battle for the city between the Peruvian defenders and the Chilean invaders.

I had originally thought it a coincidence that so many Jesuits knew of me, but that belief was ended during the war in Peru. During my assignment as neutral observer to that sad conflict, I learned that the brotherhood of Jesuits had long-standing friendships with many non-Catholics with whom they had a *quid pro quo* of assistance and service. I was one of them. Not through premeditated intent, mind you, but because of the overwhelming circumstances that compelled me to help them.

I hadn't heard from any of the Jesuits, other than some polite letters concerning Linda's death, for the last two years. Until Petrusky's appearance, I thought my connections with the Church had faded into past memories.

I got the feeling the professor knew far more about my past than he was letting on. Had he surmised my mission? If yes, what did the Church think of it? He was waiting patiently for my reply.

"Yes, I did them a service once, a little while ago," I said. "And now they think I'm in some sort of danger here?"

Petrusky never changed expression—the man would've been devastatingly effective at poker. "They do. You are dealing with a very complex situation in Indo-China, Peter. There are many sides vying for power, both foreign and Asian. There are some factions in the royal households of Cambodia and Annam who are not readily visible, and more than a few who are quite deadly. Foreign merchants and planters are very powerful in Indo-China, also. Fortunes are made by them here."

He sadly shook his head. "Not all is as it seems in Indo-China, my friend. It is, as the Europeans say, quite *Machiavellian.*"

The professor cocked his head to one side, a trait I noticed early on with him when he was about to say something profound. "That is why I have been sent by Bishop Galibert—through Father Blanc—to educate you about the situation and protect you as you make your way around the region. Bishop Cordier in Cambodia will be advised of our travel and assist us there."

"Thank you. Say, these bishops—are they Jesuits?"

"No, Peter, they are MEP, as are most of our clergy here. But back in France, and in Rome, they have many Jesuit associates."

"Rome . . ." A thought went through my mind. "I don't suppose the pope is a Jesuit?"

"No, Pope Leo the Thirteenth is not a Jesuit." He allowed another shadow of a smile to cross his face. "But he *was* raised by them in the school at Viterbo, Italy, for six years, from the age of ten. As I am sure you know, all members of the Church have profound respect for the Jesuits."

"And they can influence policy, even though they are no longer in Rome? I believe they had to leave in seventy-three."

"Yes, they still have weight even though their headquarters is now near Florence. Remember, it was Pope Pius IX who had them leave, not this pope. And, of course, ancient ties, and thus influence, are never completely severed by temporal political winds."

Well, the locals weren't the only ones who could be Machiavellian. The Italians invented it. I sensed ulterior motives from Petrusky's leadership. I also wondered just what his loyalties were within the Church. "And so I am to confide in you?"

Petrusky shrugged. "If you wish. But it is your safety that is my concern, not your secrets, Peter."

I thought about it for a minute. Yes, the Church did owe Rork and me for what we did in Peru. And they would love to know exactly why I was there—they were always affected by international political developments. No nation on earth had the intelligence gathering capabilities of the Church. But as long as I wasn't going to divulge any confidential matters, what difference did it make if Petrusky helped me out a bit at the Church's behest?

"All right, Petrusky, let's start my education right now."

"Very good, my friend. We'll begin with the overall view of

Indo-China. There are four major monarchies in Indo-China—the king of Burma, a puppet of the British; the king of Siam, a friend of the British; the king of Cambodia, a friend of the French; and the Emperor of Viet Nam, a beneficiary of the French, who has theoretical control over the old kingdoms of Tonking at Hanoi, Annam at Hué, and Cochin at Saigon. He ceded Cochin to direct French control. Now let us first discuss the surrounding foreign colonial powers, for they are the simplest ingredients in this political potion, before we delve into the Asian components . . ."

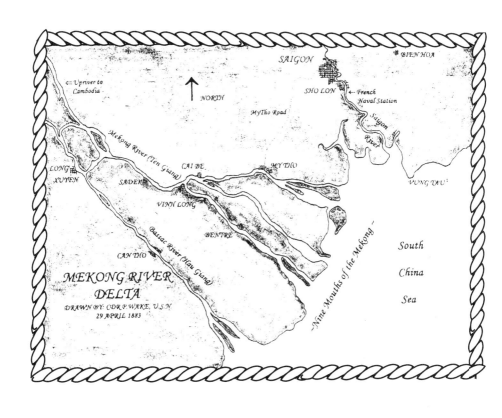

SAIGON   # BIEN HOA

⇐ Upriver to
Cambodia   SHO LON   ← French
                    ↑   Naval Station
              NORTH
                    MyTho Road   Saigon
                                                  River

              Mekong River (Ten Giang)   CAI BE   MY THO
LONG
XUYEN   SADEK   VUNG TAU

                    VINH LONG

              Bassac River (Hau Giang)   BEN TRE   South

CAN THO   China

MEKONG RIVER   Sea
DELTA
DRAWN BY: CDR P. WAKE, U.S.N.
29 APRIL 1883   ~ Nine Mouths of the Mekong ~

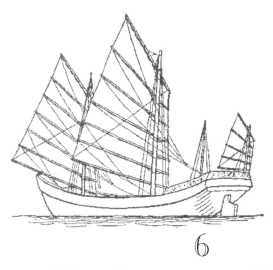

6

The Lessons of Tu Duc

Wednesday, 25 April 1883
On the Mekong River

It was an odd setting. Years later, I remembered it as clearly as if I were still there. I was in the classic conspirator's scene—dark, furtive, and fraught with consequence if discovered. Secret political conferences between a foreign naval officer, particularly one from anti-imperial America, and an educated and influential local Asian signaled potential danger for the French imperial authorities. They were always on the lookout for anti-colonial endeavors, always quashing any nascent independence movement. The French made a show of higher education of the native populations, but then controlled it closely and continually worried about the eventual effects—it gave the natives unhealthy ideas.

A dim amber lantern on the bow glowed with just enough light for me to see the shapes of cargo boxes on the foredeck, while on the deck directly over us the revelry of the bar salon was in full progress. I could hear Fountjoy's baritone and Wallace's

Scots tenor singing a British soldier's song through the open windows above—probably in an effort to aggravate the French passengers even more. Nearer to me, the bow wave rushed away along the side in a steady hiss as the slow *thump, thump, thump* of the engine's piston arms turning the great paddlewheel rumbled forward from the stern.

Up ahead I saw a maze of fishermen's candle-lit rice paper lanterns floating on buoys in the dark. The smell of lubricant grease from the steam winch beside me, and cigar smoke from above, mixed with the cooking fires smoldering from the villages of sampans and barges rafted up along the riverbanks. I intermittently caught the barest whiff of jasmine or sandalwood incense from the shore, reminding me of where exactly I was in the world.

Petrusky, as I had come to expect of the man, was prepared. He unfolded a map much bigger than the one of the delta he'd given me in Saigon. As he spread it out on his lap I saw that it covered the entire Indo-China and East Indies region. He placed thick reading spectacles on his nose and commenced his geopolitical monologue.

"The foreign powers control almost all of the area of Indo-China. First we will deal with the strongest—the British. In addition to several coastal areas of China, the British control Burma, Malaya, Sarawak, Singapore, and the Straits Settlements along the Straits of Malacca. These are extensions of their hold over India and ensure the trade route to China. They have a dominant influence in Siam, which yes, is ostensibly independent, but everyone knows King Chulalongkorn does as bidden by the British consul-general, Mr. Thomas Knox. Through the British White Raj, Charles Anthony Thomas Brooke, nephew of the famous James Brooke, they also influence the Muslims of Sarawak on the island of Borneo."

The professor swept a hand over the South China Sea on the map he held.

"The reason for all of this is, of course, the Royal Navy,

which maintains a substantial squadron of ships, known as the East Indies Station, in the area. That station is commanded by Rear Admiral William Hewitt, and is based at Hong Kong, only three days steaming from the imperial capital of Viet Nam at Hué, and five days from Saigon. His flagship is HMS *Iron Duke,* the most powerful warship in the Far East. Ships of Hewitt's squadron are always at or near Singapore, in the Gulf of Siam, and in the South China Sea, off this coast. Piracy patrol is a major part of their work. Singapore is the same distance from this coast as Hong Kong. The Royal Navy also advises—no, actually it runs—the Siamese king's small fleet of gunboats. Any questions, Peter?"

I was astounded. Petrusky was briefing me by memory, without the aid of any notes. I knew he was accurate so far regarding the British, from what I'd been told before I left Washington.

"None yet, Petrusky. Please proceed."

"The Spanish have a small, obsolete squadron of ships at Manila in the Philippines. They are only good for subduing the Muslim separatists in their southern islands, and frequently not even that. The Philippines maintain some silk trade with Cambodia and lacquer ware from Annam, but not much. They are not a major factor, but can never be discounted completely."

"Señor Altamonte is aboard, though. Do you know why?" I asked.

"We think it really is a trade mission. But we could be wrong."

I wondered whom he meant by "we," but I didn't press him. There would be time later for that. Instead, I was curious about the spice-laden islands to the south. "And the Dutch?"

"They have significant naval and military force in their area designed to maintain control over the Dutch East Indies colony—consisting of Sumatra and Java and eastward through thousands of islands, about three-quarters of which are dominated by Muslims, the rest by Hindu and animist followers. The Dutch influence is dominant to the south and east of Singapore, but not north of it. The British still worry about the Dutch impact on their Straits colonies, which the Dutch used to own a century ago. But the French further north don't have a concern about the Dutch. Other than some minor trade, they are not a factor in Indo-China."

"But the French *are*."

"In Indo-China, the French are *the* foremost factor, my friend. Directly in Cochin and indirectly elsewhere, the French control everything east of Siam, north of Singapore, and south of China on the Asian mainland. And they are expanding the frontiers and the depths of that control rapidly. You have picked a momentous period of time to visit. Change is in the air."

He paused, gazing through his glasses at me. A subtle probe? Well, I wasn't going to rise to *that* bait. "I didn't pick the timing, Petrusky. I'm just a courier."

The professor's lack of visible reaction was maddening. "Yes, of course, Peter. But just the same, you may very well see significant events while you are here."

That got my attention. "What kind of events?"

"The political situation is in transformation. No, it is more than that. It is *unstable*. I am certain of the results—the French will be victorious. But I am not certain about length and manner of the evolution to total direct French dominance. I fear it will be bloody."

"For whom?"

"For the people of these lands."

That was a verbal dodge, but I knew Petrusky was in a delicate position. I wanted him to continue, so I let it go. "Please describe the French presence in Indo-China."

"It started with French Christian missionaries, most with the MEP, in the sixteen-hundreds. By the late seventeen-hundreds, the vast number of Christian conversions among the people had alarmed the monarchies of Cambodia and Viet Nam and persecutions were begun in an effort to stop the trend of conversions and scare away the missionaries. The persecutions became deadly. Hundreds, later thousands, of Christian people were executed, both native and foreign. That provoked anger in France, which sent out naval forces from their colonies in India to protect the Christians. Of course, the local monarchies had no military to match European naval power. The persecutions stopped."

"And the French never left, did they?"

Petrusky shook his head. "No, they did not. In fact, they kept on coming. As soon as the French Navy was here, French traders started showing up. By the eighteen-fifties formal trading concessions were made to the French in exchange for some weaponry; by the eighteen-sixties legal concessions were made exempting French citizens from local laws. In the early eighteen-seventies Cochin-China became a formal French colony, ceded by the Emperor of Viet Nam, Tu Duc, at his imperial city of Hué. The French now completely control Cochin. They also have advisors in the imperial government at Hué itself and up in Tonking, at Hanoi. *And* in the kingdom of Cambodia, also. It all started in Cochin, though."

"Your mother was Cochinese—"

Petrusky completed the sentence. "And the oldest daughter of an imperial mandarin stationed in Cochin for the emperor at Hué. But he lost his position when his daughter, my mother, made two huge cultural mistakes."

"Which were?"

"She became a Christian, then she married a foreigner—a French naval officer. Upon the emperor in Hué learning of this treason my grandfather was stripped of his rank, position, and possessions. His shame was beyond recovery, and he fled his family and the empire. That was in eighteen-twenty-one and he was never seen again. I was born in eighteen-twenty-two—fourteen months after the marriage—and lived with my mother in Saigon until I was ten, when my father brought us to France, where I was educated until graduating from the university, just in time for the revolutionary unrest of the forties in France. I returned to Cochin, did work for the Church, continued my studies of languages, and began teaching. Because of *her* shame, my mother stayed in France until her death ten years ago, five years after my father's."

"Did you ever meet the other members of your Cochinese family?"

"Yes, I have met cousins. They are polite, but not friendly. I am an outcast with many—a *half-breed*, as you Americans say—in both cultures. Only the Church openly welcomes me, as a fellow Christian."

That explained a lot about Petrusky to me. Now for the difficult part—the local political stew. "I am sorry for your life's troubles, my friend. It is a difficult burden to bear, but you have certainly succeeded and risen above the pettiness of both societies. Can you now explain the situation regarding the emperor?"

"Thank you, Peter. Yes, we shall now discuss Emperor Tu Duc, Celestial King, Son of Heaven, and Emperor of Annam, Tonking, and Cochin, which he styles as Viet Nam, after the original Nguyen emperor's name for the empire. Tonking is in the north, with its capital at Hanoi. Cochin is down here in the south, with its capital at Saigon. Annam covers the long middle area, with its capital at Hué, which is also capital of the entire empire of Viet Nam.

"Tu Duc is the son of the previous emperor, Thieu Tri, and is the fourth emperor in the Nguyen Dynasty, which started at the beginning of this century, as it is measured in Western years. He assumed the throne in eighteen-forty-seven at the age of eighteen. His reign has not been tranquil. In fact, it began with violence, and violence has been a continual feature of it ever since.

"Tu Duc was not the eldest son of Thieu Tri and should not have been the successor. Hang Bao was the eldest son and rightful heir. He was moderate in religion and politics, open to new ideas. However, the mandarins of the imperial court, fearing losing control over the empire, opposed Hang Bao as being too soft to be a good successor. Thieu Tri agreed, designating the conser-

vative Confucian Tu Duc instead. The Nguyen dynasty is devout-
ly classical Chinese and as such, Confucian. Once Tu Duc took
the throne, his older brother rose in rebellion. Tu Duc crushed his
enemies and ordered his brother to be executed, but Hang Bao
committed suicide in prison instead. There are many who still
secretly revere him."

"So this Tu Duc is a ruthless man?"

Petrusky peered up over his glasses at me. "Totally. And he
hates Christians."

"So how does he get along with the French if he hates
Christians?"

"He did not get along with them—at first. Tu Duc tried to
shut off his empire from the outside world, which was futile, for
Western ideas and religion had already arrived centuries earlier.
You cannot stop ideas, and by the very act of attempting to ban
ideas, you many times propagate them instead.

"As Tu Duc's reign progressed, he instituted a return to the
repressions against Christians and foreigners, along with higher
taxes against everyone. He had a Catholic bishop in Saigon executed and ordered that all of his subjects that had converted to
Catholicism renounce their faith or they would be branded on
the face with the mark of a heretic. Resentment among the native
people and the foreigners, mostly French, grew. So did corruption
among the arrogant Confucian priests and mandarins. Tu Duc,
living in the luxury of the imperial capital inside the Forbidden
Purple City of Hué, complacently lived on, ignorant of what was
happening. He did not know the true conditions in the empire,
only what he was told by his advisors. They, as is usual, lied to
him."

Petrusky pointed to himself. "I arrived back in Cochin just
before Tu Duc's ascendancy. The imperial court was somewhat
tolerant of Christians at that point. There was even a Christian
mandarin at the court, a man named Nguyen Truong To. When
Tu Duc came into power and began his policies of isolation from
the world and religious repression within the country, Nguyen

Truong To tried to convince him that angering the French was a suicidal path. He explained that by persecuting Christians the emperor was uniting the Western world against him. Tu Duc said the French were too weakened with their own revolutionary chaos in eighteen-forty-eight to bother with troubles in the empire of Viet Nam on the other side of the world. Then he removed Nguyen Truong To from the court, stripping him of his rank. That was foolish. He should have listened to the Christian mandarin."

I remembered reading something about that. "But the French weren't that weak—they sent an expedition, didn't they?"

"Yes, a large one, with some Spanish naval support. It was sent to Saigon, where most of the Christians and foreigners lived, and it easily defeated the emperor's troops with their ancient firearms and tactics. Tu Duc then did something quite common in our history—indeed, in the history of all the monarchs of Indo-China. Pay close attention, Peter, for this same thing is going on these days too, particularly in Cambodia where you are bound."

The man's account both fascinated and alarmed me. This was all far more complicated than I'd been led to believe when given my orders. "What did he do?"

"Tu Duc called upon the Chinese emperor far to the north, the great overlord of all Asia and nominal superior of Tu Duc, for assistance against the French invaders, since by this point the European empires were against Tu Duc, even the ones who did not like the French."

Petrusky took a breath, visibly tired from his depressing narrative. He looked out over the black river ahead of us.

"The Qing dynasty emperor of China agreed with Tu Duc's request and sent troops to fight the French. They met in battle at Tonking, near Hanoi. The Chinese were defeated also. The French forced the Qing emperor to renounce his superiority over Emperor Tu Duc and all of Indo-China. They forced Tu Duc to grant legal, economic, and social concessions to the French throughout his empire. That made rival internal factions rise up everywhere against Tu Duc, who then realized the only way he would remain in power was by allying himself with the French, whom he hated."

"So the Chinese aren't involved here anymore?"

"No, they are. A few years after signing that treaty, they abrogated it, saying it was signed under false pretenses of the French. The Chinese throne still claims superiority over the emperor of Viet Nam."

"That's certainly convoluted. But back to the French—Tu Duc made a deal with them just to stay on the throne?"

Petrusky sighed. "Yes. He has become used to his lifestyle and will do anything to keep it, even deal with the hated French. The concessions included making Cochin and its capital of Saigon a totally separate French colony, and accepting a French Protectorate over the rest of his empire. Tu Duc handles internal matters in Annam and Tonking—the French handle external matters and trade in those areas. Christians are to be protected and all foreigners exempted from imperial laws.

"The emperor ended up humiliated, but still on the imperial throne, doing the French advisors' bidding. Many people from Annam and Tonking denounced him and fought on against Tu Duc and the French. They all failed. He is still there. He even made official the Romanized alphabet of our language, *Quoc Ngu*, which the French missionaries created two hundred years ago. It is widespread now—we are the only Asians using Western letters, a dubious distinction. Chinese is still the classical language of the imperial court, however. The mandarins refuse to use barbarians' script—their words, not mine."

"Are there still revolutionaries against the imperial government?"

"Yes, there are small movements against the imperial government and the French. The *Tonle Queen's* incident at Mytho will be added to the list of the malcontents' complaints, even though the instigator was neither a mandarin nor a Frenchman."

"And now, thirty-five years later, what is Tu Duc like?"

"Fifty-two years old and dissipated from debauchery. The man has several wives and hundreds of concubines, but is sick from a life-long case of smallpox, which has left him sterile and childless—thus lacking a successor. And therein lies one of the smoking fuses of the coming chaos. That is why I said you are here at a significant time. Tu Duc is very sick. They keep that secret, but I have my ways of knowing. The main question is—what will happen when he dies?"

Petrusky had a very good point. Not only was this culture complicated, I'd had no idea of the political volatility of the place. I wondered if anyone back in Washington did. The secret nature of my mission had just become more Byzantine.

"Do you have any idea of how long he has to live?"

"Nothing definite as to when, Peter, but my sources say he will probably die this year."

"Successors?"

Petrusky smiled and shook his head. "Many candidates among his nephews and cousins. None have dared raise their head above the rest at this point."

"What is the military ability of the emperor's government?" I asked.

"No navy to speak of, just some coastal customs junks and river police sampans. The army is of two classes. There is the national army, mostly of conscripts, that is stationed in different cities for domestic security and along the Cambodian border. They have light, smooth-bore field artillery, some cavalry, but are mostly infantry armed with thirty- or forty-year-old French army muskets, some with ancient flintlocks.

"Then there are the imperial guard regiments at Hué. They are to guard the Forbidden Purple City and the person of the emperor himself. No foreigners are allowed inside the walls of the city and few of the emperor's subjects have ever been inside. Only the emperor's family, imperial mandarins, the household servants, and the imperial guards live inside the walls.

"The imperial regiments man modern artillery on the city's ramparts, which were designed and built under the supervision of French army engineers back in the eighteen-forties as a gesture of friendship. There are two cavalry regiments at Hué. The imperial infantry is armed with modern rifles—"

I interrupted the professor's monologue. "Do you know what kind of rifles?"

"I have been told they are French-made Gras rifles. They are effective, yes?"

They were. I'd almost been killed by one fired by a Chilean soldier in Peru two years earlier. "There are several models dating back to eighteen-sixty-six. I imagine they have the eighteen-seventy-four model. It's very effective. Please go on."

"I am not a military man and do not know much else as far as the imperial army is concerned. Tu Duc has learned his lessons well. He is a master of survival. All of the imperial troops guarding him are disciplined and reasonably well paid. I must say that they are very imposing to see at the military pageants outside the walls."

Petrusky, like many people who are not warriors, was confusing image with substance. Parade ground soldiers meant nothing in my experience of combat on three continents. The ability to look good while marching in unison had no bearing on the ability to stand and fight—an important lesson the Army of the Potomac had been given by Robert Lee's ragged veterans early in America's Civil War.

From the professor's presentation it appeared to me that the emperor was sequestered in his cushy splendor up there in the palaces of Hué and the whole country could've, and probably had, gone to hell and he wouldn't have had a clue. The only people that would fight for him were the privileged elite, just to keep their lifestyles, and they probably didn't know how to fight. I wondered about the inner circle of mandarins' loyalty to Tu Duc, and was about to ask that very question of Petrusky, when suddenly two things happened, neither of which were good.

The first was that Rork whispered to me that Blundell was coming toward us along the starboard-side main deck. The professor and I instantly reacted by leaping to our feet and striding aft along the port side of the main deck.

Seconds after Rork's warning, the second event occurred. *Tonle Queen* abruptly crashed to a stop—catapulting my co-conspirator and I over the port side into the dark and surprisingly cold waters of the Mekong.

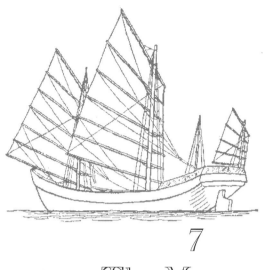

7

The Messenger

Upon surfacing I dared not shout out Petrusky's name, still fearful of anyone discovering our association, but instead swam forward against the moderate current toward the riverboat's stern—thank God it was the low water season before the monsoon torrents. As it was, I'd drifted a good fifty yards downstream. The paddlewheel was still thrashing around as it slowed down to a stop and excess steam was bleeding off the stack in a screaming jet of vapor. Angry shouts could be heard around the deck, but none related to passengers gone overboard. MacTaggert was chief among the voices, swearing a blur of brogue and rage apparently directed at Wallace, who was the officer of the watch.

Ominously, Rork wasn't in sight on the main deck. I wondered if he'd gone over too. The bosun was a strong swimmer, though, so I wasn't as worried about him as I was about Petrusky, whose abilities I didn't know.

I waited until the wheel stopped completely, all the while

treading water and peering through the gloom for the professor. Then, realizing that if alive at all he must be far away downstream of me, I hauled myself up the paddle boards of the wheel. The old wound in my chest from North Africa erupted in a spasm of pain and I nearly fell back in the water. Balancing along a spoke I carefully stepped onto the central hub, then dropped down to the deck with a squish and a groan.

"Are you all right, Commander? That must have been a nasty fall overboard."

Blundell stood there, arms folded, sardonic look on his face. At first I felt like a fool for falling in the river, then a tinge of anger grew inside, for I had the immediate and uncomfortable impression he'd been watching me the whole time in the water, but hadn't tried to help. Not wanting him to see either my pain or my anger, I kept it lighthearted.

"Yes, I'm fine. Just a bit wet. Embarrassing, really, for a naval officer to fall overboard. What happened?" The pain was receding a bit, but the ache was still there.

"We struck some rocks," he said. "There is damage to the forward part of the hull, evidently. I heard someone saying something about water coming in. Perhaps we will sink."

Struck some rocks? The hull was flooding? I looked around for Rork. Blundell must have sensed that by his next blasé comment.

"Your petty officer Rork is off in a ship's boat looking for people in the water. Seems to be a quick thinker, that man. Ah, there he is, I think."

Just then I saw a long shape in the darkness astern of us, out beyond the loom of the ship's lanterns. It was Rork, all right, rowing a dinghy upstream to the riverboat. Soon he was in the light and I saw a small man crumpled in the bow, arms dragging in the river. Petrusky's head suddenly popped up and he vomited out some water, then collapsed back into the dinghy in a coughing fit.

"It would appear he has saved someone," Blundell said, sounding to me like he was almost amused by the whole thing.

Then he looked right in my eyes. "One of the locals, yes?"

My wits were returning. "Yes, it appears so," I answered as nonchalantly as I could as the dinghy came alongside. "Good for Rork."

Right about then, Petrusky, weak and still choking, saw me on the deck and smiled as he waved. "No problem" was all I could hear from the professor, but that was more than enough for Monsieur Blundell, who looked pretty smug as he spun around and walked forward, calling back to me, "I do believe that man knows you, Commander. *Bonne nuit, mon ami.*"

So much for maintaining a quiet connection with the professor, I thought as Petrusky was lifted up to the deck by Rork, who was winded and still very weak from the malaria. The professor could barely stand up, but rise he did and pulled out his spectacles from a pocket. He focused unsteadily on me, then grinned.

"Thank God you can swim, Petrusky," I said.

"Thank God, indeed, Peter—for I *cannot* swim!"

Rork got up on deck and nodded his head. "Grabbed him as he went down, sir."

Suddenly Hau turned up, took one look at Petrusky, and gushed out in English, "Oh my, it's the professor! Is he hurt badly? Should I get some help?"

Petrusky replied evenly in the local tongue, evidently conveying that he was not hurt, just wet. Then Hau noticed my appearance and let loose another moan, started bowing and saying something in English about medical help and notifying the captain and who-knows-what-else. I just wasn't in the mood for that and cut to the question at hand by interrupting his wailing. "Never mind me, I'm fine, Hau. But what the hell just happened to the ship? Are we taking on water?"

He backed up two steps, surprised at my tone, which I must admit had becoming a bit commanding. "We struck rocks, sir. The bow smashed into them, but not to worry, the leak in the hull has been stopped. We are not sinking and they are pumping out the water that did get inside."

That didn't make sense to me. "Rocks? Rocks don't move around in a river like sandbars do. Didn't the helmsman know where they were?"

Hau nodded his head. "Oh yes, Commander, the man steering knew where the rocks are, sir. We make this journey regularly. He turned to avoid them, but . . ."

He hesitated, clearly weighing whether he should say the rest. That infuriated me. "But what, Hau? Spit it out, man!"

"The helm ropes down to the rudder were cut, sir."

No, he must've been mistaken, I thought. Hau was a steward, not a seaman. "Cut? Are you sure they weren't frayed, chafed through from wear?"

The man looked terrified at having let out that information. "Ah, well, sir, I heard Mr. Sandingham himself say they were cut."

"Sabotage," muttered Petrusky.

Rork spoke what we were all thinking. "Hmm. Someone intentionally ran the bow into the rocks? Musta' cut them ropes just as we were comin' round that bend an' approachin' the rocks—somebody who knew what they were doin'. Experienced on this river, probably on this vessel. 'Tis nothin' short o' a miracle that no one up there at the bow was hurt, *ain't it, sir?*"

That was a sobering assessment. Rork's warning that Blundell was walking forward had gotten us up and moving aft, otherwise Petrusky and I would've been thrown onto the rocks and severely injured or killed.

Petrusky shook his head and sighed. "It would appear that someone wants both you and me dead, Commander. Quite dead."

I'd only been in the Orient a month, but already knew they loved gossip and a good conspiracy story. Hau might be imagining all this about cut wheel ropes. "Yes, well, *maybe*. But who? The only other people who knew we were at the bow were Rork and Hau here, who delivered Rork's message to meet you at the bow."

I turned to the chief steward. "Did you tell anyone about that message, Hau?"

I watched him closely for deception. Hau's head wagged in the negative. "Oh no, sir! That was a private message and no one's business that you and the professor were going to converse. Indeed, I thought it an honor that you would talk with the professor, who is one of my countrymen."

Petrusky put a hand on my arm, stopping my next question. He turned to Hau, his tone benevolent. "Thank you, Mr. Hau. I know you had nothing to do with this. I think now is a good time for each of us to retire to our cabins and get out of these clothes. Good evening, sir."

Hau took the cue and departed, with considerable apologies and bowing, leaving Rork and me waiting for the professor's explanation for his abrupt dismissal of a potential suspect in the crime. When it came, I was taken aback, a feeling I was getting used to with Monsieur Petrusky.

"Peter, perhaps the time has come to accelerate your political education and discuss our fellow passengers and the reality behind some of their façades."

Before I could reply, Rork held up a hand, then pointed into the gloom on our portside. "Ahm, I do believe we have some company, sir. Don't appear friendly."

The three of us peered intently, but I heard them before I saw them—grunting in unison with the effort of rowing fast. Then four boats took form, the white bow waves looking for all the world like teeth in the blackness. A frightened shout came from the top deck of the riverboat.

"*Quan giac!*"

Petrusky shook his head with disdain. "No, no . . . the lookout is wrong. They are not pirates. Not in the conventional meaning, at least."

The four boats were separating, two heading for the bow, one for amidships, and one for where we were standing at the stern. As they grew closer I saw that each boat flew a square yellow flag edged in green from a stern staff, barely discernible in the night. I had seen that on a few river craft, but did not know its significance.

Upon recognizing the flags, the professor nodded. "Yes, just as I thought. They are with the opium warlord, Whangtai."

My incredulity emerged. "Opium warlord? Here on the lower Mekong? In the French colony of Cochin?"

"Yes, opium is officially sanctioned, licensed, and taxed here, as it is in China. In fact, they bring it in from the Chinese and distribute it in Cochin, Annam, Tonking, Cambodia, and Laos. Whangtai, who was originally from Shanghai, has five thousand men under arms to transport and guard his shipments. He has business dealings with the French colonial government in Saigon and also with the chief of the Cambodian king's opium monopoly, a Frenchman named Garnier d'Abain. D'Abain has become quite rich off opium, as has his master, King Norodom."

He paused and studied the first boat, ignoring my look of amazement and Rork's stealthy withdrawal of his revolver from within his tunic. I observed Rork paying particular attention to a man standing in the stern of the boat. *Always shoot the officer in charge first* is Rork's rule of close combat—he takes particular relish in telling me that. The man yelled out something.

"It appears we may have a confrontation," said Petrusky.

I asked, "What is going on here, Professor? Is this some sort of attack?"

Petrusky came out of his concentration and looked at me, as a teacher to a hopelessly naïve student. "No, I think not, Peter. But it most certainly is a demonstration of willpower and strength. My estimate of this situation is that it is a type of warning. You see, that man standing in the boat approaching our entry gangway is one of Whangtai's top lieutenants. He is coming here to give a symbolic message to Monsieur d'Abain, who is a passenger aboard the *Tonle Queen*."

"A message?"

"Yes. It is an unusual and dramatic message. The first part of the message is our location—that d'Abain can be touched anywhere, even aboard a European vessel. The second part will be more personal. My guess is that there has been some sort of delay in payments due Whangtai."

Rork interjected quietly, "The cut wheel rope?"

Petrusky smiled. "Very good, Mr. Rork. I believe you are correct. We now know the reason for the sabotage. They didn't cut the rope to cause a crash that would kill us up on the bow. No, Whangtai's confederates aboard this riverboat cut those ropes to stop the vessel and facilitate this confrontation. It makes the message even more indelible."

I heard a bellowing brogue fill the night with a string of foul oaths. Captain MacTaggert was on the main deck gangway, his invective aimed squarely at the boat now alongside, in spite of the five rifle muzzles aimed at his chest from only a few feet away. The Asian man in charge of the boat, dressed in the black suit common to the area, casually leaped aboard, paid no attention to the nearly apoplectic captain, and ascended the stairs to the upper deck, where the first-class passenger d'Abain had his cabin. I noted with surprise that the captain did not physically interfere with the man. As all this was happening, the other boats, including the one near us at the stern, disgorged a swarm of hard-eyed armed men, also in black, who took up station along the main deck. Their carbines were French and modern.

It was a neatly timed, professionally executed operation. The whole time I never heard any of Whangtai's men speak a word. They'd done this before. I was impressed and not a little apprehensive.

From above us came a slurry of French curses followed by more conversational tones, then silence. MacTaggert stormed up the stairs, yelling for Sandingham to get the ship under way and swearing about dope fiends and Oriental connivery.

The next moment the opium warlord's lieutenant calmly descended the stairs, nodded to his men, and jumped down into the boat. The soldiery followed into their boats. In all, no more than five minutes had elapsed since Rork first spotted the inter-lopers. Now they were rowing out into the night, a frightening apparition disappearing rapidly downstream. Message received—and not just by Monsieur d'Abain.

Within sixty seconds of the gang's departure the main and upper decks were filled with foreigners chattering about the show they'd just seen. I could hear Colonel Fountjoy pontificating above the rest: "Damned bloody cheeky, if you ask me. Little buggers need a severe lesson in etiquette toward their betters."

Suddenly the steam whistle screamed and the planking below my wet shoes rumbled with the engine's rise to life. The *Tonle Queen* backed off the rocks with a jolt and a thud, then floated in free water, the giant stern wheel behind us bashing the river as if in punishment for this gross display of disrespect to European superiority.

"Well, that was interesting," I commented.

"An instructive exhibition of opium's monetary, and thus political, power in this part of the world, Peter," offered the professor. "Only for opium would an Asian dare to do what just happened. There will be no penalty against Whangtai."

Rork was less philosophic as he relaxed and returned the revolver to its hiding place. "Looks like dope is king over everybody around here."

Petrusky sighed. "Concisely said, my friend. And now I suggest we get out of these wet clothes and reconvene in your cabin in fifteen minutes. There is more you need to know about where you are heading, the king of Cambodia, and who your fellow passengers are while en route."

I was exhausted, but the look in his eyes left no room for debate or refusal. It was then I realized that slowly, subtly, I had somehow come under Petrusky's command. That was irksome, but right then I was just too tired to make anything of it. Instead, I said, "All right," and sloshed off down the deck to my cabin.

As the three of us turned to go, I noticed a movement above me, someone leaning over the railing of the upper deck and looking down on us. Focusing on the figure, I realized with dread it was MacTaggert, glaring at my companions and me with undisguised loathing. A second later he was gone.

It had been a long day, and it wasn't getting any easier.

8

Façades

Early hours of Thursday, 26 April 1883
On the Mekong River near Sadek

My old chest wound still hurt—a dull ache that sharpened when I used my left arm to lift anything heavy. Rork expressed concern and suggested we call off the meeting, but we had too much going on at the time for that sort of thing. I needed information about the situation, and the way things were transpiring I didn't know how long Petrusky would be around to give that information.

"Oh, I'll be all right, Rork. The damned thing is just inflamed from hauling myself out of the water, all while Blundell watched with quiet glee, I might add."

"Aye, there're a lot o' that sort on this bucket. Nary a one I'd trust with me dog. If I had a dog, that is."

Rork loved dogs, always pointing out bedraggled strays to me and lamenting the fact that as a sailor he could never have one. He'd have a dozen if he ever lived ashore in a real home.

I was worried about *him*. "By the way, I noticed you were

pretty winded yourself when you got aboard. How are you doing? That fever isn't back, is it?"

"Well, me strength ain't what it used to be afore that fever got me on the road here, but I'll do the job. No worries. Besides, this here cabin's just the thing for some rest an' relaxin' an' watchin' the people on this barge. Be right as rain in no time, sir."

I let it go and switched subjects. Rork had a pretty good sense of judgment regarding people. There were several times in the past where his intuition, honed by thirty years before the mast, had proved to be a life-saving asset. "Do you trust Petrusky?"

He didn't hesitate. "No, sir, I don't trust a single solitary bugger on this tub. But we don't have much o' a choice regardin' the professor, do we now?"

Three knocks came at the cabin door. Rork opened it and Petrusky entered, looking like the academic he was in a fresh suit of clothes. He said, "Good evening, gentlemen, again," and sat at the desk while I took a bunk and Rork stood in the doorway to watch the deck. Some moths gathered near the lantern on the desk, flitting about. Petrusky watched them awhile, his eyes sad. Then he abruptly spoke with no polite preamble, no reference to the incident that just occurred, just plunged into his subject.

"Very well, Commander, let us discuss where we are going and who you are going to see, shall we?"

"Lead on, my friend," I said, intrigued by the little man's energy.

"Commander, we've discussed Emperor Tu Duc and now must address King Norodom of Cambodia. Both of them have been on their thrones for decades—not an easy accomplishment in Southeast Asia. *Do not* underestimate either one of them.

"Eldest son and successor of King Ang Duong, Norodom is forty-nine years old and has been on the throne since eighteen-sixty, following the death of his father. Educated in Siam, where he studied Buddhism, he grew up appreciating the Siamese culture, and thus had some affection for that country.

"But Cambodia was located between Siam and the emperors of Viet Nam, and was subject to both. In fact, in eighteen-forty-five, the Vietnamese emperor forced Norodom's father into relinquishing three Cambodian provinces in the Mekong delta to Viet Nam—the ones we are traveling through right now. To the west, the Siamese king forced him to hand over several provinces about the same time. The Cambodians have never forgotten those humiliations. They do not like or trust either the Siamese or the Vietnamese to this day."

"What about the French?"

"Upon gaining the throne, Norodom should have been crowned by both neighboring kingdoms, according to custom. He wasn't, due to personal animosities between the rulers. Soon after his ascension, there was civil war in Cambodia, fomented mainly by Norodom's half-brother Sisowath. Norodom finally put down the rebellion, but only by using the last resort of asking the French for military help. That is how they got their first influence in Cambodia—to help solve an internal squabble."

"Sounds like Tu Duc and his brother. And in the end the French stayed?"

"Quite so, Peter. Regarding the French, you are correct—they always stay. The price for their help was a heavy one for Norodom. France's Emperor Napoleon III developed a personal interest in Cambodia after the rediscovery of the ancient city of Angkor Wat by the French explorer Henri Mouhot. Interestingly, Napoleon had turned Mouhot's request for funding the exploration down initially. The British funded Mouhot's expedition. Then, when it was successful, the French celebrated their son's accomplishment."

Petrusky shrugged. "But I have digressed—*excusez-moi*. The price for France's help was that Cambodia would be a protectorate, like Cochin at that time. That price was paid in eighteen-sixty-three. But Norodom was too clever for his own good. He tried to play the Siamese against the French by signing a secret treaty with them, negating the one with France. That was when he gave the Siamese the western provinces of Cambodia, including Angkor Wat, in return for protection against the French. The Siamese did not live up to their obligations, however, somehow always delaying their support. Meanwhile, the French were not amused. They merely waited until the next time Norodom visited Bangkok, then raised the French flag and took over the capital at Phnom Penh. He returned to a *fait accompli.*"

Norodom sounded to me just like the rest of the local grand poobahs—greedy, egomaniacal dilettantes who would do anything with anyone to stay in power and live the pampered life. I wondered if anyone anywhere in Indo-China did anything for the good of his people. Good Lord, why in the world did the French even want this part of the world?

"So the French took over the government?"

"Ostensibly, they only handle the foreign affairs. Internal affairs are still run by the king. But the French have tremendous influence through their advisors, and dictate subtly."

"Like Blundell?"

"Yes, like Blundell."

"And what is Norodom's relationship to them these days?"

"He's a puppet. He resents them but uses them to remain in the lifestyle he enjoys."

"Why does he resent them?"

"They made him reorganize the government, do away with the Mandarin system, reduce the royal houshold—and abolish slavery, at least officially. He suffered humiliation—tremendous loss of face—with his own people."

"What is Norodom like personally?"

"He is well educated, cultured, versed in music and the other arts, well traveled. He invites many internationally famous musicians and singers to perform at his royal theater. In fact, Miss Marston is due to perform there. He has several prominent monarchs among his friends, both European and Asian. In addition to Khmer, he speaks French, English, Siamese, Annamese, and a little Chinese, I'm told. Norodom enjoys fine food and drink, and is especially fond of French cuisine. Unlike Tu Duc in Viet Nam, Norodom is interested and well versed in the outside world.

"Inside his palace, he has many concubines and dozens of children. With visitors he can be quite charming. He knows what Europeans expect, what they want to hear him say, so he accommodates their preconceptions. He has been doing it for over twenty years."

"And his view of Americans?"

Petrusky took a breath and sat there, looking at me, evaluating the chances of this newest of foreign intruders in Indo-China. "He doesn't really know you Americans, Peter. No one in this area of the world has had many dealings with your country. He may view you as a foil, an off-setting factor against the Europeans."

It was my turn to regard him for a moment. Was this shrewd half-Asian, half-European really there to help me, or there to steer me on behalf of the Church? Remembering the Church's previous relationship with me, I presumed they sent him to spy on me as well as assist me. Or was the whole Church story a ruse? Was he really working for the Cambodian royal court? Or perhaps the Vietnamese emperor? In any event, I'd have to be very careful what I said around him.

"So this Norodom is capable of double-dealing?"

The professor's face showed a momentary smile. "You Americans have such interesting colloquialisms! Yes, he is quite capable of double-dealing. In fact, I would expect nothing less than *triple*-dealing from him. How do you think he stays in power? Just assume the worst from both Tu Duc and Norodom and you will be rarely surprised."

Did I detect a flash of sarcasm from the normally reserved Petrusky? "Thank you for sharing your views on the political situation, Professor. It's a difficult one for an American to decipher."

"Yes, I imagine so. And I must not forget to enlighten you about your fellow passengers, Peter. They are not what they seem either. Let us begin with Monseiur d'Abain—"

"Who is an opium man."

"Peter, he is *the* opium man for Norodom. Has been so since seventy-four. Works with Whangtai to ensure the shipments are regular, protected, and paid for. His French efficiency has made him hundreds of thousands of dollars—the payments are in Mexican silver dollars—over the last nine years."

"Why Mexican?"

Petrusky shrugged. "Because, except for British pounds sterling, it is the purest silver coin in the world. Monsieur d'Abain probably has more of it than any other man in Cambodia, including the king."

"He sounds interesting. I haven't met the gentleman yet."

"Yes, you have met him, but have not been formally introduced. D'Abain has been aboard since Mytho and a regular in the bar salon. He is the one with the mild manner, about fifty years of age. Favors gray suits and cheap cigars. You have spoken with him in the salon several times in polite conversations, nothing of substance. Certainly nothing about his work. Yesterday after breakfast you said good morning to him on the promenade deck."

The professor saw my reaction and raised an eyebrow. "Do not look so surprised, my friend. Everything that happens in the bar salon or dining salon or promenade deck is known on the lower deck within minutes, Peter. My mandate is to educate and protect you. I need to know what is happening to do that."

"I thought the French aboard were all minor functionaries and middle-class planters—that's what Sandingham told me. He never said a Cambodian royal opium magnate was among the passengers."

The moment I said that I realized it sounded hopelessly naïve. Petrusky probably thought that too, but was kind enough not to say it.

"Peter, you are an American intruder in their midst. They don't want you to know who is who. And now for the others. We'll start with the British—Mr. Rockford."

"The blubbering old fool?"

I was ready for anything at this point, my mind reeling from the multiple façades and motives of everyone around me. But even with that, the professor managed to stun me yet again on a subject with which I was totally unfamiliar.

"Mr. Rockford may drool, but he is far from a dementia-ridden old man. Quite the opposite. He is a purveyor of gutta percha, the insulating rubber used in trans-oceanic submarine telegraph cables to protect the wire from the salt water. He operates among the British colonies on the Malay peninsula and brokers the sales, which amount to hundreds of thousands of pounds sterling. Cables are being run all over Asia and the islands these days. Very large sums of money are involved. Originally, India rubber was used, but for the past few years gutta percha has been the preferred insulation, causing great consternation in the rubber industry.

"Recently, the French plantations in Cochin and Annam growing India rubber have tried to compete by offering lower prices for their type of rubber. The cable-laying companies are paying close attention and are almost ready to make some transactions with French colonies."

He was right on that. Telegraph communications were spreading everywhere. "Professor, I know a bit about India rubber, but nothing of gutta perch rubber. Which material is better for the cables?"

Petrusky frowned pensively. "That is the subject of intense debate right now, but suffice it to say that India rubber is cheaper and easier to manage, while gutta percha is stronger and more difficult to work with. The important factor in all of this is that millions of dollars or pounds are at stake—long-range cables will be laid soon around the Pacific. Rockford is bound upriver to see what is going on. He has been sent on a commercial reconnaissance, as it were, by the British planters down in Malaya."

"Do the French know this?"

"Yes, of course, but façades are kept as a matter of courtesy."

Ah . . . so *that* explained the intensity of the rubber conversation in the salon earlier. "So amidst the revelry up there in the salon there is a serious economic competition."

"Well, the largest cable-laying companies are British—the John Pinder Company and the China Telegraph Company. The submarine cables emanating from French Indo-China are all British. The French don't have that capability right now. Fountjoy is related somehow—I am not sure precisely how—to the Australasia Extension Company, a subordinate unit of the China Telegraph Company. He and Rockford are bedfellows in the British endeavor to ascertain what the French are up to concerning rubber. That is why they are on this ship. So yes, there are ulterior motives among the passengers. And, of course, you Americans are part of all this also."

That was new to me. Feeling like a dolt, I asked anyway. "Us? We don't have a horse in this race. Sounds like the Brits and French are the only contenders."

The professor shook his head. "That's only concerning the rubber for the insulation in the creation of the cable. The Americans have recently entered the field of actually *running* long-distance telegraphic cables, having gained valuable experience in Latin America with cable-laying ships. There have been discreet inquiries from them about cable-laying contracts in Asia, from what I have been told from my sources."

Then my brain began to function at last. "So these people may think I'm part of all that? That I'm reconnoitering the area for my country's commercial interests. Specifically, cable companies."

He leaned down to brush a moth off his trousers and peered at me over the top of his spectacles. "Of course, Peter. You would too, would you not?"

"Well, I'm not reconnoitering anything for anyone. I'm just a courier."

Petrusky next addressed me like a dismissive headmaster, which I didn't appreciate. "Whatever, my friend. They will just assume that is just another façade, like all the other foreigners have. Only remember this, Peter—some façades can get you killed in this part of the world. Life is cheap here."

I was tiring of Asia rapidly. Opium, gutta percha, and debauching despots—what the hell kind of place had Rork and I ended up in? And our travel upriver had just begun, so things were bound, no doubt with our luck, to get worse. An old, bad feeling swept through my body as my companion stared at me.

I'd first felt the sensation twenty years earlier on the misnamed Peace River in Florida, as I chased blockade-runners during the Southern rebellion. Less than an hour after that initial premonition, I had a gash along my right temple and several of my crew lay dead and wounded. Over the ensuing years I'd felt the intuition a few other times. Every time it culminated in blood sooner or later. The last time had been in Peru two years earlier, as I ran through the Catacombs of the Dead with some very determined men chasing me.

Rork and I have talked about my premonitions a couple of times. He is very impressed. Tells me I must have had some Gaelic in my background, that it's a sign of great intuition. A gift from God, he says, trying to make it all sound like an attribute. I think of it as a damned curse.

The evening had worn me down. My body, drained of physical energy, was aching for some sleep. My mind was fogged with the various nuances of the intelligence I'd gained. Rest and a sunrise might make me feel better. I was tired of Petrusky and his gloomy teaching, but he was waiting for a reply. Diplomacy exhausted, I answered candidly.

"Life is cheap everywhere. And I've learned that men die pretty much the same way no matter what continent they inhabit—with a lot of screaming and begging. This is merely a messenger mission, Professor, but Rork and I will handle whatever comes up. It would, however, be particularly appreciated if you could let us know if you learn any new information. In the meantime, I'll see you around the ship, Monsieur Petrusky. Thank you and good night."

He didn't sound like he appreciated my comments. "As you wish, Peter. Good night."

After the professor departed for the lower deck, Rork whispered to me, "Do you think he knows why we're here?"

I'd been wondering the same thing.

"Damed if I know how, Sean—but yes, I think he probably does."

9

A Poisonous Stew

The river narrowed and the surrounding terrain got higher as we steamed upstream. Since tidal brackish water couldn't penetrate this far upriver, thick, dark green jungle replaced mangroves along the banks. The towns and villages were larger, and the pall of acrid wood smoke from cooking fires denser. From late morning until sunset the visibility was no more than half a mile. The crowded traffic on the river was diverse in function and form. Everything from tiny fishing sampans to lumbering, rice-filled junks and officious French gunboats made their way up, down, and across the river. In the smoke-filled air there were several near collisions, usually accompanied by the riverboat heeling over in an emergency turn and the sound of MacTaggert swearing a string of oaths in the wheelhouse.

Vinh Long, Cai Tao Ha, Sadek, and Cho Moi—we stopped at each, off-loading and taking on cargo and people, gradually getting closer to the border. Several of the French planters disembarked at Sadek, but the main characters of the bar salon stayed aboard.

The social scene in the bar remained at the same frivolous level, inane banter about carefully nebulous topics. But each evening I noticed the tension growing, the brief evaluative glances at each other getting colder. No one talked about rubber or telegraph cables or international politics. No one really talked to me much, either. It was as if they had already determined my role and reason for being, and resolved to ignore me.

Petrusky and I would see each other on the main deck but seldom spoke, and then only if he felt it safe. He and Rork talked more frequently below decks at meals; however, the professor had no more intelligence to share.

A week and a half after embarking on the riverboat, we reached the border and the Kingdom of Cambodia. It was an anticlimatic affair. Just after sunrise, the *Tonle Queen* stopped in midstream and anchored. An hour later a Frenchman, attired in an absurd yellow and blue half-Cambodian, half-French uniform, came aboard as a customs inspector and directly repaired to the bar salon. I sauntered in to watch. There, he downed the proffered sherry, gravely looked at the cargo and passenger manifests without really examining them, pounded three stamps on each of five documents, accepted an envelope from an equally solemn Sandingham, and departed—all inside of seven minutes.

Cambodia looked pretty much the same as Cochin to me, except there were fewer boats. Hau explained that to me—pirates infested the border areas. A few were renegades from the Cham, the peacable Muslims of the region; some were Chinese, supposedly allied loosely with Whangtai; but the most feared were outlaw Europeans, mostly French army deserters. Petrusky said the same thing to Rork later that day, that the French Navy hadn't quite totally pacified that stretch of the Mekong yet. The general atmosphere of apprehension made for some excitement the following night when we were anchored in mid-channel off the dilapidated thatched huts of Tan Chau, a one-dock settlement a few miles inside the border.

Rork and I were taking a stroll around the main deck after dinner, listening appreciatively to the delicate tones of the chimes and flutes coming from a tiny Buddhist temple ashore. The music of the Orient is so unlike ours, clearly meant for a different level of awareness. Even with my admitted lack of a musical ear, I found it soothing in a way I never had with European or American compositions. Just as I was succumbing to this subtle harmony, Rork spied a craft rowing toward us in the gloom.

Then we both saw another. At the same time, the topside lookout spotted them and raised the alarm in a high-pitched alert. The boats were moving rapidly and my immediate thought was that they were river pirates. Evidently, so was everyone else's. Within seconds MacTaggert, Sandingham, and Wallace were leaning over the upper deck rail above us, pistols in hand. Rork, professional that he is, quietly pointed out the make of the pistols to me—new Enfield forty-seven-caliber revolvers that the British army was using in Afghanistan to stop fanatical tribesmen. I wondered about MacTaggert's ability to procure such state-of-the-art lethal weaponry. Somebody somewhere had impressive connections.

Rork and I always carried our navy Colts hidden in those days. With things unfolding as they were, I thought it a good time to loosen my jacket to gain better access. As Rork did likewise, I heard Fountjoy on the deck directly above us muttering something about effective range. Hau showed up on the main deck and stood next to us with his pocket pea-shooter ready for action, glaring at the approaching boats, then calling out a challenge to them in Cambodian.

There was no answer from the boats. Now I could see they had several men in each. From above, the clicks of hammers being pulled back could be heard. Drawing my weapon, I moved to stand behind a thin stanchion post, ridiculous for protection or concealment, but one does ridiculous things at such moments.

Rork, of course, was far more practical. He knelt down and used the railing to steady his revolver, which was leveled at the form of a man in the stern of the leading boat.

Above us, MacTaggert growled, "Stand by and take aim, gentlemen. I will give the word to fire, and *only* I."

That was fine with me, for now I could see faces in the boats, and they didn't look aggressive to me. One of them appeared Caucasian. Yes, now I could see it clearly, a white man's face. Renegade outlaws trying to catch us by guile? Rork and I kept our pistols aimed.

Hau called out in Cochinese. A lazy-sounding reply in the same language came back and I saw Hau relax the muscles in his face, but he kept the pistol aimed. Then the white man in the first boat stood up.

"Bon soir, Capitaine! C'est Jean Dupuis, mon ami!"

Even I, with my linguistic deficiencies, could tell the man's French was slurred from drink. In the second boat, another man shouted in an Irish lilt. "Hallo there! Jim McCarthy here, Captain. You can shoot old Dupuis there, he's just a fancified Frog, but for Christ's own sake don't shoot your bloody guns at me—I'm one of Her Majesty's subjects!"

The sound of revolver hammers being backed down was attended by oaths in English, French, and Cochinese. Next to us, Hau frowned and shook his head as he put the pistol back in his pocket. The captain roared down to the boats, "You sorry bastards—I should shoot ye jes' for aggravatin' me! Get your lame arses aboard an' explain why I shouldn't put a bullet in each o' ye."

It wasn't said in jest. I thought our crazy captain just might fire a round for emphasis, but McCarthy wasn't intimidated in the least. "Because you won't spend the money on a bullet to shoot the likes o' this Irish poet, you cheap Scotch derelict. An' besides, I've got an American friend of yours along with me."

A New York–accented voice rose up. "Ah, Tag, stop showing off for the natives and gets us some rum ready—it's been a bad enough day and I'm sorely in need of it."

The three men boarded the *Tonle Queen,* ignored Rork and me standing there, and went at once up to MacTaggert's stateroom, their baggage left in a pile on the deck.

After the men ascended to the upper deck, Rork and I looked at Hau for an explanation of the bizarre incident. He shrugged his shoulders and said, "All three gentlemen are acquaintances of Captain MacTaggert. Monsieur Dupuis is a merchant in fine goods from the Far East and manufactured items from the West. He usually operates in the north near Hanoi, but sometimes comes down here. Mr. McCarthy is a surveyor, currently working for the Siamese king through the British. The American is Mr. Augustine Heard, the only one of your countrymen who is seen on the river. He is from a mercantile house in Hong Kong and sometimes visits Saigon and Phnom Penh."

I was still pondering the extraordinary show we'd just seen. Curiosity made me ask, "Do they come aboard often?"

"Occasionally. I must say, it is quite unusual for them to all be here at the same time."

"What does Mr. Heard sell?" inquired Rork.

"A little of everything, Commander."

Hau's face suddenly creased in worry. "Oh my—they will need cabins! I must beg your leave, Commander, and get some accommodations ready."

Five minutes after Rork and I subsequently retired to our cabin, there was a knock at the door and Petrusky entered. Though he'd never been what I'd call joyful, the man was damned glum now.

"This is not good, Commander. Not good at all."

Again, Petrusky was speaking in the indirect fashion so prevalent there. That sort of thing drives me mad. Why can't people speak plainly like we do in America? I wondered for the thousandth time.

"I don't get your drift, Professor. Speak up. What's the trouble?"

His head shook woefully. "Mr. Heard, the American, and Monsieur Dupuis, the Frenchman, are aboard. At the same time."

"So?"

"They are competing merchants—of guns."

Rork let out a low whistle. "Jesus, Mary, an' Joseph. An' I thought the clans o' Ireland were a thorny thicket! This place makes me beloved Gaels look positively simple-minded. Ta' think, an' I was worried about the rubber merchies causin' a row."

This was getting confusing. "All right, time for more education, Petrusky. Tell me what you know."

"Listen carefully, my friend, for the tumult I have feared would come for some time seems to be transpiring with the concentration of these various factors in one place. I am certain now there will be war here soon."

"And these men have something to do with that?"

"Yes. I will start with Monsieur Dupuis. He is one of the few Europeans who successfully deals up in Tonking with the Chinese government on the border, the Black Flag warlords on the river, the French colonial government advisors, and the Vietnamese provincial mandarins who represent the emperor, back at his citadel in Hué.

"Dupuis fought with the French navy on the Song Koi—or the Red River as you call it—against the Black Flags and has brushed death many times, but never fallen. He survives because he is ruthless. All of that has enhanced his reputation in the area."

Tonking was six hundred miles to the north. Dupuis was far out of his home area. "Why would he be down here, then?"

"A few times a year he travels on the Mekong to Cambodia and lower Laos, arranging gun sales with the local leaders. Currently there is trouble in the north. The Black Flag gangs are taking over some of the areas near the border with China. Perhaps he judged it prudent to operate in the south for a while."

"The French allow him to sell guns?"

"The guns he sells are French, but never modern weapons, only cast-off slow-firing pieces the Europeans don't want anymore. So the colonial government allows it for economic reasons. He knows many people in power, and far more importantly, he knows many things *about* those people, things they don't want to become public. So they let him come to this area. Dupuis is very cunning, very dangerous, Peter."

"Hau told me he sells manufactured items."

"Mr. Hau didn't tell you the whole story. Dupuis sells anything to anybody, including guns to both sides of conflicts. Hau works for MacTaggert. MacTaggert doesn't want outsiders to know he runs cargo for these men sometimes."

Dupuis and MacTaggert sounded like many of the ex-patriot Europeans I'd met in Asia—devoid of national loyalty and out for themselves. I was curious about my far-flung countryman's role. "And the American?"

"Augustine Heard. His father started a very successful trading company in China thirty years ago. Mr. Heard's wife is the daughter of a Belgian diplomat. Utilizing the connections of his father-in-law, Mr. Heard represented his father's company in Europe for many years, gaining quite a few connections.

"However, then things began to change for the worse. First the father died, then the company went bankrupt during that global economic panic ten years ago. Ever since, the son trades in many items all over Asia. My source tells me he has received word that includes modern American weapons. Remington rifles."

"You seem to have a varied group of information sources."

Petrusky's expression never changed. "Yes, I do."

"Is that information recent?"

"Two months ago."

I'd never been told any of this back in Washington. As usual, the people in charge back home didn't have any notion about what was happening out beyond the Potomac.

"Hmm, very interesting, Professor. And now both of them are on *Tonle Queen*. But I still don't understand. Why this riverboat?" I asked. "There are other European vessels on the river, like the French line."

"Yes, the French run the Messageries Fluviales de Cochinchine. But, for some reason I do not know, these men all have a degree of trust in Captain MacTaggert. Possibly because he has no fielty to anyone but himself. My informant says it is unusual for both Dupuis and Heard to be aboard at the same time, though."

Petrusky's informant must be in the crew, I surmised. Was it Hau?

Rork asked, "Where does the Irish surveyor come into all this, Professor?"

"I do not know. However, it is probably significant that the American, Heard, was in the same boat as the Irishman. But I am not sure why."

That didn't unmuddy the waters at all for me.

"Let me get this straight. We have competing American and French gun dealers, scheming British and French rubber planters, worried opium purveyors, and conniving colonial bureaucrats, all headed for Phnom Penh on this riverboat, where I'm to meet with a decadent king, who may, or may not, be plotting against his French overlords?"

"Yes."

"And you think all this is a sign that war is near?"

"Yes."

Rork cocked an eyebrow. "'Tis certainly appearin' to be a bad friggin' time to visit Indo-China, ain't it, sir?"

"Sean, I'm not sure there's ever been a *good* time to be here."

Petrusky stood to go, but he had one last comment to deliver. I noted the condescension in his tone. "Yes, this is a complex environment, especially for newcomers. I believe you now understand why I was sent to assist you, gentlemen. Good night, then."

We bade him *au revoir* and afterward sat down on our bunks and discussed the situation. Well, mainly it was me talking, with Rork acting as a sounding board. Nothing was like I'd been prepared for. In Washington, this had looked like a relatively simple mission: go to Cambodia, meet the king, present the president's reply to Norodom's politically explosive offer to America, and return home. Not one person brought up any of the factors we'd learned about in the last week.

Though I hated to admit it, our perpetually depressing professor was right. We did need someone like him to help us make sense of who was who. Indo-China was a poisonous stew of treacherous factions that changed form and fidelity constantly. Only one thing appeared certain to me—none of them was a friend to Rork and me.

The mission was changing into something I didn't like. Originally, I was to make an effort to have a successful conclusion to the offer and response, perhaps testing the water for an alternative offer. But now I understood that this culture had no room for an American mindset and the assignment had been naïve, to say the least. In fact, our mere presence as official Americans on the Mekong was a mistake, leading to misperceptions that could lead to who knew what.

No, this damned thing wasn't going to work out nicely at all, and there were myriad combinations of ways it could go disastrously—and maybe *mortally* for Rork and me—wrong. I resolved right then not to get sidetracked into involvement with any of these various shysters' potential calamities. Staying focused on the original mission alone, I would go through the motions of meeting the notorious King Norodom, present the president's response, get rebuffed, and then Rork and I would hightail it for home back down this river.

How was I to know then, on that dark river in the middle of a land that had never known peace, that I'd be wrong on that too?

10

Home

Friday, 4 May 1883
Upper Mekong River
Near Katom, Cambodia

The next day *Tonle Queen* stopped dead in the water again, but not because we hit anything. The riverboat had just passed the town of Neak Luong, a place whose appearance indicated nothing much ever happened. I was reclining in a chair up on the promenade deck at the time, watching some bullocks cooling off on the riverbank, their little boy attendants giggling hilariously at some joke.

One moment we were chugging along at ten knots, the next there was a piercing scream from the excess steam vent and a huge cloud of dense black smoke erupting from the stack, dropping soot and cinders over everything. The bullocks ran up the riverbank to escape the mechanic beast in the water, their little masters torn between duty to the animals and adolescent curiosity about what was happening with the riverboat. They chose watching the riverboat.

Seconds later a descending whine of steam pressure lamented the loss of propulsion and we rapidly lost speed. From the wheelhouse, Sandingham called down for the anchor to be dropped and soon we were sitting still, engine silent, the entire operation broiling in the intense Cambodian sun. I checked the thermometer mounted in the shade of the deck awning and wished I hadn't. It read 104 degrees. The humidity was worse than downriver in the Delta. I felt like I was in one of those steam bath contraptions the Europeans go on about.

MacTaggert was in his cabin one deck down when all this occurred, but not for long. "Wallace, what the bloody hell have you done now!" he barked out while climbing the ladderway three steps at a time to the promenade.

Wallace, the engineer, yelled up from an after hatch near the dormant paddle wheel, "We blew that outflow gasket I warned you about, Captain! The rocker arm's done for too. Have to disassemble the whole system and rebuild it. Three days of work at least. Maybe more."

The engineer's report was rewarded with a long, foul expletive by the captain. It covered Cambodia and her people, Wallace and his ancestors, the engine and its Glaswegian builders, and culminated in a vivid description of his own mother for bringing him into this world of woe. I must say that I was no admirer of Captain MacTaggert, but the man could pack more into a curse than anyone I've ever heard, before or since. Even more than Rork. Impressed with his creativity, I asked the steward to fetch another drink in order to reflect on it all. It was while doing so that I spied another steamer coming up fast behind us, an uncommon sight that far upriver.

Upon her approach I realized she was the *Lutin,* the Royal Yacht of King Norodom and flagship of the Cambodian Navy. That wasn't saying much—she was a third of *Tonle Queen's* size and armed with only a six-pounder smooth-bore on the bow. One evening in the bar salon Sandingham had told me about her. Her main claim was her fancy royal cabins; the secondary bragging point was her speed, ten knots even upstream. Only the French gunboats and the *Tonle Queen* could outrun her. The yacht was built by the French as a consolation present for the king in seventy-seven. She was commanded by a French naval officer with the unfortunate assignment of shepherding His Royal Decadence around the watery parts of the kingdom. Not very choice orders for a professional naval man—I surmised he'd probably failed in real duties somewhere and this was his punishment.

I noticed there was no royal standard set from the skinny mast—Norodom wasn't aboard. But an American was, as I soon heard. "Hello there, are you Commander Wake?"

I almost dropped my drink. A young man, maybe twenty-five, thin-framed in an ill-fitting heavy suit, stood on the *Lutin's* afterdeck, waving at me. He repeated his query before I could get my wits and reply.

"Yes, I am Commander Wake. And you are?"

"Ted Connally, sir. From the consulate in Saigon. I have mail for you, sir."

By this time the yacht was alongside, tying up. I beckoned to Connally.

"Then by all means come aboard for a drink and bring that mail, Mr. Connally!"

"I'm running the diplomatic mail bag up to the palace, Commander," Connally informed me, as he downed the proffered fruit juice enhanced with Bundaberg rum from Australia, MacTaggert's favorite. "We don't have a separate envoy to Cambodia. All diplomatic relations go through the Saigon consulate, and that's only a two-man office. Keeps me busy." He eyed the empty glass. "Say, can I have another of these? Helps with the heat, you know."

"Yes, of course." I motioned a steward over, then turned back to Connally, whom I'd never heard of when I was in Saigon.

"How long have you been the assistant consul?"

"Two years, sir. I was at Shanghai before that. My family has lived there for three generations."

"I see. I didn't meet you when I was in Saigon before. The consul was an older man, a Mr. Whiteside, if I recall correctly."

"Yes, sir. And he is a bit older. That's why I have to do the field work. From Quy Noh'n in the north, to Phnom Penh in the west, and down to the Gulf of Siam in the south, I handle problems and complaints. Consul Whiteside is not in condition to go out to the various locales. He's returning back to the States soon anyway. Replacement's supposed to be coming out."

Nobody had told me that in Washington, either. Put it on the list. But they had obliquely implied that I was handling the mission because the regional representative couldn't. After meeting Whiteside in Saigon, I understood. He was a good man, but tired. I understood that completely. One year out here could drain a man of energy and sanity. Hell, one month had done it for me. So, evidently Connally was it for the area. He looked energetic enough.

"When you were in Saigon, Commander, I was over on the coast at Binh Thuan. When I got back, Consul Whiteside told me an American naval officer had a courier assignment to King Norodom. You're a rare sight. We haven't seen one of our naval officers around here in a while."

He was obviously curious about me—like everyone else—but refrained from being blunt. The Orient had probably rubbed off on him, I figured.

Changing the subject, I asked, "How often do you get to Phnom Penh, Mr. Connally?"

In Saigon, Whiteside said *he* hadn't been there in a year. There were no Americans, no trade for the States, no reason for him to go, he'd said. When he found out I was heading upriver, he'd given me a lackluster "good luck."

However, perhaps this young man knew things that could be helpful to my mission. He sounded intelligent. "I get upriver two or three times a year, Commander. Usually it's to deliver mail and put in a brief appearance at the royal court. Show the flag, as it were."

Hmm, that didn't sound promising. I thought the timing of our mutual journeys interesting. Did Whiteside send him to spy on me? Or was I succumbing to professional paranoia? "Are you headed for the court now, or is it just a mail run?"

"Just a mail run, sir. Unless *you* would like to deliver it, since you're headed there anyway. I have to get down to Ca Mau, back in the Delta, to handle a trade disagreement and I'd appreciate it mightily if you could escort the mail, sir. It's a small bag, not heavy at all. And, of course, I don't want to get caught upriver this time of year. Too many things to get done back in Cochin, like that problem at Ca Mau. If you take the mail, I can take passage downriver on a native boat today and get back sooner."

Wait one minute. *Get caught upriver this time of year?* He said it nonchalantly, a well-known point, apparently. But one that I didn't know. Well, I didn't want to be caught in Cambodia either. In fact, I was aiming to get the hell out of Cambodia as soon as I could, once I met with the king. What was the problem—revolutionaries? Bandits? The opium warlords?

"I don't mind delivering the mail at all, Mr. Connally, but why is it that you'd be caught up here this time of the year?"

"The monsoon, Commander. It doesn't come for another month, maybe six weeks. This time of year the water levels are falling fast. River traffic will probably end soon. This may well be the *Tonle Queen*'s last trip for over a month, probably two. From here on up the river to Phnom Penh, it gets very shallow."

Connally saw me sigh in disgust and said, "No one told you?"

I intended to be pleasant, but I'm afraid an edge crept into my tone. "No, they didn't. Is there a way out of Phnom Penh other than the river?"

"You can go overland to the coast, but that coast has pirates."

Pirates? The whole damned place evidently had pirates, on

the river and on the coast. Was there anywhere without pirates? I sat there trying to remain positive, but inside I was seething. Why hadn't Petrusky advised me of this? He'd told me about every other friggin' negative thing under the sun.

Connally was sitting there, drink in hand, waiting hopefully for me to reply.

"Very well, I'll take the diplomatic mail to Phnom Penh, and I thank you for the word about the monsoon, Mr. Connally."

"Thanks for taking the bag, and thanks for the drinks, Commander. Your mail is in there, by the way. It's not locked," he said a little too cheerfully for my liking. Ten minutes later, young Ted Connally, America's real representative in Indo-China, was aboard a passing river junk and already disappearing downstream, waving goodbye.

I just nodded my head in return, for MacTaggert was walking my way, appearing even more irritated than customary after our face-off at Cai Be. "Ye river passage'll be in the royal bleedin' tub alongside, Commander. Our engine's gone arse o'er hell on us. The first-class passengers are transferred to *Lutin* an' leavin' in ten minutes. Get to your cabin an' move your stuff out."

I looked at *Lutin*. It was going to be crowded. "Very well, Captain. Thank you for arranging passage—"

"Stow it, Wake. I've not the time for your bleedin' lies."

Rork and I stayed on *Lutin*'s deck and watched the sun going down, silhouetting a distant line of tall palms along a rice paddy dike. Petrusky had somehow schemed a transfer to the yacht and sat aft of us, saying nothing, taking in everything. The deck was preferable to the elegant but stifling cabins below, which even ten knots of apparent wind over the deck couldn't cool down. As the other passengers concentrated on getting drunk enough to fall asleep in the cramped conditions below decks, Petrusky, Rork, and I sat on a deck box and watched the sky turn luminescent blue, then greenish-lavender.

"Looks like the color in them mangos back in Florida, durin' the war," Rork said softly. "Remember them? Aye, it was hot like this, but the bugs were worse. An' the afternoon thunderstorms were somethin' outta hell an' tarnation. But, oh, those island mangos, sweet an' perky . . ."

I tasted them in my memory, too. "Yep, especially the ones from Useppa Island. Linda always had them ready for us."

"I miss those mangos. That I surely do, sir."

I was dreaming of more than mangos now. "So do I, Sean. Those were bad times, but there were some wonderful moments."

I'd just read a letter from home. Rork had waited for me to tell him the contents. He never got letters. His family was all gone, except for some cousins in Wexford, Ireland. It was a sadness he seldom mentioned, instead focusing on my family. He was the godfather to both my children. They called him "Uncle Sean."

The letter was from my daughter, Useppa, born on and named for that very island we'd been remembering. It had taken seventy-four days to reach me. She and my son, Sean, lived at Don and Martha Boltz's travelers' inn on Chain Bridge Road by Fairfax, Virginia, just outside Washington. We all moved there after Linda died. After living in a dingy apartment in the city near the navy yard, it was a pleasant change for all of us—a safe place for my children to grow up and a tranquil place for my heart to grieve.

Useppa was getting older now, though. She'd be eighteen soon, and I had the same worries as all fathers. She was always headstrong. I thought that a good quality in a girl, one that would protect her from unscrupulous types. She also had a crippled leg from birth, a malady she was able to mostly hide during social functions, but one that still gave her pain. We'd tried everything the doctors had suggested, but nothing cured it. Linda said once that it would make Useppa stronger in other ways. She was so right on that. My daughter was one of the most intelligent and insightful people I knew. Her knowledge of history and current politics was nothing short of phenomenal. I was extremely proud of her.

I gave the letter to Rork to read.

14th of February, 1883
Dear Daddy,

I'm sending you a Valentine wish in this letter—that you know how very much I love you. I don't know where you are in Asia, but I know your spirit is in my heart, right here in Virginia.

Now for the local news. Aunt Martha and Uncle Don are well. Uncle Don says when you get home he needs help with the willow tree. The kitty Sheba is just as lazy as ever. Miss Kathie says hello and to let you know that she has all the gentlemen patrons at the Inn's tavern firmly under her dominion. She had to cudgel Dirk the other night for attempting to take liberties, but the next day he apologized for his behavior and brought her flowers.

Sean is fine, though he still acts like such a pestiferous little brother at times. He wanted me to tell you he got a letter from Annapolis last week in response to his query in November. It had the procedures for application and he has started by writing the senators from Virginia and letting them know he's looking for sponsorship in 1886. Sean is very determined and says, "Now, Useppa, it's never too early to get things under way." Daddy, even though he's only sixteen, he sounds just like you!

And what about me? Well, I have some exciting news of my own. Remember when the church decided to send missionaries out to the Bahamas and Florida? I'm joining the missionary group that is going to Key West. We are going to help the Negro freedmen in the Keys and in lower Florida—they are in desperate need of education. When we were at Useppa Island two years ago to scatter Mother's ashes, I began remembering how much I missed Florida from my childhood.

They need teachers and I am almost a fully trained teacher, so they were happy to have me volunteer. Martha and Don think it's a wonderful opportunity and I hope you do too, Daddy. I'll be with decent people and safe, so don't you worry about that sort of thing. Most of all, I'll be helping people. I know that you'll understand that, too. I leave the third week in April and will send you my new address once I get it. In the meantime you can send me letters care of our church—Foundry Methodist in Washington—and they'll send them along.

With lots of love for my sailor Daddy,
Useppa

Rork looked up from the letter and put a hand on my shoulder.

"Aye, she's a fine lass. You an' Linda did well by her, Peter. I'm proud as peaches o' her."

"That's a brave front, Sean. You're really as scared as I am for her."

Rork let out a sigh. "Aye, a wee bit. But she's a grown woman now, Peter. An' she has to make her own way in life. Linda surely did, during a war, an' with a Yankee officer, no less."

I cringed at the memory. Those were perilous years during the war. "You don't need to remind me of that."

"Ah, but methinks somebody should, friend. You're thinkin' o' the worse an' forgettin' Useppa is Linda Donahue Wake's daughter. Linda taught her better than that—she'll be just fine. Now let's talk about the lad, shall we? All those years o' yarnin' to him about the adventures o' bosuns, an' he still wants to be an officer? I feel I must've failed, somehow."

That brought me out of my funk and got me laughing. "Sean Rork, you incorrigible rogue, for years you *did* try to convince him to *enlist,* didn't you?"

Rork shrugged and flashed that famous grin. "Bosuns have far more merriment than you officers, Commander. *Far more.* Just wanted the lad to enjoy life at sea."

"Well, from the stories I know about *your* liberty ashore, I think you're right about that! Still, officer or enlisted, this navy life is hard on a man. Not healthy, Sean. Bad on marriages. We've both seen a lot of men regret it."

It had been very difficult, indeed, on my marriage. Throughout the long separations, Linda had been a saint, keeping the family together, raising the children.

Rork nodded. "An' now the lad is about to do what you never could. Graduatin' from the academy. Things're changin' in the navy. Changin' even more in the future. We'll need bright young officers like him. No telling what little Sean will see an' do. Just think, your son'll probably make admiral one day."

My little boy, an admiral. It was difficult to even think of him in my profession, let alone an admiral.

"Aye, sir. He'll make a right proper officer. An' with that Annapolis ring there'll be no limitations in his career."

Rork didn't say it. Didn't have to. My career had always been shadowed by my lack of formal naval education. I came up the hard way. My son would come up the right way.

I looked around me at the unchanging landscape—tangled jungle, rice paddy, thatched village, coffee-colored river. A lethargic mass shaded in green and brown. Every person and animal moved slowly, the wet heat weighting their bodies down, sucking the vigor from them. The very air of Southeast Asia relentlessly killed men as they toiled, one deliberate step at a time. "I'm feeling tired, Sean. And old."

"You're only forty-three."

"Forty-four in a little more than a month. Sailors age faster than landsmen. Must be the salt air."

"Aye, but we do love it though, don't we?"

"Occasionally."

Then I broached the subject I'd been mulling over for some time. "I'm thinking of buying some land on one of the islands on that southern Gulf coast. Maybe Patricio Island—remember that one? Just northeast of Useppa Island. I inquired last year and found out it's available; the Cuban who was the last titled owner never paid the taxes."

"Aye, that's a good island. Got a high ridge."

"Yes, it does. You know, Sean, I don't have a real home of my own. Haven't for years, since I left Massachusetts in the war. I think I need that now. A place where I can go on leave and get away from the navy for a while each year. You're always welcome and expected. I mean that, Sean. I'd want you there with me. You need a home, too."

His eyes got distant and he smiled. "A place o' refuge. Aye, that's a fine notion, indeed. Mark me down as volunteerin' on that idea, Commander Wake."

"There's no house there, though. We'd have to build one. A real one, not some palm-thatched thing, like during the war. Two would be better. One for you and one for me."

"Clinker or lapstrake?" he asked with a sly grin.

I'd been getting maudlin, but Rork, always the sailor, always the jester, had turned the mood lighter. I laughed at his reference to boat-building. "Well, as long as it doesn't spring a leak I'm fine with either!"

"But a bilge pump just in case, I'd suggest. You know those storm tides down there . . ." His attention was diverted by a commotion behind me. Rork stood and said, "Good evenin' to ya, Mr. Heard."

I turned to face the American trader.

11

Phnom Penh

Friday, 4 May 1883
Upper Mekong River
Cambodia

My first, and lasting, impression of Augustine Heard was the man's hairy head. He was in his mid-fifties then, with thick brown hair. The top was more than compensated by the bottom, which sported a huge mustache and outsized jaw-line whiskers. After perfunctory introductions, he got right to the point, those bushy side-whiskers bouncing with emphasis. Heard was not happy. I could tell by his tone of voice that the man was used to getting answers.

"Forgive me for being blunt, Commander Wake. I've been told you're aboard as some sort of courier, but I've also been told no one believes that. Why exactly, pray tell, are you on the Mekong, bound for a potentate little cared for back in the States?"

It came out as an order. I wasn't about to engage in coy banter about my mission, either the overt or the covert, with someone like Augustine Heard who thought he could bully me because of his perceived influence, so I projected my own self-confidence.

"Your candor is refreshing, Mr. Heard. I'm not as well-versed in the ways of the Orient as you, so I like blunt people and appreciate your curiosity. Yes, it is uncommon to see a U.S. naval officer here. The reason for my arrival is quite simple, though evidently the others aboard prefer more deceitful motives, a style in line with their own. I am delivering a message to the king regarding piracy on the coast."

"Well! Is our navy finally going to do something about it?" he demanded.

"We're hoping the king does something about it, Mr. Heard. It's his country."

"*Hoping?* Anyone out here who *hopes* for anything is a fool. And as for the king, he's essentially powerless. Only the French or British can accomplish anything in that regard. They have real navies. I fear you are wasting your time, Commander. And taxpayers' money."

I ignored the jibe and sent one of my own, just to shake him up and see his reaction. "And what about you, Mr. Heard? Are you selling guns to the king, or is it to the warlords in the area?"

It was quite a reaction. What little skin on Heard's face not covered by fur turned red in rage. His eyes bulged until I worried he might keel over from a seizure of apoplexy.

"*Guns!* Did you say *guns* referring to *me?* That's not only preposterous, it's an insult to an honest merchant, Commander. My family has traded in Asia for thirty years and we do not—repeat, do not—deal in *guns*. The secretary of the navy will hear of your impertinence!" With that said he strode away, muttering about the government wasting tax money on highly paid delivery boys.

Rork offered his opinion, which wasn't helpful right then. "Always such fun to make new friends, ain't it, though? Got a wee bit testy about the gun thing, didn't he? Methinks we've got ourselves one more enemy, sir."

Hmm, he had a point. Maybe Petrusky was wrong about Heard. The man certainly reacted like he was innocent of my accusation. And if the professor was wrong on that, what else? We were a long way from friendly territory and I'd just managed to alienate the one man who might be expected to show some semblance of nationalistic support for us in Phnom Penh.

It didn't take long to confirm Heard was an enemy, either. He spread his opinion about me around the *Lutin's* cramped salon cabin within an hour. That evening, over drinks and dinner, I was studiously ignored by the entire assorted menagerie of characters making their way upriver. Everyone, that is, except the pathetic French commander of the Royal Yacht, a scrawny sublieutenant who tried to engage me in chummy conversation about technological trends of weapons. My French and his English weren't equal to the task, so we both gave up after a few minutes.

To this day, I still remember the smug look on their arrogant faces when I left the table that evening. Yep, this Yankee navy man was a newcomer in Asia and those pompous asses were the Old Hands. It was all I could do to repress my intense desire to remove those smug looks. Fortunately for me, I didn't yield to desire.

The first we saw of Phnom Penh were the Royal Palaces of Cambodia. Set back from a bluff along the river, they weren't at all what I expected after days of watching mile after dreary mile of that impoverished country go by en route to the place. Quite the contrary, it was a fairy-tale scene that unfolded before us. Rork and I were on the bow at sunrise as *Lutin* rounded a bend to the right, then ducked into a smaller waterway on the left, the Tonle River, which joined the Mekong and the Bassac Rivers at the nation's capital.

The palaces' golden spires, lit by the sun's early rays, pointed like brilliant exclamation marks toward the sky, with carved claws and elephant trunks accenting the gables. The massive roofs of a dozen buildings were ornately trimmed in vivid tiles of azure blue, gold, white, and green. More strange shapes protruded up from the rooflines, snakes and birds and animals I didn't know. Every building was raised upon a pedestalled foundation with at least ten, maybe twenty steps leading to an elaborate colonnaded entrance. In the morning sun, the whole place was illuminated as if from within, shining brightly and accentuating its architectural artistry.

The grounds surrounding the palaces were manicured gardens of green grass and stone, with flowers of every hue all over the place. The closer we got, the more details we could make out, and the more awestruck we became.

"Me God above, sir. 'Tis fancier than the Dublin cathedral, it is. I saw some sights in China, but nary a thing like this."

"I've never been anywhere over here, Rork, but this surpasses anything I've seen in Europe, let alone the States."

And the buildings were just the beginning. *Lutin* tied up at the Royal Dock, where tiny brown servants in bloused green trousers and bare chests padded up and down the gangway in tiny steps to unload the passengers' luggage. Serious-faced warriors in yellow tunics, folded arms holding wicked-looking swords and lances, watched from the top of the bank, their comical pointed hats incongruous with the cold looks in their almond-shaped eyes.

To the right of the palaces was an area of European buildings. They were functional and drab, without the Oriental flair for architectural delicacy. Where the palaces were a mosaic of colors and pleasing to the eye, the foreigners built grayish-white monotone structures with a minimum of trim. I suppose they were meant to impress the locals with the strength of modern France, but I thought it just a sad, stark reminder of who was doing what to whom. The hotels were further along the river road. I could see the Grand Hotel's sign in the distance. It didn't appear very grand to me.

Our fellow passengers were disembarking into the noisy crowd around us, hailing rickshaws to take them to the French-owned Grand, ordering the laborers to pick up this or that bag from the general pile, and just generally being loud and obnoxious. Except for McCarthy, the gentlemen were attired in the tropical European uniform for civilians—straw hats and white linen suits with ties, the jackets of which were already blotched with sweat stains. McCarthy, the jungle surveyor, wore an open shirt and ragged trousers as he called out in Irish-brogued Cambodian to the surrounding throng of local gawkers, apparently asking something of them. Above all the pandemonium, Miss Marston's falsetto could be discerned as the feather-boa'd celebrity flitted around like some large flightless bird, imploring in English to laborers who didn't understand her, "Oh, I *do* say, whatever *are* you doing there, my good man?" "That one there—get that bag this instant!" "Fragile! It is fragile!"

I considered it comic, as did the onlookers, though the upper-crust folks at the dock wouldn't agree. No, they were just enduring Oriental ineptitude and confusion, all part of the white man's duty in the darker parts of the world. As with the night before, no one was speaking to *us,* which suited me.

Heard gave me a disgusted glance, grabbed his own luggage, and rickshawed off down the main riverside road. McCarthy finally found what he was searching for and cried out to a very well-dressed Cambodian lady whom he obviously knew intimately—he gave her a big laughing hug, a luscious kiss, and away they sauntered. D'Abain was whisked down the road to a palace by an official-looking carriage, as befitting a king's royal opium general, and Dupuis demanded a rickshaw in rapid Cambodian.

The Catholic contingent clambered aboard a wagon powered by a sway-backed horse that looked as if it might keel over at any moment. My last sight of them was memorable for the look of fright on the nuns' faces—this was where most of them would spend the rest of their lives, and not in some opulent palace, either. They were good people and I felt sorry for them.

Petrusky had some farewell words with Father Blanc, both glancing at me, then he wandered back over toward where Rork and I stood. I must say he didn't look overjoyed.

The Brits put on quite a demonstration of imperial efficiency. Gathered with their belongings in a circle, they attentively listened to the colonel tell them precisely what they would do next. Rockford gave an approving grunt and Miss Marston twittered about thanking God they had the colonel to look after them. After that, Colonel Fountjoy loudly commandeered a servant from the *Lutin* and ordered him to procure four rickshaws, each of which was to have two large seats, decent stowage for cargo, a strong man to pull it, and for only half the price the other foreigners were paying, which was too bloody much. The bewildered servant tried his best, haggling for several minutes with the rickshaw men, none of whom wanted to pull Miss Martson or the colonel for the price offered.

Much gesturing and yelling later, the carts were piled high with baggage, the diva was lifted onto her very own rickshaw, the vehicles were formed up into a convoy, and at the colonel's order of "Forwaaahrd, *march!*" the entire show trotted away, pulled by straining rickshaw men toward the Grand. The servant fled from view shortly afterward. No telling what price he'd settled on, but I suspect it wasn't the bargain Fountjoy expected.

It was pleasantly calm on the dock now that the happy bar salon crew from the *Tonle Queen* had disappeared, leaving only *Lutin*'s perplexed sub-lieutenant; the confused Spaniard, Altamonte; and my own small but diverse party of three. Rork and I stood there, seabags on our shoulders and valise in my hand, surveying the scene.

Petrusky asked me where I was supposed to go, which meant all of us. It was a reasonable question, given that I'd already journeyed thirteen thousand miles around the globe specifically to get to that spot, but I'm afraid I didn't know the answer. There'd been no advance plan for accommodation in Cambodia, and I had to assume that due to the unforeseen nature of our arrival, no one in authority knew we were coming. However, it soon transpired that I was, as was becoming all too common on this mission, wrong yet again. Not only did the authorities know we'd arrived, but they were coming for us.

Petrusky pointed out the carriage first. It was coming out of a gate in the low wall surrounding the palaces and moving at a clip, right for us. The various functionaries—servants, soldiers, and minor bureaucrats—who had attended the arrival of the Royal Yacht *Lutin,* took one look at the coming carriage and scattered. I took that as a bad sign. Petrusky shook his head enigmatically, as he was prone to do, as Rork quickly scanned the horizon for trouble and slid a hand into his coat.

The French naval officer, and titular head of the local navy, presumably decided he had something better to do than be around when his seniors arrived and retreated to his yacht. Meanwhile, our befuddled Spaniard Altamonte was gazing at something downriver, unaware of the excitement behind him.

The approaching carriage was rapidly overhauled by a cavalry escort of traditionally attired troopers in green and yellow, but equipped with modern weaponry and accoutrements. Somebody important was coming.

"Those are French Gras, sir," advised Rork. "The eighteen-seventy-four models, same as we saw in Africa."

He was referring to the rifles each cavalryman was holding at the ready in his left hand, and to our mission in northwestern Africa years earlier. The French Gras rifle had a deadly reputation. Paris supplied them free to friendly potentates around the world for use in their personal guard regiments—usually for use against their own disgruntled people. This was an elite guard unit heading our way.

The officer commanding the escort galloped up, reined his horse, and shouted for the troop to halt, which they did with notable precision, having transformed into a line abreast, arrayed in front of the carriage. He then trotted forward and announced in French, "*Bienvenu au Cambodje, messieurs, de la roi . . .*" After that much he lost me, his Cambodian accent mangling the words even worse than my feeble attempts at French. I did catch the word *"Americains"* in the middle of it, though. Petrusky kindly translated for Rork and me.

"The colonel is commander of the imperial guard and welcomes you to Cambodia and the palaces of His Majesty, King Norodom, who is pleased the Americans have arrived and who has personally issued orders that the American visitors are to be shown every courtesy."

While Petrusky and the colonel spoke some more, I noticed that Altamonte's face drooped—evidently no one was expecting the Spanish. I was sympathetic to him, a fish out of water even more then Rork and I. "Señor Altamonte, I would be honored if you would agree to join our party, in the spirit of American-Spanish friendship."

That was a bit of bunk, really. Altamonte knew as well as I that our two countries had nearly gone to war over the Cuban revolution of sixty-eight—we were in favor of the Cuban patriots—and the Spanish atrocities on the island in seventy-three, but I thought a little generosity was in order. What could it hurt? He was just a bureaucrat visiting there to talk about silk tariffs. Might help the American image in the world.

My offer brightened him up. "Thank you, Commander. I would be delighted and honored."

"Very well, then. Professor Petrusky, would you please let the colonel know that we are impressed by our welcome, honored by the colonel's hospitality, and humbly anticipating our visit with His Majesty. Also, tell him that you are serving as our official interpreter and that we have taken the liberty of inviting our friend Mr. Altamonte to join our party."

Petrusky did as asked, certainly sounding like he was doing a good job. My doubts about his motives, never solid, began to wane. Yes, he might have been wrong about Heard, but I thought he was right on most everything else, from what I could see. On my long journey to Asia, I'd figured the Cambodians would provide an interpreter. Having one of my own, who also understood the politics and history, was a luxury.

The professor counseled me, as an aside, that the colonel hinted he was a distant cousin of the king, something I should keep in mind. The colonel, whose name was unpronounceable for me, bestowed a smile at my reply and grunted something to his men, who sprang into action.

The line abreast parted to show the carriage, a gilded affair obviously built by the French, then adorned by the palace's artisans. Golden elephants, goddesses, and a giant serpent decorated it. Two minions in outlandish purple outfits with curled toes and conical hats—apparently some type of classical costume and not the court jesters—jumped down from the carriage, opened the doors, and bade us to enter with swirling gestures and a bow that reached the ground. The four of us took our cue, climbed aboard, and away we went, into a world Petrusky informed us few Westerners had ever seen.

By that point in my life, I had been in the White House several times, viceroys' mansions in Cuba, royal palaces in Spain, castles in Italy, and sultans' kasbahs in Morocco. I'd hobnobbed with the elite in Europe, America, and Africa, and conceitedly thought myself inured from further jaw-dropping awe in my life.

But I had never seen anything like the home of King Norodom of Cambodia.

"Not bad a'tall, sir," observed Rork when he met me later in my room, which was beyond opulent. "Very comfortable billet, as befittin' a man o' your position. Me own quarters're right frilly, but the stewards are the best part o' the bargain. Have you seen the stewards, sir? I fancy them quite well, sir."

I had indeed, and I didn't like the look in his eye. "I presume by that you mean they are pretty girls."

"Oh, nay, nay, sir! Why, that would be an insult to them, an' their lovely mothers. These lasses are truly *beautiful*. Most beautiful in all the world, an' I've seen a fair bit o' it to know. An' quite friendly to boot."

Uh-oh. I smelled trouble coming—Gaelic-lover trouble. Rork had been the center of turmoil with lasses around the world. It was clearly time for my patented Rork-don't-get-us into-something-I-can't-get-us-out-of lecture. He'd been the recipient of that talk on four continents, always said thank you, and then usually ended up ignoring it.

"Rork, remember the army major's daughter back in sixty-four? And the Italian girl whose daddy turned out to be the mayor of Genoa? And, of course, we mustn't forget that admiral's niece in Washington. You get in trouble with these young ladies by promising them far too much, my man—then they give *you* far too much. Then I end up in trouble along with you and your problem becomes *my* problem! Not here, Sean. Not now. We're on the far side of the world, by ourselves."

I could tell he wasn't getting my meaning. At times Sean Rork could be very thick-headed. Time to be blunt. "No girls, Bosun Rork. That's a direct order."

His brow furrowed in concern. Mock concern. "Why, Commander, methinks you're worried about *me*, o' all people, doin' somethin' improper. Now don't you worry a hair on your head about ol' Sean Rork. I was raised by Catholic priests back in the Sainted Isle to be a proper gentleman at all times with the members o' the fairer sex. Aye, an' that I was, sir."

"You left Ireland at thirteen, Sean."

"An' a perfect gentlemen I was, while I was there, sir."

I gave up. "All right, you're warned."

I had expected to be in the capital a few days before obtaining an entrée to the king, affording me the opportunity to formulate an appropriate plan of addressing the reason I was there, the king's offer to the United States. But that was not to be—it turned out we were expected that very evening at a royal soirée. Two hours later I was reclined on my bed listening as Petrusky, sitting ramrod straight in a satin upholstered chair, explained what would happen in about forty-five minutes. He had been alerted by our guard colonel friend as to what protocol to expect and asked to pass it along.

It was interesting for me to note that now we were in a social setting controlled by Asians, the professor was no longer relegated to second-class treatment. Though he was still looked down on because of his European father, his educational accomplishments and linguistic skills were appreciated. He would be accompanying me and Altamonte throughout the entire evening.

Rork, however, was still considered my servant and would be restricted to a back room with a view on the proceedings, which didn't bother him a bit. He was frequently treated that way and preferred less limelight anyway. It allowed him to ascertain pertinent information from the servant class, a caste long underestimated for the intelligence value of their knowledge. Rork portrays the role of servant well, for short periods of time. He says, without a smile, that it comes from "hundreds o' years of survival while bein' occupied by English barbarians."

Rork stood easy by the window while Altamonte sat quietly near the door. The Spaniard unsettled me a bit, too introverted for any commercial attaché I'd ever known, incongruously content to let us manage things. Oh well, it was the Orient and every color and kind was there.

I was in full dress uniform and noted the fact that Petrusky, unlike Altamonte and most people, wasn't surprised by my medals. They were unusual for an American—the Legion of Honor of France, the Order of the Lion of the Atlas of Morocco, and the Order of the Sun from Peru. Obviously, the professor knew more about me than he'd let on. Altamonte was surprised and respectfully asked how I had obtained them. I answered that each was a long story, but suffced it to say that they were thank-yous from governments grateful for a service I'd rendered them at one point or another. I didn't mention that each trinket carried bad memories and painful scars along with the commendation.

Petrusky cleared his throat and began his instruction.

"Gentlemen, there will be a general soirée this evening in the grand reception ballroom of the Throne Hall, or the Preah Timeang Tevea Vinicchay. All of the finest inhabitants of the city will be there, including the royal family, the Cambodian upper-class, the foreign residents, foreign visitors, and the French advisors."

French advisors. Blundell! I'd lost track of him when we disembarked from *Lutin*. He had been cool to me for the last few days of the river journey, but then so had most of them. In the salon he'd been in deep conversation with Dupuis, d'Abain, and several French planters, and several times I'd noticed them watching me as they talked. Not kindly either. I wondered—what did he really do in Cambodia? For whom? Did he go with d'Abain the dope peddler to the palace? What had he told the royal leadership about me?

Petrusky droned on, "At precisely six-fifty, we will be escorted by a subaltern of the guard from this guest residence and arrive at seven o'clock, entering the main doors at the head of the steps. You will be interested to know we are considered special guests of honor. Upon entering the hall, we will walk clockwise once around the main room and stop in a receiving line, where we will stand until His Majesty appears before us."

I had to ask. "Why clockwise?"

"It is conducive to good fortune and a sign of respect in this culture. May I continue?"

"By all means, Professor."

"Very well. The king and his entourage will be announced and appear upon the dais, whereupon all will bow, and the king will acknowledge our presence, and signal us to come forward. Just *after* members of the royal family are acknowledged, the three of us—Commander Wake, Mr. Altamonte, and I—will come forward and bow deeply. That is a position of immense honor to us. It will be a solemn moment. As we bow we will fold our hands, as in prayer, against our chests."

"Sounds sort of like church," I offered pleasantly, hoping to provide a little levity to our instruction. Rork chuckled. Altamonte was busy scrutinizing a lampshade.

"No, Commander. It is a *royal audience.*" For a man of many languages, Petrusky's understanding of Western humor was severely limited. I ended my attempt at wit and assumed a properly attentive demeanor. The professor, undaunted by my interruption, continued for the next half hour until he had covered every facet of the evening's four-hour protocol. It was another feat of memory on his part—he'd only learned this an hour earlier and never referred to any notes. Memorization is a valuable skill in my line of work and I respect it in others. Wish I could do it myself. When he had finished, I complimented him and said we would follow his lead throughout the affair. We'd have to—I'd lost track of the bewildering rules, orders, and strict expectations early on in the briefing. Poor Altamonte never absorbed any of it.

After tutoring us in what was expected, the professor announced it was time to make our appearance. I readied myself to represent my country, knowing one and all would be watching the American's every move. The plan in my head was to keep the whole thing trouble-free, fulfill my mission that very evening, then look for a way out of Cambodia as soon as possible. With any luck, Rork and I could catch a ride on a small boat—like Connally had done—and be heading downriver the next day. With no further difficulties, at the end of a week we could be aboard a steamer at Saigon.

And if truly exceptional luck should shine upon us, we might even meet up with USS *Juniata* if she put in at Saigon. Rumored to be headed home from duty with the Asiatic Station, she was commanded by Commander George Dewey, an old friend from my days at Washington Navy Yard. I knew George would be glad to get an experienced officer and petty officer to add to his watch bill, and that Rork and I would get home much faster than trying to catch various passenger steamers heading eastward.

12

Norodom

Amazingly, to my cynical way of thinking, everything unfolded just as Petrusky had predicted. With an efficiency a
Prussian general would admire, the courtiers kept the hundreds
of guests moving in the proper directions while a buzz of conversational anticipation filled the room. And what a room it was—
fully two hundred feet long and one hundred wide, with seven
double doorways along either side, outside of which hundreds of
the Cambodian elite watched the foreigners arrive first, while
they waited their turn to enter.

The Throne Hall, built in 1870 by the French for their
newest regal puppet of the empire, was nothing short of magnificent. A pleasing blend of modern European construction and
ancient Oriental decoration, the high, frescoed ceiling immediately drew one's eye upon entering. The scenes were from
Cambodian history, from the ancient Angkors to the current

Khmers, with Norodom's dynasty figured prominently in the most recent panels. Then one's view descended to take in gold everywhere in various textures—gilt paint, solid gold fixtures, golden fabrics. The whole effect shimmered in the glow of a dozen giant golden lamps, six enormous golden chandeliers, and yellow rice-papered lanterns placed around the room. There was golden gilt trim over the doorways, a golden silk tent above the golden thrones for the king and queen, and golden uniforms on all the court officials. I had never seen so much gold.

All this radiance accented the background of crimson silk tapestries, swirled-marble floor tiles covered in the main by huge embroidered carpets of green and red designs, and cream-painted walls. Flowers in brightly lacquered vases provided dashes of dramatic contrast.

Even the people added to the scene. The graceful Cambodian ladies of the court wore silk bodices over bloomed trousers, mostly in the color of the day. This being a Saturday, dark red was the expected hue of their dress. Were it Friday, etiquette would've demanded blue—other days were yellow, violet, green, and so on. The elegant Brahman gentlemen of the palace, properly self-impressed with their station in life, were attired in gold-trimmed white tunics over golden puffed trousers. The somber mandarins were the most impressive, plodding solemnly in their snow-white uniforms with golden shoulder boards, sashes, and imperial decorations, like elderly Western admirals.

From somewhere in a far corner, classical Cambodian stringed instruments and chimes performed gentle melodies that echoed amorphously around the chamber, occasionally accompanied by the slow beat of a deep wooden drum. The chimes were of high pitch, but sometimes a gong would be added to the tune. Incense of sandalwood and cedar, earthy and thick, filled the air, the perfect accessory to the mystical music. I am no aficionado of tunes, but to my ear this was soothing, unlike the see-sawing of some Western orchestras to which I've been subjected.

The explanation of this pageantry was provided by Petrusky,

who was as enchanted with the wealth of stimuli to our senses as Altamonte and I. He was also proud of his regional culture. Cambodia was different in many ways from his native Viet Nam. But it was all Asian, so dissimilar to my eyes, ears, and nose. When I asked what a particular new waft of incense was, our tutor's eyes widened in awe as he took notice of it also. Then he murmured, "It is dragon's blood incense, made from the red resin of the croton plant. Very rare, Peter. Symbolic of *courage and power.*"

I'd only been there five minutes and felt like an inexperienced school boy on his first visit to the city. No wonder Norodom made a deal with the French to be able to stay in power and live this way. Could any man resist this?

Soon the entire procession had packed into the room, the three of us standing in the front rank facing those imposing thrones. Petrusky nodded toward a group of ancients near the dais. "Those are the superior mandarins of the Council of Five Ministers—the prime minister; the minister of justice; the minister of finance and fine arts; the minister of the navy, commerce, and agriculture; and the minister of war, public works, and education. They really run the internal affairs of the country."

The gentlemen looked nearly dead to me. The minister of the navy was an emaciated octogenarian with a permanent scowl. Petrusky nudged me to look at the other side of the room. "And there is the French resident superior, His Excellency Paul Foures; along with the bishop of Cambodia, His Excellency Bishop Courdier. And I think that is the German-born collector of customs standing next to them. Oh, look, there is the opium general for the king, Monsieur d'Abain, whom you met briefly on the boat."

That group definitely appeared more energetic, or should I say vigilant, by the way they were eyeing the guests, especially Altamonte and me. D'Abain had a particularly malevolent look when our glances met, and I wondered why an opium lord would concern himself with me. Petrusky saw it too, and said in a stage whisper, "They do not trust you, Peter."

Well, I thought, that's entirely mutual. By this point, I

didn't trust *anybody* on the Asian continent. I studied the bishop, looking for signs of recognition of Petrusky or me, but saw none. What threat was I to any of these people?

Then it hit me. Somehow they knew why I was there.

I wasn't a threat to them, it was my country that was a threat to their way of life. Earlier I'd wondered if Petrusky had surmised the true purpose of my mission, figuring with his knowledge and insight he probably had. But would he have shared his suspicion upon reaching Phnom Penh? And with whom? The bishop? Yes, probably—more than anything else, Petrusky was loyal to the Church. Had the bishop gossiped his suspicions to the others? Or was I getting obsessed by mistrust?

A gong intruded upon my deliberations. The sound shimmered like the gold all around me, silencing the guests and echoing down the hall and back. The music stopped and it seemed as if there was a collective intake of breath, with all eyes on the western end of the hall. Another gong announced the arrival of the king. It was more of an unveiling, really. Saffron silk curtains were pulled back to either side of the throne dais to reveal his presence, fifty feet in front of me, standing in front of the royal seat.

The Europeans all bowed their heads or curtsied, the foreign Asians folded their hands in front and bowed deeply from the waist, bending over as far as they could. The Cambodians, except for the Brahmans and superior mandarins, got down on their knees and lowered their heads to the floor—the famous *kowtow*. Even the Brahmans and mandarins genuflected deeply, not out of fear, I noticed with interest, but almost procedural respect. A younger mandarin, perhaps of sixty years, commenced a booming announcement to the hall.

"*Luong Trong Reach! Chau Krung Kampuchea! Preah Ammachas Chivit Loeuh Thbaung! Machas Karuna Viseso! Preah Bat Norodom!*"

That was followed by a French army officer stamping to attention over on the side, bemedaled and self-important, intoning a translation in French. Then, to my great surprise, from the opposite side of the room came an English translation with a heavy Cambodian accent. "The Reigning King! King of the Kingdom of Cambodia! The Eminent Supreme Lord of Life above All Heads! Master of Compassion and Mercy! His Majesty . . . *King Norodom!*"

Everyone turned to me for my reaction.

Obviously, the translation was done just for me. Petrusky hadn't covered this possibility. However, I realized this was one of those moments that called for more than merely bowing one's head, so I bent over from my waist and tented my hands, touching my chest and bringing them up to my lips. Then, hoping I was doing it right, I forcefully said, "*Awkun . . .*"

That meant "thank you," as I'd heard the locals do. I waited for a reaction, keeping my eyes downcast. Fortunately, the Cambodian leadership displayed approving expressions. A high-toned buzz filled the room and I received a rare congratulatory whisper from the professor.

"Well done, Peter!"

Another gong signaled us to stand tall again as Norodom mounted his throne. I had a chance to study him during his ascent and noted that he was in good physique for a man of forty-nine years. His face was starting to show his age, but the eyes were absolutely inscrutable, studying everything and everyone around him without even turning his head. A trim mustache of French influence framed a decisive mouth and chin, while the hair was short, thick, and parted down the middle.

His uniform, golden silk with much inlaid gilt, was of French design as well, a tunic and trousers with medals, sashes, and jewels hanging all over the chest—a good twenty pounds of baubles, which might explain his fitness. Despite the fact that he wasn't a military man, he did look the part, and I found myself intrigued by this Norodom fellow.

His Majesty intoned some words which were lost on me, then dismounted—as everyone cast their eyes down—and made his way to group of important people standing on the side of the room. The ensuing reception line was similar to official reception lines the world over that I've been ordered to attend. The only people who enjoy those things are the fakes and the fawners, and there were plenty of those present that evening. Due to my apparent seniority on the guest list, I was near the front of the line, which stretched all the way around the room along the walls.

Norodom, *sans* the queen, whose whereabouts I never did ascertain, stood with the mandarins and the French resident superior, receiving his due respects, nodding slightly, occasionally deigning to smile. I noticed he didn't shake hands with his subjects and guests, presumably because of his exalted station, so when my turn came up next I was taken aback to see a proffered hand. At the same time he surveyed the medals on my chest, lingering on the Legion of Honor.

Then His Majesty said, "*Bienvenu au Cambodge, Commander Wake.*"

I wasn't the only one taken aback. The whole place saw it. For the first time since I'd met him, Petrusky was speechless. It devolved upon me to think fast in French, which in my case is always dangerous.

"*Merci beaucoup pour votre hospitalité, Votre Majesté.*

I shook the royal hand and was shocked for a second time. Norodom, clearly pleased with the stir he was causing, palmed me some sort of folded note. Not to be outdone, I employed a skill in card-sharking I'd picked up from Rork back during the war, using my fingers to slide the note up my sleeve. Rork's words at the time he taught me the trick were "Never know when dastardly skills might come in handy, sir." How right he was.

After that it was time to move on to the French resident superior, Foures, who didn't appear to have noticed the illicit transaction. He did notice both the Legion of Honor and my attempt at his language, though, and launched forth in fast French. I happen to think French is the most beautiful language in the world and am embarrassed by my deficiency in it. This version was completely beyond my powers of comprehension, but

Petrusky had recovered his wits enough to translate for us. The statesman had uttered the usual inane claptrap, but his comments weren't important. The look on his face was, however. It was undisguised curiosity about that medal on my uniform.

I was intrigued to notice my fellow former passengers standing much farther back in the line once I left the royal area. I hadn't seen them from the front row earlier. They didn't appear amused at my elevation in social status. I didn't much care what they thought or did. Later I found out I should have. Never underestimate a peeved ne'er-do-well. Especially a group of them.

Next on the agenda that evening was dinner for the most favored guests, about two hundred people, which was to occur in a separate palace nearby. The *Tonle Queen's* social elite were also attending, but kept away from me. Still smarting, I supposed at the time, from my rise in royal affection.

I transferred the note from sleeve to pocket during the procession next door, but it was too dark outside to pull it out and read it. My questions were answered once inside and under the light of an enormous chandelier.

Commander Wake,
 Please meet my man at the stupa for King Ang Duong at midnight. He will take you to me.

 N

I quickly put the note away and racked my brain to make sense of it. A *stupa* was a conical memorial monument. Petrusky had pointed out an entire courtyard of them as we'd made our way to the Throne Hall earlier. I remembered that Ang Duong was Norodom's dead father, the previous king. And yes, now I remembered that individual *stupa.* It was in a corner, under the shade of some orange trees.

A servant guided Petrusky, Altamonte, and me to our places. Tables a hundred feet long ran perpendicular to the royal table athwart the room. We were seated at the head end of the middle table, nearest the royal place settings. When the dinner, consisting of nine courses, finally got under way, I surveyed the king for signs of conspiracy. None. The man was engaged in conversation constantly and never looked my way.

Shrimp, fish, and pork were the main entrees, broiled and spiced with cinnamon, ginger, and nutmeg, along with a myriad of other condiments unknown to my simple palate. A fiery sauce called *nuoc cham* was prevalent on most of it, with a sweet sauce composed of ginger and molasses balancing it nicely. Of course, the foundation for the entire dinner was rice, both brown and white. I am a bit plain in my culinary preferences, but must admit I liked that dinner. The letdown was the drink, a bland rice wine and a watery version of beer, neither of which impressed me. Rork sampled both later and pronounced them forgeries of real liquor. My opinion was that it was a true cultural failure—a tropical country like Cambodia should be able to come up with a decent rum.

After dinner came the last phase of the evening, the most memorable of all for me. The final sixty of the most valued guests were invited to go to the next palace on the grounds, the legendary Chan Chhaya, or the Moonlight Pavilion. Checking my pocket watch, I saw that it was almost eleven o'clock. An hour to go until I was to slip away from my colleagues. Petrusky and I accepted the invitation to the pavilion, but Altamonte had disappeared. I assumed he returned to his quarters, possibly with some digestive ailment.

The Moonlight Pavilion has a magnificent roof, similar to the Throne Hall, but no walls on three sides, only columns. There was no moon that night, but the starlight shone in and subdued torch sconces provided an amber glow. Jasmine incense drifted among the guests and in the dim light everything gradually seemed to lose its urgency.

Norodom was seated upon a mound of pillows, surrounded by females who served him and older males who sat back and kept quiet. Petrusky informed me they were eunuchs and concubines.

For the briefest instant, Norodom nodded to me, then resumed his monologue to a uniformed Westerner I hadn't seen before.

Blundell had shown up and was sitting with d'Abain across the circle from me. Fountjoy, Rockford, and Miss Marston were close to them, the opera star looking decidedly worse for the wear and the other two uninterested in the festivities. I wondered how the rubber rivalry was going, and also what effect Whangtai's little warning foray against d'Abain had on the governance of opium in Cambodia. But happily those concerns weren't in my realm of responsibility and soon were replaced by what was transpiring around me.

Once everyone was seated around the central stage, a special after-dinner drink was served—cobra liquor. Just to allow us confidence in its authenticity, the glass jugs from which it was drawn were displayed on nearby tables. Inside each jug were several dead cobras, along with scorpions and spiders, all fermenting nicely in a clear liquid.

It was the first cobra I'd seen since an exceptionally evil man in northern Africa had done his best to have one kill me nine years earlier. I still have nightmares about that undulating dance of death the damned thing did inches in front of my face, while two giant Senegalese cutthroats held daggers to my back. As I studied the snakes rotting away in their jars and watched others drinking the stuff, I decided it was time to overcome my memories and be sociable. It was sweet at first taste, then packed a secondary explosion once it descended to one's stomach. The locals were impressed that I tried it—the Brits recoiled in horror when it was shown to them—so I garnered some approval there.

The show that night was going to be classical Khmer dance, the style of the ancient empire of Cambodia, followed by something called *Bokator*, a performance by warriors. Petrusky was excited by the prospect but I was feeling a little odd, probably because of what I ate for dinner. Three cups of cobra liquor did the trick, though, giving me enough energy to endure the rest of my social obligation and putting a pleasing tint on the proceedings.

The classical dancers were beautiful girls, clad in gauzy blouses that showed trim bellies and enticing bosoms. That brought Rork to mind. I wondered what he was doing at that moment. Probably backstage helping them with their costumes, I imagined. The dances were slow and sensual, unlike any I'd seen in Christian countries. But they weren't obscene, just gracefully balanced and feminine, moving with deliberate poise in time with the rhythm. It was a fantasy setting and I was entranced, lulled into a state of tranquility I hadn't known for years, since my wife passed away. I made a mental note to remember everything, for it was becoming a lovely evening.

My disposition was further enhanced by a few more cups of the cobra liquor, which wasn't so bad once you got over the ingredients. The stuff engendered a nice glow inside, allowing me to philosophize to my good friend Petrusky about our place in the world as Christians, and how we should learn to appreciate other cultures. He'd only had two cups of the elixir, so he wasn't able to assimilate all of this as well as I was, which I thought a shame. Therefore, it was obviously time for *me* to be the teacher, so I bade him to catch up on the intake. It was apparent to me that if he was understand all I was about to teach, he'd be in need of some constitutional encouragement. But alas, no, the professor remained true to his nature.

"Sobriety is always the best policy," is what he said, if I remember correctly. How very boring, and what a waste of good cobra liquor.

But I wasn't bored for long, for I regret to report the pretty girls were ushered away, replaced by a troop of somber men with fighting sticks—the promised *Bokator*. There were twenty of them, wearing black pantaloons and no shirts, each with a long scarf Petrusky called a *kroma*. The scarf was wrapped around the waist, and red and blue silk cords were tightened around biceps and heads. He advised me that *Bokator* was an art form of warriors, not a sport, and the color of a man's *kroma* gave his rank within the order, black being the highest most of them could attain. All of these men wore a black *kroma* except two, much older than the others. Their scarves were golden. Petrusky explained the older men were the masters, having devoted their lives to the art, and that all of the men had pledged their lives to the king.

It opened with a circle of dancing, evolving into two teams that whirled the sticks within inches of their opponents. Every spectator was riveted by the action, their sweaty faces shining in reflected firelight—even more so when the warriors tossed their sticks to the side and four of them engaged in a melee, using every part of their bodies as weapons against others, drawing blood and causing sickening bone-breaking thuds. This was no game at all.

The four left the stage and six more came up, facing the two golden-scarved warriors. After bowing in respect, they launched an attack against the masters. Dancing, whirling, arms and legs striking out, they went after their betters, without holding their punches and kicks. Blood sprayed, bodies grunted with pain, and it looked like the masters had taught their pupils too well.

But, as Rork frequently says, old age and treachery will win out against youth and skill every time. So, it was with a roar from the crowd that the golden-scarves did some tricks they probably hadn't taught the youth of the clan. Soon one of the attackers was done for and carried away, another limping badly off the stage. The guests showed no mercy on the youngsters, though, and urged the old men on with shouts in several languages, social decorum forgotten. No one was immune to the building passion. The seething crowd, including even the staid Professor Petrusky, became part of the action, yelling encouragement and screaming approval.

A hand touched my shoulder from behind, surprising me. I turned to see a servant nodding toward the courtyard beyond. My watch said twelve-ten. The king! I checked the imperial pillows— he was gone. Now I'd kept the man waiting, after traveling thousands of miles just to meet with him. Petrusky was shouting with the others as I got up, pointing to my stomach and indicating I would return soon from a visit to the necessary room, or whatever they called it in Cambodia.

Then I swayed unsteadily through the audience, those wonderful drinks disturbing my equilibrium fearfully. Somehow, I'd managed to get drunk and be late for a king. Not good at all. Cursing myself, I followed the servant to the entry steps and started toward where I thought I remembered the stupa of Ang Duong lay. The servant didn't follow and I stumbled my way in the near dark until I heard a dainty female voice, the accent making her English hard to understand. Or maybe it was the cobra juice.

"Commander Wake? Please follow me."

I did so, not knowing that my days of lethargy in Indo-China were over.

13
The Mission

Monday, 7 May 1883
Royal Palaces
Phnom Penh, Cambodia

I was led by the hand through the dark hallways of a building on the far side of the royal grounds. My guide never said a word more to me, just pulled me along at a steady pace while I struggled to regain my wits and figure out what I would say to the king when I did finally meet him. I had, of course, planned it all out well in advance—but for the life of me, I couldn't remember a syllable of my intended speech. This would have to be extemporaneous.

We opened a heavy door and entered another hall. Flickering light showed at the end, from a side door. The guide gestured for me to go forward, then she departed back through the door. I advanced down the hallway, sober now and wary. I was all alone, with enemies of various nationalities surrounding me in a forgotten kingdom in the middle of nowhere. My hand gripped the butt of my Colt inside my coat. The medals on my chest jingled with each step. Then I was at the doorway and slowly peered around the wall into the room.

It was a simple room of modest size. Four wall sconces presented decent light on the scene, which was a bit Spartan compared to the opulence around us in other parts of the palaces. The room looked to be an anteroom of some kind, a temporary holding area.

Norodom was seated on a plush European sofa, a bottle of Australian rum resting on the coffee table before him, with two snifters laid out beside it. Four comfortable chairs flanked the sofa. He beckoned me to one. I was wondering how we would communicate when the king lifted his glass and surprised me yet again.

"Thank you for agreeing to my rather eccentric request, Commander. I speak English, so we have no need for an interpreter, even one so distinguished as Professor Petrusky. I have here some Bundaberg rum, which I am told naval men appreciate. Please have some."

"I didn't know you spoke English, Your Majesty," I said, while pouring a gill of the rum. After that cobra liquor, it was the last thing I needed in my stomach, but how do you refuse a king?

"I learned it as a young student in Siam. The British advisors to the Siamese king taught me, though I wasn't supposed to learn anything but classical Buddhist scripture and the sacred canons of Theravada." A royal eyebrow rose at the memory. "Even at an early age, I discovered that sometimes one needs to be flexible in regard to expectations, or regulations. The British also taught me about rum."

I didn't know what to say to that, though I agreed completely, so I mumbled, "You certainly learned well, sir—about the English language, not the rum, of course."

The king's manner abruptly hardened to business. "Well, our time is limited tonight and you've come a very long way, Commander, so I suggest we dispense with the petty customs of salutations and get to the point of your visit."

This was it. "Very well, sir. I have a message from Chester Arthur, President of the United States of America, regarding your kind offer of January fifteenth."

"And where is it?"

"In my mind, sir. Your communication stressed the secrecy of the dialogue, so my superiors decided that it should be committed to memory rather than chance a document falling into the wrong hands."

I could tell he didn't like that. I had to admit, it *was* highly unusual and might smack of a lack of trust, or—as I now knew—as a lack of *respect* in this part of the world.

"I see," said Norodom coolly. "Then please repeat President Arthur's reply."

"The president respectfully thanks Your Majesty for the exceedingly gracious offer of a naval coaling and supply station on the Cambodian coast for the next ninety-nine years, and understands that it would serve the interests of both countries. The president acknowledges your point that the United States Navy has need of a permanently dedicated supply and repair base for our Asiatic squadron, particularly these days with the advent of machinery-driven ships. The offer of a large station with a ninety-nine-year lease, along with extra-territorial authority, at Phu Kwak Island would serve that purpose quite well."

I paused for a breath, but he was impatient, holding his glass in mid-air, waiting.

"And, Your Majesty, the president further realizes that the presence of an American naval station on the coast of Cambodia would probably reduce the piracy problem in the general area of the Gulf of Siam and the South China Sea, and on that coast specifically. All of which is in the interests of Cambodia and all the peoples of the region."

Norodom's gaze intensified. "And now you are about to say, '*however*,' Commander, are you not?"

The man was shrewd. And correct.

"Yes, sir. I am. The 'however' regards the perception of the

British and most especially the French. What would they think of this agreement? Would it violate any bilateral treaties between France and Cambodia? Would it be seen as a provocative threat to the Royal Navy's dominance in the region? In essence, it would create more international problems for America than it solves for our navy."

Norodom leaned back. "The French and the British have failed to eradicate piracy in the Gulf of Siam and in the greater South China Sea region, Commander. The addition of more naval assets in the area would be seen as a benefit, not a threat. America is well known as a neutral nation in Asia; your policies in China have proven that. You have no colonies and no plans for colonies, so the Europeans will have no fear of encroachment in their spheres of influence and control. This agreement is for a supply and repair facility for the American navy, which has had a squadron in Asia's waters for the last seventy years to protect their merchant ships. That is nothing new, nothing provocative."

He put his glass down and bent forward, elbows on his knees, hands spread wide in earnest.

"The Asian people see America as an example of what a European colony in Asia might one day become. What your countrymen have accomplished is a miracle, Commander. A model for the world. And may I have the honor of addressing you as Peter?"

Whew, he was good. Very good. Minimizing the negatives, emphasizing the positives, and appealing to my patriotism, not to mention my own ego. It was a strange situation for a lieutenant commander in the United States Navy. And one fraught with political peril.

"Your Majesty, I am honored. Yes, sir, please call me Peter. As to the reaction of the Europeans to an American naval base in their midst, I fear they would view it far more strongly. I think Paris would think it an attempt by Cambodia to reduce the influence of France in this country."

He flashed a disarming smile. "Peter, you are accurate on

that, they might. But you are not the only foreign nation we are speaking with. This is my decision, not France's."

"Your Majesty, forgive me if I am wrong, but it is my understanding that France directs your foreign policy, as per the agreement of several years ago. Therefore, it appears they will be quite upset by this offer and even of our mere discussion of it."

The face hardened again. "They direct what I *allow* them to direct, Peter. Phu Kwak Island is internal territory of the kingdom of Cambodia, and it has been for the last thousand years. When the French and British were running around in bear skins during what Westerners call the Dark Ages, we had the largest city in the world at Angkor Wat, and an advanced civilization which the Europeans could only see in their dreams. Whether it is for America, or Spain, or some other nation, Phu Kwak is an excellent location for a naval station, and a potential solution for the piracy problem on our coast."

"Spain, Your Majesty?"

The king changed demeanor once more, now he chuckled. "Why do you think Señor Altamonte is visiting me, Peter? He was just here, in this room. I left the ceremony early to discuss options with him. The Spanish are very interested. They need some new stimulus for their East Indies colonies."

Norodom clearly enjoyed the joke on me. So Altamonte had been playing the simpleton, but was in fact a high-level envoy? And all this was happening on the sly, out of the view of Paris's man on the spot, the resident superior, who would be less than amused. "But, Your Majesty, the French—"

The king interrupted me, raising a hand dismissively. "The French do not intimidate me or my people. They are newcomers here and Cambodia will retain her independence of policy, make her own friends, and decide her own future."

Well, *that* was all hot air, or did he really believe what he'd said? As I tried to assimilate all this maneuvering, he poured me more rum and continued, "The French and British need some political and economic competition in this region, Peter. America is a natural candidate and can gain some very lucrative trade. I can help with that in various ways. There are many fields where the well-known American ability of innovation can be profitable. I believe you call it 'Yankee ingenuity.' Refined textile products, shipping, artistic goods, and easily transportable raw materials like rubber, copra, and sugar—these are all available, directly or indirectly, to the United States."

This discussion was far beyond what I'd expected. It was also way out of my realm. Norodom was suggesting a major political and economic shift in the region, and was obviously trying to play another foreign power off against the French. He paused, expecting me to say something, so I muttered, "Ah, yes, Your Majesty, I've seen that the rubber trade rivalry is quite heated in this area."

"Yes, for right now, it appears that way. But the British will lose that contest—Fountjoy and Rockford just don't know it yet. The British will make money off their gutta percha, to be sure, but the French rubber plantations in Indo-China will get the large telegraph cable contracts. The British cannot sell their type of rubber cheaply enough."

It was amazing. Before meeting him, I'd thought Norodom some sequestered hermit, softened by a pampered life and kept in the dark about current affairs by his own manipulative mandarins and French advisors. I was completely wrong. This man was smart and anything but soft. To my mind, he was also very dangerous.

It was time for me to get back on the subject and conclude my mission, even if it made him angry. By noon the next day, I was planning to be heading downriver for home.

"Yes, well, Your Majesty, we seem to have progressed beyond my area of responsibility or expertise, which is the offer of the island for a naval station. I'm afraid that the concerns of the United States are such that a deal doesn't look viable anytime soon."

"Peter, you can't make a professional recommendation about this subject to your president without seeing the location. Can you?"

"Your Majesty, the political concerns outweigh any professional advantages, so the matter of a personal survey is moot. My president wanted to show his respect by sending a senior envoy to convey that message and to thank you for the offer. Pursuant to your wishes, it's been done in a low-key fashion, so as not to disturb any other parties. That was my mission, sir, and I have completed it."

Norodom's tone was still pleasant, but the eyes grew cold. "No, Peter. Your mission is not completed until you get home. How do you propose to do that?"

Was that a threat? I kept calm. "Down the river tomorrow, sir."

"Oh, no one has told you? I am sad to say that will be impossible. No riverboats are steaming on the river now, the water is too low. Even the *Tonle Queen,* which should be repaired and moving by tomorrow afternoon, will not be coming upriver to Phnom Penh. She is heading back down to the Delta."

"A ride on a small boat, then."

"Also impossible, Peter. Some bandits near Banam have stopped all river traffic. They may even try to capture *Tonle Queen,* if she doesn't get downriver fast enough. I have ordered three regiments of my army to go to Banam, search for the brigands, and attack them, but that will take some time. Probably weeks, possibly months."

I didn't like this. He'd been baiting me to enter his trap. "Then what do you suggest, Your Majesty?"

"A simple solution, Peter. And one that serves our other topic as well. You will accompany me on a royal visit to Kampot, on my southern coast. It happens to be very near Phu Kwak Island. From Kampot we will find you transport to Saigon or Singapore, or anywhere else you desire."

"Ah, well . . . thank you, but . . ."

"Peter, you are thinking perhaps this will be an arduous journey, like the one you had upriver? Then I think you have never traveled with a king, my new friend. It will be comfortable, educational, and far more enjoyable than sitting in Phnom Penh, waiting for things to eventually happen so you can get downriver . . . someday. And, of course, your servant and the professor can come along also."

Hmm, put that way, did I really have a choice? It did sound like a quicker way to get to Saigon than sitting around waiting for the rains to come and raise the river level. Or wait for the bandits to be overwhelmed by military force. And he was right, I never had traveled with a *king*. It sounded like a pretty classy way to travel—Rork would be pleased and Petrusky intrigued. And we might still make Saigon in time to embark on *Juniata* if she came. Norodom fidgeted, unused to waiting for answers to his offers.

I managed to stammer out, "Well, ah . . . I suppose that does seem to be the obvious thing for me to do. Thank you for the generous invitation, Your Majesty. When were you planning on leaving, sir?"

He clapped his hands in delight and stood. "Excellent. We leave at dawn, Peter. The elephants will pick you up at your quarters at sunrise."

Elephants? Rork and I were incompetent with *horses*. I was about to get that part clarified when His Majesty King Norodom, the Supreme Lord of Life, Master of Compassion and Mercy, et cetera, et cetera, got up and unceremoniously left the room.

I sat back down, thinking. None of this was in my plan.

14

The Coast

Saturday, 12 May 1883
Kampot, Coast of Cambodia

The king was right. It was a very classy way to travel, once you got used to the elephant's motion. Fortunately, Rork and I were used to that movement—it was just like being at sea sailing downwind. A slight pitch up and down, combined with a roll from side to side.

Unfortunately, the professor was not, and fifteen minutes into the journey he ended up with a case of *mal-de-mer,* while he was still ninety miles from the sea. I must say, the man never complained. In any event, the choices were limited to either riding the elephant or going by foot.

Horses, we were told, were far too skittish to make their way through the dense jungle. When I asked why, an officer explained condescendingly that it was because they are afraid of snakes, as if I were an idiot to ask. And snakes, we were further advised, were rather numerous in the jungles of Cambodia. Turned out that cobras were plentiful, but the real rascals were something slithery called a *krait,* which apparently loved to nestle close to humans, then kill them for sport. This intelligence made the elephant idea look pretty good to me and Rork. No doubt that officer is still regaling his comrades about the time he had to answer stupid questions from the Yankee sailors who didn't know anything about horses or snakes.

After all three of us mounted our colossal long-nosed steeds, the escort officer added with great enthusiasm that we were now safe from all *ground* snakes, but to still be on the lookout for something called the green tree viper, which looked just like a vine and would bite an unsuspecting traveler in the face. Right about then, Rork began to doubt my decision to depart the royal palace. He didn't say anything, but I could tell by his expression, which was rather cross.

As it was, by my navigation, we made between five and eight knots through the jungle paths—about twice as fast as a man, even without snakes in ambush. For the first two days Rork attacked every overhanging vine near us with a long stick, then gradually relaxed and settled on only attacking vines that moved. None of them proved a valid target, however. We never did see the infamous tree viper.

Other than worrying about deadly serpents, it was a fascinating journey, mainly because of the lifestyle. Each day there was a stop for meals that took two hours to set up, what with the tents and kitchens and tables and chairs. The column contained about forty elephants and must have stretched for a quarter mile—a daunting logistical endeavor. Dinners were truly extravagant; the tents were converted into miniature palaces, with a musical and dance performance each evening, before we retired to our sumptuous quarters, the most elegant of which, of course, was Norodom's.

An interesting omission struck me on the second day—the French advisors weren't along. I asked the king about that. His reply was attended by a quick wink. "They were invited, but declined. They are far more partial to the palace lifestyle than the jungle."

"Are they aware I'm along, sir?"

He pulled on his chin thoughtfully, his face in a pseudo frown. "You know, Peter, I believe someone must have neglected to tell them. I am fairly certain that if they knew you were with me, they would be here too, even in this jungle. For some reason, the French foreigners don't like *other* foreigners to visit my country. They are worried about you, but they are angry about the British colonel and the other one."

Norodom laughed and said, "And their feelings were hurt that I asked Miss Marston to perform at the royal theater. They informed me there were French opera singers who were twice as good." He sighed. "Ah well, I am in the jungle and will not be able to see her performance, so perhaps the joke is on me."

Our host took many opportunities to point out animals and places to us. We only passed through one town of any size, Chhouk, where the road was lined with cheering subjects. Norodom basked in their glow, but I registered the sharp-eyed men in uniforms behind the crowd and speculated on just how genuine the adoration really was.

When we started out, I was told that Kampot was ninety English miles from Phnom Penh. As we plodded through the jungle I realized that estimate was "as the crow flies." The trail wound around swamps and hills and rivers, so we probably traveled at least two hundred miles. Finally, at the end of five days, we arrived at Kampot, a scruffy little town of slums gathered around a fork in the Kampong River, a mile inland from the mangrove coast. It was a squalid place, and unlike elsewhere in Cambodia I could smell no incense, only sewage. The miserable inhabitants duly cheered their ruler, although with lackluster effort. Most of them had a sullen look about them. I observed several giving their king downright surly stares. The place was unsettling, with a tense atmosphere, but nothing definite formed in my mind as to why it should be different from the other towns.

When we reached the central square—an overstatement of the place—along the riverfront, I inquired among the entourage as to the passenger potential of the port, chiefly to Saigon. One courtier turned to a nearby provincial official who shrugged his shoulders and said, *"Navire? Il n'y en a pas."*

I didn't need Petrusky's help to translate that—the man said there weren't any ships. My secondary plan had come to a distinct halt. The professor stood silently staring at the ground, while my stalwart assistant struggled to contain his emotions. To his eternal credit, Rork said nothing overtly, but I did see him exhale mightily and caught a Gaelic sound or two slipping out.

This would not do. It was worse than staying in Phnom Penh. One does not confront a king in his own country, though, especially a feudal king who can have you killed if he desires, so I submerged my anger and went to politely ask him what the new strategy was, now that we knew no ships were coming to take us away.

Norodom was unfazed, declaring nonchalantly, "Peter, my friend, I realize that you are eager to go home and we will do our best to help you. Tomorrow morning we will embark upon another of my royal yachts and travel to Saigon. And since we are in the area, I will show you Phu Kwak Island while we are en route."

He had another yacht? Around here? That was hard to believe, but my options had dwindled to zero. "Thank you, Your Majesty. I know the president of the United States will be grateful for all you've done to get us to Saigon."

The king was distracted by an aide and walked away. Then it dawned on me that I didn't really know where we were. I approached the one court official I knew spoke a little English. *"Excusez-moi,* do you have a map of this area, sir? A *map?"*

"Oh! *Une carte? Oui, monsieur."*

A British map of Indo-China was brought to us. Rork and Petrusky came over and watched as the courtier spread it out on a camp table. It covered from China to Malaya to Burma, including all of the Gulf of Siam. I traced the coastline from the parrot's beak of Cochin around to the northwest. I found Phu Kwak Island, the largest in the Gulf, then I found Kampot.

I wish I hadn't.

They say that ignorance is bliss. At that moment in time I would have enjoyed some ignorance. Rork groaned when he studied the coast where my finger had landed. Petrusky nodded and sighed. The Cambodian saw their reactions and focused on the map. He turned away, embarrassed. The British label on the map of that coast meant the same in French: THE PIRATES.

Rork glanced at the crowd of brooding faces around us and said, "Remember back on the river when I told ye I had *that feelin'*—that we'd run into some nasty buggers? Well, here we are, sir. If these ain't pirates, I'm no son o' Erin. I know that look."

He was right. We'd both seen pirates in Central America and North Africa—there was a look, a dead-eyed coldness—that was common to them the world over. As I surveyed the locals watching us, I realized they were, in fact, *evaluating* us. Our strengths, our weaknesses.

"Rork, you're right. I've been feeling uneasy since we arrived here. Now I know why. But maybe they'll steer clear of the king's yacht. They might not want to attract that much retribution."

Rork put a hand on Petrusky's shoulder. "What say ye, Professor? Got any word on these shifty blighters?"

"The pirates on this coast are mostly Malay Muslims and Chinese renegades, led by Chinese with affiliations to the opium warlord Whangtai. They also have some loose connections with pirate gangs in Malacca, Borneo, and the southern Philippines."

"Whangtai? The bandit who runs dope on the Mekong River?"

"Yes, Mr. Rork, the very same Whangtai, who you may recall sent his man to pressure Norodom's opium chief d'Abain with the demonstration that night on the riverboat. Whangtai is not afraid of the French, much less any Cambodian king."

Rork looked at me and wagged his head. "Well, sir, this ain't gettin' any better, is it?"

No, it wasn't, so why would Norodom, who'd impressed me with his knowledge of the intricate goings-on in this corner of the world, want to venture into a hostile area? It was fairly evident he'd set this up to get me to see the damned island, but why come here without a strong protective force?

Whatever lingering small doubts I'd had about Petrusky's motives were secondary now. Until we reached Saigon, the three of us were alone among these mongrels and had only each other for mutual defense. There was no diplomatic paper trail—all the details of my mission were in my head. Connally thought I was upriver at Phnom Penh. No one knew we were on the coast. No one would look for us. No one was going to help us.

"No, Rork, it's not getting better. So we'd best stay together and stay alert, gentlemen."

Five minutes later I had reason to support Rork's assertion. A disheveled local French priest—I'd seen no church, so his congregation must've been tiny—walked up to me and gave me an envelope with a wax seal embossed with a cross. On the outside was written "Wake." The priest, who appeared jaundiced and walked unsteadily, spoke no English. My French chose that moment to desert me as he rambled on in an odd accent, so I asked Petrusky to communicate.

"He says he received this from a runner who came from the church in Chhouk. It originated in Phnom Penh and was sent by relay through the churches to us here. It is a confidential message for you, Peter, from Bishop Courdier."

The priest trudged away, his duty done. Petrusky examined the envelope. "The seal is that of a bishop and is unbroken."

I opened the envelope. The five-page note was in French and dated May sixth. Bishop Courdier's small personal card was enclosed also. I got the gist of the meaning of the letter but asked Petrusky to translate, just to make sure. He read it aloud.

Dear Commander Wake. It was an honor and pleasure to meet you last night at the royal soirée; however, I regret that we did not have the opportunity to speak at more length. I was aware you were coming to Phnom Penh, since Bishop Galibert at Saigon had written to me of your impending visit, and that he had asked Professor Petrusky to accompany you. I had hoped you would be in the city for a while so I could invite you to dinner.

Now I see that you have departed with the king on an impromptu excursion to Kampot and will probably not return, so this letter will have to suffice. While I do not know of the precise reason for your mission to Cambodia—and it is certainly not within my purview to know—I feel it incumbent upon me to pass along some information regarding your visit that has come into my possession. Please forgive its lack of detail, but as I suspect you may understand from your profession, frequently such sources are not the types who can or will provide specifics.

You apparently have stimulated considerable speculation about why you are in Indo-China. The ostensible explanation of simple courier with a message to Norodom in reference to complaints of molestation of American shipping has not resonated with the numerous factions, several of whom are unsavory, which have conducted said speculation. Thus, rumors have been started, some of which have implied American interference with the status quo. Because of this perception, it has been determined by some of these factions that the potential American interference should be terminated before it can develop into a problem for them. One of those areas of contention has to do with underwater telegraph cable contracts and the subsequent subcontracts for the cable's insulating rubber. They think the Americans might get the cable contract, then decide to use the British plantations' rubber. Fortunes rest upon these issues and, sadly, life is not held in great value in Asia.

There are regrettable associations in Indo-China between legitimate endeavors and criminal enterprises. Sometimes the law-abiding need the protection of the law-breaking. And sometimes, when the perception of a threat is strong enough, that protection comes in the form of preemptive violence against the threat. Commander, you are perceived as the threat by the rubber interests.

Therefore, I have reason to believe that your life, and those of your companions, is in grave danger. My sources tell me that an evil combination of forces is at work. The warlord Whangtai, who *receives funding from certain interests for his protection, has been given the task of eliminating their perceived threat—you and your companions. His efforts along the Mekong to trap you have failed, but he has associates among the scoundrels of the coast and if I know where you are, they do also. Considerable money has been authorized for your head.*

And now some other matters. I have been led to believe that you have the impression Mr. Augustine Heard is a dealer in weapons or possibly opium. You may take my word that he is not. It would be wrong if you returned to your country with that false impression and inadvertently disseminated it. He deals in legitimate items of trade. I am sorry to say I cannot say the same about many of the other merchants in Indo-China.

You should also know that I have just received disturbing news this morning that the French military position in the northern part of the Vietnamese empire, at Hanoi in Tonking, is in peril. The Black Flag insurgents, led and aided by the Chinese army, which has crossed the border, have surrounded the French garrison at Hanoi. They have recaptured most of the area along the Red River that the French pacified in March and April. Captain Henri Rivière, the famous naval officer, is in command at Hanoi and fighting on, though the French are overwhelmingly outnumbered. My informants report that many in Cambodia and in Viet Nam are fearful the violence will spread, as the anti-Western Chinese have much influence in various parts of the region. Some are even predicting disaster for the French. Some are hoping for it.

Your host, King Norodom, is a brilliant man, well-versed in political machinations. He lives a lifestyle of heathen decadence, it is true, but do not mistake that for lassitude. The king has had to always be several steps ahead of his opponents to remain in power, so what is apparent with him is not always what is real. Never underestimate him. He tolerates the Church because of his fear of the French, but he does not like Christians or Europeans, nor trust Westerners in general. The aforementioned news from Hanoi will interest him greatly.

A final thought, sir. You have influential friends in the Church, Commander, who have let it be known that you are to be assisted in every way possible. I am a man of God and have no temporal powers, only my indomitable faith that good will prevail. Unfortunately, passing along this information is all that I have available to me. I am praying that being forewarned will make you forearmed, and that we will be able to meet again, once this unfortunate episode is over, and enjoy that quiet evening I had so hoped would occur.

For the obvious reasons, please completely destroy this letter immediately upon reading it. Also, please keep my personal card and present it to any clergy you might chance to meet in Indo-China. There is an inscription on the reverse they should read.

My son, I pray fervently that in this time of uncertainty, God grants you the wisdom to know what to do, the strength to do it, and the good humor to get through it. Until we meet again,

Petrusky finished with, " Peter, it is signed *Marie Laurent-Francois Xavier Courdier, M.E.P., Bishop of Cambodia.*"

The three of us stood there, each contemplating what the bishop had written me. The professor sighed. "It is as I feared. Many Asians will be encouraged by the news from Hanoi. The French side will be enraged. The war will spread."

I was thinking of *us* right then. "Hanoi's far away, Professor. The primary question for us is how will any of this affect our chances to get to safety at Saigon."

He thought about that for a moment, then said, "It will hinder us. Remember, the pirate leaders are mostly Chinese, with distant ties to the victorious Black Flags. The pirates will be emboldened to take action against Westerners while they are perceived to be weak."

Rork harrumphed and pulled out a match, flaring it off his brogan's sole and lighting the letter afire. I looked at the back of the card, where a line was handwritten in French. It was simple and I could get it, but Petrusky translated for Rork.

"*Mr. Wake is a friend of the Vicar of Peter. Help him.* It is signed, *Bishop Courdier.*"

Petrusky looked up at me. "You are not Catholic, Peter, so you may not know what that means. Do you?"

"No, not really, Professor. I supposedly have a personal vicar someplace?"

He shook his head no, then murmured, "The 'Peter' on the card doesn't refer to you, Peter. It refers to Saint Peter. 'Vicar of Peter' is the ancient original title given to the first popes of the Vatican, and sometimes to their successors. This refers to the current Vicar of Peter: Pope Leo the Thirteenth, *himself.*"

Rork was staring at me. "The Holy Father? You, a heretic, have him as a patron? Peter Wake, now I *know* the end times have arrived . . ."

Well, of course, we both knew that I, a Methodist of all things, had friends among the Jesuits. Maybe a bishop here or there, but the Pope? I'd never even been to Rome, nor met the Pope, and figured the professor might have blown things a bit out of proportion with his translation. However, since it obviously impressed both of my Catholic companions, I concluded it might be useful with the few clergy we chanced to meet.

The two of them stood there, gaping at me. I, on the other hand, felt ridiculous about the whole thing. "Let's just hope it impresses the scoundrels on this coast as much as it impresses you two."

With that said, we set off to find King Norodom and see how the transport was lining up for the morning. After half an hour we still hadn't found him and no one knew where he was, though the town was full of his baggage train elephants.

I had a sinking feeling we'd been abandoned, but didn't let on. Rork was already upset with me for agreeing to leave the capital with Norodom and thus getting us into this fix, there was no sense in aggravating his annoyance. Then, after we'd circled the small town for the third time with no success, the bosun announced, "That bloody flamin' rogue's marooned us, sir—sure as a hooker's icy heart."

"It does seem so, Peter," remarked the professor ruefully, nodding his head in sad accord.

I ignored them, trying to maintain the fiction of confidence. "All right, it's getting dark. Let's find a place to sleep within the royal entourage. Either Rork or I will be awake at all times. In the morning we'll find a way out of here on our own, king or no king."

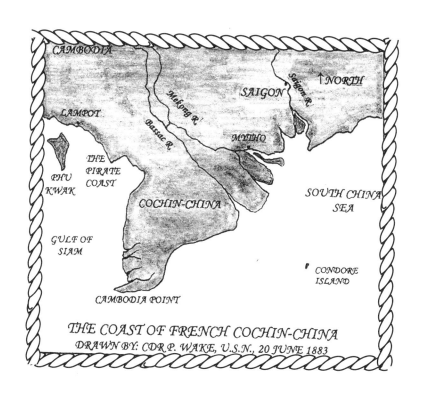

CAMBODIA

↑ NORTH

SAIGON

Saigon R.

Mekong R.

LAMPOT

Bassac R.

MYTHO

THE
PIRATE
COAST

PHU
KWAK

COCHIN-CHINA

SOUTH CHINA
SEA

GULF OF
SIAM

CONDORE
ISLAND

CAMBODIA POINT

THE COAST OF FRENCH COCHIN-CHINA
DRAWN BY: CDR P. WAKE, U.S.N., 20 JUNE 1883

15

Phu Kwak

Sunday, 13 May 1883
Off the coast of Cambodia
Gulf of Siam

We billeted in a tent with some of the senior courtiers. They tried to give us our own accommodations, but I insisted we stay with the others, thinking there might be some safety, and possibly anonymity, in numbers. As it was, I closed my eyes but didn't sleep much. Too many things were swirling in my mind, too many scenarios, too many probable endings for this nightmare. Most of them resulted in our deaths.

Late that night, while all around us were snoring, the three of us whispered our appraisals of the situation. Petrusky, having read the bishop's letter, apologized for his prior description of Heard as a gun dealer, saying he'd gotten it from a Chinese boatman on the Mekong. He maintained his characterization of Dupuis, though. And said he found it interesting that just as the French fortunes in Tonking were waning fast, Dupuis had found it convenient to head south and seek new partners along the Mekong.

In regard to our future, Petrusky was worried about Whangtai, citing the warlord's ties with the pirates, who would be delighted to curry favor with the warlord by killing us and to make some money in the bargain. He felt that Norodom, assuming he truly was innocent of collusion with the evil forces at work in this, did not have the strength along with him on this journey to deter or resist the pirates. When asked why he thought the king brought so few soldiers, he supposed it was to not alarm the French advisors in the capital. Major military force would've done that and the French would've insisted on coming along. It was obvious that Norodom wanted this to be a trip with just the Americans, and he wondered why.

Well, of course, I knew why. It had to do with the king still trying to get the Americans to commit to a ninety-nine-year lease at Phu Kwak. But to change the subject I asked the professor his opinion on what we should do now, stay on land or go by sea? Petrusky said we'd have better chances at sea than to return to Phnom Penh on that long trail full of potential ambushes.

Rork suggested that we might go by sea in the other direction, north along the coast to Siam, confusing the enemy. He added that we could, if need be, steal a boat and escape on our own. He didn't trust Norodom at all and preferred to be rid of him and the royal minders.

I was leaning toward Rork's idea. We'd done that very thing in Peru two years earlier, when all around us looked hopeless. The problem in Kampot was that if we were able to steal a vessel, we'd have to get it downriver and away before the alarm could be sounded, and the chances of that occurring were slim. I told them both that in the morning we would check the waterfront for suitable craft, but if the king's yacht looked appropriate we'd use that and forget any thefts. I ended by saying we must at all costs not offend the king or his officers, for they were the thin ray of hope we could get through this without desperate measures.

The Master of Compassion himself showed up at dawn at the doorway of our tent in a decidedly good mood, dressed in semi-regalia and demanding to know why we had slept with his underlings when we could have reposed in the solitary splendor our stations in life allowed. He never favored us with an account of his whereabouts the evening before and we didn't dare ask.

In answer to his query about our sleeping arrangements, I explained that we were wary of the locals and more at ease in the company of his entourage, learned and refined as they were. Norodom accepted my meager rationalization with grace, waving his hand and saying, "No matter. The day is dawning. We are off." Then, like a boy with a new toy to show his pals, he changed the subject with a cheery invitation to breakfast—on the royal yacht.

It was a skeptical trio who followed His Majesty through the morning crowds, the courtiers shushing and clucking the disgruntled common folk out of the way, and down the filthy main street to the bamboo jetty on the riverbank. And there, to our amazement, we saw a steamer.

Well, it really wasn't much of a steamer, but it was floating and smoke was coming out from the stack, which was vastly superior to everything else on the waterfront. We didn't have much time to view the vessel from afar, for the king was in a hurry and therefore the household staff was scurrying to get the baggage and supplies aboard. We followed the rush of people behind Norodom as he strode up the plank and arrived to the applause of the yacht's rather odd-looking crew.

They were tricked out in French-style uniforms, which appeared to be new, making me wonder how long the boys had been in the king's navy. I suspected that until that morning they'd been in the elephant corps of the army, probably as the groomers. The captain and engineer were swarthy half-breed–looking fellows, even more incongruous in their uniforms. I guessed they were the steamer's former master and engineman, now decked out in gold lace, but still reeking of arrack liquor and in serious need of a bath.

The crew lined up on deck for an imperial inspection. If you ignored the fact they were incompetent, they did look relatively good. The same could not be said for the royal yacht. Petrusky asked around and discovered that until the day before, the steamer had been a rice barge tug, utilized to tow boatloads of rice along the coast and up rivers. Now she flew the king's standard from her tiny foremast. The vessel was perhaps seventy feet in length and propelled by an ancient walking beam engine that drove two side wheels. She was locally built of teak and probably at least forty years old—archaic for a vessel in debilitating tropical waters. We found out that Norodom had chartered her the night before sight unseen. Now, here he was, inordinately proud of the newest addition to his fleet, pacing back and forth with hands clasped behind his back, scrutinizing the shine on the buttons and shoes of his sailors.

"Oh, I don't fancy this a bit, sir," grumbled Rork as we stood watching from the stern. "This tub'll be slower than one o' them elephants—assumin' she stays afloat. Not one little bit do I fancy *this*, sir."

I surveyed the dugouts and small sampans lining the shore. "Well, it's a tub, all right, Rork, but still, she's a damn sight better than the other choices."

Petrusky gestured forward. "Breakfast is ready for us, Peter."

And so it was. On the foredeck, in front of the tiny wheelhouse, tables had been set up together with white linen, crystal, and silverware. Stewards of the royal kitchen, who a week earlier had been serving in the opulence of a palace, were decorously going about their duties, the surroundings notwithstanding. The king was already seated, beckoning to me and the professor. Rork, who was not invited, muttered a Gaelic oath and said he was going to look around a bit.

Going downriver on a derelict hulk while lounging in majestic grandeur would've been comical if we'd been in a peaceful country. I wasn't feeling any mirth, however, for the atmosphere was anything but tranquil. There was a malaise in the air, a sense of hopelessness, of resentment. I was sure Norodom must've have felt it, but if he did, he didn't reveal it. Instead he kept up a show, combining imperial paternalism and jovial optimism. He was the only one buying it. The crew and household entourage, with the few soldiers we had, were nervous. No, they had transcended that when we left the dock—now they were scared.

Along the banks, the grim townspeople stopped whatever they were doing, which wasn't much, and stared as we passed by them. Norodom was their king, but in name only. These people had no allegiances beyond what terror or greed could produce. I checked Petrusky's reaction. He saw me and shrugged. He felt it too.

We reached the mouth of the river after the meal, crossed the bar, and swung southwest against the gentle swells in the Gulf of Siam. King Norodom loved it all, standing near the bow and announcing to everyone that he was a sailor at heart and would henceforth spend more time at sea. Many of the imperial followers didn't share His Majesty's newfound love of salt water, however, and started to look a bit green about the gills. Petrusky was beginning to share their fate and I suggested he take some ginger, an old sailors' cure. He procured some and thanked me profusely an hour later.

Rork and I, back at our perch at the stern, felt better now, as sailors always do when away from the confines of land. Land spells danger for seamen, be it reefs or diseases or politics. The sea represents freedom, even such a dangerous part of the sea as the one we were steaming through.

Steaming, by the way, turned out to be a relative term—the

engine coughed and wheezed as much as it steamed. The stack exhaust alternated between gray and black, depending on what they'd found to burn, and periodically the steam vent would scream in protest at a surge in the pressure. Our engineer, now without the encumbrance of his heavy new coat, spent the time swearing in Malay and beating the rusting iron beast in certain places with an equally rusted iron bar. Curiously, I did not see a lot of lubrication going on, something most engineers do constantly to ensure the thing works.

When I mentioned that to Rork several hours later in the afternoon, he took barely concealed delight in informing me that an hour earlier he'd been down in the engine room and up close to our means of power. His prediction was that it might last a hundred miles, at the most. He further cheered me with the knowledge that we had fuel, a tiny bit of coal but mostly wet mangrove wood, for only about twenty hours of steaming, which corresponded with his estimate of the engine's life expectancy.

And according to his navigation—he'd had another look at that British map—this all meant we would be dead in the water somewhere around two-thirds of the way to the large cape at the southern end of Cochin. To get to Saigon, we had to round that cape and then steam another two hundred miles. He ended his opinion with a reiteration of his suggestion to go north along the coast toward Siam, instead of our present course to the southwest.

Now I must admit that Sean Rork isn't the best navigator I've known, but I decided to humor the old boy, for he is without a doubt the very finest man I've known. So I asked, "How, please tell, do you propose we do that?"

"Simple—seize the vessel an' turn the bitch around," he replied matter-of-factly.

"And the little matter of the king?"

"Present him with a *fait accompli*," Rork said, proudly using a little French to make his point. He threw a glance of defiance toward His Majesty still standing up at the bow, grinning at the world.

"I think not, Rork," I said calmly, not wishing to get his Irish blood boiling. It was already simmering and he could be devilishly difficult when he got all worked up on a subject. "We already have enough enemies and I don't wish to expand the list to include a reigning monarch. Our mission here was to nicely pass along the president's decline of Norodom's offer—remind me to tell you later what that was. Operational security seems to be moot by this point—we can't kidnap the man and create an international debacle. No, we'll ride this bucket as long as she floats, then improvise something. Besides, I still want to try to rendezvous with George Dewey's ship at Saigon and ride her back to the States. I know he'll be passing by Saigon and probably'll stop there. A warship's the easiest and fastest way to get back home."

Sean Rork can be very persistent. Some would call him stubborn.

"Oooh, it'd be easy to take her over. Agin' these fools, the two of *us* could do it in less time than a tinker's song, sir."

Occasionally, I have to be firm with the bosun. "No, Rork. Mutiny is not an option."

My old friend should've had a career on stage. His hands went up in the air and eyes widened innocently as he took a step back in mock horror.

"*Mutiny!* Why, sir, I'm duly scandalized—aye, sir, I say *scandalized*—at such a word to describe anythin' that Sean Rork would say!" he protested, the last part a bit too theatrically for my taste.

But he wasn't finished. "Why, Sean Rork's been a bosun for me beloved Uncle Sam for nigh on twenty-three years now, an' would never counsel such a thing, sir. I was merely suggestin' a . . . decisive act . . . a *liberation* . . . for everybody's own good, that I was. Nary a mutinous bone in me body, sir."

Just as I was about to explain the finer points of admiralty law to my deniably mutinous bosun, Petrusky arrived at our perch and pointed toward a distant lump of green on the starboard bow.

157

"Peter, there is Phu Kwak Island, on the horizon. Do you know much about it?"

Up forward, King Norodom was peering through a long glass at the island. Sensing another sales pitch coming, I inwardly groaned and turned my gaze to the professor, still wondering whether he knew the true point of my mission. He and I had never discussed Phu Kwak and the man was so damned hard to read. I kept going back and forth about his loyalties and his knowledge about my true purpose for being there. The general air of pessimistic wariness in Indo-China raised mere suspicion to an art form. In any event, I supposed I really should know more about the place.

"No, I don't, Professor. Can you enlighten me?"

The teacher in him came out. "It is the largest island in the Gulf of Siam and known as 'the island of ninety-nine mountains.' The largest of them are in a ridge along this side of the island, with Mount Chua being the highest at six hundred meters. The people there are Malay, Cambodian, or Cochinese. Also some Chinese merchants, naturally. There are pirate lairs, Malay and Chinese, along this side of the island. Since eighteen-sixty-nine, there have been two small French rubber and copra plantations on the other side, facing the west. It is rumored that the pirates do not molest French ships, that a *quid pro quo* is said to exist. I do not believe the French would do that, but many do believe it."

"Hmm, very interesting." I was reminded of Norodom's portrayal of the island. "And it's been Cambodian for a thousand years, I would imagine?"

"A thousand years ago it *was,* but its current ownership is the subject of disputes. Right now the island is generally considered to be part of French Cochin, even though it lies off the Cambodian coast, because it was part of the provinces granted to Cochin by Cambodia in the eighteen-sixties. The Cambodian king denies this, however, and maintains that the island is still Cambodian. The French colonial government of Cochin in Saigon believes it is theirs; however, they deem it not worth fighting over at this point—which may truly explain why the pirates can still operate there and on the mainland in this area. There is no real rule of law here."

Petrusky provided his explanation indifferently, which was important to me. I was certain that if Petrusky had somehow guessed the genuine nature of my mission his voice would've betrayed him when discussing Phu Kwak. I now decided that Petrusky probably was what he originally said he was—an academic whom the Church had asked to assist me.

But the professor's information revealed something else— King Norodom lied to me about the island's current sovereignty. The intent was obvious. My new pal the king was trying to stealthily present a *de facto* American counterbalance to France's domination in the region, which was precisely what President Arthur had worried about. It was brilliant of Norodom, in an underhanded sort of way, but it also showed me the true extent of the king's desperation to fend off the French, who were inexorably taking control of everything in the region.

Rork handed me a tarnished old telescope he'd gotten from the captain, then pointed at Phu Kwak. "Take a look to the left o' the island, sir."

Three sailing junks were bound northeast with the wind on their quarter, heading for . . . *us*. I focused the lens, which barely turned, and was able to enlarge the view slightly. Yes, three junks, their high sterns crowded with people, their dirty woven sails straining out on either side, were running fast downwind and rolling in the seas. There were the usual streamers from the mastheads to ward off evil spirits, but no flags that I could see.

"Tell me what you know of the pirates of Phu Kwak, Professor," I asked while studying the junks.

"I know a little bit, Peter. They are led by Chinese renegades, some of whom have ties with Whangtai. Some have ties with the Black Flag gangs up in Tonking. In southern China, piracy was very organized and flourished until the eighteen-twenties and thirties. That was when the British pressured the Chinese emperor to end the corruption and collusion by the provincial government, which had looked the other way for centuries. At one point there were supposedly tens of thousands of pirates in and near the large island of Hainan, off the southern coast of China, that roamed the seas from the Philippines to Java to Siam. But by the end of the Sino-British Opium War in the eighteen-forties, many had been pushed out of China and established themselves elsewhere. Some ended up in this area. There are various stories about the ones here, but I do not know the veracity of the stories."

Puffs of smoke rose from the island, which I judged ten miles distant. The puffs were in a pattern—three, followed by three more. To my mind they looked like signals. Several puffs bloomed on the junk farthest away, the smoke swept away on the wind, but the dull thuds coming across the water to us. Yes, they were blank signaling charges.

"Have you heard anything about their leadership?"

"They are ruthless. I do not know their names or anything about them personally. Oh, wait . . . except for one. It is an extraordinary tale, but it just may be true. I do not know."

The three junks were spreading out in line abreast, the classic attack formation. They didn't look like fishing or cargo junks to me. At the combined closing speed, we had about an hour before they'd be on us. At the bow, King Norodom was watching them too. He wasn't grinning anymore.

"So what's the tale, Professor?"

"There is a female pirate leader with several ships who sails in the Gulf of Siam. She goes by the name of Shu, which means 'tender kindness' in Chinese—it is an evil play upon words, for she is reputed to be very cruel to those who oppose her. Shu is supposedly the granddaughter of a very famous Chinese woman pirate called Cheng Ay Sao from Canton who died in eighteen-forty-four. Cheng Ay's son was himself a pirate who sailed south and tried to build a lair at Borneo, but was driven out by the Muslims and came to the Gulf of Siam, where Shu's mother met him. Shu was subsequently born somewhere around here. The mother was killed by the childbirth and people say it was Shu's first murder. Shu purportedly has a hideaway on Phu Kwak somewhere and preys only on non-French Westerners' ships in or near the Gulf of Siam. That is the general meaning of the story as I have heard it."

"Yep, I agree. It sounds like a tall tale, all right."

I handed him the glass to take a look. Rork whispered, "Heads up, sir—His Ownself is comin' this way."

King Norodom approached us, nodded toward the junks and asked, "Do you think they are pirates, Peter?"

"Yes, sir. They look like pirates to me. They're headed for us."

"And do you have any suggestions as to what we should do when they arrive here?" he asked calmly, sounding like friends were coming over for dinner.

"You have a dozen armed soldiers aboard, sir. I would suggest that they shoot with deliberation at the junks from the extreme range of accurate fire—about a hundred yards in this sea—aiming for the leaders at the stern of each junk. And keep firing as long as they have ammunition available. Depending on the soldiers' accuracy, that *may* deter the pirates, sir."

He looked dubious of our chances. So was I.

"I see," he asked. "And if they keep coming?"

"Then the pirates will try to swarm aboard us by ramming all three junks into us at once, Your Majesty. If the captain can maintain evasive maneuvering we can possibly thwart their attempt and get to windward of them."

"Explain that, Peter."

"They are sailing downwind fast, sir, but they can't go directly up against the wind. So once we get past them and upwind, we can use our one advantage to its fullest."

"Which is?"

"Our steam engine, which allows us to go up into the wind."

The king perked up, then frowned. "But if they do succeed

in ramming and swarming aboard us?"

"Then we engage in close quarters combat, sir, and everybody fights. Both Rork and I have revolvers. Your sailors can use the ship's tools, the soldiers their bayonets, the courtiers the royal silverware. I see that you have a dagger."

The royal head shook curtly. "I would prefer we not engage in that, Peter. It would appear that the captain's role will be crucial in this situation. I will personally order him to not fail."

Well, I certainly preferred we not engage in personal combat too, but one glance at our captain told me he might not be up to the task at hand, even with the boost from a royal morale speech. Then I had an additional thought. A very uncomfortable one.

"Ah, Your Majesty, there's something else we need to consider. I just thought of it. And it's not good news."

"What is that?"

"The captain may be in on this. He and the engineer are locals. The locals are in fear of the pirates—it's the same all over the world. How did the pirates know to come at us? This is just a rice tug, seen frequently on the coast. Rice tugs don't carry wealthy passengers or valuable cargo. So why are the pirates choosing today to intercept this vessel? Were they warned by messengers this morning, after you chartered this vessel last night? Perhaps the captain and engineer will be spared during the attack and get a finder's fee, as it were, later on from the loot. Of course, maybe it's that big flag that got their attention." I glanced at the royal standard flying above us.

Norodom shouted something at a sailor, who ran to the mast and hauled down the king's flag. Then His Majesty turned to me and straightened up to full height, his tone an octave lower, the eyes boring into me.

"Peter Wake, I agree with you. I am offering you the rank of commodore in the Royal Navy of Cambodia, and as such, the immediate command of this ship, with back pay for a year to be given at a later date. You will take over command from the captain immediately. I further offer the position of chief engineer in the Royal Navy of Cambodia to your man Rork, to commence now. He will take over for the man in the engine room immediately also. Shoot them if you need. Professor Petrusky shall be an ensign and assist Commodore Wake."

Then, in a loud voice he announced to everyone, "As the Sovereign of the Kingdom of Cambodia, I command you to take charge of this ship and outrun those junks to windward." He repeated that in Cambodian, then smiled benevolently and continued in English to my companions and me. "And upon completion of this task an endowment from the imperial treasury will be awarded to each of you."

For the umpteenth time since we'd arrived in Asia, I was amazed. The man really thought that was all there was to it. Just issue an edict and it would happen. Rork, who'd had his fill of kings and queens as an Irishman, stared off to windward and began softly humming "Yankee Doodle Dandy." Petrusky studied the deck as he backed away toward the stern railing. I was going to have to do this alone.

"Your Majesty, thank you for your gracious offer of rank and privileges. However, Bosun Rork and I swore an oath not to be subject to any foreign state or potentate, so we must regretfully decline. And, as the professor is a man of peace and not trained for war, I believe he respectfully declines also. Regarding the captain and engineer, relieving them from command is your purview, not ours, so I would suggest you have your men do that, but only if the captain and engineer demonstrate some proclivity to facilitate the pirates' capture of the vessel. They know her capabilities better than any of us, so as long as they are loyal, I say let them do their jobs. We don't know how to run that old engine anyway."

I couldn't think of a more decorous way to say no. It must've been a while since the last time someone refused a royal order from the king of Cambodia, for Norodom wasn't taking it gracefully, as evidenced by his next gesture, which was to stalk off to the bow and fume. Along the way he said something to the senior soldier aboard, a subaltern who straight away posted soldiers near the captain, who had also removed his uniform coat, and the engineer. The action was seen by everyone and the intent was doubted by no one, especially the captain and engineer.

Petrusky was scared. "It appears the situation is not optimistic at all—I will pray for us."

Rork put it in sailor's jargon.

"*Phu Kwak* . . . who'da thunk it? After all me trials an' troubles o'er the last twenty-three years servin' me dear old Uncle Sam, 'tis one hellova place to get deep-sixed, ain't it, sir?"

I was looking at the island just as Rork said that. I was tempted to tell him then how Phu Kwak entered into the mission, but didn't. Still, I couldn't help wondering if someday President Arthur would see the irony of his messengers getting killed near the island he refused to take, from a king who didn't have it to give.

16
Chaos

Sunday, 13 May 1883
In the Gulf of Siam

We could see the pirates clearly now. And hear them as well. The shouts and screams needed no translation from Petrusky—they were taunting us, describing our impending deaths in vivid detail. At first the Cambodians were terrified, even the soldiers fumbled with their ammunition pouches and bayonets.

Petrusky had been praying the Catholic prayer for courage non-stop in several languages for the last forty minutes. While doing so he also armed himself with a kitchen knife and a belaying pin, pausing to sheepishly apologize for his lack of skill with firearms.

Norodom, his anger at me concluded, went about the vessel with admirable stoicism, calmly preparing his men with stories from the Khmer empire, seven centuries earlier, where the Siamese and Annamese enemies always outnumbered the Cambodians but were always defeated. Petrusky, who knew Asian history well, interrupted his praying long enough to translate for me, adding in a disapproving whisper that not a word of it was true. But, true or not, I could see that it was working—the men were standing straighter, gripping their weapons tighter. Norodom ended his speech with a promise of jewels and rank to those who fought well and became the heroes of Cambodia. He sounded like he actually meant it.

Rork and I took the time to make sure all hands were stocked up with items that could club, stab, or burn the enemy. Fortunately, the royal cutlery was ideally suited to the job ahead, and each man carried two polished knives embossed with the imperial seal of their sovereign, making our ship's company a very elegant crew indeed. Except, that is, for the hapless captain and engineer, whom Norodom decided were far too busy to be bothered with that sort of thing. He wanted them attentive to their primary duty. He also wanted them unarmed in case they turned on us.

The final minutes were nerve-racking until Rork, ever the bosun, went forward where everyone could see him. Standing tall, he began the age-old custom of petty officers before battle, bellowing out in a deep steady tone his orders, even though not a single man beyond Norodom and Petrusky and I could understand him. He glared at the approaching pirates, then stared wild-eyed at his shipmates.

"All right, lads, come gather 'round an' listen to your old Uncle Sean! Well, we're about to earn our money now, aren't we? Those loud-mouthed heathen arses're tryin' to frighten the likes o' us. Hah! They can bloody well just bugger off, 'cause that ain't gonna happen! No, not while Sean Clooney Rork is standin' among ye.

"Now what is gonna happen is that we're gonna make every bleedin' shot count, an' shoot 'em right here in the chest. Right here in the chest! Knock 'em down like ten-pins, we will, mates. An' when those poxy-arsed sonsabitches get nice an' close, we'll feed 'em raw friggin' metal down their gizzards and watch those scurvied scumbags head back down to the Devil's own hell where that sort o' sewage belongs . . ."

It was an awesome sight and a hell of a speech, one I'd heard before and always marveled at. Not a man moved or spoke. Not even the king. They didn't get the words, but each one of them knew exactly what Rork meant.

Next, my old friend looked to windward, pointed at the three junks, and laughed. It was one of those deep, rolling, Irish belly laughs. It ended abruptly as his face grimaced in rage. He paused, timing the effect perfectly, then roared one last shout to the men—to *his* men, for they were bonded to him now and he knew it.

"So who among ya poor bastards is with me?"

And then, by God, every man-jack son of the Orient on that decrepit craft stood and cheered, including His Majesty, the King of Cambodia. They whooped and hollered in their strange high-pitched lingo for that crazy American bosun, and for themselves. They yelled and screamed until they were hoarse, pounding on each other's shoulders and brandishing their ridiculous weapons. Petrusky, kitchen knives in his hands, was right with them, cheering on Rork's invocation in, of all things, Latin.

Yes, I'll admit that I succumbed to the mob's frenzy too, and wielded my Colt high above my head, while screaming every vile oath thirty years at sea had taught me. Near the king, the servant boys were jumping up and down, waving their forks and knives at the enemy. Even the tug captain and engineer were cheering.

Making his way aft, Rork slapped each man on the back, howling Gaelic curses of defiance at the pirates and laughing maniacally.

I pounded his back and said, "Well done, Sean Rork—one of your very best."

He chuckled, then grinned slyly. "Well, sir, the lads looked like they could use a little cheerin' up. No sense in takin' all this *too* serious, now is there? As me sainted daddy used to say—we can't live forever, now can we?"

The first shot was from a cannon. Fortunately, it wasn't much of a cannon. The shot ricocheted along some wave crests far in front of us. Some of our men nervously looked aft for Rork's reaction. He harrumphed and proclaimed, "Why that's just a baby's pea-shooter, lads! Probably a three- or four-pounder at the most."

The men saw his response and smiled. If the big American sailor wasn't frightened, why should they be? Rork and I decided it was time to put on an example of how to go about picking off the enemy's leadership, so we went forward, took two rifles from the soldiers, and set up a firing position just in front of the wheel-house. The king and Petrusky came along. I asked the professor to translate Rork's instructions to the others as the bosun demonstrated.

"All right, lads. Let's go o'er the basics. Hold your rifle sight as steady as ya can on the center o' the target's chest, take a slow breath, an' squeeze that trigger on the uproll. *Squeeze,* don't jerk it. 'Tis just like caressin' a pretty lass's fair charms, 'tis."

That got the laugh he was hoping for, while I wondered how Petrusky translated it into Cambodian. Rork called his shot as calmly as at a billiard table. "Center junk, tall man in the stern."

The rifle banged and all heads swiveled toward the junk. There was commotion on the afterdeck of the junk, a form fell, and our boys cheered again. Now it was my turn. I lined up on the junk to the right. The main sail was blocking sight of the stern, so I picked a man on the main deck who was yelling at someone. *Bang.* The man disappeared from view.

By then Rork was centered on the main junk and firing repeatedly, methodically marking his targets and putting lead rounds into the mass of pirates. I kept up fire on the right-hand junk and told the king to have his men concentrate on the left-hand junk.

King Norodom was ready, eager to show his men what he could do. By that point the range was a hundred yards and closing fast. Several more cannon shots came our way but all went harmlessly alongside and bounced past us. The pirates began firing, but their shoulder weapons weren't as long range or as accurate as the royal guard's French Gras rifles. A pirate's round of grapeshot impacted the bow, and a few of the smaller pieces hit the deck around us. Astoundingly, none struck a man. That kind of luck wouldn't last long.

In the five minutes after we started firing, we'd gotten perhaps fifteen of them, which left another hundred and fifty from what I could tell. All twelve of the soldiers, plus Rork, the king, and I, were firing. We were not behaving like any rice tug those pirates had ever seen, but the junks didn't alter course and I had no doubt that they knew who and what was aboard. Still, we weren't killing enough of them and they'd be alongside in seconds now. I turned to Petrusky and asked, "Are you ready with your weapon?"

The professor's measured academic personality had disappeared, replaced by a madman. "Yes, sir! Just tell me when to launch it."

"Very good, Professor. Stand by. We'll wait until they are right next to us, then I'll give you the word."

Petrusky was in charge of our secret weapon, a jury-rigged version of Greek fire, Cambodian-style—four casks filled with a soft mudlike mixture of rice husks and palm oil, enhanced with several jugs of rum as an accelerant for the flames. On either side of the tug, two casks were ready to be launched by a simple bamboo catapult affair. Petrusky was in charge of lighting the mixture and tripping the restraining rope to launch the flaming mess into the pirates once they came alongside. When I'd explained what his duties would be, he beamed, remembering his classical studies.

"It worked well for the Byzantines, Peter, and so shall it work for us! And, of course, it is quite *apropos* that we use it against Chinese-led pirates."

"How so, Professor?"
"The Byzantines learned it from the Chinese!"

The pirates quickly closed to the point where accuracy wasn't needed and their cannon grapeshot and musketry began peppering us with deadly effect. Several of our men fell in screaming heaps on the deck, clutching a head or arm or leg, and the servant boys rushed up to drag them aft and away from the action. As the junks got closer we lost more and more men, the enemy's fire sweeping the decks until half our number were down. I saw blood on Rork's upper left arm and was about to call his attention to it when the professor pointed to the other side.

On the starboard bow, the right-hand junk was about to strike us, its bow swarming with half-naked men armed with every sort of bladed weapon.

"Not yet—but light the fires!" I cried to Petrusky before my eyes were drawn to the port side.

The center junk, which I assumed held the pirate leader, swerved at the last second to hit us on our port bow, where the left-hand junk was also headed. It sparked an idea in my mind and I yelled for the king to tell the captain to bear off to the port, and possibly cause the two junks to collide before they reached us.

Norodom did so, then turned to fire at the oncoming junks, but the captain never responded with the course change. Instead, he stood out of the wheelhouse, waving his arms to the pirates, bawling something plaintive to them. I fired at the right-hand junk and glanced back in time to see the king raise his pistol and fire into the face of the captain, whose head snapped back as his body crumpled.

"Steer the ship!" I yelled across to Norodom, who waved acknowledgment and spun the wheel, turning the tug to the left.

I heard a crash near me and felt the tug lean over to port,

then settle down to starboard. The right-hand junk had hit us, riding its hull up and over our low deck. Pirates quickly dropped down among us, with more massed on the junk's foredeck.

"Greek fire to starboard!" I barked out and instantly heard a thud as the catapult lifted the two burning casks up, flinging them into the air. Upon landing on the junk they burst into a whoosh of flame, mostly in the sails and rigging. The woven thatch sail went up like a bonfire, the burning debris raining down over the junk's main deck, hopefully to start other blazes.

Rork was portside, right where the two junks were set to hit us. Our last-minute tactic confused them sufficiently to lessen their impact on us, but both eventually hit our vessel. He was down to his revolver—aiming at the men perched on the bows above him, firing, pivoting to a new target, aiming, and firing. I saw him reload, then I had to shoot a huge Chinese in front of me, putting three rounds into the chest to stop the brute. When I turned back, Rork was on the deck, pulling a lance out of his thigh and swearing to high heaven.

"Greek fire to port, Professor!" I yelled, but nothing happened. The professor was nowhere in sight. Running to the lanyard, I tripped the line, launching the casks into the two junks to port. They landed in a flash of fire on the leftmost, one cask bouncing down onto the central junk. The evil concoction spilled over everything, spreading the flames among men, sails, and rigging. Some of it spattered onto our port side, but not enough to begin a conflagration. Thick black smoke soon covered all four vessels, however, and I couldn't see the decks of the junks clearly anymore. But the bandits were still over there, for shots were continuing from them.

I desperately looked around for my companions, but saw no sign of Petrusky, or anyone else around me—I was alone on the starboard deck now, the junk above me a blazing cauldron of screaming men. Several Malay pirates, dazed by our resistance, stood unsteadily on the starboard deck, looking at their own ship afire. Frantic to get them before they recovered their senses, I emptied the last of my revolver ammunition at the thugs, hitting two and forcing the others overboard.

I felt a tug on my arm and turned around, thinking it Petrusky, but it was a near miss from a cutlass, wielded by some Oriental maniac in a loincloth. Terrified, I used my pistol to desperately parry his next thrust, and with strength I didn't know I had, pushed him overboard. Those feral eyes raged at me as he sank below the surface—a haunting sight. I'm shivering now, writing this.

The tug was still moving, slowly pushing past the junks arrayed on our sides. Norodom wasn't steering anymore; I saw him recklessly slashing his dagger at two of the pirate gang who'd dropped down on our portside by the paddlewheel. The pirates laughed at him—the king's dagger was a plaything compared to their long cutlasses—then they both lunged at him. He dodged one, but the other scored a slashing hit, blood instantly covering Norodom's left trouser leg. The king staggered, about to fall on his wounded leg as the other brigand, eyes wide in demented wrath, screamed and swung a roundhouse blow for Norodom's head with his cutlass.

It missed by inches, for suddenly Rork deflected it with a belaying pin thrust upward from where he lay on the deck below Norodom. That was when I understood that the king had been defending Rork as he lay wounded on the deck.

The pirate glanced around him for support, but he was alone, his comrades having jumped overboard. He hesitated, a fatal mistake, for one of the king's soldiers ran at him from behind, skewering him with a bayonet against the side of the wheelhouse, where he squirmed in agony.

The junks were no longer against our foredeck by this point, they were sliding aft. I saw the smaller one to port drift away from us, the larger one still scraping our side, denting the paddlewheel box. I yelled to fend off to port—we had to keep the junk from crushing that paddlewheel box. Two royal servants understood and shoved a pole against the hull looming over us.

To starboard, our foe was ignoring the battle, engaged in trying to save their ship from the fire that was engulfing it. An explosion rippled out from it as some gunpowder went up. They were losing that fight.

Meanwhile, heads bobbed in the water all around us. I had an immediate fear of counter-attack, should they climb up our low sides. Pointing to them, I got a Cambodian soldier to stab two coming aboard.

Stunned by the violence and noise, it took me a while to recognize that our forward movement, initially retarded by the impact of the junks, was picking up again. I could see that in a moment we should be free of the enemy's grasp as they fell astern of us. Stumbling over to where Rork and Norodom lay, intent on seeing to their wounds, I noted with bewilderment that I didn't have any. Then a shriek brought my attention to the stern of the large junk.

That was when I knew that Petrusky's tale was real.

It was Shu—the woman pirate of the legend. She stood atop the gunwale, silhouetted against the sky, wearing a crimson robe trimmed in gold lace and pointed golden hat, the peak of which flopped over to one side. She turned her gaze to me from sixty feet away as she shrieked again. It wasn't a cry of pain or fear—it was the primal cry of an enraged female animal.

One's brain does odd things at moments such as that—my mind slowed down the action around me, capturing that instant in time as a mental photograph. Our decks were a pandemonium of chaos, but my eyes focused on that terrifying woman. I will see that unfolding tableau in vivid detail for the rest of my life.

She was about my age and of average size for an Asian woman. The very act of having the strength and agility to be able to stand on a gunwale railing was a feat in itself and impressed me at the time. Smoke roiled around her, but there she stood, not flinching at all, like a magnificent beast, cornered and mortally dangerous. I remember thinking that she'd be a formidable adversary in a hand-to-hand fight and hoped she'd stay on her vessel.

In one hand she held a pistol, in the other a cutlass. There were other pistols in her belt. Shu screamed again at her crew, now aiming the pistol at me.

It was ludicrous—here I was, on the far side of the world locked in a death struggle with a *woman*. It all seemed so fantastic, so unreal. Belatedly, I registered that someone near me was shouting something to me, trying to get my attention, but I was mesmerized by that form standing against the sky.

And that was my mistake. Rork was the one yelling at me, telling me to get the hell down, that they were sharp-shooting at me. Coming to my wits, I comprehended his warning five seconds too late—just after the first round hit me in the center of my chest. It felt like a red-hot poker jammed into me, just like the previous chest wound nine years earlier, in Africa. That made me angry. How dare they shoot me there? I was already wounded there. I searched around the deck for a rifle to shoot the bitch, but I never found one, for I was interrupted again.

The second round struck my head.

I didn't feel any more pain. Instead, I lost control of my body and began falling. It seemed to take a long time to fall to the deck. Then Petrusky's face was close to mine, swimming in and out of my vision. I wondered where the hell he'd been. The professor looked scared and I remember him saying, "Peter, what have they done?"

My last memory of that day was an absurd notion—my brain must have been affected by the wound in such a way that I hallucinated that the professor would be in a lot of trouble with the Pope for letting Peter Wake get killed. There would be a Papal court-martial. And poor Professor Petrusky would be convicted.

I remember feeling sorry for him, then I passed out.

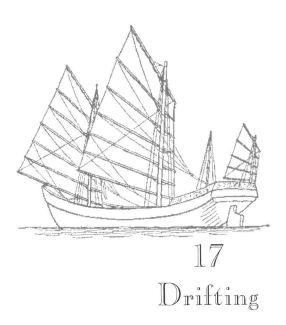

17

Drifting

Bright sunlight pierced my eyelids, bringing me into consciousness, instantly engulfing my head in the worst pain I've
ever endured. I opened my eyes into slits and rolled my head to
the left, aware of a human form close by me—sounds were coming from that direction. Words in a foreign language. It hurt just
to hear noise and I wished they would please stop, but then they
saw me moving and the words got louder.

Norodom came into my view, smiling down at me, gesturing for someone else to come. I was lying on a deck and everyone
else was standing up, looking so far above me. Others came into
sight. It was Rork and Petrusky, both limping.

Rork grinned at me as he leaned over. "Well, me dear old
friend, ya had me goin' there for a while. You managed to scare
the knickers off us, an' I thought for certain your Yankee luck had
run out this time. Oh, that I surely did, sir."

I heard someone croak out the words "shot . . . chest . . .

head." I realized it was me. Yes, I had been shot in the chest and the head, during the battle. Everything suddenly began to hurt.

Petrusky knelt down slowly, favoring his right leg. "Yes, Peter, you were shot in the chest and the head, but a miracle has happened, thank God and all the saints in heaven. Mr. Rork tells us that the bullet that struck you in the chest had lost its momentum—I believe he used the word 'spent'—and thus it did not penetrate far. The bullet that hit your head did likewise. Though you have puncture lacerations at both wound sites, they are not deep. Your chest may have a cracked rib and the head wound was mostly a concussion."

"What? The bullets were . . ."

Rork leaned over again and laughed. "Aye, Commander! Those piratical Malay thugs either didn't charge their muskets enough, or their powder was stale, probably both. Either way, they had just enough way on 'em to knock you down, but all should be right as rain in no time. Why, you had worse at that bar riot o' sixty-four. Remember that one?"

Norodom got down close to me, his voice sounding distant as he clasped my hand. "Commander, you did it. You saved us. The Greek fire was brilliant. We have gotten past the pirates, left them burning behind us. Thank you, Peter, on behalf of all Cambodia. Thank you."

I tried to get up, but a throbbing arc of pain stopped me. Petrusky spoke again. "Please rest, Peter. You can get up later, but for now, stay down."

Things were coming back to me, memories of the fighting. I surveyed my surroundings and knew we were on the tug, but where *was* the tug? Where were the pirates? The sun was high in the sky, but the battle had been fought in the late afternoon. What day was it? And where had we ended up?

"Where are we?" I asked.

The three of them exchanged worried glances. Something was wrong. Then it came to me. There was no noise, no engine. I tilted my head to either side. Land wasn't in sight on the horizons. We were drifting at sea.

I asked again, "Where are we?"

King Norodom answered. "Somewhere off Cochin, Peter. We don't know exactly where. But no matter—we are alive and you will soon be recovered from your wounds. Now rest easy, my friend."

"Engine?"

"It stopped. Now please rest easy."

Petrusky put something sweet tasting under my tongue. Minutes later I was out.

It was dark when I regained awareness. Just a few feet away, I heard a conversation in English about our situation, which was sounding rather dire.

Norodom had an encouraging tone. "Obviously, the currents are taking us closer to land. That would be French Cochin. There will be help there."

"With respect, but I dunno, sir," countered Rork. "I've heard tell there's pirates all along this coast. Phu Kwak's below the horizon astern o' us, so we don't have no worries about that evil-hearted whore an' her crew from hell, but there's probably more o' the same all around us. We best be careful when approachin' land."

Petrusky sounded exhausted. "Bosun Rork is correct, Your Majesty. There are renegades from many cultures along this coast. And remember, according to Bishop Courdier's information, there is a price on Commander Wake's head, so others may come searching for him."

Hmm, I'd forgotten *that* salient fact. Norodom's voice lost its confidence.

"Yes, Professor, I agree that Mr. Rork is right, of course. We have been drifting for two days. But if we do not get medical assistance, some of my men will die from their wounds. And we are running out of water and food."

Rork sighed. "Once a fair wind from the southwest or west pipes up, I can jury-rig a sail an' we can head easterly. Until then, with no wind, the current is it, sir. An' nary a thing we can do about it."

"Except pray," added Petrusky.

I lifted up on an elbow. My head was groggy and ached, but the excruciating pain in my head was gone. Movement in my arms and torso, however, caused the center of my chest to convulse with a sharp twinge that took my breath away. I had to proceed slowly, but I made it to where I was leaning on my elbow and could see around me.

Even in the dark I could make out that the deck and wheelhouse were in shambles. Scattered around the deck were a dozen men and boys, some sitting up but most were lying down, curled up in pain. A couple of them moaned pathetically. I couldn't get the lingo but it sounded like they were begging for help. There was no lantern showing, the light to see came from a half moon that was high in the night sky.

"Rork . . ." It emerged from me in a hoarse whisper. I tried again, with better results. The bosun came over and sat beside me.

"Feelin' better, sir?"

My voice came back to me. "Yeah, I'm moving slow, but I'm moving. Whatever the hell the professor gave me worked. I feel much better now."

"He put a ball of opium in your mouth. Said it would take the edge off the pain and let you rest."

"Opium? Well, it got the job done. Now, how are you?"

"Got stuck in the leg an' shrapnel in me left arm, but no infection, so I'll be fine. The king got shillelaghed somethin' fierce—got a hellova purple bruise on his guts an' skewered in his left leg—but he's a tough bloke an' makin' it through. The professor had a nasty gash on his leg, but that ol' boyo's got more guts than most I've seen. He'll do all right. We've got a bunch o' wounded men, though. Some're hit bad. Lost a bunch, too, sir."

"All right, please give me a report on our circumstances, Rork. Start with what happened when I was shot. I still don't understand that."

"Well, I was yellin' for ye to get down, the enemy was markin' you as a target, sir. But you couldn't hear me an' was standin' there directin' the action as cool as a county squire. Then you clutched your chest, an' after that your head damn near came off from the impact o' that second round. Whiplashed right back on your neck, it did. Those pirate bastards were cheerin' that loud enough, but they soon had other things to worry more about—like their junk ship burnin' up.

"Still, you scared the beejesus outta this old Mick when you got shot. Aye, that you did, sir. I couldn't get to ye, they was still aboard, an' our lads had to lance 'em overboard. Oh, I's proud as peaches o' the lads, sir. They fought like little tigers, they did. 'Twas a sight to behold, our brave little fellows against that horde o' heathen sonsabitches. Afterward, I finally got o'er to you an' saw the wounds were shallow. Said a big prayer o' thanks to old Elmo just then."

"Huh?"

"Patron saint o' sailors, sir."

"Oh, yeah, right. Tell me what happened after I got shot."

"We steamed to windward an' left them scum behind us. Oh, remember the tug engineer? A shyster if ever there was one. Knew *that* the minute I saw the slimy bastard."

"Yes, I remember him. Where is he?"

"Dead as a salted mackerel, courtesy of our little academic, sir. Right in the thick o' things—before you got shot, an' when all hell was breakin' loose—Mr. Petrusky saw the engineer slowin' down the machinery an' yelled at him. Well, that poxy scoundrel had the bad judgment to ignore the professor an' tried to shut down the steam valve, so as to blow this crate to kingdom come. No doubt about it, that bugger was part o' the scheme with them outlaws.

"Ah, but Mr. Petrusky was havin' none o' that—oh, no, sir. He up an' flung that great big galley knife he was wearin' in his belt at the fella, an' as luck would have it, the blade stuck right in the traitor's gullet. Prettiest blade toss I ever did see, an' by that wee little teacher, too. But that ain't all! Then the professor conked him o'er the head with a belayin' pin an' pushed the rascal into the water. 'Twas then that the professor manned the engines an' got us out o' that mess once an' for all. Damned if I know how, but he figured out how to make the rusty ol' beast go. A fine job o' work he did."

So that was what had happened. Now I knew why Petrusky hadn't fired the portside catapult—he was busy fighting the engineer.

"The engine's stopped. We ran out of fuel?"

"No, sir. We was steamin' at full speed and the ancient bugger couldn't take it. Just packed it all up an' died. Professor says it can't be resurrected, not out here with what tools we've got, anyway."

"So we're drifting?"

"Aye, sir. Near as I can tell, we're about six miles off the coast o' French Cochin, but it's the pirate coast, with nary a gov'mint presence. I'd be mightily glad to see even Monsieur Frenchy Frog right about now. Might even let him do his kisses an' hugs, if he'd just get us outta here. An', oh, how I could surely use a dram o' decent rum, right about now. Nary a drop to find aboard. All went for the fire bombs."

I was still trying to get my bearings, and the timing in my mind was off. "How long's it been since the fight?"

"Two days, sir."

"And we're off Cochin?"

"Aye, sir, along the Gulf o' Siam coast o' Cochin. By my estimations we're close to a place called Kiang Rach Dina. Thirty miles northwest o' the big cape. The professor agrees with me, sir."

"Who's in charge?"

Rork shyly said, "Uh, that would be me, sir. The king said I was the senior sailor that was able—you was down an' out o' it, sir—so he'd follow me orders. Offered to make me an officer, a lieutenant, in his navy, he did. Can ye imagine that? Me—*Sean Rork*—a lieutenant."

"Yes, actually I can, Sean. You'd get the king's navy whipped into proper shape."

"Well, no need now that you're up an' kickin', sir. I ain't no officer material an' don't wanna be. You officers don't have half the fun us bosuns do. No, sir, you're in charge now."

Spoken like an old-school bosun. They were an odd, rough breed. Thank God we had them. Rork helped me up so I could get a better fix on things. The moon was hazy but still provided a faint contrast between sky and water. He pointed out a thin dark line on the eastern horizon—the French colony of Cochin. Saigon lay over there somewhere. Nothing else was on any horizon. We were very much alone.

Petrusky and the king had gone forward and were lying on the deck. It was quiet, except for the moaning of the wounded and the slap of water on the hull.

"Rork, is there a watch set?"

"Aye, sir. The king, the professor, an' I have been standin' two-hour watches. I'm on now. Just started."

"Very good. I'll be on the watch bill, too. I'll relieve you at the end of your watch. Wake me up then. I mean that."

"Aye, aye, sir."

"The food and water—how much do we have?"

"Not much, sir. Some rice, salted fish. Couple o' casks of water. 'Bout a week's worth."

"Very well, I want the man on watch to guard the food and water."

"Aye, aye, air. No stealin' yet, but I see what you mean. The water's the worst, the wounded men need it bad, but there's not much to give."

"As far as the water goes, we can get more out of the condenser tubes of the boiler. It'll be rusty but should be drinkable."

"Damned good idea, sir! Wish I'd o' thought o' that."

"At dawn we'll have a meeting and go over what we know and what we'll do. All hands at the meeting, from the king to the cook. I'm going to get some rest now. Get me up in two hours, no more."

"Aye, aye, sir. Two hours."

Once Rork walked away, I gingerly lowered myself to the deck and stretched out on my back. The moon shone down like a long lost friend from another place, another part of my life. How many times had I been on a deck and looked up at that same moon? If a man hadn't been groaning in agony twenty feet away it would've been a tranquil setting, just drifting with the current. The current. I had to figure out where we were.

I tried to remember what I knew of the currents and wind patterns. On our passage to Saigon from Singapore we'd come near here. The first officer of the packet ship and I had spent an evening discussing the navigational hazards in various parts of the world. I told him about the Caribbean Sea, he told me about the South China Sea.

I learned that the currents in that region change with the monsoon seasons. Now, as I lay there, I tried to remember what he'd said. My mind was slow, having difficulty concentrating. What the hell were the wind and current directions in May? Southwest monsoon, yes, that was it. But no, May was too early. May was the transition time from the northeast monsoon of winter to the southwest monsoon of summer. So that meant currents and winds would be weak and out of the west.

And that was good, because we needed to go east. The packet officer had said the currents ran up to a knot or more, but that wouldn't apply now. Probably half a knot in May. That meant twelve miles drift a day, or twenty-four so far. Another day and a half to the big cape—what was its name? Cambodia? Yes, Cape Cambodia. Named that when this area was still part of Norodom's kingdom. And beyond the cape? Another two hundred miles to Saigon, but we'd see a port or a ship long before then. The shipping lanes ran close by there. A ship? That reminded me of *Juniata*. We'd miss her port call at Saigon. Oh, well . . .

My body and brain were drained of energy. I'd never been that dead-tired in my life, but I forced myself to think. Had to figure it out. A week of rations left. We should be able to make it if we drifted fast enough, and the westerly winds should pick up any day now. I started to drift off myself. Couldn't help it, my eyes just wouldn't stay open. My mind worked for a little longer before I finally gave up and succumbed to sleep, feeling confident that we'd only have another five to seven days before rescue—at the most.

I was wrong about the wind and the current. Dead wrong.

18

Dugong

Friday, 25 May 1883
South China Sea
off the coast of French Cochin

It wasn't five more days. Or seven days. The west wind didn't come for ten agonizing days. Ten days of glaring, white-hot sun that split our lips, broiled us inside our skins, and singed our eyes. Ten days to drift thirty miles. Even the current had dwindled to almost nothing.

On the morning of May twenty-fifth—I kept track of the date with notches on the mast—I felt a zephyr. Three hours later, it piped up to a gentle breeze. By then we were off the cape at the bottom of Cochin. In those ten days we saw only three junks in the distance, dazzled specks on a dazzled sea.

Debate ensued about whether to signal the first two we sighted. Most legitimate cargo vessels didn't venture this close to shore on the pirate coast. We didn't signal. The third junk was seen on the ninth day. By then there was no debate—struggling to even stand, we signaled with smoke, deciding that if they were pirates we would ask for food and water before they killed us for sport. The junk ignored us. Rork said it was probably because they were legitimate and thought *we* were pirates laying a trap. No one laughed at the irony.

I was wrong about the wind and the current. I was also wrong about the food and water. The water in the condenser tubes of the boiler was rusty, but when strained through the king's silk shirt it was potable. Most important, there was more than I had imagined, so that water rationing was not a problem. The food would've been, but I had miscalculated our usage. Forgot the attrition factor—dead men don't eat.

The professor, who had some academic knowledge of physiology and medical science, had rendered what aid he could to the wounded. In spite of Petrusky's care—he was distraught by the absence of any medicine or surgical tools—most did not make it. The wounded were dying fast by the fourth day. By the sixth day, all who had been severely wounded in the battle were gone, and the last funeral was held by those of us who remained barely among the living.

The funerals were Buddhist ceremonies presided over by King Norodom, since there was no monk to perform the expected rites. As a youngster studying in Siam, he'd become expert in the teachings and rituals of Buddhism. As the leader of his people, he was also held as a leader of the faith and both the dying and the survivors considered it a great honor to have him officiate. Due to our dismal state, the funerals couldn't be done exactly to the rules, but the king pronounced a royal dispensation of the usual procedure and approval of certain adaptations.

Rork, Petrusky, and I, as Christians, did not participate, but watched from our usual place at the stern while the professor explained the solemn services in a low voice. It was quite a spiritual sacrament and one that has stayed in my mind, like so much of that culture, all these years since.

Norodom went to each man before he died and chanted the *sutras* of the faith, to better fix the man's mind on the beauty of the faith and ease his transition. He would whisper in an ear one of the various names of Buddha, mostly *Phra Arahant,* then he wrote on a piece of paper the four syllables that are considered the heart of the belief—*ci, ce, ru,* and *ni*—which represent heart, mental concepts, form, and *Nibbana.* Petrusky described *Nibbana* as the end of suffering in this life. The king then put the paper containing the four syllables in the mouth of the dying man, where they remained until he was gone.

As Norodom gently held each dying man and whispered the ritual, the groaning from the pain of horrendously gangrenous wounds gradually stopped and the man's facial expression softened. Minutes later he slipped away. Petrusky always led Rork and me in a Christian prayer at that moment, asking God to have mercy on that man's soul. The other survivors noticed that and smiled their thanks. The lines of politics and religion blur at death, no matter where you are.

There were no coffins or flower wreaths or fresh water to bathe the corpse according to tradition, of course, so those were officially dispensed with by the king. We did have plenty of incense sticks in the royal entourage's supplies, though. They were liberally burned as a symbolic crumb of food—there wasn't enough real food for the customary offering. The symbolic offering was given as the *mataka* gift from the deceased to the officiate, or *sangha,* as the crew murmured a chant to their king, acting as a monk. Even the other wounded joined in the eerie hymn. The professor translated for me.

"Reverend sir, we humbly beg to present this *metaka* gift. May you, the *sangha,* receive this food in order that benefits and happiness may come to us to the end of time."

A crewman then raised a white ribbon on a boat pole as the others took the body to be cremated. They used the boiler's firebox fuel, and since the engine had stopped before we'd used it up, we had enough wood for it to serve the purpose. There were no ceremonial urns, so the ashes were placed in some of the king's personal silver service—tea pots, chalices, wine decanters, bowls.

They were placed safely below, to be sent to the men's families when we were rescued.

As the days drew out under that merciless sun, the line of silver containers got longer and discussions about being rescued diminished. Talk itself diminished. Grunts and nods were enough, thinking and speaking took too much effort. The salted fish in our rations did more harm than good, making us desperate for water, making our mouths very painful. It was used up by the fourth day after I'd taken over. From then on we each had a cup of rice, boiled in salt water, in the morning and the evening. Hope evaporated, and we now just existed, slowing dying of hunger and exposure. We moved only as much as we had to, waiting for the inevitable.

At each day's sunset, Petrusky would say a prayer, asking God to ease our pain and to please just let us die in our sleep that night. And every morning he would say a prayer thanking God for allowing us another day.

When the sea breeze came late in the afternoon of the twenty-fifth, Rork was too exhausted to make a sail, or move at all. None of us did, instead letting that river of air wash over us and cool our blackened skin a bit, reveling in the delusions our minds created.

But the wind continued through to the next day, strengthening at sunrise. We realized it wasn't a dream, it was real. Because of that moment, when the reality of that wind set in, for the rest of my life I will know that the limits of my endurance are far beyond what I had always believed. We thought—*knew*—we were dead men and were struggling to try to die with a shred of dignity, but the wind that morning reminded us we were alive and needed to set a different goal. To live.

Rork was the first to smile. I could see that it hurt his cracked lips, but the smile enlarged to a laugh. Soon Norodom joined him, and the sound of hysterical men laughing at sea filled the air. It was impossible to resist, and I let out a shout and giggled like the rest. Even Petrusky chuckled. We, who couldn't even move an hour earlier, rolled in mirth on the decks at the absurdity of it all.

And then the king saw something that made us cry with joy. To windward, over the distant Gulf of Siam, he pointed out a dark cloud. Within an hour, it was one of a line of clouds, pregnant with rain, approaching us. By noon, we were lying there, soaking up water from heaven.

It was incredible. I could actually feel my skin expanding as it moisturized. We let it rinse away the salt that had solidified in our clothes—which were little more than rags now—and had crusted in our crotch and armpits and hair, producing terrible boils. Leaning back, we opened our mouths and drank it in, filling our bellies with life-giving water. Letting it soothe our skin and bathe our eyes. More than one of us cried at how decayed our bodies had become and how wretchedly thankful we were for the most basic of nature's gifts—rain.

Sitting there in the downpour, the wind pushing us east past the great cape and out into the South China Sea, each man thanked God through his own faith. I have known danger—imminent death—at the hands of men who were desperately trying to kill me in my life. But that slow death from hunger and thirst and exposure to the elements, of feeling your body inexorably shrivel away, and your mind lazily fade into nothingness, was the worst foe I have ever faced. I had reached the edge of the eternal abyss and am sorry to admit that I'd given up, ready to plunge over. Until that rain.

Then it all changed. Our bodies, our minds, our outlook—all improved. Within an hour we were talking about our location and possibilities for rescue. By that nightfall optimism had taken root once more.

"You saved us with your idea of the water in the condenser tubes," Norodom said to me in the dark, later that evening. The others were asleep and I had the watch. The king was in an expansive mood and couldn't sleep. "That gave us enough to last until the rain, Peter. We would have died days ago if not for your idea."

I've never liked fawning, not even from a king. "Nonsense, sir. The professor or you or Rork would've thought of it."

"But we did not think of it. You did."

There was nothing to say to that. And we weren't out of the woods yet. By my estimate, we were being pushed by the southwest monsoon winds in a northeasterly direction at two to three knots. The coast lay to our north, on the port quarter, and was getting farther away. Rork understood, but neither of us let on to the others. They couldn't take another setback.

"Peter . . ." Norodom's buoyancy disappeared. "I must apologize to you."

"Apologize? About what, sir?"

"Leading us into this sad circumstance. I wanted to get away from the palace, from the sycophants, from the French so-called advisors. I wanted to get out among my people without the trappings of office. I needed to see the distant horizons of the ocean, so I used taking you by sea to Saigon as an excuse to escape my duties. That is why and how we have arrived at this point in time."

He took a breath and looked away. When he continued, emotion choked his words. "I owe everyone aboard an apology. And all of my dead men."

Not totally convinced by this new candor, I said, "I thought you did it because you wanted me to see Phu Kwak."

He sheepishly nodded. "That also entered into my mind. In my arrogance I didn't think pirates would dare touch my small entourage. I was mistaken."

I decided it was time to find out the truth. "Phu Kwak isn't yours to give to the United States in a lease."

"Yes, there are some who say that."

"Including the French?"

"Yes, including the French."

"And that was why you didn't have your French advisors like Blundell along, or even a regular guard regiment?"

"Yes. I wanted to do it on my own, to have the freedom my father knew as king. The French tell me what to do, where to go, what to think. They pretend it is merely advice, but I know better."

Norodom gazed off at the horizon again, unable to face me. His humiliation was real. And heartrending. "Peter, I know what is said about me—'the Frenchmen's puppet' or 'the king who gave away Cambodia' is what I am called behind my back. Blundell condescends to me and my own people despise me."

I couldn't help but have sympathy for him—this man, this king, this vassal sovereign of a quasi-state that clung to past glory. "Your Majesty, the people who might say that sort of thing have no idea of the pressure you are under from many sides. That is why you tried to bring the United States into the region—to offset the French pressure. Yes, I know that. It was obvious."

He began to speak, until I held up a hand. "But back to the situation at hand—you've been absent from the palace for weeks now and they've probably tracked your trail down to Kampot and the rice tug. Blundell will be searching the coast to rescue you."

The king shook his head. "I am not so certain of that, my friend. It would be in Blundell's best interest to have me dead and my half-brother Sisowath installed on the throne in my place. Sisowath is openly pro-French and would end all pretenses of independence for Cambodia. They have been grooming him for years to take over and are just waiting for an excuse. And, of course, Blundell wants *you* dead also."

"What?"

That made no sense to me. I hadn't even spoken with

Blundell since the lower Mekong. I revealed something to Norodom I thought he didn't know. "No, it was the rubber planters who wanted me dead, according to the Bishop Courdier's intelligence source. He sent me a warning."

The king smiled and shook his head. "You are naïve in the ways of Indo-China, Peter. Your nemesis is Blundell. He was very worried about *you*—an American naval officer—becoming a close friend with me. You became his rival, possibly replacing his influence over me."

"The rubber planters . . ."

"Yes, you seem to have caused many people concern, Peter. They thought you were spying for the cable companies and upon your return would recommend the British gutta percha rubber in Malaya. Or that your country would try to influence me to allow the United States into Cambodia. They all had a good arrangement and didn't want any other foreigners, and most especially liberal Americans, here to spoil it. So who do you think they went to with their complaints? It was Blundell. He saw your elimination not only as a way to keep the planters calm, but as a convenient solution to your perceived meddling in his political arena, as well."

I found that hard to believe. "The planters I can almost understand. But Monsieur Blundell is a French official. He wouldn't get involved in something as sordid as the murder of a foreign naval officer."

Norodom raised an eyebrow. "No, Blundell's hands would be clean. He would have someone else do it—Whangtai and his henchmen. Whangtai would get an opium run upriver without an imperial tax fee in exchange."

"What about Resident Superior Foures? Is he in on this too?"

"No, no, he is a decent man. I cannot believe he would be involved, or condone, or even know of this. It is Blundell. He is the real power among the French. A man with malevolent ambition, with an evil core to his heart."

"But how do you know this all to be true, sir?"

"Because my spies in the palace tell me what Blundell is up

to. I have paid informants in many places. It is how I live day-to-day, constantly having to be aware of who is plotting what against whom. That is how I have managed to stay in office for twenty-three years. It is a cheerless manner of life."

He sighed, and I wondered about his "manner of life." At first glance it'd looked pretty comfortable to me, but upon reflection it was an incessant gamble. A contest of Norodom alone against the French, against usurpers from his own people, really against everybody. A solitary life of doubt.

The king laughed quietly and said, "Blundell used *my* opium general, d'Abain, to deal with Whangtai and get *him* to go after you on the river. Blundell knew there had been animosity between the two, that Whangtai was angry at d'Abain for some supposed double-dealing. Whangtai being given a free run upriver, without the tax, would heal the conflict between them."

"But the killing of American officials—me and Rork—would bring disrepute to the French government here."

"Oh, of course, there would be the usual official French statement of regret after they learned of your death. They would lay the blame on the local barbarians—just another reason the civilized French are needed to be here. I can see the newspaper quote now: 'Lamentably, the scourge of banditry has risen once again on the Mekong, and has killed one of our gallant American brothers-in-arms, a diplomatic courier on a mission of peace.'

"Whangtai's name would never be used. Foures would be genuinely shocked. Strong military responses would be sent—unfortunately arriving in the area long after the bandits had departed. Your body, and that of Mr. Rork, if ever found, would have an escort of full military honors aboard a French warship back to the United States. Professor Petrusky would receive a wonderful Catholic funeral in Saigon. But the most important result would be . . ."

I completed the king's thought. " . . . that the Americans would be scared off from getting involved in Indo-China—a place the French hadn't quite totally pacified yet." I was getting angrier by the second. "You *knew* about all this?"

The king held up his hands in defense. "Yes, Peter. I did not tell you before this because I did not want to erode your confidence in me, and in Cambodia, and thereby lose a leasing deal for Phu Kwak. Besides, I thought you would be safe with me, and that I could show you the island, then take you to Saigon. That on this journey we could become friends and, through you, I could sway the American president into approving the Phu Kwak lease. Yes, yes . . . I know there might be jurisdictional arguments about the island, but thought I could conquer those once I truly had the American president interested."

What a tightrope Norodom had been walking. It wasn't what I wanted to hear, but it sounded plausible, once one considered it from his viewpoint.

"You really think Blundell would have *you* killed?" I asked, still astounded at that notion. It was too bold, too fraught with consequences if discovered.

Norodom shrugged. Ironically, it looked almost Gallic. "And why not, Peter? Once Blundell found out I was away on the coast with you, and without any French advisors as witnesses, just turn the pirates loose. That way he ends the American meddling, satisfies the planters, and gets his own man to be king. Quite a bargain, I would say."

The king sighed. "However, I did not realize when I took you to the coast that this would happen. I hoped we could preempt Blundell's plan for Whangtai on the river and be untouchable at sea on our way to Saigon. Never did I think Whangtai would bargain with that she-devil pirate woman Shu. Blundell must have offered a substantial amount of money in addition to a tax-exempt opium run upriver."

Sitting down on a deck box, he held his head in his hands. "I was wrong. I am sorry."

In my current state I was tempted to be sarcastic, but I held it. He was already distressed. But this new revelation made me question *what else* I didn't know about the people around me.

The distant smudge didn't go away. Instead, it got darker and bigger, broadening out along the eastern horizon. The morning sun had been up for two hours when Petrusky first spotted the island. Now we were getting close and the professor told us where he thought we were. Everyone was excited—salvation was in sight.

"Condore Island is actually a small group of islands that are administratively part of French Cochin. There is a small French-run prison on the main island and a fishing village. That is all I know."

"How far offshore?"

"I do not know exactly, Peter. Perhaps fifty miles from the nearest mainland, one hundred from the coast near Saigon."

Rork had jury-rigged a small sail two days earlier and we'd ridden the southwest monsoon winds at an estimated hourly average of three knots. Now, seeing that we were going to go past the northern end of the islands, we tried to adjust the trim to get the tug to go a bit more to windward on a reach, but the derelict tug had no keel to speak of and kept sliding off to leeward. I had a thought that we might make it if we put everyone and everything on the starboard deck to balance her better. I ordered Rork to the helm.

We'd have to try—there was no choice. Even though we now had fresh water from the daily squalls, none of us had eaten in a week. We'd tried fishing but the sea life just mocked us, frequently swimming around our hull but for some reason not taking our bait or venturing close enough to be lanced. Everyone had rashes and our bones hurt when we moved, signs our bodies were shutting down. Several had early symptoms of scurvy, their mouths a bloody mess. If we didn't make that island, the next land was in Borneo—six hundred miles to the east.

We continued to eke out every yard to the southeast we could as we sailed for the northern point. It was two miles distant at sunset, and it was obvious that we were going to miss the island. I struggled to think of a solution. All hands, from the king to the one surviving servant boy, sat there on the deck gazing at me, waiting for some brilliant idea I would have to get us those two miles to safety. My mind wouldn't work. It was too much for them to think me capable of conjuring up a new plan and I felt resentment creeping into my sentiments. I almost broke down in tears under the weight of their stares.

The sunset behind us was a beautiful display of colors, but I thought it a cruelly paradoxical omen of death—our last sunset with land nearby. In the last two hours I had grown even more melancholy, seeing what the others couldn't. I couldn't shake the feeling of despair. When one of the men pointed directly down into the water on the starboard side and muttered something, I snarled at him to shut the hell up. Rork shot me a reproving look, making me instantly regret the outburst. I was losing control.

The man, it was Hong, one of the royal household's servants, cried out again, only louder. "Dugong!"

Now a bunch of them were pointing at something. We'd had many fish dart around by the hull during our voyage through hell on that ship, and in all that time everyone had missed with a lance. Out of curiosity and to make up for my earlier rudeness, I went forward and looked down in the water. Stunned for a moment, I stood there, then looked up to the sky and murmured, "Thank you, God."

The cry of *"Dugong!"* was spreading among the Cambodians, who were beside themselves with joy and ran forward, crowding around me.

Rork called up to me from the helm, where he sat on a crate. "What is it?"

"Rork, it's a huge friggin' manatee!"

Rork leaped to his feet. "Good Lord, a sea cow—get a lance into him quick!"

Hong was ahead of everyone on that design and had a lance in his hand, the attached coiled rope in his other.

"No, wait! We may get only one chance lads, so I'll do it," shouted Rork, who turned to Norodom and said, "King—take this bleedin' helm while I get dinner!"

The crew gathered around as Rork hefted the lance—left by the pirates during the attack—then steadied himself and aimed for just aft of the animal's head. With a grunting oath he plunged it down, the line snaking over the side after it.

The dugong dove and swerved to the right, just as Rork took two turns of the rope around the Sampson-post at the bow. He stood there straining as he held on to the rest of the line. It slipped twice and he lost ten feet of line. Others, led by King Norodom, grabbed on behind him, holding it as the bow swung around and the tug slowly trailed the beast.

It was then that the impossible happened.

Petrusky said later that it was divine intervention, a logical train of events that could be seen with hindsight and only coordinated by a supreme omnipotent power, but never predicted ahead of time by mere mortal men. Norodom said the same thing. Rork declared it the damnedest thing he'd ever seen and that Saint Elmo had reported in for duty again. Well, I'm not certain of all those explanations, but I do know what I saw.

The dugong was heading for Condore Island.

19

Bizot's Domain

Sunday, 27 May 1883
Puolo Condore Island
South China Sea

"This is an astonishing story, something from Verne or Dumas!" said Petrusky, translating Commandant Bizot's comments after hearing the tale of our journey to his island.

The professor, the king, Rork, and I, were sitting in wicker chairs on the verandah of the commandant's cottage, sipping wine and nibbling cheese, trying hard not to gulp. The professor had been adamant that we not gorge ourselves, repeatedly warning that it would harm us greatly in our weakened state, and that we must quench our thirst and hunger slowly. It was damned hard to do.

Bizot spoke again and for some reason my French failed me. Perhaps it was the wine, but I had to rely on Petrusky's rendition of the commandant's words—"What a tale of God's mercy."

The stone and frame home was situated on the hill overlooking an anchorage devoid of vessels. Our "royal yacht" was beached on the sand three hundred feet below us, barely visible in the half-light of dusk. An hour earlier we had been brought up from the beach in wagons, after having been towed in by the tiny harbor's cutter.

The dugong—God bless his mammalian soul—had gotten us within half a mile of the island, then died from his efforts, sinking below the water. With tears in his eyes, Rork let the ten-foot-long corpse take the lance and line with it to the bottom, saying the creature had earned those accoutrements of honor.

I contemplated that dilapidated tug hull and answered Bizot, "*Oui, Commandant. Merci à Dieu.*"

Bizot was an interesting man. He was in his late forties, quiet, with a firm manner. You could tell from afar he was the commanding officer by his confidence. A professional naval officer whose career had deposited him at Condore Island twenty years before as a young ensign, he'd never left. Promoted up the ranks *en situ,* Bizot was France's man in charge of the tiny garrison of sixty marines, the prison of two hundred criminals turned virtual slaves, and governor of all the islands in the little archipelago.

His eyes sparkled as he explained that a love affair with a native girl had fueled his decision to stay, and that the consequent marriage had produced seven lovely children, who were far more reward than any glory the navy could give him. It was a lonely outpost, with a prison supply ship sailing out from Saigon only once a month, but Bizot seemed to enjoy his position—as much, if maybe not more, of a king than Norodom with his millions of subjects. At least on Condore there were no usurpers.

The supply ship had visited three days earlier, he told us. We would be his guests there until early July when the next one would come. The king and I would have Bizot's quarters. He would take his family to the in-laws for the month. We protested—me more than the king, I noticed—but the commandant was insistent. Bizot said with a sly smile that his mother-in-law owed him the gesture. Petrusky and Rork would bunk in at the first officer's quarters. The Cambodians in the entourage, a bedraggled lot who looked a far cry from their previous finery, would recover at the barracks.

There was a small hospital with no doctor, but Petrusky would have medicines to work with on his patients. What we all needed most of all, the professor announced, was rest, decent food, and water. Time would take care of our ailments. Bizot agreed, saying that everyone, and everything, on the islands was at our disposal.

He was as good as his word. At the end of two weeks we were all able to walk the steep hills of Condore, albeit carefully. The two-thousand-foot mountain I declined, but on the third week of our stay one of the Cambodian courtiers, possibly to impress his sovereign, made the ascent one day and garnered a royal pat on the back upon his return.

I knew that Rork and I had missed connecting with the possible Saigon stop of *Juniata,* but was confident that once we reached Saigon we would find passage with a packet steamer to Singapore and thence homeward. Petrusky was so close to his home in Saigon he could smell it, and was nervous as a cat waiting for the weeks to go by. King Norodom was the most distraught of our band of refugees.

During an evening stroll he confided to me that he was convinced Blundell had completed his cunning *coup d'état* and that his brother Sisowath—whom he could never stand, even since childhood—was now king and had probably already signed over the last vestiges of independence to the French.

"No doubt the memorial service for my death was a beautiful affair," he muttered. "I am sure Sisowath and the French shed copious tears."

"They'll be shedding tears of sorrow for their own plights when you return to Phnom Penh and the truth is told of what transpired, Your Majesty," I suggested, using his title to cheer him.

"Time will tell on that matter, Peter," he said doubtfully, then abruptly snapped his fingers and grinned. "But wait! Allow me the pleasure of changing the topic to a far more positive one. I understand from Mr. Rork that felicitations are in order, my friend."

"For whom?"

My question made the king laugh out loud, which made me wonder even more what in the world he was talking about.

"Rork said you would probably say that!" The man was laughing so hard he had tears in his eyes. "Peter, my dear friend and comrade in arms, today is the twenty-sixth day of June in your Western Christian calendar—and the forty-fourth anniversary of your birth! It is good to be alive and be able to celebrate another year, yes?"

Rork knew I've always disliked surprises and celebrating my birthdays, so the wily jokester got a king to do it for him. But I had to admit, it was funny. Plus, Norodom had a point.

"Yes, you are very much correct, Your Majesty," I replied with a chuckle. "It surely *is* good to be alive and able to have another birthday."

At the end of June, after four weeks of leisure and recuperation, the professor judged us medically and gastronomically competent to handle the feast that the commandant had been planning since our arrival. On Tuesday evening, we would be officially welcomed, as honored guests and new friends, to Bizot's little bit of the French Empire. The supply ship would be arriving a few days afterward, so it would be one of our only opportunities for a celebration.

It was to be, we were informed, a *grande soirée traditionnelle*. We had been dressed in donated clothing since our arrival, but now Commandant Bizot ordered his four officers to furnish us with dress uniforms approximating those that had disintegrated during our ordeal. For Rork and me, French blue and U.S. Navy blue were remarkably alike. My tarnished insignia were polished, medals recovered from my seabag and cleaned, shoes that fit us were found, and by the end of the effort I can say, with no little pride, that my bosun friend and I were able to represent our country with an impressive degree of *panache*.

Petrusky was presented with a fine suit, constructed by skilled prisoners who declared him ready for the *salons de Paris*. As handsome as Petrusky's suit was, the king's attire was nothing short of magnificent—a copy of his regalia of the palace, based on his description. The prisoner-tailors were warmly congratulated by all of us and rewarded with special privileges by Bizot's first officer. All was ready for the big night.

The much anticipated evening commenced with hors d'oeuvres and champagne on the verandah of the officers' quarters, the scene back-dropped by a gorgeous sunset framed by the puffy monsoon clouds. The colors of the sky reminded me of pastel versions of the fruit Rork and I knew back in Florida—orange, mango, banana, key lime, they were all there, brushed across the sky. When I mentioned my opinion to Rork, he laughed and said, "Aye, sir, you're feelin' a good sight better now. Now you best be careful with the wine tonight, or you'll be drunk as an English lord afore the grub is served. An' that's a mighty steep hill outside to fall down!"

I *was* feeling much better—surviving a close call with death will considerably improve one's outlook in regard to minor irritations. I answered in a similar vein. "Then I solemnly promise to be on my very *best* behavior, Rork. God knows I want to spare you any embarrassment!"

An inmate string quartet played music by famous French

composers—Bizot refused to listen to German compositions because of what that country had done to France thirteen years earlier. It was all of no matter to me, of course. I couldn't tell a French composer from any other. Norodom and Petrusky, however, certainly could and were in heaven, beaming their appreciation and yelling "*Bravo!*" after each piece.

For this auspicious occasion, the entire population of single ladies on the island had been invited to be our consorts. All four of them were petite Asians dressed in the beautiful *ao dais* of their country, each in a different color. They demurely picked out a conversational partner among us and stayed with him during the evening's festivities. Watching them, I got the impression they had decided among themselves—everyone on the island knew the four of us—long beforehand which of them would get which one of us.

Rork, unaccustomed to formal affairs—especially where French was the common language—handled himself admirably, I am particularly pleased to report. He has always underestimated his social abilities for such situations, but I know that my friend is a natural *raconteur* and can mix in with the best of them once the ice is broken. His boyish looks and good-natured Irish humor overcame the language barrier quite easily and he soon had half the room laughing with his description of a Moroccan whirling dervish.

As it pleasantly turned out, my partner was a charming lady named An, whose soldier husband had died of disease three years earlier. An had no family left on the mainland and nowhere to go, so she stayed on the island, doing chores to get enough money to make ends meet. In a place where prisoners do most of the labor and servant duties, that meant she was just barely getting by, but one would never know it by her dignity and allure. An could've outshone any society dame in New York. I was utterly taken by her charm.

She had taken the time to learn some basic English phrases for the evening. Between that and my fractured French, we got along quite nicely. She explained that her name meant "peace," which I thought lovely, and that her family name, Trung, meant "loyalty to one's king and country." Her family was from Cochin and she and her husband had ended up at Condore when his army battalion had come for guard duty ten years prior. Mr. Trung had been the sergeant major of the battalion.

An hour into the evening, I realized that it was the first time I'd been in a social setting intimately with a lady in two and a half years, since my Linda had died. It seemed much longer than that to me. Possibly it was my weakened physical state, or the effects of the alcohol, but I didn't feel guilty or saddened by being with An.

Quite the contrary, I was profoundly grateful for truly feminine company, from which I had been sequestered for so long. An's beauty was complemented agreeably by her character, which was attentive and respectful and supportive—so unlike some women I had met in Washington and in Europe, whose coquettish ploys seemed so counterfeit. The ladies of the East were either supreme actors or were fully authentic, and I could easily see how Bizot had become enchanted by the local girl who'd become his wife. As the evening progressed, I too felt under their spell.

Petrusky had an older lady for a consort and together they had an intense discussion about religion—her Confucianism and his Catholicism. His Majesty escorted an exquisite girl, statuesque and refined, who had clearly practiced her etiquette for a European social gathering. Norodom, equally at home with both the subservient role of women in his court and their more equal position in Western society, was enthralling not only his companion, but the other ladies attending as well.

Dinner followed the sunset session on the verandah. Prisoner cooks created a wonderful dinner of game hens and vegetables and custards, accompanied by some good Bordeaux—as French a repast as one could have on an isolated island in the South China Sea. It was done with a conglomeration of plates and glasses and linens, but the attendants were elegant in their synchronized serving of the dishes.

Our host regaled his guests by recounting his meeting with Captain Raphael Semmes, the famed Confederate ocean raider who put in at Condore in December of 1863, just a few months after Bizot had arrived on the island. They looked for my reaction, which was appreciation for a good story, well told. Semmes was a legendary seaman and gentleman.

At the conclusion of the meal, Commandant Bizot stood, cognac in hand, and proposed a toast to the long reign of King Norodom—who glanced ruefully at me—and the bravery of men who overcome the ravages of nature and survive.

Two quick rounds of cognac later, Norodom countered with a speech about the hospitality of the wonderful life-restoring people of Condore Island, whom he compared to angels in the Christian heaven, and decreed the undying affection and loyalty of the kingdom of Cambodia for every single inhabitant of Condore. He also invited everyone to be his guest at the royal palace and said that special presents would be sent from Cambodia to the people of Condore. It was a performance worthy of a New York Tammany politico and accomplished its goal—there wasn't a dry eye in the room when he finished.

Dancing music started up after the speeches. None of that choreographed minuet-style dancing for Condore Island—this was slow waltzing music. The French officers led off with their ladies, followed by the king and his. Petrusky, overpowering his limp, squired his companion around the floor splendidly well. Rork, whose leg was wounded worse than Petrusky's, begged off, fearing he'd fall if he tried it. Instead, he and his lady conversed in halting French.

That left me. Physically I was able, but my emotional courage absconded just then. An and I were at the dinner table, she sitting there waiting patiently and me flustered and tongue-tied. It had been so long since I'd danced with a woman, and that had been with Linda.

Rork leaned over and whispered, "It's all right, Peter. Linda would want you to live life again."

My eyes misted at that, but finally I summoned the gumption to inquire of An, *"Voulez-vous danser?"*

Seconds later she was in my arms and we were gently swirling around the room. An was a talented dancer and forgiving of my missteps. I'd almost forgotten how it felt to hold a woman close. It was delightful.

Rork winked at me from his spot on the sofa where he and his lady were apparently going over the French words for the parts of a face. I knew he meant well with the wink, but it still disconcerted me. Then An moved closer and I shut the world around me out, thinking only of the music and the woman in my arms, lost in a dreamy state where nothing else mattered. We danced three waltzes, with me feeling giddy—or maybe just dizzy, by that point.

We were both warm after the exercise and she suggested going out to the verandah to cool off in the night breeze. That sounded perfect. Everybody else was dancing and we had the place to ourselves, lit only by a dim table candle in a glass.

The night sky had cleared of heavy clouds somewhat and a few stars winked through the remaining overcast. The moist earth and tropical flowers smelled incredibly vivid to me—I will never take those for granted again after my ordeal—and I drank in the scent of life itself. In the background, the French music was incongruous with the jungle around us, but it made the setting even more exotic in the candlelight. I knew it was one of those scenes that would stay in my mind forever.

An stood there with her hands on the railing, gazing out to sea and the world beyond the island. Her lavender *ao dai* seemed to float in the gentle wind. She turned to me and I saw a lone tear on her cheek. Suddenly I realized that they were all prisoners of one kind or another on the island. I would soon leave, but An would stay, doomed to a remote speck in the sea for the rest of her life.

Without conscious decision, I leaned down and kissed away the tear, then held her closely. She softened and molded to my body, then kissed me deeply. All semblance of anxiousness departed me. I surrendered to the moment, to my weakness. How long we stood there, not saying a thing, I do not know. We just held one another, reminding ourselves that we could still feel emotions, still attract affection, still open our hearts just a little. Her body responded to my caresses, and my body followed its instincts as she touched me. Silently and softly, we touched intimately. An and I knew where the evening was bound. Neither of us protested. I needed to get us away from there. A plan formed in my mind.

Then it all ended. Our bond and our embrace were broken by a slamming door, the clattering of voices inside, the fading of the quartet's music until the place was quiet.

Rork bellowed out, "Commander Wake, come quick!"

With a muttered curse, I raced around the corner and found Rork, Petrusky, and the king, grouped around Bizot. He faced a young messenger heaving from the exertion of running up the hill. The boy looked at me, then babbled out his message between gasps for air. I caught the gist of it, but Petrusky translated it fully for Rork and me.

"An American warship named *Juniata* has just rounded Haon Cau Island and will be entering the anchorage in an hour. When they found out from the guard boat that you were here, they said they will anchor for the night and come ashore in the morning."

All eyes were on the Americans. Someone applauded, igniting an ovation that ended with a cheer for the United States of America. The professor shook my hand and said, "I must say, tomorrow is the most appropriate day for a reunion of Americans!"

"What?" I asked. I could see that Rork didn't understand either.

Petrusky laughed. "Peter, it is the anniversary day of your independence from Europe!"

"Why I'll be damned—it'll be July the fourth, Commander!" exclaimed a beaming Rork. "'Tis Independence Day for all o' us Yankees, both born Americans like you, sir—an' new lads such as me."

The musicians started up again, playing the Tennessee waltz. I hadn't heard it in years, since a ball one night at the White House. Everyone looked to me to celebrate the news, but damn it all, I was fuming mad. Why the hell did Dewey have to arrive right then?

An smiled at me and held out a hand. There was nothing to do about the news, and escaping the attention of the others would be nigh impossible now, so I took her hand and we waltzed for hours. A sorry substitute for what we both wanted and needed, but the only option. Part of me was angry we'd lost the moment, part of me was grateful we still had the chance to hold each other, even if only politely in public. And part of me wondered if it all was an omen, a reminder that my life wasn't meant for normal contentment.

At midnight Rork came over during an intermission and quietly suggested we go back to our quarters, adding, "We need to be bright-eyed an' bushy-tailed for Captain Dewey in the morning, sir."

I knew he was right, but damned well didn't want to stop. Resenting his interference, I grumbled, "*No.* Another dance, Rork, then I'll go."

The instant I said it, I knew it sounded stupid. Rork said nothing, just looked at me. I sighed and shook my head in resignation as An approached us. She saw that something was wrong.

Reluctantly, and more brusquely than intended, I bid An goodnight, saying, *au revoir,* that I would see her the following day. It came out as a command.

An nodded understandingly, but her chin quivered as she said, *"Merci pour cette soirée merveilleuse, et pour la tendresse ce soir."* Then those eyes, those beautiful eyes, looked up into mine and she said goodbye, not *au revoir.* *"Adieu, Peter Wake. Bonne chance avec la vie . . ."*

I never saw An, the loveliest of the angels of Condore Island, again.

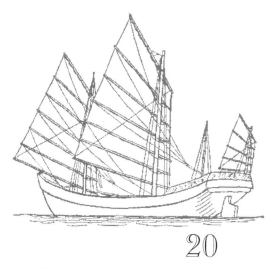

20

Necessities of the Service

I first met George Dewey during the Civil War, when he was passing through Key West en route to his home in New England on leave. He, unlike me, participated in some great events during that war of rebellion, the most salient of which—the battle of New Orleans—had already happened by the time we met. George was known back then as a go-getter, a man not content with less than total success in any endeavor.

He stood out among his peers not because of his stature—he had an average physique and wasn't tall—but because of those wild eyes and an enormous mustache that dominated his otherwise clean-shaven face. He also had a tremendous laugh—one of those genuinely infectious laughs—that was frequently the result of one of his practical jokes. He was just another lieutenant passing through back then, in a navy town full of lieutenants passing through, and we were introduced over rum at the bar of the

Russell House. Later that evening, I introduced him to the quaint Key West custom of rum-infused coconuts and he introduced himself to five of my precious dollars at an impromptu game of cards. We kept up an on-again–off-again friendship over the next few years, mainly seeing each other at naval headquarters in Washington while on temporary duty there.

Our next meeting was at Washington in January 1873, after I returned from duty in Panama and just before I shipped out as executive officer aboard *Omaha* in the West Indies. George's wife had died in childbirth three weeks before and he was anguished, pouring his heart out to me over dinner. A month later he relinquished his assignment with the torpedo station at Newport, where he worked with my old friend, Gunner's Mate Durling, and went back to sea. While grandparents raised his son, George accepted command of *Narragansett* and plunged himself into work, surveying the desolate California and Mexican coasts.

During my years stationed at Washington Navy Yard in the late seventies, George returned to duty there as secretary of the national Lighthouse Board, a convenient billet for officers without ships in those lean days of the navy. He would come over for one of Linda's dinners and we would talk about the way the navy ought to be run and equipped. There were quite a few of us thinking about that sort of thing, preparing for the future; the now well-known U.S. Naval Institute was formed back then to provide precisely that sort of forum.

But he was bored at his shore assignment, telling me the Lighthouse Board's major occupation seemed to be a prolonged debate about which was better for lighthouse mechanical operations—lard oil or mineral oil. I wasn't enthralled with my shore assignment either at the time, and leaped at the chance to go to sea as an observer at South America's War of the Pacific in '79. George, who had far more connections than I did, envied me that opportunity and tried to wrangle some sea time of his own, with no success.

That was when my Linda died—while I was on my way back

from Peru in '81. At the same time, George got sick from some apparently undiagnosable ailment, recovering slowly. I remember him telling me that we now shared a common tragedy as widowers, and that I would be healed with time. I never thought it possible then.

Though George despised his mind-numbing assignment at the Lighthouse Board, he was intrigued by the intellectual stimulation of Washington life and enjoyed the interaction with colleagues there. But even with that, I saw George's vigor declining. He told me one evening that he recognized a professional change was needed, one that might also help his health. So he lobbied hard for a command and was given *Juniata*, which had orders for the Orient.

That was the last time I'd seen him, at the Navy Department in October of 1882, just before he took command of her. That walrus mustache twitched mightily as he slapped me on the back and said it was his turn for adventure now, joking, "Maybe I'll see you over there on the far side of the world, Peter. By the way, first drink's on you!"

Remembering that comment, I put a bottle of the local Condore version of rum in my seabag, in preparation for boarding *Juniata* that morning. Old Gideon Welles—the secretary of the navy notoriously despised for ending the grog ration—would've scotched that idea posthaste, of course, but I've always felt that occasional violations of minor regulations add spice to life.

I'd already said my farewell to the king and Petrusky. They wanted to take the more covert supply ship to Saigon in a couple of days. The king's plan was to quietly return to Cambodia and his throne. He didn't want to advertise his intentions.

It was a bittersweet moment—we'd become more than friends during our ordeal. Parting was difficult, but each of us wanted to get away from Condore and go home. None more so than Norodom, who assumed he would face, quite literally, a fight for his life upon returning to Phnom Penh.

I'd been wrong about the king and the professor, letting suspicion get the best of me, and admit I was pretty contrite at our goodbye. It was with genuine concern that I wished them both the very best fortune and assured them of my everlasting friendship. Petrusky's last words were that he would pray for me every Sunday. Norodom told me that he was forever in my debt.

It was clear that An had said her goodbye at the soirée and didn't want to see me that morning, so there was no reason to delay my departure on that account either, though I would have if she'd wanted. No, as it was, I planned to have Rork and myself aboard by six bells, greet my old friend Dewey, have breakfast in the wardroom, and watch the island fade away an hour later as we steamed east toward the rising sun and home. My time in the Orient was done.

It didn't work out that way. George beat me to the punch and arrived on the front stoop of my quarters at five minutes before sunrise—ten minutes before I was going to descend the hill and see *him.*

"Peter, what the hell kind of trouble have you gotten into now?"

He didn't look very well, tired and gaunt. "Why in the world did you get up and over here this early, George? I was just going to see you. And are you all right? You look ill."

"Yes, I'm all right—just haven't completely beat that sickness yet. I came over because I wanted a walk ashore. You know how it is. Now, don't try to divert me anymore, you slick-tongued devil! You answer me first, Peter Wake, or I won't let you on board my ship."

Rork came in and George greeted him, remembering him from dinners at my home in Washington. Like most officers, Dewey respected veteran petty officers, particularly bosuns. Unlike many, he didn't mind my off-duty friendship with Rork. Some others called it fraternization and condescendingly dismissed it as a weakness of mine, ascribing it as yet another result of my lack of proper naval education as an officer and a gentleman.

And they were correct—I didn't graduate, or even attend, Annapolis. I entered the navy as a volunteer officer during the war and commanded small ships on the blockade, doing the unsung dirty work close inshore. Of the six thousand of us who got temporary commissions then, only a hundred thirty-three were retained and given regular commissions after the war. And of those, only a handful were left in the navy twenty years later.

By 1879, my career had reached a plateau and I realized that in a navy with few ships and too many officers, non–academy graduates would probably never obtain a decent command. That was why, at the suggestion of the senior admiral of the navy, the venerable David Dixon Porter, I'd migrated into the intelligence field after returning from Peru.

In those days, the Office of Naval Intelligence was a little-known back room on the second floor of the State, War, and Navy Building, next to the Executive Mansion. In official operation for only a year, we collected maritime information from distant squadrons and sometimes went overseas to check on things ourselves.

Thus, I was assigned to go to Cambodia on a mission described to me by Porter himself as "brief and mundane." In fact, he'd apologized at the time that he didn't have something more exciting for me to do. At the briefing, President Arthur told me, "It might be a nice holiday, Wake. Exotic. I rather envy you."

Well, that sentiment certainly turned into rubbish once reality was met. The American executive leadership had no idea of what was going in Indo-China. But they would once I got home; I'd make sure they did.

I gave Dewey a brief rendition of what we'd been up to—without the confidential parts concerning a possible deal on Phu Kwak. It took me an hour to tell the story, by which time the room had filled with the king and the professor, who wandered in when they saw the commotion. The king, being a king, couldn't help adding his own impressions of the events, but also omitted the Phu Kwak lease idea, taking his cue from my warning glance. I pestered

George to tell me how he'd found me at Condore, but he deferred until later, making me, and everyone else, exceedingly curious.

When Commandant Bizot joined our group, he decided that a farewell breakfast was needed to celebrate this unforeseen gathering, so we all adjourned to the officers' mess, the location we had left only hours before. Over our meal, my old friend filled us in on his illness and how *Juniata* came to be at Condore.

"I'd been a bit ill back home in Washington, as you know, Peter. Well, we found out later I had typhoid. It further developed that this particular typhoid is evidently hard to shake. As a matter of fact, the Royal Navy's doctors at Malta last year predicted I wouldn't last a month, but I thought that forecast a bit premature and managed to muddle through and fool 'em all. I'm still feeling poorly, however, and have asked for a relief. As soon as he arrives out here, I'll be homeward-bound on sick leave to fully recover from this damn thing."

"So *Juniata's* not heading eastbound toward home?"

"No, only me in the near future. The ship's due to rotate home later in the year."

Dewey, his eyes sunken and bloodshot, stopped and looked at the men gathered around him.

"So, I'm sure everyone wants to know why I'm here at your island paradise, Commandant Bizot. It was an odd confluence of events, really. We were in Singapore, bound for Hong Kong, where my relief is supposed to be sent. Departing Singapore, we shaped a rhumb line course northward, which took us close to Saigon. Peter, you know the reputation of old *Juniata's* engine. Isherwood had a good idea with that design, but the damned thing for one reason or another is always breaking down. It broke down off Indo-China and we put into Saigon briefly for repairs. That's when we heard you were missing, along with the king."

Norodom leaned forward. "How did you hear this, Captain?"

"From Connally, our man at the consulate, sir. He said they were concerned because Commander Wake hadn't returned from

Cambodia and there were rumors of bandits closing down the Mekong. Also that Your Majesty wasn't in the Cambodian capital, the name of which escapes me, I'm so sorry . . ."

Norodom's eyes hardened as he educated Dewey. "The capital city of the kingdom of Cambodia is known as Phnom Penh, Captain. Please expand on the rumors regarding me."

"This is third-hand, Your Majesty, so I don't know the details, just that you had left the capital and that our man and his petty officer assistant were missing. There was some information that you had gone to the Cambodian coast, so Connally speculated that perhaps Commander Wake might be with you and asked me to have a little look-see in that area, in case there was some misfortune. Of course, I would've searched for any American naval officer, but when I heard who it was, I just knew that Peter had gotten himself into another dicey jam and would have a great story to tell."

Dewey turned toward me. "You always seem to find interesting ways to get into turmoil, my friend."

That got a laugh from Rork and quizzical looks from the others.

"Oh, and one more thing, Peter. It seems that the powers that be back home had been trying to contact you—Connally had some official correspondence for you. I have it here, along with your other mail."

Dewey handed me four envelopes. I quickly perused them. The largest one was the standard blue of official naval mail, another was from the consulate in Saigon, the third was from my daughter, and the fourth from a lawyer in Key West. I resisted opening Useppa's right away, instead returning my attention to George, who resumed his explanation.

"Once we got repaired, courtesy of the French Navy—thank you, Commandant—I got under way and took *Juniata* south and around the cape at the bottom of Cochin, thinking you might have shipwrecked along that coast. We steamed a couple hundred miles, to within sight of an island named Phu Kwak, but had no sighting, so I decided to turn around and head for Hong Kong. Yesterday evening we spotted these islands and I thought we might as well take a look. Long odds, but you'll be pleased to know I judged you and Bosun Rork were worth it, Peter."

Dewey cast a sideward glance at me. "Then, to my great surprise, the guard boat told us you were actually *here*. Hmm, now I had to do something, so I decided to stay overnight and give you a ride in the morning. For which you owe me greatly, my friend."

"That I do indeed, George." I pulled out the bottle of rum and gave it to him. "Here's the first installment."

My gesture received a round of applause. George stood and bowed in appreciation.

"And now we have to go, Peter. I need to get under way."

Another session of thank yous and good lucks began among everyone, with Dewey looking on. It was a struggle to contain my emotions regarding Norodom and Petrusky. They were choked up as well—an unusual sight among the Orientals I've seen. And then, finally, we descended the hill to *Juniata's* gig waiting at the dock, relieved beyond words to be leaving the Eastern parts of the world.

"You need to read your mail, Peter. Right now," George said ominously, once we were out of earshot of the others. He looked grim. "Start with the blue one we all know so well."

I opened the navy envelope and examined the contents as we walked down the path to the landing. I wasn't pleased with what I saw. Rork looked concerned at my expression, which must have been hardening as I read.

"Do you know about this?" I asked George when I finished reading.

"Yes. I got a similar one, but I didn't want to say anything for the obvious reasons in front of the others. Now read the one from Connally."

I did, and it didn't make me any happier. Rork's questioning glances were becoming glares, so I handed him both envelopes.

Dewey didn't say anything, which was unusual—officers didn't normally give their orders to enlisted men to read, but Rork would be alongside me, so he had a right to know about these orders.

He read the official navy communication first, then handed it back to me without comment. I read it again, thinking perhaps I'd misunderstood, but the message, typed with one the new writing machines, was to the point—obviously dictated by Admiral Porter himself six weeks earlier.

United States Navy
Naval Headquarters
Washington, D.C.

27 May 1883
To: Lt. Cmdr. Peter Wake, USN,
Temporary Duty with Asiatic Station
From: Adm. D.D. Porter, USN, Senior Adm. Cmdg.,
Navy Dept., Washington D.C.,
Priority: Urgent Copies: Cmdr. G. Dewey, USS Juniata
Classification: Secret
Reference: Change in original orders
Time of effect: Immediate upon receipt

Lieutenant Commander Wake—

Preamble:
Should you receive this communication when east of Longitude 135 East in the Pacific Ocean, you will ignore these orders and proceed directly to U.S. Naval Headquarters at Washington, D.C., according to your original directive of 22 January 1883. However, should this communication reach you while you are still in the Pacific region west of Longitude 135 East, you will immediately comply with these orders.

Orders:
Due to the necessities of the service, upon receipt of this com-munication you will conclude your previous assignment with haste and by any means immediately proceed without delay to Hué, the imperial capital of the Empire of Viet Nam.

At that place you will ascertain the whereabouts and safety of the newly assigned U.S. Minister to the Court of Emperor Tu Duc, Mr. Beauregard Strom, who has been incommunicado since his arrival at that place on or about 5 May 1883. Once you have locat-ed Mr. Strom, you will assist his return to Saigon, in French Cochin China. In addition, you will obtain from him his judgment of the situation regarding the rumored imminent fall of the French military forces in the Indo-China area, and the probable French response to such a scenario. You will also attempt to ascertain from local native sources, from local imperial sources, and from French colonial and military sources, their views on this matter, and what the prognosis is for the near and distant future in that region. Finally, you will deter-mine what effect these events will have on the political and econom-ic situation in the Chinese heartland.

After obtaining this information you will proceed as soon as pos-sible to the nearest non-French telegraphic station, either in Singapore or Hong Kong. You will communicate the results of both your original and the new assignment by telegraphic method, utiliz-ing standard cipher, to the specific attention of this officer at U.S. Naval Headquarters.

Expenses:
All appropriate local and transit expenses incurred in the execution of these orders are authorized, either by standard departmental voucher, governmental bank draft, or documented personal reimbursement. Upon conclusion of the above assignment you are authorized to engage any means of transport to Washington, D.C., preferably by way of Panama, where you will ascertain the progress of the French Canal. You are also

authorized to include Sean Rork, Boatswain's Mate, U.S.N., in your
assignment and expenses.

Receipt of Orders:
You will send confirmation of receipt of these orders as soon as
possible by any means available, including plain text in open tele-
graph, omitting any references to details of said orders.

By direction of:
D.D. Porter, Admiral, USN

Admiral D.D. Porter
Senior Admiral Commanding the
United States Navy
Naval Headquarters
Department of the Navy
Washington, D.C.

Usually such orders were signed by a senior aide to Admiral
Porter. This one was signed by Porter himself. That did not bode
well. Obviously he wanted me to know he was involved in this.
And because Porter was involved, it probably meant the secretary
of the navy and the president were as well.

Rork handed me the note from Connally, which I also read
again. His handwriting was in the careful style typical of most
diplomats I'd known.

Lt. Commander P. Wake
June 28th, 1883
U.S. Navy, French Cochin China

Dear Commander Wake,

Because it is anticipated that American trade in this region will increase, six weeks ago (three weeks after I last saw you on the Mekong) the U.S. diplomatic mission status in French Indo-China was upgraded to that of a ministerial mission, with the new Chief Minister (the previous Consul General retired and went home) to be located in Hué, the imperial capital of Viet Nam. I am now the consul in Saigon. All U.S. diplomatic services in the Vietnamese regions of Annam and Tonking, the French colony of Cochin, and in Cambodia, will come under the new Chief Minister to the Court of Emperor Tu Duc.

Beauregard Strom, the Chief Minister, arrived at Hué and I went to brief him on the area. When I mentioned that an American naval officer named Wake was on the Mekong couriering a message to King Norodom, he indicated he knew you from a previous assignment in Europe and that you were friends. His wife is due to travel out from the United States and join him this summer.

Now there is a problem. Minister Strom has been incommunicado for well over a month. There are rumors circulating that he went north into the Tonking region near Hanoi, where the fighting has been heavy, to determine the situation there. I am very worried.

The French have had reverses along the Red River and in the Hanoi area, and have lost the commander of their forces at Hanoi, Lt. Cmdr Henri Rivière, who was killed in a battle with Chinese Black Flag insurgents on May 19th. The Chinese are threatening the French with incursions all along the border and ships of the Chinese fleet have assembled at ports in southern China, including Hainan.

Among the Tonkinese, there is widespread hatred of whites and the current speculation is that the French will withdraw from Tonking. Across Indo-China all foreigners are seeing increased hostility, and I fear things will get far worse with any further French defeats.

I have cabled the State Department of the situation and they were going to request the Navy Department send you to look into Mr. Strom's disappearance. Should you be anywhere near Saigon and receive this note, please stop and meet with me in regard to this situation.

Respectfully,
Theodore Connally
U.S. Consul
Saigon, French Cochin China

Reading between the lines, something I'd become adept at over the years, I got the distinct impression from the correspondence that President Arthur was wondering how the fighting in the southeastern part of Asia would affect foreign, especially American, trade status in China.

We'd reached the landing. As I followed Rork into *Juniata's* gig, I asked Dewey, "You got one of these from Connally, too?"

"No, just the one from headquarters. Connally briefed me in person. Evidently you know this Strom fellow—any ideas as to what this mess is all about?" asked Dewey, as the coxswain told the crew to pull for the ship.

"Yes, I know him. But I don't have a clue about the situation, George. I do know the one man who can educate us both and help get this done, though."

Rork, seated at the bow, heard our conversation and shrugged, then nodded resignedly at me.

"Turn the gig around, George," I said. "I need to head back up that hill."

Dewey chuckled nervously. "Uh-oh, that sounds ominous. Very well. Coxswain, turn her around." He glanced at me. "And I thought we'd have a pleasant Fourth of July today."

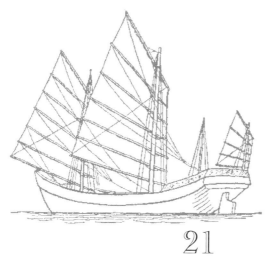

21

First-Class to Binh Thuan

Wednesday, 4 July 1883
Puolo Condore Island
South China Sea

The professor was less than his usual poker-faced self as he replied to my request. The man looked positively incredulous. "Peter, you want me to go with you to *Hué*?"

There was no way to sugarcoat it—not with a man like Petrusky. Rork and Dewey looked on from the side as I answered.

"Yes."

"From your description of how events have transpired, Peter, I might not be welcome at the court. I am seen by some in Cochin and Annam as too pro-French. And I am a Christian, a Catholic Christian. Remember, Peter—Tu Duc allowed the killing of Christians. And you, as a foreigner, certainly might not be welcome at a time like this."

"Yes. All true. Will you come?"

He exhaled while thinking it over. I had only told him of my task to find Strom, not of my mission to gather intelligence from various sources about what was happening, and what would happen in the future. My request was for him to be my guide to the numerous factors and personalities of the court, and my trusted interpreter.

"Very well. I will come," he muttered. "God please help me, but I will come."

I took his hand and said the phrase I'd learned from him on the Mekong. *"Cam on, nguoi ban cua toi."* Thank you, my friend.

Petrusky cocked an eyebrow ruefully. "I am beginning to regret teaching you my language, Peter Wake. I fear it might result in trouble for both of us. And I have a premonition that this will be as dangerous as our confrontation with the pirates."

I hesitated before replying. In my career, and in my personal life, I have always abided by a policy of candor whenever possible. Sometimes, though, one only exacerbates a situation with unguarded comments. This was one of those times.

"Nah, it won't be that bad, Professor."

An hour later I was on the weather deck, standing near Petrusky at the rail and finally taking time to read Useppa's letter. It was a short note, only two pages. She usually wrote five or more. Useppa said she loved Key West, had met several people who knew her mother when she was Useppa's age, and was enjoying the challenge of her work at the mission home. I found it a very affirmative letter and I could easily visualize her standing there in front of me, smiling and laughing.

I noticed there was no mention of any young man, probably in deference to my sensibilities, which I appreciated. There had been one in Washington, a clerk at the Interior Department named Fred something or other, but that flame obviously had flickered out. Just as well—I had thought him a bit too oily and smooth-talking. I wondered if Fred's romantic decline accounted for her desire to leave Washington. I wished Linda were there to reassure me about young ladies; I worried all the time about my little Useppa, who wasn't so little anymore. It disturbed me to realize that other girls her age were getting married and having their own children. Egad, me a grandfather? I was far too young to be a grandfather.

When I mentioned that casually to Rork, he gave me the do-you-actually-believe-that? look. Further inward reflection, along with a throb of pain from that damned old chest wound, which aggravated the new chest wound, reinforced that I really *was* old enough to be a grandfather. A very sobering thought.

Then I checked the lawyer's note. I'd met Mr. Maloney in Key West during the war. His son was serving in a Florida regiment with Robert Lee's army in northern Virginia at the time, but he wasn't bitter at all toward the federal occupiers at Key West. He was still there, a prominent and respected man. Nine months earlier, back in November when I had decided to buy the island, Maloney was the one I trusted to get it done correctly.

The note was as I had expected, confirming my purchase of Patricio Island on the lower Gulf coast of Florida, very near Useppa's namesake island. One hundred and forty dollars and twenty-two cents for the land, twenty dollars for the lawyer, and ten dollars for the Monroe County records clerk down in Key West.

This would be a surprise for Rork. He knew I was thinking of it; he didn't know I'd done it. There was still another three hundred left in my savings to build the basic house. Maloney was trying to find a carpenter in the Fort Myers area to construct it for me, but was having difficulty. I planned on Rork and me doing some additions once we got some leave. With any sort of luck, within two years it could be a nice home.

I gazed out over the South China Sea and allowed myself a dream, a vision of my island home. So different from the tensions of my work, a real refuge. And close to tranquil memories of a younger time for me, with Linda. She would've understood completely. The professor caught me grinning at the realization that for the first time in the forty-four years of my life, I owned land.

The *Juniata* was a jinxed ship if ever there was one. I was last aboard her in Key West during October of 1863. Infamous even then for malfunctions, she'd been extensively refitted before her current deployment, including new guns replacing the old ones. I say new ones, but they were really obsolete smooth-bore nine-inchers, converted from the old Parrot design but still without any rifling. They were still useless against most foes. In any other navy belonging to a sea-going nation, they would've been relegated to the scrap heap. It was beyond merely embarrassing—it was dangerous.

That sort of stupidity angered me greatly. Good God, even the *Chinese* navy's armaments were more modern, since they had taken possession of newly-built German and English warships only the year before. And the Chinese knew they had ships to be reckoned with, from their new pronouncements about national pride and foreign encroachment. That wasn't idle chatter, either. According to what Dewey had heard in Singapore and Saigon, the Chinese imperial authorities were backing both the Black Flag warlords and the Vietnamese emperor in their defiance of France. A Sino-French naval war was not out of the question.

During a discussion in Dewey's cabin my first night aboard, I shuddered to think of what might happen if we had to fight our way in against fortified land batteries, or the Chinese fleet, to rescue Strom in Tonking. George was more direct—he said flatly that we couldn't do it and that he wouldn't try.

The next morning that discussion was rendered meaningless by two events. First, the engine seized up again, the engineer explaining to his captain between four-letter words that the bearings on the cross-head had overheated and welded themselves into the arm guide, causing that to seize up, which made the engine contort and ultimately shut down. All of that meant nothing to me, but the fact we were dead in the water did.

With a weary voice, Dewey ordered sail to be set and a course made for the mouth of the Saigon River. He told me that he was not going into a war zone *under sail,* that unfortunately I would have to get to Hué, and maybe even on up to Tonking, by land from Saigon. I understood completely, and we both cursed the fools in Congress who had put our navy, and our country, in that ludicrous position by failing to build and arm modern ships.

It took us four frustrating days to sail the hundred miles to the coast by Saigon. It should have taken overnight, but the breeze and current were against us and we were forced to tack back and forth to get upwind. That was when I learned that *Juniata,* with all her other problems, didn't like to tack. She frequently would stop in mid-turn, going into "irons" with all sails aback. Then the damn old bucket sat there drifting backward until the crew could get her around and the sails filled again. We would lose miles toward our destination each time that happened.

Finally, on the morning of Monday, the ninth day of July, 1883, we met with the pilot boat off the Saigon River bar and arranged a tow upriver. That evening after sunset, *Juniata* docked at the French navy station just south of the city, near a Chinese settlement called Cholon. Our naval hosts were very careful not to laugh at our less-than-impressive arrival. I could see that they had to make quite an effort.

I'd been there when I first arrived in the colony in March and remembered the naval station as a rather relaxed place. Not any longer. Now I noted there were more guards patrolling and the place was a scene of much activity. Obviously on a war-footing, the officers were openly nervous around the native laborers who did all the manual labor at the yard. I didn't see why the French couldn't do their own, but kept my mouth shut.

Dewey and I said our goodbyes at the gangway—he apologizing for the short ride, and me wishing him good luck on his travel home. Neither of us thought we'd ever see each other again.

That probably sounds silly from the perspective of hindsight, but at the time I could tell he thought I'd get killed in some jungle fight, while I was sure he'd die of his disease halfway home.

An agitated Consul Connally met us at the dock. Within five minutes the energetic young man had paid his respects to Dewey, got the gear organized into a horse-cab, and whisked Rork, Petrusky, and me off to the consulate. At his office, Rork and Petrusky busied themselves with finding us something to eat from a street vendor while Connally filled me in on the state of affairs inside the convoluted empire of Tu Duc's Viet Nam. As to be expected in the Orient, the situation had not improved. I seriously wondered if it ever would.

Connally didn't beat around any bushes. "Mr. Strom is still missing, Commander. Other than persistent rumor that he's somewhere in the Tonking area, I have nothing new on him. This is extremely strange—we should have heard something by now."

"Are the imperial authorities in that area helping?"

"They say there are looking, but I don't believe them."

"Do you think Strom is being held by them?"

"No. There's no reason for them to hold an American diplomat. America is not seen as a colonizing power in Asia. We're seen as the ones who promote the open trade policy in China and restrain European excesses. My guess is that perhaps a local warlord or the Black Flags might have him—they align themselves with anybody convenient. The problem is that on first glance most Asians think we're Europeans, so Mr. Strom may have been mistakenly taken by people ignorant of the difference between Americans and the colonial Europeans."

I hadn't thought of that. "What a mess. All right, Rork and the professor and I will head north in the morning. I'll need your help on transport to get to Hué."

Connally pointed to a map on the wall. "It'll take you a while to get there by land, but passenger steamships aren't going north now. The railroad can get you the hundred and fifty miles up to Binh Thuan. That'll take three days. Once past the railhead, you're on the old imperial coastal road, which isn't maintained very well at all. And at that point you still have another four hundred miles to go—by cart. I can get you passage on the train, but beyond Binh Thuan you'll have to arrange your own transport. I have no contacts up there. Sorry, Commander."

Not what I wanted to hear. "Damn. This doesn't get any better, does it?" I took a deep breath and tried to sound optimistic. "Well, apparently there's no choice, so we'll just have to try it."

"Ah, well now, that could still be a problem, Commander. Travel by foreigners in that area will be risky. Binh Thuan isn't in French Cochin, it's in Annam. Cochin is still pacified and under France's direct domination as a full-fledged colony, but they have no real troop formations in Annam."

"We'll make it. And having the professor along is a great help. He's briefed me in detail about this Tu Duc fellow, so once we get there I'll try to get the emperor to really put forth an effort to find Mr. Strom."

Connally's hands were shaking. The man had been under a lot of tension, waiting alone for weeks for help to arrive. All he'd gotten was me and my two assistants. His tone got gloomier.

"Yes, well, that's the second thing I wanted to tell you. The situation in Hué has gotten much, much worse. Emperor Tu Duc is dead. We got word by telegraph that he died yesterday at the citadel in the heart of the Forbidden Purple City."

No wonder he was nervous—that changed the equation for the worse. Or did it? "Wait a minute, Ted. Tu Duc hated the French. It should be *good* that the emperor is dead, right?"

"No, it's not good for the French, or for Westerners in general. Tu Duc, as anti-Western as he was, had a restraining influence on the *real* hotheads at the imperial court—the mandarins. They are pro-Chinese, by the way."

Was *nothing* simple in Asia? "I'm afraid to even ask at this point, Ted, but who is taking over as emperor?"

"No one knows."

Petrusky would know, I thought, and decided right then that our trio would leave at sunrise. The sooner we could get under way, the sooner we could get to Hué, and thence up to Tonking if need be. I also had a hunch that once beyond Binh Thuan, the professor could get us traveling faster than the twenty miles a day by donkey cart.

"Ted, get me three tickets aboard the earliest train in the morning. Now I need to fill you in on what happened to us in Cambodia, so you'll know who is who in case you run into them."

I proceeded to advise him about various characters aboard *Tonle Queen* and their conflicts, the effort by Blundell to eliminate Rork and me on behalf of the planters and his own political security, and our escape from the pirate assassins on the Cambodian coast. I could tell it was all new to him by the stunned look on his face. He pondered the situation, then said, "This greedy infighting puts a new complexion on the situation—a weakness the enemies of the French might exploit. We may be getting close to total anarchy."

I agreed, and then, remembering my orders, I picked up a pencil and began writing on a piece of paper on Connally's desk. Then I handed it to him and said, "Please get this sent in the morning."

He nodded and glanced at the paper.

9 July 1883
To: Adm. D.D. Porter
US Naval Hdqtrs, Washington DC
From: LCDR P. Wake

In Saigon now. Received new orders—implementing immediately.

Wake

Connally looked up at me. "Mr. Strom said you knew each other in Europe."

I didn't feel like delving into it, so I just said, "Yes, we did. Genoa in seventy-four. Now you'll have to excuse me, Ted. I need food and rest, and you need to get those tickets."

We reached Binh Thuan late on the night of the twelfth after a very long, and somewhat eerie, ride. The train had one first-class carriage, which Connally had bribed the train depot dispatchers to get us on. First-class was a gross misnomer. Other than the exorbitant price, there was nothing first-class about it, from the wooden seats to the lack of a toilet to the putrid food. But I must say that it was better than the only other passenger carriage—the second-class coach. That had animals in it, although they were limited to fowl. Aft of those two cars were another six, laden down with rubber. Lots of it. Sheets of rubber were piled high in wood pallet loads, which were piled high on the flat cars. On top of the rubber sat the third-class passengers, along with their pigs, chickens, goats, and mangy dogs—for eating, not as pets.

The countryside consisted mostly of rubber trees, from what I could see as we trundled along. The jerky swaying and lurching was a motion far worse than any I've felt at sea. At least on the ocean you could stand and walk around—in the rail car there was no room to stretch one's legs.

Halfway to Binh Thuan, we left the colony of Cochin and entered Annam, where the French had no direct rule. There we changed to a smaller train on a narrower gauged track. The crowded interior conditions were the same, but the ride wasn't as bad. Petrusky said that was because the train wasn't as fully loaded—the planters were waiting until things calmed down before shipping their valuable product.

Other than at the infrequent depots, I didn't see any Frenchmen through the windows once we entered southern Annam. In fact, as we got further north, I didn't see many inside the train. Only a priest was with us on the final leg, from Kim Ngoa to Binh Thuan, and even he declined to talk, instead just sitting there preoccupied, fingering a rosary.

On our second night we arrived in Binh Thuan, a bustling

city composed mostly of slums. The first order of business was to find the telegraph station, for Connally promised to send an update on conditions in the Hué area and any new intelligence he'd found.

An old Annamese in a disheveled Western suit grudgingly searched for the telegram among the pigeon-hole shelves, making a show of what an imposition it was to comply with my request. Since Connally was to have sent it that afternoon, I thought the theatrics a bit much—how many telegrams did this fool in Binh Thuan get in a day? Then he grunted out that he'd discovered it and rudely read the thing in front of me. In a monumental exhibition of self-discipline, I did not succumb to my frustration and deck the arrogance out of him, but calmly took it out of his hands once he condescended to give it over.

Most of it was a rehash of what we already knew or surmised, but the last part about Blundell got my attention. I handed the message sheet to my colleagues.

12 JULY 1883, 2 P.M.
TO: P.WAKE—BINH THUAN—ANNAM—EMPIRE OF VIET NAM
FROM: T.CONNALLY—SAIGON—COCHIN—FRENCH COCHIN CHINA
-X—FRENCH ARMY PUSHED BACK AGAIN INTO HANOI BY CHINESE SUPPORTED TONKINESE FORCES—X—FRENCH NAVY BLOCKADING HUE AND TONKIN COAST—X—NO NEW EMPEROR YET—X—CONFUSING RUMORS FROM HUE—X—FRENCH HERE ARE WORRIED—X—GENERAL WAR BETWEEN FRANCE AND CHINA/VIET NAM EMPIRE EXPECTED SOON—X—US ENVOY TO CHINA JOHN RUSSELL YOUNG TRYING TO DEFUSE SITUATION BETWEEN CHINA AND FRANCE BUT NO LUCK SO FAR—X—US POSITION IS NEUTRALITY—X—YOUR ROYAL FRIEND ARVD SAIGON—X—HEADING TO PHNOM PENH—

X—HIS SOURCE IN PP ADVSD BLUNDELL & DUPUIS
NO LONGER IN CAMBODIA—X—UNK WHERE—X—
UNK ABOUT OTHERS YOU TOLD ME ABOUT—X—
GOOD LUCK—X—PLS GIVE SITREP WHEN YOU
CAN—X

"Monsieur Blundell has connections everywhere. With the violence in Tonking and the political unrest in Annam, perhaps he is taking advantage of the situation for personal gain in Cochin," suggested Petrusky. "There are many possibilities— moving opium, guns, rubber, rice."

"Or maybe he's looking for us," said Rork, none too nicely. "He probably knows by now we're alive an' might have figured his treachery. There's a wee bit o' a score I've got with that scallywag."

After twenty years with Rork, I knew that tone well. Rork never bluffed about what he would do to a man who had incurred his wrath. If we ever did meet up with Blundell, there was definitely pain in his future, something I had no problem with at all, as long as it was done quietly.

"Time will tell, gentlemen. Now we have to figure out a way to get from here to Hué."

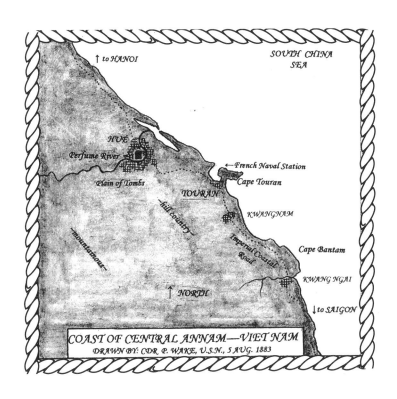

to HANOI

SOUTH CHINA
SEA

HUE
Perfume River

Plain of Tombs

French Naval Station

Cape Touran

TOURAN

hill country

KWANGNAM

mountainous

Imperial Coastal
Road

Cape Bantam

KWANG NGAI

NORTH

to SAIGON

COAST OF CENTRAL ANNAM—VIET NAM
DRAWN BY: CDR. P. WAKE, U.S.N., 5 AUG. 1883

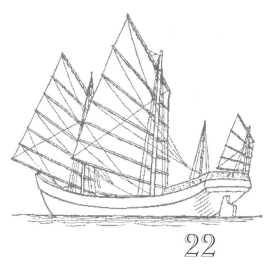

22

Damned Skawly People

Thursday, 12 July 1883
Binh Thuan, Annam
Empire of Viet Nam

While bouncing our way north along the tracks in Annam, Petrusky and I had talked about what to do once we arrived in Binh Thuan. My thought was to give a warlord a fee to take us up the coast road. The professor shook his head at that, saying this area was different from Cambodia. He explained that other than the imperial army—which probably wouldn't help us and might imprison us—there were no real warlords in Annam powerful enough to get us the whole distance or even a long way, only local district chiefs. That meant paying off one after another, with a great possibility of being stranded or robbed in the middle of our journey.

He suggested paying for a boat to sail us up the coast, bypassing the political troubles on land. After our last excursion on the "royal yacht" along the Cambodian coast, I was dubious of that idea, to say the very least. However, the professor countered that piracy was rare along this particular part of Indo-China, that it was a far more civilized shore. He also said a junk could slip through the naval blockade, since they were probably looking for steam vessels. That made sense and I reluctantly agreed.

After arranging for our food, Petrusky left us sitting on the ground in a fishmonger's stall at the Binh Thuan town market and headed off to find a boat. That endeavor took him all night, during which neither Rork nor I slept a wink, what with all the locals eyeing us suspiciously as they walked past.

We kept our revolvers visible and leaned our backs against a wall—the only one made of stone I could find—and returned the evil stares with some nasty ones of our own. Rork can appear particularly malevolent when he wants to, an asset he employed well for the entire evening. The professor returned just before dawn and reported that he had found a captain and bargained a decent price. After eating some rice and fish balls—with a horrid sauce that tasted like it may have been poison—we walked five miles to a little village nearby, boarded an old sailing junk, and set sail.

Seated amidship among bales of sugar cane, animal crates, and other assorted freight, Petrusky enlightened us about our transport. The junk was named the *Binh Hai*—Peaceful Ocean—and the captain went by the name of Hung, which meant prosperity. The junk looked the same as the others in the harbor, filthy and decrepit, but that made me feel a bit more at ease. We could blend in with the coastal traffic and evade the blockade as hundreds of other vessels were doing. Having been on the other side of that equation during our own civil war, I knew that naval blockades were far easier said than done.

The professor reported that Hung was already heading up the coast to take on a cargo of fruit at a village on a bay called Kam Ranh, then bound further north to offload at someplace near a city called Kwang Ngai. None of that signified anything to me, but the fact that for ten Mexican silver dollars Hung would take us past Kwang Ngai and on up to Hué did catch my interest.

As the crew of ten set sail and got the *Binh Hai* under way,

Rork and I examined our new home while the professor gabbed with the captain. Rork had served on the Asiatic Station before and knew about sailing junks, but this was my first opportunity to really study one close up.

Basically, our sixty-foot ship was the same type as the pirate junks that had attacked us, but of course, we'd hadn't the leisure to study those at the time. By Western standards these craft look ungainly, but Petrusky said junks had sailed all over the Pacific and Indian oceans and were regarded as very seaworthy. The stern was high off the water, like an old-fashioned Spanish galleon's stern castle, and fully six or more feet higher than the bow. On the sloping main deck, there was a tiny cabin forward of the stern, used mainly for the captain's personal possessions, and a huge cargo hold full of sugar cane. The rig of each mast was simple. A large sail with bamboo battens, slung fore-and-aft on a mast, lanteen style. There was a tall one amidships, balanced by a small one perched at the stern and another one on a platform at the bow. Rork noted that lazy jacks from the boom to the masthead enabled the seamen to easily lower the sail in place, effectively reefing it in seconds.

Binh Hai was steered by a massive tiller and could sail surprisingly close to the wind, as demonstrated by a grinning Captain Hung, who deftly slid between dozens of other vessels in the harbor. Like seamen everywhere, he knew when he was being watched by professionals and cut it pretty fine a couple of times with anchored junks just to show off, but managed it without disaster. Within minutes, Hung brought us out into open water, where we met the southwesterlies. Soon we were riding the monsoon winds, our sails slung out to either side wing-and-wing, and scudding north along the coast, rolling to beat the Devil but making good time.

Petrusky said, "Peter, the captain says we have the sea and wind helping us—a good omen for the voyage."

"I dunno, sir," offered Rork. "That there Hung looks a bit dodgy to me."

I had to agree. Hung *did* look dodgy, probably because his left eye was sewn shut—and not done neatly, either—an apparent consequence of the scar that ran from his forehead to his left cheek. The right eye darted around in a disconcerting manner, as if it were loose in Hung's head. He wore the standard pajama outfit of Asia, of course, but with one additional accoutrement that instantly drew one's attention. An ancient blunderbuss-pistol-looking affair was jammed into the cowhide belt across his front and a dagger and sheath were installed on either side. Curiously, several teeth dangled on jute strings from each sheath.

The pistol seemed a historical artifact, possibly from the Spanish explorers three hundred years before, and I wondered if it worked. The daggers cast no doubt, however, for I'd seen the man slicing an orange with one of the razor-edged things. If he'd been displaying the ugly thing for my benefit, it worked. They were wicked weapons, with blades that serpentined from tip to hilt, like a flat snake, obviously capable of creating a horrific wound. I asked the professor about them.

"Ah, yes. Malayan *kris*—very effective in the hands of an experienced man. Quite frightening to behold, and for good reason. It produces an interior wound almost impossible to suture closed, one that becomes infected quite easily," Petrusky informed us.

"And the teeth?" I asked, already guessing the answer.

"One for each man killed, Peter. Captain Hung is a very experienced man."

I counted seven teeth. Rork looked at me and groaned, saying, "Well now, that makes me opinion o' our captain a wee bit different, sir. Change it to *extremely* dodgy."

I couldn't argue that. "The roll-call of dodgy characters in Indo-China is getting rather long, but while we're on this junk he'll top the list."

"Right, sir. An' unless otherwise directed by yourself, I'll shoot the evil-lookin' bugger if he looks about to skewer one o' us."

The coast was a ragged succession of points and bays and islands. It was a green coast, beautiful, lush, and alive with small sampans, sailing junks, even a few junks with steam engines. We made good time, passing a cape called Pandaran and wearing across the wind onto the port tack with a great clatter from the bamboo battens. By the next afternoon we were sailing up a deep bay at Kam Ranh.

It took two days to unload the sugar cane at the town and then load the fruit. When the professor saw what kind of fruit was about to be brought aboard he kicked the deck and said something in his native tongue that sounded pretty vulgar. Quite a display for him. I looked down into the punt alongside and saw nothing that would cause such a violent reaction from our normally composed academic companion. It was a mound of green oval-shaped fruit, each about ten inches long and covered with dull spikes. Then I got a whiff of our new cargo.

"Durian," sputtered Petrusky as he glared at Hung at the stern.

"Smells pretty bad," I said.

"It will get worse, Peter. I am sorry that I did not ask what kind of fruit we were to carry. Durian fruit is a prized dish here, but the odor is terrible, especially when a large quantity is confined, as in a cargo hold."

That, as I quickly comprehended in disgusting detail, was an understatement. The closest analogy I can provide for the stench is that of a sewer. A large, stagnant sewer. We got under way the following morning, bound north again, everything and everyone stinking to high heaven. With the wind from behind us, the very stern became *Binh Hai*'s sole place of somewhat clean air, and the captain claimed it as his own, glowering at the rest of us. Rork mentioned that he was considering killing Hung just to be able to dump the cargo. I laughed, then studied my friend closer. He wasn't jesting.

"Oh, belay that kind of talk and stand easy, Rork. It's not worth it."

"One more day o' this stink an' it *will* be, sir."

Hung told Petrusky that the voyage from Kam Ranh to Kwang Ngai would take four days if the wind held steady. On the second day, I thought perhaps I could make it; we were halfway there. The monsoon wind was a constant twenty knots and we were doing at least seven or eight. The professor, trying to bolster our spirits, advised that this far into the monsoon season the wind never slacked. He predicted we'd be at Kwang Ngai ahead of Hung's estimate.

Two hours later the wind died.

Petrusky almost cried. Rork got quiet. The crew moaned. The captain cursed. I fought the urge to swim to shore, five miles distant. Without the ventilation of the sea breeze and with the hot summer sun baking it, the durian reeked even worse. Rork suggested killing Hung and the entire crew, dumping the cargo overboard, and sailing the junk ourselves to Hué. He was serious. I thought the idea was beginning to have merit.

After two days of sitting there, drifting north at one knot, Petrusky gave us even more depressing news. Hung had deduced that the cause of the wind's demise was the approach of a typhoon, early for the season, which had sucked the wind from the coast. The captain went to the bow, sniffed the air, twirled slowly around studying the horizon, peered off to the northeast with that one eye, and announced somberly that within a day or so we would have all the wind in the world from the west. I thought it a theatrical moment for the benefit of his disgruntled passengers and crew. That night, just after our obligatory rice and salt-dried fish dinner, I found out that Captain Hung was no charlatan regarding weather prognostication.

The wind went from nothing to force four out of the west in

five minutes. Within an hour we were at force six—twenty-five knots, gusting to well over forty. The sailing junk of Asia is an odd-looking craft, but both Rork and I have said this about them ever since that journey—they scud before the wind in a storm better than most Western designs. With that high poop, easily reefed sails, and big rudder, a sailing junk was the best vessel to weather a storm going downwind.

And downwind we went, off to the northeast on a broad reach. They first doused the after mast, what we would call the mizzen. I forget what their tortuous native names for the masts were. Next, they reefed the great main sail halfway, tying down the ends of the bamboo battens in the quickest reefing job I've ever seen. By midnight the wind was piping higher, force eight at least, and the main came down completely, leaving only the reefed foresail and three men straining at the heavy tiller. Throughout it all, we never shipped a major sea aft of the main mast, though the bow was pretty wet the whole time with solid spray and some seas.

Fortunately the wind was off the land a few miles to the west, so the seas were only fifteen feet—far less than they'd be if the wind had come hundreds of miles unfettered across the South China Sea. Rork stayed forward with the crew while Petrusky and I stood aft with Hung. Using the age-old seamen's trick for determining the center of a cyclonic storm in the northern hemisphere, I faced the wind and put my right arm out at right angle to the wind—that pointed to the storm's eye, which was somewhere to our north. Petrusky confirmed that, explaining that in July the storms usually came across the South China Sea from the Philippines and hit the mainland in the southern China or northern Viet Nam area of Tonking. Right where Strom was thought to be.

Heeling far over—that high freeboard that kept us relatively dry couldn't escape the wind—we did at least nine or more knots, surging down the waves, the tiller vibrating and the shrouds screaming up and down the musical scale with the gusts. By dawn the gale had moved the wind to the sou'southwest and Hung kept his ship on the same course relative to the wind—a broad reach, now heading northwest and following the curve of the coast. It was a neat trick on his part and allowed us to maximize the storm's assistance to us.

What we'd lost in the doldrums we more than made up for with this burst of speed. Hung coolly forecast to Petrusky that we would be in Kwang Ngai the next day, though how the hell he knew where we were in that chaotic watery world where the visibility was measured in feet, I never knew. He was taking soundings, but beyond that the man saw no stars, no land, no other vessels, not even a horizon, for the sea and air were a blended mass of liquid. It astounded me. I would've run off downwind two hundred miles to get away from the dangers of land in the storm—Hung simply used the tempest to further his voyage.

That night the moon came through as visibility improved and the wind lay down to only twenty knots from the south. Hung set more sail and *Binh Hai* easily pressed on to the west. At dawn, green mountains littered the horizon over a turquoise sea, a beautiful sight illuminated by golden shafts of the early sun. Three hours later we glided several miles up a small river with the flood tide and a fair breeze to Kwang Ngai, the setting incongruously serene compared to the tumult the day before. Our captain nonchalantly called out hellos to acquaintances among the junks and sampans, as if he'd merely been on a Sunday sail at a Long Island yacht club.

"He's a dodgy character all right, but one hellova seaman," declared Rork as we tied up at a dock already piled high with durian fruit. "By God, I'll give the bugger that."

Durian doesn't smell any better wet than dry, and it was with grumbling relief by everyone aboard that the last of the stuff was finally off-loaded at the end of the day. Hung returned to the junk to announce we would depart the next morning, after loading our new cargo. Our piratical-looking leader informed us he had bartered to haul some pottery and lacquer ware, packed in crates filled with straw, to Saigon. With a short side trip to Hué to drop us off.

The evil eye winked at us as he told Petrusky our new cargo would smell much better—more like goat dung than human sewage. Turned out he'd gotten the straw from a barn nearby. A barn full of goats. He added that the sail to Hué would take maybe two days.

Petrusky had his ear to the ground for pertinent intelligence while we strolled about the docks that day, during which Rork and I again received less-than-affable stares from the locals. They were so hostile that my bosun and I decided to curtail the geography of our ramble and remain close to the junk. The professor, however, was all over, talking with everyone and getting the scuttlebutt on what was happening in the country.

The news wasn't good from our standpoint. The professor subsequently informed us that people were making disparaging comments about foreigners. Imperial troops were conscripting young men to fight for their country. Petrusky suggested Rork and I stay aboard the junk and not wander around—war was definitely coming and we looked a lot like the enemy.

In the political arena, people were talking about the new emperor that had been proclaimed days before. The court mandarins at Hué had decided that a man named Duc Duc, nephew of Tu Duc, would be the new sovereign and had disseminated the word across the country. Evidently Duc Duc didn't have a big following. Most folks had no idea who he was.

Petrusky, however, knew something of Duc Duc and wasn't impressed. He said the new emperor had a very bad reputation for debauchery that made Tu Duc, with his hundred and four wives and two hundred concubines, pale in comparison. I thought that quite an accomplishment, even by Oriental standards.

At ten the next morning, Tuesday, the twenty-second of July, 1883, our *Binh Hai* was riding the ebb tide down the river to the sea. Everyone in the crew was happier than I'd seen them so far. The faint odor of goat dung didn't bother anyone aboard—once you've carried durian, all other cargo is pleasantly fragrant. The passengers were not happy at all, though, because Petrusky had been out and about early at dawn and returned with fresh news from Hué, which he shared as the three of us sat on the tiny foredeck watching the verdant countryside go by.

"Duc Duc has been deposed. He was considered too soft. The mandarins are in charge again and will choose someone else, but all is uncertain. There are rumors that the French killed Duc Duc, or that some of the mandarins deposed him to curry favor to the French. There are also rumors that French reinforcements are arriving in Saigon and Hanoi, and that Hué will be attacked at any day. People think many will be killed."

Rork frowned, his voice rumbled, "Oh, aye, a simple assignment to Cambodia, then return back to home, 'twas what I heard months ago. In an' out. Sweet as an angel's cake in me girl's hand. Home by the summer, we'd be. Right, Commander?"

No argument to that. "Yes, that *was* the plan originally, Rork."

His words quickened. "Well now, so far, we've been caught in the middle o' a bunch o' bloody opium peddlers, rubber conflicts, pirate attacks, palace intrigues, deadly doldrums when there should be monsoon winds, damned near dead from starvation, endured typhoon storms, stuck on a boat with fruit that stinks to high heaven, an' every inch o' the way have been surrounded by lyin', thievin', murderin' scoundrels an' renegades."

"Yep, that about sums it up, Rork."

I was hoping to change the subject, but he wasn't done. Sometimes my Irish friend has to let out his dissatisfaction with the way events are transpiring for us. Cursing is the least violent way. Besides, he had no appropriate targets around anyway.

He was warming to the subject now, the snarl becoming a tone of incredulous wonder. "An' so here we are—bound into some sort o' bloody friggin' hornet's nest to find a missin' striped-pants diplo type wanderin' in circles with his thumb up his hawse-hole, an' only God knows what-all's a comin' our miserable bleedin' way from these nasty scalawagin', sonsabitchin', foul-smellin', dead-eyed brigands who're every damned place you look."

A huge booted foot stamped the deck. "Hells bells in Killarney! Why I used to think those poxy-faced villains down South America way was a pretty mess o' evil-doers—but as God is my holy witness, Commander Peter Wake, this whole *entire* corner o' the world's got the *worst* bunch o' damned *skawly* buggers I've ever seen! An' every swingin' lug in Uncle Sam's sufferin' bloody navy knows I seen a fair amount o' them, man an' boy, for over forty long years o' me miserable life."

I noticed Rork's right fist was clenched. Just then he pounded the fist on the bulwark, harrumphed mightily, and glared off to windward. The tirade—compared to some I've seen, it was one of Rork's milder ones—got the total attention of the Annamese crew, who stopped what they were doing and looked on warily as the big bosun growled something further in Gaelic. The crew then jumped back in fright when he abruptly pounded the bulwark in frustration again. Hung fingered his blunderbuss.

"So vividly put, Sean. Feel better now?" I asked quietly as I studied his hand for damage.

His face relaxed, showing just the trace of a smile. "Yeah . . . I suppose so, Peter. But I'll be feelin' a bloody sight better when I see this friggin' arse-hole of a place is hull down astern o' us . . ."

Petrusky, who'd been sitting there wide-eyed with awe and fear, nudged me and whispered, "Peter, if you please. I was able to follow along for most of it, but what is the definition of this word *skawly*?"

I chose the gentlest meaning for the word. "Ah, that would be the Irish word for *horrible*, Professor."

He turned back to the bosun, shrugged his shoulders, and shook his head apologetically. "Yes, Mr. Rork, I am afraid that you are entirely right in your assessment of the situation. This place *is* full of damned skawly people."

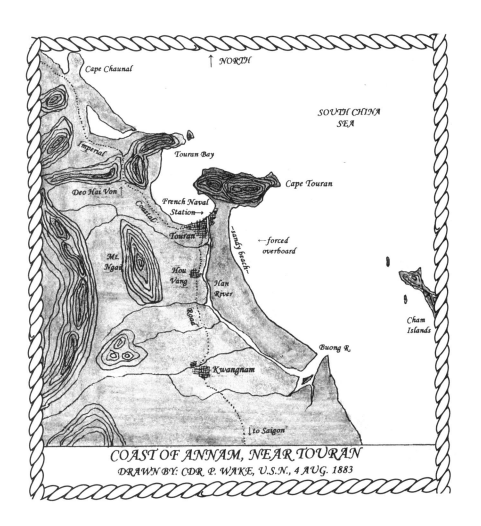

NORTH

Cape Chaunal

SOUTH CHINA
SEA

Imperial

Touran Bay

Deo Hai Von

Cape Touran

Coastal

French Naval
Station →

Touran

←forced
overboard

sandy beach

Mt.
Ngan

Hou
Vang

Han
River

Road

Cham
Islands

Buong R.

Kwangnam

↓ to Saigon

COAST OF ANNAM, NEAR TOURAN
DRAWN BY: CDR. P. WAKE, U.S.N., 4 AUG. 1883

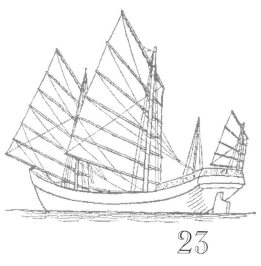

23

The Poet-Warrior

Binh Hai had an easy downwind sail for the next day and night. The morning after, however, things changed yet again and, as usual, not for the better. I should have been warned by the fact that for the first time on that section of the coast, no other junks were in sight. Instead, I was entranced by the beauty of the scenery around me, with the professor acting as tour guide as we stood by the bow.

We were sailing close along a golden-sand beach that stretched across the low-lying verdant coast and had just sighted the mouth of the Buong River to port. Well behind the coast, a series of five lumpy, red-rocked mountains curved away from the sea. Far offshore to starboard I saw the gray smudge of Cham Island and ahead of us was a large cape jutting several miles out into the South China Sea. Petrusky said it was Cape Tourane, one of the most famous in Indo-China. A bay on the other side contained a French settlement of the same name. The Vietnamese name of the place was Da Nang before the French bombarded it to ruin in 1847 and renamed it. The cape had a substantial green-clad mountain rising from the surrounding low land, giving one the false impression that it was an island off the flat coastline.

Rork, Petrusky, and I were remarking on the navigational consequences of that illusion when the lookout aloft screamed, *"Tau be chay bang hoi!"* and pointed to the end of the cape.

"Steamer warship," said the professor quietly.

Sure enough, rounding the cape was a small gunboat, maybe four hundred tons, smoke pouring from her lone funnel. The French tricolor appeared at her gaff peak and floated in the wind. That was when I realized—far too late—we were alone on the sea and not mixed in with a large fleet of fishing junks. The locals in that area obviously knew something we didn't.

"Xu toi!" muttered Captain Hung as he strode over to the helmsman back at the stern.

"He said *damn,*" Petrusky dutifully interpreted for me, adding unnecessarily that the gunboat was heading directly for us.

I glanced at Rork, who lamented, "Kinda stick out like a sore thumb, don't we, sir? Oh, Saint Patrick, help us now—I feel like a lone Dago on Plymouth Hoe. Any ideas?"

"Not yet."

I didn't have any, but Hung did. He pushed the tiller to starboard, making *Binh Hai* swerve toward the beach. At the same time he yelled at the crew in rapid-fire Annamese and I had the unpleasant sensation of seeing Petrusky's jaw drop in recognition of the captain's orders. Various crew shouted at each other, their voices a jumble of anger and fear. They began a frenetic effort to drag the cargo crates over to the side, some breaking open, spilling broken lacquer ware and straw on the deck. The three of us went amidship to see what was going on.

An argument soon ensued between the professor and the captain. I caught the words "American" and "Remington" from the captain. Hung ended it with a roaring curse at Petrusky and walked forward from the tiller to the ship's waist, where his men were now heaving crates overboard. The crates sank immediately, the broken ones leaving a trail of straw floating behind us.

The professor let Rork and me have the bad news. "Gentlemen, it seems that Captain Hung is carrying more than lacquer ware in those straw-filled crates. He is transporting American rifles from a Chinese merchant in Kwang Ngai to an imperial army colonel in Hué. They are intended to arm a battalion to fight the French."

He paused and took a deep breath. "And we must now jump overboard or the captain will shoot us. He will let us take our bags and suggests that we swim for the beach."

Rork and I instantly spun around to face Hung, drawing our revolvers as we did so. We were too late, though—that blunderbuss was already leveled at our guts. I glanced left and observed two crewmen held pistols on us from the stern. Two others by the crates held rifles.

"*Roi!*" bellowed Hung as he motioned to the rail.

"We must go now, gentlemen," Petrusky said, leaning down to pick up his bag from the pile on the deck where we slept. "There is no other choice here. He is dumping everything that could be contraband—and that includes us."

"All right, Rork," I said. "We can't win this, so we need to keep calm. Put your revolver back and get your seabag and I'll get mine. Time for a swim."

Rork didn't say a word, but kept his eyes on Hung while getting his seabag. The three of us walked to the rail, Rork and I tightening the draw on our bags. Petrusky had a canvas luggage bag and I remember thinking that it probably wouldn't float and hoped that the professor would. Then there was a popping sound to seaward and two geysers fountained up on our port side. The French were close and had our range, signaling for *Binh Hai* to heave to.

Hung's eye flared and he cocked the flintlock's hammer. I

announced the only thing I could think of at the time. Calling out, "Follow me, boys," I jumped overboard into the clear green water a quarter-mile from that pretty beach.

I heard two splashes next to me. Both of them surfaced and I was pleased to see the professor's luggage was indeed buoyant, somewhat anyway. Inverted, our navy seabags floated as they were supposed to, acting as life preservers.

Binh Hai was already a hundred yards off, having altered course to seaward in an effort to get some distance from the tell-tale floating trail of straw. We treaded water for a moment to get organized. Rork brushed away a piece of drifting goat dung-clumped straw and pointed out to the professor that he had one in his hair, then declared with a grin, "At least the water's warm," and struck out for the shore, followed by Petrusky.

Behind us, the gunboat came up to the junk with angry shouts in French to stop and be boarded. No one on the junk looked our way. I could see Hung on his main deck, protesting his innocence. I turned and swam for the beach behind my companions, waiting for the gunshot that would end my life in that wretched country. None came.

"Where are we?" I asked, while gasping for air.

"Somewhere southeast of Tourane, Peter. Perhaps four kilometers—about two and a half of your English miles."

The three of us sat under a palm tree just in from the beach. Offshore, the gunboat was steaming away from *Binh Hai*. The junk had tacked back to the southeast and was close-hauled into the wind, bound away from the war zone.

"So Hung pulled it off, eh? He's one devious bastard, all right," said Rork. "Reminds me a bit o' me ol' cousin Aongus—a shifty devil o' a smuggler if ever there was one. Talked his way out o' prison many a time with the king's excise men on the coast. Aye, that he did."

When Rork is angry he gets quiet. When he's nervous, he talks. I could tell he was about to regale the professor with Aongus's exploits back in the old country. I'd heard the tales of cousin Aongus many times in twenty years and wasn't ready to hear them again.

"How do you recommend we get to Hué from here, Professor?"

He stopped cleaning his spectacles and stroked his chin. "Hmm. We should definitely not go into Tourane or the French will stop us, detaining you both as foreigners and probably imprisoning me as a provocateur. No, we will have to walk around Tourane, then on to Hué. It will be forty English miles, at least."

Not what I wanted to hear, but that was becoming the norm. I realized he was correct. The French would never let any of us go into the imperial capital of Hué, and Petrusky, even though he was Christian and part-French, was still an Oriental and therefore suspect. Then there was the fact that if the French ever found out there were American rifles being smuggled into the emperor's troops, they might think Rork and I were part of that operation, especially if they learned we were on the vessel carrying the weapons. Yes, avoiding Tourane was a priority.

"Very good," I agreed. "Two days, maybe three if it's mountainous."

Petrusky looked apologetic for his country's terrain. "I am sorry to say that it will be, Peter."

Rork rolled his eyes and moaned. Sailors hate walking in mountains.

We were adhering to the professor's plan—dress like the locals, put our bags inside of burlap rice sacks, move only at night, walk on the side roads, and get off the road upon sighting a French patrol. I considered it a good plan, but it made our progress slow, for there were many detachments out scouring the coastal plain around Tourane. The French were taking no chances of surprise attack on their interior defensive position at the town.

I must say that Rork and I looked ridiculous. It was hard to believe our black pajama outfits fooled anyone within a hundred yards of us. There are large men in that part of the world, but not many and none as big as Rork. Petrusky bargained for some clothes, then got a village woman at Houvang to sew extra lengths on the trousers and sleeves meant for Rork and me. My sartorial embarrassment didn't diminish the success of Petrusky's efforts, however. Not a single person, French or native, questioned the two lumbering oafs walking next to the professor.

It took two days just to sneak our way around Tourane. None of us knew the back way around. Petrusky had been to Hué and Tourane several times before as an interpreter for Church officials, but he'd always traveled along the imperial coastal road constructed by order of Tu Duc in the eighteen-sixties. We were moving cautiously, with the professor frequently scouting ahead and reporting back.

Then we hit that line of mountains I'd seen from the junk. There was no way around them. They curved around all the way to the coast, north of Tourane Bay. The second evening I stood on a low hill as the setting sun gave the colors of the forests around me a golden hue. It was a beautiful, tranquil vista spread out like a painting. Rice paddies and sugar fields in the lower areas, vegetable fields and pastureland in the higher elevations, then that rock on the mountain slopes peeking through the jungle vines and hardwood trees. At places it was white, like marble. At the top, the peaks were all rock, jagged and angry, defying anyone to try to get past them.

That was where the beauty stopped for Rork and me, for now we had to climb those mountains. From the sea, the ridges had appeared lumpy. Close up they were nothing short of torturous. A solid barrier from west to east, right to the shore. Petrusky explained that the mountains rose to over fifteen hundred meters, then did the mathematical conversion in his head and explained they were five thousand feet high.

He saw my reaction and laid a hand on my shoulder. "Do not worry, my friend, there is a pass through the mountains."

I scanned the line of crests and sure enough, there was a dip just a few miles inland from the coast, evidently a pass of sorts through the wall of rocks.

"There?" I asked.

"Yes. It is called Deo Hai Von—the Pass of the Clouds in your language. Only five hundred meters, Peter. Only one thousand six hundred feet."

When he heard that, Rork muttered, "You think Strom is worth all this friggin' climbin', sir? Hell, the lad's probably sippin' champagne somewhere with a bunch o' trollops slippin' him grapes an' whisperin' how manly he looks. You know, we may just be interruptin' a good time for the boyo."

"Yes, Rork—he's worth it and even if he weren't, it's our *mission,* so we go. I don't like this any more than you do."

"I thought you'd say something like that."

I ignored his reply and turned back to our guide. "Professor, the sun has set—kindly lead onward . . ." I looked at that mountain. "And upward."

There was only one road through the pass—that imperial road that linked Hué with the cities to the south, all the way to Saigon. Even at night, the traffic was heavy—carts, wagons, horses, mules, elephants, and two French army patrols. In the middle of the gap there was also a French army post, checking all who were passing through. Petrusky said it was new, that he hadn't thought of that possibility.

Fortunately others had. We back-tracked half a mile and joined a line of people who didn't want to be perused by the French army—they scaled the cliff to the left of the gorge and climbed to the overlook, then descended on the other side. Curiously for me, the worst part was going down in the dark, my imagination providing a multitude of scenarios for my death. It was with shaking knees that we congratulated ourselves afterward, holing up in a grove of pine trees where we built a camouflaged lean-to and collapsed. To my knowledge, and profound relief, the French never found the detour used by hundreds to get around their checkpoint that night.

We entered the southern outskirts of Hué at dusk on the afternoon on Tuesday, the thirty-first of July—six and a half days after washing up on the beach and twenty-five exhausting days after leaving Saigon. What had seemed a difficult yet straightforward mission in Connally's office had turned into a nightmare of uncertainty and peril.

Actually, by that point I was beginning to doubt we'd made it in time to find Strom alive, assuming he was in Hué. If the rumors about him being in Tonking—another five hundred miles to the north—were true, I didn't think we could even *get* there, much less rescue him or recover his body. But our orders were such that I had to try. There was no alternative.

The southern outskirts of the city bordered a strange sight that unfolded to the west—the Plain of the Tombs. A vast area of small rolling hills with forested parks and meadows among lakes and streams, it was populated by mausoleums of mandarins, imperial nobility, and—most imposing—the gigantic memorials for former emperors.

Across the imperial highway, on the seaward side to the east, lay miles of rice paddies. Ahead of us, to the north, lay the foreign settlement clinging to the southern bank of the River of Perfume. And beyond that on the far shore, visible for miles, were the fortified walls of the Citadel of Hué, imperial capital of the Nguyen dynasty emperors of Viet Nam. Petrusky explained all this with palpable awe. French-educated and Christian-believing as he was, there was still a sense of reverence and loyalty for this place and all it represented.

We crossed the Phu Cam Canal and entered the foreign settlement, mainly French traders and missionaries and the ancillary townspeople that supported them. Petrusky suggested that we hide at his friend's home at the edge of the town, not in the foreign quarter where Rork and I would be more visible. That sounded reasonable and I acceded to his proposition. His friend Hhom, a local teacher, was plainly not enthusiastic about having foreigners, but bade us a grudging welcome and gave us the first decent food we'd had since Saigon.

After an intense discussion between Hhom and Petrusky, the professor told me, "I will be back with a friend from the imperial court. Stay here and do not let yourselves be seen by anyone."

With that, he was off into the night. When he'd gone, Rork made a "hmm" sound and said, "I noticed our scholarly companion made that a command instead of a request, sir. Didn't you?"

"Yes, I did too," I answered, while wondering who this mysterious friend of importance was that the professor never mentioned before.

I got my answer seven hours later. Rork and I were woken up by the professor at two in the morning. By the dim yellowed light of a lone paper lantern, Petrusky introduced the man standing beside him.

"Commander Wake, I have the honor of introducing you to His Excellency, Nguyen Khuyen Mien Chi, Royal Mandarin, Scholar of History of the Third Rank within the Can Chanh Palace of the Kings who are Sons of Heaven, in the service of the Emperor of Viet Nam and Sovereign of Annam, Tonking, and Cochin."

It was a grand title for a history teacher, and one I noticed that omitted an important detail—the name of the current emperor. But fortunately, I didn't bring that up, for I was to learn why in a moment. What I did do was use a phrase I'd been practicing in my mind in case I met a high-ranking gentleman of the court. It was a formal greeting.

Bowing from the waist, I said, *"Chao ban, thua on."*

Petrusky flinched a bit at my pronunciation but nodded his appreciation and glanced at Khuyen. His friend paused in his reaction while regarding me as one might a novelty brought home from a carnival. While I was being inspected, I in turn studied him.

Mandarin Khuyen was a little older than me, thin to the point of emaciation, with a skull-like face, tired eyes, oiled-down hair, a permanently down-turned mouth, and a white goatee that must have been five inches long from chin to tip. He wore a formal Oriental suit of orange tunic and trousers, with puffed shoulders and an elaborately designed chest cloth embroidered with dragons and serpents.

Khuyen smiled slightly at my linguistic effort, then dumbfounded me by replying in very good English, "How very kind of you, Commander Wake, to address me in my language, which I know is difficult for you to pronounce. It is particularly noted and pleasing that you used the formal address of 'Sire.' Thank you. With more practice, your accent will be quite good. You obviously have an ear for foreign tongues, so I hope you also have an eye for my country's well-known artistry."

I hadn't really seen any artistry in the country to that point— I'd been too busy dealing with the rather malevolent citizenry; however, I said as sincerely as I could muster, "The artistry of Annam is renowned throughout the world, Your Eminence, and I am humbled to be in the heartland of the finest practitioners of such skills. And your English, also a difficult language to learn, is absolutely perfect, sir."

Khuyen smiled, which translated into a grimace on that face, and said to Petrusky, "You are correct, my friend, Commander Wake is articulate and intelligent—a dangerous combination. I think him a poet-warrior. You have my permission to present the invitation." Then he spoke to me. "Commander Wake, this is a difficult time to visit the imperial city; however, your nationality and charm have lubricated an entrée. I hope you accept and fulfill my wishes. Please excuse my haste, but I must now depart and attend to other pressing duties."

I was trying to think of how to say thank you formally in Khuyen's lingo but only got out a simple *"Cam on"* before His Eminence glided out of the tiny room. When Petrusky returned from escorting the mandarin, I asked, "What the hell was all that about, Professor?"

"That, Peter, was a test, which you passed. I have known Khuyen for twenty years, so he trusted my portrayal of you, but he was curious to see for himself."

"What's this about an invitation?"

"We are going to stay at Khuyen's house. It is an extremely special honor and granted to very few people outside of royalty. We will go in two hours."

This was happening pretty fast for me. "And where is it that he lives that makes it so special?"

I will always remember the tone of reverence in Petrusky's reply as he stood there in the murky loom of that small lantern in a poor teacher's house.

"Within the Forbidden Purple City."

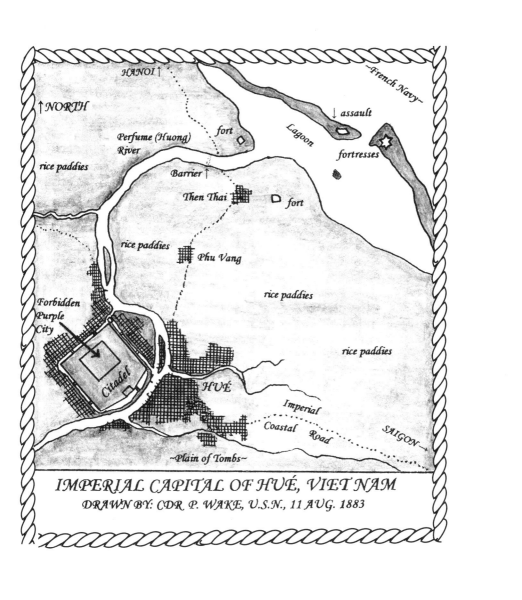

IMPERIAL CAPITAL OF HUÉ, VIET NAM
DRAWN BY: CDR. P. WAKE, U.S.N., 11 AUG. 1883

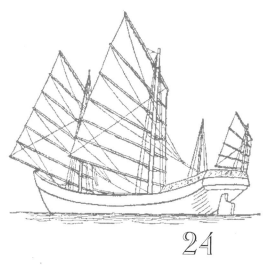

24

The Forbidden Purple City

Wednesday, 1 August 1883
Hué, Annam
Empire of Viet Nam

The professor said a carriage would come for us, so while we waited I asked him who was the current emperor of the land. He exhaled tiredly and said, "The younger brother of Tu Duc. He is named Hiep Hoa, was formerly known as Hong Dat, and was proclaimed the new emperor yesterday."

"How long do you think this one will last?"

"I do not know, Peter."

"Is he as depraved as the last one?"

"No, I think not. From what I have heard, he is far better educated and mature. He is thirty-seven years of age. In fact, he declined the throne, but the Empress Dowager Tu Du convinced him that he has a duty to his people to govern."

"The Empress Dowager?"

"Yes, she is the mother of Tu Duc, and of Hiep Hoa. She authorized the mandarins to remove Duc Duc from the throne.

The Empress Dowager is a very powerful woman."

She certainly sounded like it. I had more questions, but let it go at that. We were all too tired. Just before dawn a carriage—Mandarin Khuyen's personal transport—arrived and took us to the Perfume River, where we floated across to the north bank on a ferry barge. I smelled none of the legendary flowery scents and inquired why. The professor said the scent comes from flowers upriver in the parklands of the imperial tombs. Downriver where we were, all I smelled was sludge.

Moments later I peeked out a curtained window and saw one of the most ominous sights in my life—the thirty-five-foot-high outer walls of the Citadel of Hué. The walls were lit by great flaming torches set on the outward slope every twenty yards. The flickering light was reflected in the broad moat circling the fortification. I'd seen the walls from a distance as we approached the city the day before, but close up they were impressive, and would be very difficult to breach without large-caliber modern artillery. In the east the sky lightened, silhouetting the fortress and giving some notion as to the scale of the place. The grayish-brown battlements seemed to go on forever and I asked Petrusky just how far the city's walls went.

"The large wall you see encloses the Citadel of Hué for ten kilometers, or six of your English miles."

"My God, I had no idea. So where is this forbidden city?"

"Inside the Citadel, Peter. It is a small rectangle, with walls just as strong and tall, but only one and a half kilometers long—perhaps a little shorter than one mile. We will enter the Citadel soon through the side gate of Dong Be, then we will enter the Forbidden Purple City by the mandarins' gate at Hien Nhon." He reached over and closed the curtain. "This will be dangerous. Please keep your face hidden. Mandarin Khuyen has taken a great risk in allowing you and Mr. Rork inside the walls."

I would soon learn the truth of that statement. But right then I was mesmerized by the world I was entering, which dwarfed Norodom's palatial estate in Phnom Penh. Norodom was supposed to pay an annual nominal homage to the emperor of Viet Nam in the form of a tribute. During our ordeal on his "royal yacht" he'd mentioned to me one evening that he had visited the imperial palace in Hué, but he never described it in any detail. Now I wondered if it was because of envy.

Crossing the fifty-yard-wide moat on a bridge, we entered the outer wall through a four-story-high gate structure that was more like a palace. The huge mahogany doors were twenty feet high and a foot thick. There was much shouting and saluting by the soldiers on guard, clad in French-style uniforms and carrying the ubiquitous Gras rifles that I'd seen everywhere the French had influence and the locals had money.

Inside the Citadel, the carriage clattered through a park of extraordinary horticultural specimens, with bursts of color and scent pleasing one's eyes and nose, and the greenery manicured into all sort of shapes and designs. There were no flaring torches inside the walls—delicate red and yellow lanterns lit every wall, street, and footpath, illuminating the creative patterns of light and shadows among flowers and shrubs that branched off in all directions. The gardens were divided by rows of trees and small monuments until we started passing homes of the rich. We saw block after block of multi-storied pagodas where the wealthy elite dwelled.

In the half-light, I noted many servants scurrying about, their impassive faces revealed nothing of their thoughts. It was an unreal world compared to the squalor everywhere else in Indo-China, a fairy-tale existence, and I knew those thick walls were meant to keep out more than a foreign foe. What would the common folks think if they saw this opulence?

After traveling through the streets for perhaps ten blocks, we made an abrupt right turn and crossed a smaller moat, then the brakes squealed us to a stop when someone close by shouted, *"Bat lai—bai gio!"*

The professor scowled. "This is not good. They shouldn't be saying that."

Our driver was explaining in rapid Annamese something to

the guard who stopped us. The guard sounded angry. More voices from nearby, none of them especially respectful toward our vehicle. I dared not look out, but murmured, "What was it they said to us?"

"They ordered us to stop—now. That doesn't happen with a mandarin's carriage; it is a gross insubordination. Something may be happening in the city."

"Like what?"

"A coup, a French attack, a royal procession about to pass by. I do not know." He paused to listen. "The driver is telling them a royal lady-in-waiting is inside. If they believe him they will not dare to look inside the carriage. However, if they do not believe the driver . . ."

He paused. It infuriated me when Petrusky did that.

"What?"

"Then we are doomed."

More heated discussion ensued outside, the guards' tone becoming sarcastic. The professor sighed, then nodded. "Ah yes, it is as I suspected. A possible coup attempt among the mandarins was rumored for tonight. The guards are nervous."

I could literally feel my heart pounding against my ribcage. Rork's eyes were darting to either side, his Colt ready for action. Petrusky began silently going through the Hail Mary. I watched the door of the compartment, trying to remember the way out of the city if we had to run.

Then the driver switched tactics, laughing about something. A soldier laughed. Maybe the confrontation was defused? Then Petrusky confused me by groaning, "Oh Lord, I cannot believe he said that . . ."

"What?" I demanded again. "Finish your damned sentences, Professor."

A guard yelled off to someone else in a questioning tone. There was a reply.

"The driver said that it is not just a lady-in-waiting inside here, but a concubine of the third rank and auxiliary attendant to

The Most Treasured Lady. This is quite dangerous, Peter. Our executions will be excruciating torture for taking the name of The Most Treasured Lady in vain. The soldiers will expect at least two eunuchs to be inside here, guarding her attendant concubine."

Petrusky crossed himself and went back to the Hail Mary.

Over the years, I've discovered that in tense times of mortal peril, Rork can always be relied upon to add a bit of levity. This was precisely *not* the time for that sort of thing, of course, but that didn't stop him. He shook his head in mock disgust, then prodded my elbow and whispered, "Eunuch, eh? Hmm, I suppose ol' Sean the Mick'll get that dirty duty, too. No clippers though, lads, I'm rather attached to me boyos. I'll just fake it as a eunuch."

I *really* wish he hadn't said that.

For then one of those stupid things happened, the kind that are very embarrassing to divulge later. I had an immediate mental image of Sean Rork, the Court Eunuch. And that got me laughing. Which got Rork laughing. Which started Petrusky groaning in fright. Which, for some demented reason, Rork and I found even funnier. Outside the discussion stopped, as did my heart when I realized they must have heard us giggling. Booted steps came up to the door. A fist knocked on the wood and inquired something. Rork, deadly serious now—actually, he looked terrified—kicked Petrusky in the shin and gestured for him to answer. The professor hesitated in befuddlement, then said something petulant-sounding to the guard, followed by an order to the driver.

This was it. The silence must have only been five seconds, but it seemed an hour to me. I got ready to die for the tenth time since arriving in Indo-China.

The guard instantly snapped out a subservient reply and there was the loud squeak of hinges as large gate doors were opened. The carriage started moving and the three of us let out a collective sigh of relief.

I asked Petrusky what it was he said to the man.

"I told him the concubine was expected to be in the emperor's bed chambers precisely at the moment the day's new sun mounted the eastern wall of the Forbidden Purple City and that his delay of our passage would jeopardize that—and incur the wrath of the new emperor." The professor allowed himself a satisfied smile. "I presume I did a serviceable enough rendition of a eunuch, Peter, for the guard called ahead to clear the way for our carriage."

He turned to Rork and kicked him lightly in the shin. "Sorry to steal your show, Sean Rork, but I realized that my concubine impersonation is just not that good, so I went with the eunuch imitation instead."

Rork broke into a huge grin and howled with laughter, slapping Petrusky on the knee. "Well, *I'll be,* Commander. Seems our academic lad here has himself a sense o' mirth! Damned good on you, Professor. Bloody well done, in spades! The rum's on me, by God, when we next get to a *civilized* waterin' hole."

I sat there watching the two of them and tried to get my heart back in rhythm. Rork—there's only one of him in the world. Thank God.

Fourteen hours later, after a day of nervous repose, we sat on pillows around a low table covered with plates of rice and seafood, at a clandestine meeting in Khuyen's private study. It was a unique room, a blend of academia and subtle artistry, one that still provides an indelible memory.

Intricately formed miniature pine trees were fashioned into a tiny forest on a corner table, balancing the far corner where a vase of flowering bamboo was set in a pan filled with water and yellow lotus blossoms. The walls were paneled in oiled teak and sandalwood, the gentle scents of which combined with the jasmine incense smoking near the forest. Bookshelves lined two walls and brass racks for scrolls lined the other two sides. The whole effect of the room was meant to calm one's senses into a state of intro-spective tranquility. My senses were far too elevated by events to be tranquil, however.

I wasn't pleased. The mission of finding Strom was being sidelined with this meeting that the professor had insisted upon us attending. I agreed reluctantly to participate in his enterprise, but I was worried. Not only was this wasted time probably not going to assist me in my assignment, it was foolhardy on its own. As Petrusky reiterated before all the conspirators sat down, the penalty for what we had already done was death—slow death.

I use the word "conspirators" because it is the most applica-ble for the affair in which Rork and I found ourselves. Everything we were doing was not only a violation of our standing naval orders to remain neutral in foreign internal conflicts, it was an active endeavor to thwart the policies of a sovereign Oriental potentate and of a powerful European nation. The gathering had the ostensible goal of avoiding the impending bloodshed, of course, but the problem was that certain factions within the imperial household could consider this a *de facto* mutiny against the standing policies of their government in time of war. Rork and I would be considered spies—for the French, of all people.

Actually, my prime motive in attending was the impression I had that one or more of these men were the key to finding Strom. Once I'd found him and gotten Rork and me out of there, the whole place could be filled with gore and anarchy for all I cared.

Besides the three in my own party, there were three other conspirators at the table—Mandarin Nguyen Khuyen; Mr. Bui Vien, a diplomatic emissary of the court; and His Eminence Marie-Antoine-Louis Caspar, Catholic Bishop of Annam, whose youthful appearance was no illusion—the man was two years younger than me.

Looking around at the faces—Mandarin Khuyen's cadaver-ously sad eyes, Bui Vien's trimmed French-style goatee and side-burns, Petrusky's bespectacled intellectuality, Bishop Caspar's intense attention—I realized that they had pledged their lives to this. Once their effort became generally known, they weren't going to be able to leave the country. Their options had just run out.

Servants padded into the room and deftly removed everything but our cups of rice wine from the table. When they had cleared the room, Khuyen spread his hands and said, "My friends, thank you for coming. I suggest that we speak in the one language common to us all—English—and that we dispense with ponderous formalities. I will begin by summarizing the situation, since some of you may not be familiar with the latest events."

He stood, his frame trembling. "But first, let me say this: we are at a moment of history that will shape this country for the next ten generations or more. Our failure will be catastrophic and reach far beyond the boundaries of this land. Mistakes in perception and judgment have been made by all sides. My esteemed friends, as I speak, well-intentioned men of power are reacting to this situation by following their traditional instincts. Those instincts will lead us all down a path of no return."

He paused to take a shaky breath, then looked each of us in the eye.

"Within days, thousands of Frenchmen and Vietnamese will die in battle, France and China will be at war, blood will flow across the continent of Asia, and our independent Empire of Viet Nam will cease to exist."

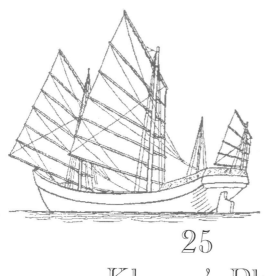

25

Khuyen's Plan

Thursday, 2 August 1883
Inside the Forbidden Purple City
Hué, Annam
Empire of Viet Nam

Khuyen certainly got us riveted with that bold statement. The mandarin must have had many diverse sources of intelligence, for he proceeded to support his prophecy with a detailed recitation of what was happening in Hué, Hanoi, Saigon, China, and the South China Sea. Every man in the room leaned forward to see and hear as Khuyen unrolled a map of Asia across the table.

"Five months ago the French reinforced Hanoi and the Tonking region with soldiers under Rivière. Emperor Tu Duc felt this a violation of his sovereignty and various treaties with France, so he appealed to his superior sovereign, the emperor of China, for support."

Khuyen turned aside to Rork and me. "My American friends, you may not know our relationship with China or that the emperor of Viet Nam is a nominal vassal of the emperor of China, who is lord over all of Asia. Just as the king of Cambodia is a nominal vassal of the emperor of Viet Nam, we bow to the north. The Chinese emperor is only twelve years old and in the care of regents—but the real decisions are in the hands of the wily Empress-Dowager of China, Tzu Hsi. She is very cunning and for thirty years has been constantly vying the Europeans off against each other to keep herself, and now her youngest son, in power in Beijing.

"She realized the French were weak in northern Indo-China and authorized support to Tu Duc. Fifty thousand Chinese soldiers were sent to reinforce the hundred thousand in Tonking already. Their mission? To foment confusion and intimidate the French by their numbers and their ferocity."

Having filled the Americans in on who was who in China, Khuyen returned to the general subject. Pointing to the map, he continued.

"Meanwhile, Emperor Tu Duc paid for Chinese Black Flag mercenaries—who are former Chinese imperial soldiers and now nothing more than bandits—to surround the French and force them out. Some of our Vietnamese imperial troops assisted them. The French counterattacked and met heavy opposition. Out of frustration Rivière hanged fifty Chinese Black Flag bandits he had captured, along with many Vietnamese prisoners. That solidified the resolve against the French.

"In May, the Chinese-Vietnamese forces ambushed Rivière at a bridge outside of Hanoi, killing him and fifty of his men. That was followed by attacks on the French everywhere. The French pulled back into Hai Phong on the coast. They had a thousand men—surrounded by almost two hundred thousand. The Chinese and Emperor Tu Duc thought the French would leave. That was a major error in judgment, for they did not.

"Instead, they moved nine thousand reinforcements from overseas into Tonking to recapture the region. Those soldiers have not made much progress. Now sixteen thousand more French soldiers under General Bouet, and a fleet of warships under Admiral Courbet, are approaching Hué from the sea. We expect them here at any day to reinforce the warships already blockading the coast. When they arrive, there will be an attack on Hué and general war will erupt everywhere."

I was impressed with his knowledge. That naval information was significant. I knew that the French squadron in the area, known as the Naval Division of Tonking, had eight modern ships, from large cruisers to torpedo boats—more than enough to deal with any indigenous regional warships or fortresses in the region. But that they were being reinforced even further meant they were planning war with China who, unlike Cambodia or Viet Nam, had the ability to put up a real naval fight.

I thought about the French in Tonking. A thousand men against two hundred thousand? With *millions* more available, not far away. The thought in my mind was why would anyone in Paris want this place to begin with? Was the trade on the Red River up into China that important?

But the imperative point for me was how any of this affected Strom's location, or his life. Petrusky had cautioned me earlier not to interrupt with questions until the Mandarin Nguyen Khuyen had finished his talk. I swallowed my frustration and waited as Khuyen sipped from his cup, then began once more.

"The Chinese now have their honor at stake. So do the French. So did Emperor Tu Duc. The Chinese asked for American mediation months ago, which has been given, but nothing has resulted, for Emperor Tu Duc died in July and Duc Duc, a regrettable choice, was installed on the throne. That was when the French military authorities, seeing our void of leadership, decided to take advantage and send overwhelming forces to this region. They had no incentive to negotiate, and pride dictated they revenge Rivière's death. The French want blood, we Vietnamese want our sovereignty, and the Chinese want to save face and get out."

I looked at the bishop, who'd been silent so far. "And what does the Church want, Your Eminence?"

He held up a hand and looked at the ceiling, then back at me. "Something quite uncomplicated, my son—we want *peace.*

There is no reason to have a war."

"That's the most uncomplicated thing I've heard since I arrived in Indo-China, sir."

Bishop Caspar laughed. "I know what you mean, my son. The Church stands ready to do whatever we can to prevent this coming bloodshed."

"Even against the French government?" I asked.

He nodded. "I love France, but I love all humanity even more. Let us try to stop this from happening."

Khuyen sighed and put a hand on the bishop's shoulder. "That is what we all want, my friend. However, the momentum of events is against us. And not only will there be more bloodshed than has already occurred up in Tonking, but it appears that unless the Chinese want to engage in total war in our defense, the French army will overrun us easily, within days. My country will fight, and our soldiers will die, but the ultimate outcome is not in doubt.

"Fortunately, there is some good news. Our leadership crisis is solved. The imperial Council of Regents and the Mandarin Ministers of State have prevailed upon our own most gracious Empress-Dowager Tu Du to approve a new emperor. It is Hiep Hoa, a wise and just man. He is not as anti-Christian as Tu Duc, and is seen as far more decisive than Duc Duc. He ascended the Dragon Throne two days ago."

"What about the British or Americans?" asked Bishop Caspar.

Khuyen shook his head. "The British have their hands full in China and want no part of this. And what of the American influence? Not only was the famous and respected Mr. John Russell Young trying to bring all parties together in Beijing, but the United States sent a special envoy to Viet Nam, a Mr. Beauregard Strom, their new Chief Minister. He was to coordinate efforts with Mr. Young in China and try to end this madness. Those efforts have failed."

What? Rork and I perked up. Khuyen noticed and gave us a ghastly smile.

"You have been told, Commander, that he is in the north, in Tonking. That is not correct. He was there in May and June, but he has been here for the last month."

I was thunderstruck. "Here?"

"Yes, outside the Forbidden Purple City, but inside the Citadel. Mr. Bui here spoke with him when he first arrived."

Bui nodded. This was absurd—something was very wrong. "Is he all right? Why hasn't he communicated with anyone? We thought he was up in Tonking, dead or taken prisoner by the Black Flags."

No one answered. An awkward look came over Bui's face and I got wary. "He's alive, right? And *not* a prisoner?"

Khuyen raised his eyebrows and pursed his lips. "Yes, Mr. Strom is alive, but the rest of it is quite discomforting for us, Commander. I shall request Mr. Bui to explain, since he has the most knowledge of the matter."

"Chief Minister Strom is alive and very well cared for, Commander. After his arrival, he met Emperor Tu Duc and offered his services to mediate the growing conflict. That was accepted and he traveled to Tonking, but the emperor died shortly thereafter. The peace efforts broke down in Tonking and Mr. Strom was able to return here to the capital before chaos closed Hanoi. The French High Commissioner, Dr. Francois Jules Harmand, invited Mr. Strom to stay in Hué and assigned one of his senior staff to host Mr. Strom.

"The staff member is a man with whom I believe you are acquainted—a Monsieur Maurice Blundell, formerly of the colonial administration in Cochin and recently an advisor to King Norodom in Cambodia. Mr. Blundell and his friend Monsieur Jean Dupuis arrived here a month ago, just before Mr. Strom arrived back from Tonking. Dupuis has gone on to Tonking by a back route; Blundell stayed here."

Blundell—here? Rork's jaw tightened. Bui gave us an inquiring look.

"You know him, yes?"

"Oh yes, I know Blundell only too well," I replied. "Look, why all the hemming and hawing here? Why hasn't Strom let us know he's all right? I want to see Beauregard Strom right now."

Bui wagged his head. "Ah, that will not be possible, for Blundell will allow none of *us* to see him. We have informants among the servants who tell us that Mr. Strom thinks his telegram messages have gone out of Hué to his office in Saigon, but in actual fact, Blundell has them intercepted before they get to the telegraph station. He has also provided false ones in reply, to keep Mr. Strom calm. Blundell also told Mr. Strom it is too dangerous for him to leave Hué, due to the unrest, so the gentleman stays there, comfortably ignorant of the real situation and that he has been incommunicado all this time. We do not know if the High Commissioner is involved, but think not, by all indications."

"But that's kidnapping! And it doesn't make any sense."

"Ah, but Mr. Strom does not think he is kidnapped. He thinks he is a guest, a very-well-taken-care-of guest. Blundell merely has to create the illusion that Mr. Strom is in communication and the pretense can continue until the French military arrives."

"Why the hell would Blundell take the chance to do all this? Strom's an *American diplomat,* for God's sake!"

"We are not absolutely certain of his motives, but we think it is because he is concerned about the Americans getting involved and mediating a peaceful end to the crisis. You Americans have no real commerce here, no stake in the outcome. You want to help avoid a war. The Vietnamese want to avoid a war. That is not what the French government wants at this point, though."

I glanced at Bishop Caspar. He quietly indicated agreement.

Everyone in the room agreed, but it didn't make sense to me. "I still don't understand, Mr. Bui."

"That is because you are thinking with an honorable man's mind, Commander. Please place yourself in Blundell's position.

Once the heavy French military forces get here, they will immediately crush us completely and finally have the excuse to take over everything in what is left of our country. It is the domination they have tried to obtain through attrition for the last forty years."

Petrusky leaned over and expanded Bui's point. "The economic consequences of a total takeover are enormous, Peter. We are an area rich in resources, much of which goes into the imperial treasury, not so far from where we sit. If the French take absolute control of Annam and Tonking, as they did in Cochin, some of them will become very wealthy. Blundell has private investments in the rubber, sugar cane, and copra plantations. Through his friend d'Abain, he has an interest in the opium trade. Through his friend Dupuis, he has a percentage of the merchant trade with China along the Red River in Tonking.

"He already makes money, now he stands to make a fortune—really several fortunes. And all he has to do is make sure there is no mediated settlement that preserves imperial authority over the internal affairs of Viet Nam. To do that, he merely has to keep Mr. Strom ignorant for a few days more. Once the French military has subjugated the city, it doesn't matter if Strom finds out—he will have no mediation job left to do."

The professor nodded. "Yes, it will be embarrassing to the French government if Blundell's plot becomes known, but they can deplore it as the action of a malcontent and the ensuing occupation will be a *fait accompli*. Or, like Blundell's plan for you and Rork, if Mr. Strom protests too much he could meet with a deplorable death, most certainly accidental, of course. Or perhaps at the hands of bandits."

If true—and it was appearing more plausible by the minute—it was an incredibly nervy scheme on Blundell's part. "*Damn*," I blurted out. "This is incredible. And you're reasonably sure the French high commissioner's not in on all this with Blundell?"

Khuyen answered that. "We *think* not. He hasn't been here

in Indo-China as long as Blundell and isn't known to have the same commercial investments as Blundell. We think Blundell is . . . *c'est tromper, en francais* . . . how do you say it in English? To deceive? He is deceiving his superiors as well as Mr. Strom. It is my opinion that Commissioner Harmand probably assumes that Mr. Strom is, like most diplomats, merely content to *try* to achieve his peace mission, but not to particularly exert himself or ask many questions."

I knew Beauregard Strom, and knew he wasn't the sort that refused to "exert" himself. Strom, who'd fought the American Civil War in a Louisiana infantry regiment, would be hopping mad when he found out he'd been hoodwinked. He was a large, powerful man, too.

Bui ignored Khuyen's remark about diplomats and added, "You see, Commander, in the current situation, the French diplomats do not have to *do* anything, just merely do *nothing* and stall for time, a few days. Time is on their side."

"And what does your emperor think of all this?" I asked Khuyen.

He shook his head. "The emperor probably does not know, either. Until three days ago, he was a member of the nobility who lived in a comfortable villa in the countryside, well outside the Forbidden Purple City. None of this is his doing; he just ascended the throne. I doubt he has even met any of the French delegation yet."

The more I heard, the angrier I was getting. The whole damn thing was outrageous. And I couldn't believe these people were allowing this to drag on. "Thank you for this information, gentlemen. I'm going to Blundell's place right now. Where is it?"

Bui shook his head. "We know he is at the French legation compound, but do not know precisely where he is inside. Our informants say Mr. Strom is in the part that has only French servants. Our people are not allowed inside that area."

Bishop Caspar said, "Even we in the clergy are allowed only in the public social areas. I fear we are a bit suspect among some of the government officials. They think us too liberal and pro-Vietnamese, so we also are not allowed in that most secure area."

He was about to prattle on some more, but the insanity of the whole thing had gotten my blood heated up to the point where I was tired of listening. It was time to end this charade. "Well, Rork and I will damn well be allowed in there, or somebody's going to die stopping us! I'm not putting up with this one minute longer."

I felt Rork's hand on my shoulder. "Perhaps we should listen a bit more, sir."

"No, Rork. I'm tired of listening and not doing. Let's get Strom and get the hell out of here."

"Aye, sir. That's just my point. This is a very strange place an' I don't fancy traipsin' around in the dark without a good plan. I'm rememberin' the mess o' a time we had gettin' *in* this place, an' I think we'll have a hellova time tryin' to get *out* if we're on the run. Mr. Strom's not in danger, sir. No need to rush."

I'm usually the one who has to calm *him* down, but I had to admit Rork made sense. I blew out a long breath and decided to forgo the curse on my lips. Instead, I said, "Very well, Rork, I'll slow down. So, are there any ideas among you gentlemen?"

Khuyen smiled at Rork. "Thank you, Mr. Rork. I understand your annoyance at all this, Commander, but yes, I do have an idea. One that will fulfill your assignment of making sure Mr. Strom is not in danger and telling him what is occurring—and that will also fulfill my wishes that this matter be resolved without war, in a way that will preserve our independence."

"How?"

"Quite simple, really. We do not go in search of Mr. Strom—we have Mr. Strom brought to us. To be more specific, to a diplomatic reception hosted by the new emperor. No one has seen Mr. Strom outside the French compound for weeks, but he must respond to a royal invitation from the emperor to attend a reception. And that is where Commander Wake will meet his countryman."

Khuyen smiled at his own brilliance. "And our aspiration of

achieving peace can also be met, for Emperor Hiep Hoa must hear the truth, so that he may make a wise decision. But he must hear the truth from a credible party. It should be a neutral professional warrior—that would be *you*, Commander Wake—who will explain that he cannot vanquish the foreigners and that, therefore, it is best not to fight the French military and thereby give them the excuse to annihilate the imperial authority in Viet Nam. The mandarins around him now are urging battle, something they know little or nothing about. The emperor must hear the truth that mediation is the best way to resolve this dilemma, and hear it from a man he can trust.

"A reception is the best way, no, the *only* way, to further the goals—" he gestured around the room, "—of everyone here."

"What a wonderful idea," said the bishop. "Avert a war with a party."

"All right," I said, wondering about the bishop's sanity but too mentally fatigued to care much. "I agree. When is the reception?"

"No reception is planned right now, but Mr. Bui and I will see to that." Khuyen's brow furrowed. "It must be done with finesse, for Mr. Bui and I are currently not favored within the court and this could be viewed by some as a conspiracy to circumvent the protocols of the court—and the official policies of the emperor. We are seen as tainted by our friendships with Christians and the West in general. The Confucian mandarins of the imperial court who want to isolate the empire are wary of us.

"But do not despair, there are things we can do. I have a protégé in the office of protocol who can arrange some special invitations and keep them confidential. It will take two or three days to implement this plan. In the meantime, no one must know that Commander Wake and Mr. Rork are within the Forbidden Purple City. They will stay inside this house, guarded by my servants. Their invitations will be held in secret until that evening. If Blundell should find out, he may be tempted to do something drastic that we could not prevent. An accidental death might befall Mr. Strom and you two naval men."

Khuyen had been standing the whole time. Now he sat down, clearly exhausted, but added one last thing. "And it will be quite something when Blundell sees our two newest American guests at the reception. If we go about this carefully, he will not know until after you meet and brief Mr. Strom, and then the emperor. Then, if this plan succeeds, Blundell will be too late, for war will have been averted. At that point, Blundell will be exposed."

Rork chuckled at that. It was an evil little chuckle.

Khuyen asked for questions and got none. As we all stood to say our goodbyes, Bishop Caspar took me aside.

"Professor Petrusky has been a valuable asset to you, has he not?"

I remembered my initial doubts about the professor, which had been more than allayed. "He has been beyond value, sir. I understand I have the Church to thank for his presence. I fear it was far more dangerous than either of us imagined at first."

Caspar gave a little shrug. "We arranged a hiatus from the college for him. It was deemed important. And yes, it did turn out to be full of mortal peril, but you had a powerful force on your side, my son. God has smiled upon your endeavor—blessed are the peacemakers, remember? It appears the decision to assist you was a correct one."

"And whom can I thank for that decision, sir?"

"I regret I am not at liberty to say. But I will say this—I will be sure to let your friend in Rome know of your appreciation."

He turned to go, then stopped. "It is interesting, is it not, my son, that the paths of so diverse a selection of men can meet for such a noble purpose, in so unlikely a place as this? Ponder the complexity of it. Truly, it is the work of God. I will pray for Mandarin Khuyen's plan to have a successful conclusion."

And then he was gone, to be smuggled out of the Forbidden Purple City and back across the river to his church. I thought then it might be the last time I'd see Bishop Caspar, but like so many other times in Southeast Asia, I was wrong. Once everyone else left, the professor, Rork, and I lay down on our cots, each of our minds contemplating the immediate future and what it held. It took me a long time to get to sleep.

I remember that for some reason, sitting there around that table with my co-conspirators that evening, Mandarin Khuyen's proposal seemed like a logical plan, the best idea in a bad situation. But three months later, when I tried to explain our actions to President Arthur at the White House, it sure did sound like the dumbest idea I'd ever heard. At the time, in Khuyen's study, I had no idea what the consequences would be. They have weighed heavily on me ever since.

26
The Gong

Tuesday, 14 August 1883
Inside the Forbidden Purple City
Hué, Annam
Empire of Viet Nam

By now I should have known that upon being given an estimated time frame of when something might happen in Asia, one must at a minimum double it to approach accuracy. In this case, tripling the estimate would be closer to the mark. It didn't take two or three days for Khuyen and Bui to set up the reception—it took nine days, during which time Rork and I dutifully hid out in our comfortable prison. And the irony didn't escape me that Strom was in a similar condition close by us, he just didn't know it.

The delay was caused by the current Celestial Son of Heaven. Hiep Hoa suddenly found himself in a very lonely position as emperor confronted with imminent war. It seemed that the new emperor was in need of some martial ardor after ascending the Dragon Throne. Having been briefed by the senior mandarins about the enthusiasm of his army, he wanted to join the lads for a while, possibly to absorb a little *esprit pour la guerre* himself. So off he went on maneuvers with the soldiers to soak up some of that fervor and perhaps boost morale among the boys actually carrying the rifles. Or at least, that is what he thought he was doing.

I have been in the field with soldiers in battle, and Khuyen's description of the emperor's excursion smacked more of an elegant picnic outing of dilettantes than a serious inspection of the imperial guard regiments' professional abilities and an opportunity to increase their *élan*. In any event, he soon tired of roughing it with his household entourage of five hundred courtiers and minions and departed the bivouac of the Fourth Guards Regiment, returning to his palace in the Forbidden Purple City on the eleventh of August.

There he'd received the request of Mandarin Khuyen for a reception and given his approval for a gathering in the throne hall of the Can Chanh Palace on Tuesday, the fourteenth of August. Due to the convoluted nature of his ascension, Hiep Hoa hadn't had his coronation gala yet, so the reception would be the first chance for foreigners and lesser-ranked mandarins and ministry officials to see the empire's newest sovereign. This would be a simple gathering. The big gala would be held later.

No wonder it took so long to plan and implement, I thought as I entered the palace. The reception was "an informal event" without the full royal regalia of office, but even then, it made Norodom's soirée look sophomoric in comparison.

Rork was spending the evening at a side door with Khuyen's servants. He'd picked up a smattering of Annamese, and between that and his gregarious nature could get along with basic communications—and gather intelligence from the proverbial "lower deck people" as well. Petrusky was by my side in the middle of it all, both of us in our best attire, he in a borrowed black tie dinner suit and me in my dress uniform.

In all candor, I must admit that I have, as do many of my brother naval officers, a hearty dislike of wearing that cumbersome dress uniform, which was apparently designed as a punishment centuries ago by our predecessors in the Royal Navy—especially so in the debilitating atmosphere of August in the tropics. Nonetheless, perspiring heavily the whole way, I got myself into the rig and made a proper entrance and show of decorum.

An American naval officer wasn't expected—the invitation arranged by Khuyen had my name but omitted rank, service, and nationality—and I could see my appearance was stirring no small reaction. True to Khuyen's plan, I continued on nonchalantly touring the room and ignoring the stares and murmured words, which mainly centered on the shiny things decorating my chest. Earlier, I'd debated whether to wear my French medal and finally decided I would—there would be French officials there and my *Chevalier* of the *Légion d'Honneur* always impressed that type.

The Cam Chanh Palace pagoda was fully decked out for the occasion, with red and yellow lanterns everywhere, gold gilt trim on everything from the spittoons to the ashtrays, and red and gold tapestries and tiles covering the walls and floors. A smoky kind of incense—sandalwood, according to the professor—hung in the air. The main hall was probably over a hundred yards long and fifty wide, in the center of which sat the famed Golden Dragon Throne of the Nguyen Dynasty, under a canopy of golden silk.

To the rhythm of gongs and drums, hundreds of court mandarins—including Mandarin Nguyen Khuyen—were all done up in their best gold-embroidered and -brocaded gowns, parading in from the side palace. Solemn as cardinals and loving every minute of the attention, their procession moved clockwise around the hall to the awe and bows of the hushed audience. They would look silly in Washington and even London, but here they lorded it over the lesser ranks with a feudal power unknown in modern Western society. Woe be it to a subordinate who offended or displeased, even unintentionally, a mandarin of the upper class. Come to think of it, they did remind me of several admirals I've known over the years.

The entire effect was far more opulent and Oriental than Norodom's palace, which was more open in architecture and more Indo than Sino in style. My friend Norodom's displays were simplistic when measured against his fellow monarch in Hué. In Hiep Hoa's bastion, the overwhelming influence of China and Confucius was noticeable in every overt and subtle sense. Even the language spoken by the courtiers among themselves was classical Mandarin Chinese.

With more than a trace of empathy, Petrusky informed me there was an added intention and benefit to the Chinese look of the place—it reminded the French leadership that hundreds of thousands of Chinese troops were poised to help out their imperial friend to the south. I thought that a bit overstated and countered that I doubted if any of the young conscripted Chinese troops doing the *fighting* cared a wit about Hiep Hoa, considered him a friend, or even knew his name. I learned long ago that military *quality* makes up a lot for cannon-fodder quantity.

The emperor hadn't arrived yet, and neither had Strom or Blundell, but the French authorities had. Their smiling presence symbolized the peculiar environment in Hué. Total war between France and Viet Nam was expected literally at any day, its ominous cloud of death and destruction permeating every conversation and thought in the massive room, yet both official parties acted as if nothing untoward was happening. The Vietnamese and their adversaries laughed and toasted in French with champagne and wine provided by the French—*naturellement*—while discussing the wet weather lately. I found it absolutely insane.

Petrusky told me about each of the Frenchmen as they came into view at the main entrance. There was High Commissioner Dr. Francois Jules Harmand, a former French navy physician and the senior French civil authority. A tall athletic figure, the thirty-nine-year-old Harmand's close-cut hair, firm jaw, and serious eyes gave the immediate impression of a man who was no one's fool. I thought of Blundell and whether he had in fact duped this man. If he had, the consequences for Blundell of an exposé would be unpleasant. If, however, Harmand was in on the scheme to keep Strom ignorant and incommunicado, then my problems grew far more formidable.

Next was forlorn-faced Louis Eugène Palastre de Champeaux, age thirty-three and, until recently, the senior man in Tonking. Now that the military had taken over that area, Champeaux was relegated to Hué, which also was getting rather dicey as far as the near future was concerned. Champeaux'd had a rough time of it over the last couple of years—captured by the Black Flag rebels a year earlier and finally released, harassed in Hanoi for the last six months and almost captured again, and now chased out of his assignment by everything falling apart. No wonder he looked haggard.

After Champeaux was Pierre Rheinart, a career colonial administrator in his middle forties and a ten-year veteran in Indo-China. The knowing eyes set deep in his congenial countenance indicated a man who had seen much and was fazed by little. The professor said Rheinart was well-known and respected at the imperial court. I marked him as a man to make the acquaintance of that evening, with the view that he might be of some assistance should I have to organize a hasty exit for my little group, hopefully to soon include Beauregard Strom.

Petrusky pointed out a raft of tense French merchants that followed the leadership, all staying quite literally close to the coattails of Harmand and Champeaux. Jules Ruff was the virile twenty-nine-year-old founder of the Messageries Fluviales de Cochin-Chine riverboat fleet—main competitors of the *Tonle Queen*—and current organizer of a railroad venture to link Saigon and Mytho. He walked like a soldier and I wondered if he'd had military experience. Many of the colonials did, and I guessed he might have occasion to use it when war came—Ruff certainly stood to lose a lot if the Asians successfully threw off the French yoke.

Auguste Pavrie looked very much like one of the French renegades on the Mekong. He was in his sixties, with hard eyes and raw-boned cheeks, his graying beard long and unkempt, wearing a suit that hadn't seen an iron in decades. Pavrie was obviously out of place in the genteel surroundings, but more importantly, he appeared not to care. Petrusky said he was an explorer, military scout, minor colonial authority, and spoke most of the languages in the region. Then the professor paused, his eyes on mine.

"In addition, Monsieur Pavrie is owner of the telegraph company that has lines across Indo-China."

That had interesting possibilities. "As in the India rubber versus gutta percha dispute for insulation on telegraph lines under water?"

"Yes, Peter. Pavrie is a friend of the rubber planters across Annam and Cochin. Also a close friend of Blundell. I would think he knows about Blundell's effort to kill you. Perhaps he is involved in it. Be careful around him, he might try to collect some money with your head."

"From what I understand, he'll have to get in line."

"You jest, Peter, but these are dangerous men."

Before I could reply, the professor said, "Uh-oh, look who is entering now. It is our old friends Dupuis and Blundell, no?"

Dupuis went right to the bar table, but Blundell was hanging back, saying hello to Pavrie, then talking to someone obscured by the crowd. I caught a glimpse of the third person from behind, a massive man with gray hair standing at least eight inches above the surrounding Vietnamese. Evidently Blundell was conveying a joke, miming with his hands. The man with him was laughing. I could hear it from eighty feet across the room and recognized it instantly. Glancing around his companion's shoulder toward me, Blundell's expression went from jollity to surprise to terror in seconds. The large man turned around to see what had frightened Blundell and I was able to see him clearly.

Beauregard Strom—the man I'd come to find.

Strom and I went back nine years, to my assignment as flag lieutenant to the admiral commanding the United States Navy's European Squadron operating in the Mediterranean. He'd been the American consul at Genoa in 1874 and initially we'd had a somewhat adversarial relationship. Many in his profession thought naval officers were a bit too uncouth. Like most naval officers, I detested the state department crowd as being too effete, commonly known in navy circles as "the diplos" or "the striped-pants set."

But I was wrong about him. Strom was different from most others in his line of work—he'd been a warrior in that infantry regiment. He knew war and the military profession. Once we gauged each other and had readjusted our first impressions, I learned quite a bit from him. It took me about a week to realize that the diplomatic jungle of Europe was every bit as dangerous as the military world, and frequently salted with incidents that had consequences far more wide-reaching.

As a Venezuelan diplomatic friend once elucidated to me, "Peter, the captain of a warship can kill hundreds of men with one broadside. But a diplomat can kill hundreds of *thousands* with the war he starts while sipping champagne and nibbling caviar."

So Strom and I became grudging friends, then close allies as he taught me the subtleties of international relations in that snake pit of intrigue—Europe. When I nearly came to grief in Italy because of a French woman who had entered my life, Strom first chastised me, then made sure I was extricated from any public harm. Later, when I returned from a hazardous mission in Africa—to rescue that very same lady, with her husband along-side me, no less—it was Strom who had arranged a tremendous celebration for my award of France's Legion of Honor. Since then, we had been in annual correspondence and occasionally dinner companions when he and his charming wife Christine were in Washington. I'd last seen him three years earlier, over dinner at Billy Ebbitt's in Washington. Both our wives were with us.

Linda wore that green satin dress that I loved to see her in . . .

My mind jerked from the past to the present, where events were developing swiftly. In Khuyen's plan, Petrusky and I would remain in the background of the crowd, spot Strom first, and quietly get him away from the French into a side room, where we could alert him to what Blundell and company had been up to. That plan fell apart right about then, for my nemesis had noticed me first.

Strom, the unwitting victim, stood there dumbfounded, staring at me. Then he grinned and raised a hand in greeting, waving to get my attention. Blundell glared at me and backed away to Pavrie. Seconds later I saw him quickly walking toward Dupuis at the bar, elbowing people out of the way. A subtle contact was now spoiled, so I made haste toward Strom. Petrusky followed right behind me through the densely packed people, calling out *"excusez-nous"* to the French guests.

The scene got even more exciting when I was still ten paces away from Strom. He is a big man and abruptly bellowed out, "Good God, it's Peter Wake, as I live and breathe!"

Well, that got the attention of everyone within a hundred feet and dashed Khuyen's plan completely to hell. Out of the corner of my right eye I saw Pavrie circling around behind me. Petrusky saw him too, and quietly warned me. Just as I arrived at Strom, none other than Commissioner Harmand walked over and said peevishly, "Beauregard, my dear friend, you did not tell me your navy was visiting."

"I didn't know! But I'm glad to see Commander Wake anytime. Peter, why are you here?"

The whole thing would've been funny if we'd been in a civilized place—but we weren't, and I was already worried about what Blundell and company were up to. And how exactly does one tell a prominent man he's been the victim of a Machiavellian scheme, in effect kidnapped, even though he probably blissfully enjoyed every minute of it?

No, this was not the time to be diplomatic, so I leaned close and whispered, "I've been sent to *rescue* you, Beau. You're in danger. We need to talk in private—right now."

To be fair to my friend Strom, my unexpected appearance and now my startling comment would be hard for anyone to fathom promptly, but he reacted with a dramatic double-take, his jaw dropping open. While the senior diplomatic representative of the United States of America recovered from his shock, the French reacted faster, and not too nicely, I might add. Ruff and Pavrie stood on either side of me, both looking like they wanted to bodily throw me out of the room. In this desperate moment, I noticed that none of *them* had the Legion of Honor, so I puffed out my chest in an effort to deter anything too violent from being started.

Ruff asked in good English, "You were that American on MacTaggert's boat on the Mekong, were you not?"

At the same time Pavrie, who Petrusky had told me earlier spoke a little English, inquired rudely in French why I was there, *"Pourquoi êtes-vous ici?"*

Champeaux added in a sad tone, "Have you news from Hanoi? Was your squadron there?"

Harmand, meanwhile, was waiting for his formal introduction to this foreign naval officer who suddenly showed up in the middle of a French-dominated region, just as they were about to elevate that domination to a new level. He clearly was not amused by Strom's breech of diplomatic courtesy.

Strom had finally gotten back on course, however, and reverted to his usual charming self. With a beaming smile he intoned a wonderful introduction in French, albeit couched in his Louisiana Creole accent, which I was glad to see made Harmand cringe, just a little. *"Est-ce que, messieurs, je peux vous présenter le Lieutenant Commandant Peter Wake, de la Marine des Etats-Unis?"*

I looked at the high commissioner and did my bit with, *"Enchanté, Votre Excellence,"* followed by my best imitation of a curt European bow, without clicked heels, of course. Strom taught me back in seventy-four to never click my heels at a Frenchman—it reminded them too much of the Franco-Prussian War, when the Germans overran them back in seventy.

Harmand was equally polished in his smiling reply, though his eyes were less than kind as they bored into me. *"Bienvenu au l'Indochine, Commandant."* Then he switched back into British-accented English. "And what may we honor as the reason for this most unusual but welcome visit by a naval officer of America, who is also a *Chevalier* of the *Légion d'Honneur?"*

That was neatly done, I thought. Strom was eyeing me just as intently, obviously wondering the same thing. I replied with as straight a face as I could muster, "I am but a courier, Your Excellency, taking a message to Chief Minister Strom. I have no ship or squadron here."

The veracity of my courier story had probably been long expired for the French authorities, but it was the only thing I could think of at the moment, so I continued with it, nodding to Strom. "And now I must beg the forgiveness of you gentlemen, for I am duty-bound to pass along the communiqué to my superior."

Harmand looked perturbed at that absence of good manners and Pavrie muttered something dark in French, but that wasn't what worried me the most. No, the immediate threat was Blundell, who was waving to Strom and beckoning impatiently for him to come to the champagne bar. Needless to say, Strom did not know anything yet of Blundell's scheme, and my friend was pleasantly gesturing back—Beauregard did love good French champagne.

I had to think fast, get him away from these Frenchmen, warn him of the plot against him, and make arrangements for an exit from Hué. But how? Right then the victim of the crime was about to go have a drink with the perpetrator.

That was when I was saved by the largest, loudest gong I've ever heard.

The gong—all seven feet of it—boomed out three times, signaling the grand entrance of the man everyone was there to see.

Petrusky translated the major-domo's announcement: "*The Revered Hiep Hoa, His Royal Highness, King of Annam, Emperor of Annam, Cochin, and Tonking—of all the people of Viet Nam, Sixth of the Nguyen Dynasty of Celestial Sons of Heaven, Sovereign of the Golden Dragon Throne, and Beloved Royal Vassal of the Emperor of All Lands under Heaven in the Middle Kingdom of Earth.*" The last referred to the Chinese emperor, another reminder for the foreign guests.

All heads turned to the royal entranceway, where a procession of the highest-ranked mandarins, along with senior eunuchs, imperial guards, and court servants, led a guard of honor carrying a palanquin, atop which sat His Royal Highness. At the same time as the mesmerized audience was taking all that in, a golden brocaded arm reached around Strom and tugged at my sleeve—Mandarin Khuyen. He nodded to the wall behind us and started off in that direction.

It only took seconds, but Harmand and the rest of the French, even Pavrie and Ruff, were all watching their newest imperial opponent, Hiep Hoa, enter the hall and missed it. Petrusky caught the gesture, however, and headed that way while I leaned past Harmand and whispered casually to Strom, *"Porto Fino."*

He understood the inference. Porto Fino was the site of a seaside castle in Italy where I once almost made a huge mistake in my life, but was saved by a timely warning, which enabled me to leave with my honor intact. Strom had been at that castle that night and knew the story.

Without comment or question, he sidled through the gathered assembly and met us by a huge red tapestry against the northern wall. Khuyen glanced around and slipped behind the tapestry, followed by the professor, Strom, and me. I glanced back at the French—they were still watching the emperor like hawks, but Blundell was nowhere in sight.

Suddenly a large form came around the curtain, startling me

out of my wits. It was Rork. "Saw ye duckin' behind this big ol' wall rug in a wee hurry, sir, an' thought maybe an extra hand might be needed."

"We need all the help we can get, Rork. The plan just fell apart. Blundell spotted us and we're getting Strom out of here fast."

"Aye, where to, sir?"

"Hell if I know, Sean. Just follow the mandarin."

By the time we got to where others were standing behind the tapestry, Khuyen had a mahogany panel opened in the wall and was stepping into a dark passageway. As the imperial subjects of Hiep Hoa began to kowtow in the throne hall, literally bending down to the floor in subservience to their new emperor, my little band slipped away down that murky corridor. Each of us was acutely aware that our lives were in the hands of a man immersed in the treacherous world of the Forbidden Purple City.

I fervently hoped I'd judged Mandarin Nguyen Khuyen rightly.

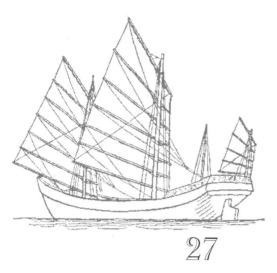

27

No Recourse and No Escape

Tuesday, 14 August 1883
Inside the Forbidden Purple City
Hué, Annam
Empire of Viet Nam

The passageway was dimly lit from the left side by little cracks of light showing through the paneling, just enough to discern our way. The applause and music—and that incessant gonging—from the throne hall on the other side of the panels reverberated through the darkness, heightening my sense of dread about what was coming in this most exotic of places. Because the nature of my work is frequently clandestine, I've been forced many times to trust my life, and Rork's, to strangers in foreign countries—but often the trepidation itself is what damn near kills me. I suppose only my innate stubbornness—that's what Rork calls it—allows me to carry on during those moments. This was surely one of them.

Our route took us behind the northern wall to the Left House of the Can Chanh Palace. Once there, we emerged into an open room the mandarins used as a private antechamber, then crossed to the southern wing of the Left House, where the working offices of the imperial cabinet staff were located. Khuyen stopped and explained all of that, then opened a door to an office and announced we would stay in the room for one hour, then go to another building for a special meeting. He was sticking with the original scheme.

"If all goes well with Mr. Bui's part of the plan, in an hour we will have an opportunity to save this country and thousands of lives," he added. "If it does not go well, we may die in here within an hour."

We were in the office of a senior clerk in the excise department, Khuyen continued, motioning for us to sit in the chairs arranged around a table. Piles of tax records covered the table. Bookshelves and scroll racks lined the walls, and I noticed a type-writing machine on a side table. Maps of Annam and Tonking spread across one wall, above a large desk. Two wall oil lamps were already lit, shedding a modicum of light and a maximum of smoke. After asking Petrusky to stand at the door as lookout, Khuyen sat at the head of the table and pointed to the other end for Strom. Rork and I sat on the sides. Strom had been quiet to this point. Heaving with the exertion and anxiety, he was visibly displeased with me.

"I hope to God you've got a good reason for all this, Peter."

Khuyen spoke before I could answer. "Allow me to belatedly introduce myself, Chief Minister Strom. I am Nguyen Khuyen, Mandarin of History for the imperial palace, and I sincerely regret that recent events, of which you are not aware, have necessitated this unusual departure from normal diplomatic protocols. And may I say on behalf of my people that I appreciate your journey to our land to try to avert a war. It is a noble deed."

That didn't alleviate Strom one bit; he was growing angrier by the second. Beauregard Strom's physical size and deep voice could be daunting.

"Mandarin Nguyen Khuyen, of all people here, you know

the repercussions of the insult we just caused. We probably just caused an international incident by our rudeness to the hosts back there and I want answers, *right now*. What is going on here?"

Khuyen wasn't intimidated and replied evenly. "Which hosts would that be, Mr. Strom? The French? They are *not* your hosts. This is *not* their country. Do not confuse the French with your true host, which is Emperor Hiep Hoa, emperor of all the people of Viet Nam. The reason you were led away from the reception in this unorthodox manner is so that Commander Wake could inform you about the plot against you and your country."

Strom swung his glare onto me.

I nodded. "It's true, Beau. By the way, the gentleman at the door is Professor Petrusky, a linguist who has helped Rork and me in Cambodia and here in Viet Nam. I trust him completely."

Petrusky nodded hello, but Strom wasn't in a social mood. "Explain all this, Peter."

"Please bear with me and answer some questions first. You've been in Blundell's custody since you arrived in Hué, correct?"

"*Custody?* I've been a guest in the man's home, Peter. He's treated me with every courtesy. I consider him a friend and a decent man."

"Did you ever leave his home or the company of his men?"

"No, I suppose I haven't. The streets are unsafe around here," Strom glanced at Khuyen, "for foreigners, and I was appreciative of Maurice Blundell's offer of protection and hospitality."

"And did you send telegrams to Connally at Saigon?"

"Yes, I've sent half a dozen at least, reporting on the events in Annam and Tonking. He forwarded them on to Washington by way of the Singapore line."

"No, he didn't, Beau. Connally never got any telegrams from you. In fact, he reported you missing, and most probably still in Tonking, two months ago. No one has heard from you. No one knew you've been in Hué for over a month. Rork and I were heading home from a courier assignment to Cambodia a month ago when we got orders from Washington to find and rescue you."

"That's absurd. I've received telegrams from Connally. Several of them—in direct answer to mine."

"Connally never sent you any, Beau. No one has known your whereabouts for months. Blundell read your communiqués to Connally, then conjured up some appropriate replies to make you think all was well."

"Peter, that is a very serious allegation. How do you know this?"

"Connally told me himself you were missing. Mandarin Khuyen has informants that told him about the false telegrams from Connally that Blundell created to trick you. And here are my orders from Washington."

I handed him the blue envelope and continued speaking while he read Admiral Porter's orders to me. "Beau, we thought maybe a Black Flag warlord up in Tonking had gotten you. When Rork and Professor Petrusky and I made it this far, we found out you'd been ensconced here with Blundell. By the way, your Mr. Blundell tried to have us killed in Cambodia. Came damn near to it, too. He doesn't want any American meddling in this region. That includes you."

He looked up from the papers in his hand, his voice edged with rage. "Who the hell all is in on this damn thing?"

Khuyen answered. "Blundell and probably his two assistants, Courcy and Briére. Probably Dupuis, possibly Ruff and Pavric. We do not think Commissioner Harmand or the senior diplomats are part of this design. At least, we have no proof."

Strom turned to me. "When I arrived in Saigon, Connally told me you were over in Cambodia on a courier assignment. So why would Blundell want to kill you and Rork?"

"Because he thought the Americans were getting involved in the telegraph line contracts and would favor the British gutta percha rubber over the French planters' India rubber. He is closely allied with the French planters. Has a lot of money tied up in various agricultural products. He also feared the local governments turning to the United States for aid, with the French advisors—

that would be him—thereby losing their influence and, most importantly, a substantial income."

"That's pretty far-fetched, but I see—I think. However, what possible reason could Blundell have to keep me, *an American,* out of communications with my own people over here in Viet Nam? I'm only here to try to prevent bloodshed on both sides. My assignment is concurrent with John Young's efforts in Beijing to slow this ridiculous march to war between the East and the West. For God's sake, we're Americans. We don't want any empire—this is a *peace* mission! Everyone wins if we succeed."

"Not everyone, Beau," I said. "The private French companies in Indo-China will make much more money once the French completely take over Annam and Tonking after defeating the Vietnamese, which won't take long. Blundell has investments in rubber, sugar, rice, copra, you name it, in both Cambodia and Viet Nam. Once the French take over—those companies will expand, without any imitations. He stands to make a fortune. But if there is no war, then the Vietnamese retain some control over the French companies inside the empire and the status quo continues, or possibly a backlash would increase Vietnamese control over them."

"How much time is there?"

"The French fleet is reported to be approaching here from Singapore, so the war could erupt at any time when they arrive. Once it starts, Blundell's gang wins. All he had to do is stall any peace talks. You see it now?"

Strom's jaw tightened. "Blundell told me Emperor Duc Duc refused to talk. Gave me letters to that effect—probably forged too. He said the new one wouldn't either. You're right about Courcy. He told me the French would wait another couple weeks for the emperor to negotiate, but that it wasn't looking good. That other one, Briére, was right in there with Blundell too. I heard Pavrie and Blundell talking about consolidation of rubber plantations. Thick as thieves, all of them."

"I am ashamed to say our side has its problems also, Mr.

Strom," admitted Khuyen. "We have men in authority who have counseled the emperor to go to war. That the time has come to defend our land. Unfortunately, he is listening to them. The emperor does not understand that we are not strong enough to resist the French militarily. We must rely upon nonviolent guile and diplomacy. Violence on our part will play right into the hands of Blundell and those like him—giving them the excuse to crush us."

Strom's open hostility toward Khuyen faded. He sighed and said, "All right, I understand this mess better now. So what do you propose we do at this point, Mandarin Khuyen? Is there a way to stop this lunacy?"

"Yes, there is, Mr. Strom. Mr. Bui of our foreign ministry, whom you met upon your arrival weeks ago, is at this moment handing a message from me to the emperor inside the reception, requesting a confidential meeting with him. I will be bringing all of you with me, though he does not know that. Together, we will try to persuade the emperor not to do what the French are counting on him to do—fire on the fleet when it arrives and thereby give them the excuse they need and expect. You, Mr. Strom, can speak to the political side of this dilemma. Commander Wake will speak to the military side. But I must report that there are three major obstacles to this enterprise of ours."

"Which are, sir?" I asked.

"The first is the Council of Regents, the highest royal advisors. Three out of the four have counseled war. They were the ones who deposed Emperor Duc Duc because he was considered too weak, too debauched by French wine and culture—one of the charges included against him was that he had a French priest as a friend. Another obstacle is Viet Nam's Empress Dowager, Tu Du, who is pushing for closer ties to China and their empress dowager, which means war. The third obstacle consists of the four senior mandarins operating the government—the so-called Four Pillars of the Empire. They, like the regents, are worried about French encroachment on their authority and lifestyles with modern ideas and methods of government. They want the empire to turn away from the west and return to the ancient ways. They hope the French will just go away if there is fighting. It is naïve of them, but sadly true."

I didn't understand. "How are those people obstacles to us speaking with the emperor, sir?"

"Because they control whom he sees and where he goes. If they find out about my message tonight, there will be no meeting. But that, of course, will be the least of our immediate concerns."

His voice trailed off and I asked, "How so, sir?"

His gaze was unnerving. "They will kill us all, Commander. We are defying the rules of the court and the wishes of the senior-most leaders of the court. Death will keep our transgressions quiet. Remember, you are within the Forbidden Purple City, where guards kill those who have angered the regents and senior mandarins. Duc Duc is being executed as we speak, slowly starved to death not far from here."

Khuyen reached inside his gown and pulled out a watch. "The emperor has received my message by now. Mr. Bui, if he is still alive, should be here shortly to give us the reply so that we may move to the meeting place."

Khuyen gazed around the room at us, his monotone betraying no emotion.

"From now on, gentlemen, there is no recourse and no escape for any of us if things go badly."

"Sweet Jesus," muttered Strom. "They didn't tell me about any of *this* back in Washington when I was given the assignment."

"Join the crowd, Beau," I said. I gestured toward Rork. "We didn't know either."

Ten long minutes later, Bui arrived. He was out of breath, as if he'd been running for his life. "The emperor said yes! He will meet at the gaming place behind Can Thanh Residence at the appointed time. I just came from there and the way is clear."

All eyes were on Khuyen. "Very well, gentlemen. We have passed the first impediment. Please follow me."

The six of us filed out of the office, Khuyen in the lead and Bui in the rear. Strom pulled me over to him. "This whole thing is sheer madness, Peter. Are you sure we can trust this fellow?"

I looked up at the diminutive figure in front showing us the way and shook my head. "I'm not entirely certain, Beau. But he has gotten us this far."

"Well I don't trust him any farther than I can throw him."

"Yeah, I know that feeling real well, too."

28

Stone Walls

Tuesday, 14 August 1883
Inside the Forbidden Purple City
Hué, Annam
Empire of Viet Nam

We waited in the gardens at the rear of the heavily guarded emperor's residence, evidently a place no Westerner had seen, not even the senior French authorities. There was a small torch-lit clearing around a lotus pond, paved in stone with manicured bushes surrounding the whole affair. Khuyen said that Blundell and his associates wouldn't dream of going into the area without a regiment of infantry. That comment hardly made me feel any better, but by that point things were far out of my control. I really didn't expect to survive the night.

An hour later, six guards appeared—all wearing side arms and three with rifles—and spread out in a perimeter, one standing ten feet from my hiding place behind a bougainvillea bush. Moments afterward, Hiep Hoa arrived with two young concubines, or wives—I never could tell who was who in Oriental royal households. He was attired in a heavy gown of golden silk, upon which were ornate patterns embroidered in gold thread, each apparently symbolically important.

Hiep Hoa had a long face with a trimmed moustache, the ends of which wrapped around his mouth and met a pointed goatee. His eyes were set close together and mere slits, showing no sign of his thoughts. The hair piled atop his head was oiled down and decorated with golden jewelry, and even at a distance of twenty feet, I could smell the scent of roses emanating from him. He was thirty-seven but looked in his early twenties, a trick of the powder and rouge that covered his face. The whole effect was one of petulant softness, but after what seemed like a year in Southeast Asia, I knew better than to judge on appearances. That was a perilously foolish thing to do.

The emperor picked up a pile of sticks and started tossing them into some pots a few feet away. They bounced out of a small pot and landed in a larger one, eliciting a chorus of approving squeals from the females. After acknowledging their accolades, the emperor called out to someone beyond the range of the torch light. A heavyset eunuch arrived and ushered the girls away. At the same time, the guards moved farther away, leaving Hiep Hoa alone in the garden.

Khuyen stepped out and greeted his sovereign, bowing deeply. They had a quiet conversation for several minutes, then Khuyen called out in our direction, *"Nhap vao."*

Bui and Petrusky stepped out of the bushes and bowed down, kowtowing to the ground. Rork, Strom, and I entered the clearing and bowed from our waist.

Khuyen said, "His Majesty does not speak French or English, so I will translate. I have told him the general overview of how we came to be here, of Blundell's plan, that our lives are now at his mercy, and that Chief Minister Strom and Commander Wake have defied death to be able to speak the truth to him, in an effort to save the lives of our people and the authority of his throne. I will request that Chief Minister Strom speak first."

It was quite an introduction to follow. Remember, only an hour or so earlier, Strom had been delightfully unaware of all of this sordid chaos. However, I'd seen Beauregard Strom charm and sway the dead-eyed diplomats of Europe and had no doubt that if anyone could, he would get the emperor to see the political consequences of the impending war. I was far less certain about my own powers of persuasion.

Strom started out with a bow, then straightened to his full height of over six feet. "Your Majesty, I came here seeking no land, no commercial concessions, no political gain, and no military influence for my country. I came here only to seek peace for this region. And why was I sent to do that? Because peace is prosperous, and war is detrimental to trade. The United States is a trading country and believes in open doors."

He waited for the translation. I watched Hiep Hoa as Khuyen explained. The emperor showed no emotion. Strom continued.

"Mandarin Nguyen Khuyen has demonstrated to me that I was the victim of a hoax and a cruel plot to thwart my mission. Apparently, this was done by private Frenchmen and not the French diplomats. The reason they did that is quite simple—they want to take complete control of this country in order to make even more money than they already are. War gives them that excuse. A military action by Viet Nam gives them such a war.

"What would be the results of such a war? It will be portrayed as the Christian French defending themselves against Oriental barbarians. The European diplomatic corps will immediately support France. The Americans will stay neutral. The Japanese, who have expressed interest in supporting you against the West, are too far away and not powerful enough at this time. The Chinese, who say they support their loyal Vietnamese vassal, will find it inconvenient and delay, possibly making their own deal with the French for those Tonking border districts they have coveted for so long. You will be very alone in this confrontation. King Norodom in Cambodia is too weak. Likewise the Siamese king."

Khuyen translated and I thought I detected a slight sigh from Hiep Hoa.

Strom spread out his hands, a gesture of peace and inclusion. "But a negotiation—what would be the result of trying that? First, it would take time and that is good. Time allows men to think. Second, it could involve more countries than just China, you, and France. The more countries that are involved, the more options you will have. Third, and this is most important, Your Majesty, it will demonstrate to the world the graciousness of your reign and the peaceful intent of your government, particularly to the press organs of the world. It will allow you to use those journalistic organs to influence the people of France and the other European countries, to show them you are not a backward and savage land that needs European culture to move forward in history. Invite the journalists from these newspapers into your presence, show them your intentions, make them understand the great culture that is Viet Nam. They will tell the French nation.

"And once the people of France understand that, they will pressure their governments to back away from war, to have a relationship with your empire based on equality among nations. Please remember, Your Majesty, that France's motto is liberty, equality, fraternity. Use the press to appeal to that and make the French *people* your allies."

It was a masterful performance, especially when one considered Strom pulled it off extemporaneously. A glimpse to my right showed that Petrusky, who was pretty articulate himself, was nodding in appreciation. Mr. Bui pensively dipped his head in agreement. Rork played the role of servant, standing at parade rest in his usual spot one step behind and to my right, his face as impassive as the emperor's.

Strom ended with a flourish. "Your Majesty, it would be the greatest honor of my life if you would allow me to coordinate such a peace process. The United States of America stands ready to provide such a mediation and is confident of a successful outcome."

Hmm, that last part was a bit optimistic and I noticed that Hiep Hoa frowned when it was interpreted for him. He stepped forward and spoke, looking at Strom as the mandarin put it in English.

"I thank the diplomatic representative of the United States of America for his thoughts on this matter between my empire and the French. It saddens me that your noble hopes do not conform with the reality of the moment, however. The time for talking has regretfully passed."

Strom made to speak, but the emperor held up a hand and said something to Khuyen. The translation was, "I will now hear from the American naval officer."

I bowed. "Yes, sir. Well, I am a warrior, and as such I do not look at things like politics and personalities. I only look at the strengths and weaknesses of myself and my enemies. In this case, the strengths and weaknesses of the French forces and of yours."

I knew ahead of time it would be delicate, but when I actually faced the cold eyes of a man who can order your instant death, a man who has been surrounded by sycophants and yes-men, then I do acknowledge a certain amount of apprehension built up in my belly about giving the emperor an unwelcome dose of reality. What loyalty did I owe this man? Or this country? Should I say *anything* in order to come up with a way to get us out of there?

Strom settled that for me when he sensed my hesitation and said, "Give it to him straight, Peter. Thousands of lives are at stake."

Khuyen translated that too. Hiep Hoa pursed his lips and studied me even closer. I took a deep breath and said it plain. "Your forces are a sad joke, Your Majesty. The conscripts will run even before the first shot is fired; the imperial guard will run when they go under their first modern bombardment. I predict the French will overrun your forces not in days, but in hours. To send your soldiers into battle against the French would be sending them to slaughter. A useless slaughter that will serve no purpose."

Hiep Hoa's eyes blazed when he heard *that* in his language. I doubt anyone had spoken to him in such a manner. The emperor spat out a reply. Khuyen told us his answer.

"You have seen this great fortress of Hué. There are also great fortresses on the river east of the city, and large fortresses along the coast—all designed for us by the French themselves, years ago. The river is too shallow for the large ships of the French fleet, with their big guns, to navigate and we outnumber their men ten to one, should they dare to come ashore. In addition, my imperial guard regiments have modern rifles and only four days ago each soldier fired his rifle ten times at a target to become ready for battle. Now he carries twenty bullets with which to shoot down the enemy. Twenty!"

Hiep Hoa stood there, waiting for my rebuttal.

"The fortresses are protection against infantry only, Your Majesty, not against the French warships' guns. Modern large-caliber naval guns will destroy them in minutes. The French fleet doesn't have to come up the river—they can fire on this palace from the sea, many miles away. *Some,* but not many, of your men have modern rifles and have the ability to fire five or six rounds a minute. That gives them a total of four minutes fighting time at the most. All of the French sailors and marines have modern rifles, and each carries one hundred bullets. Behind them will be carts loaded with thousands more bullets.

"And they also have Hotchkiss revolving cannons, each one capable of firing forty-three separate thirty-seven-millimeter exploding rounds"—I showed him the size with my fingers—"each *minute*. And they have dozens of those with hundreds of thousands of rounds ready to mow down your men like a scythe through waves of grain. The French also have smaller gunboats that can and will go up the Perfume River, getting close enough to bombard this very place we are standing with explosive shells. You have no modern field artillery, no machine guns, and no large army capable of maneuvering in the field against a well-equipped and well-trained foe."

He didn't want to hear that either. "Commander Wake, you describe us as weak, but we have already beaten the French in battle. The Chinese and Vietnamese were victorious against the vaunted French in Tonking."

"Yes, Your Majesty, overwhelming numbers of men went against a small French force that had no heavy weapons. This is different. The French now have a modern fleet and army coming. As many men as you can send against them, they will have more than enough ammunition to kill them with."

This wasn't going well, and had sunk into an adversarial debate. I paused for a moment and looked him in the eyes. "I speak not to insult you or your brave soldiers, Your Majesty. Their bravery and your honor are beyond question. The point here is that they cannot win and their dying will not accomplish anything. It will be in vain. I am here as an American, one whose country threw off the yoke of European colonialism. I completely understand your fervent wish for your people to stay independent and free, but this is not the way. Use your head and not your heart, sir. Mr. Strom has made sense. His is the best way."

Hiep Hoa approached me, appearing to almost glide with his steps hidden beneath the hem of his gown. He stopped directly in front of me. I could tell the man was exasperated with me, controlling his irritation. He took a deep breath and explained the secret behind his reasoning. It came out sing-song in his lingo, but there was no misunderstanding his face as it was translated.

"You know much of the machines of war, Commander. But what you do not know is that a week ago my astrologers *assured* me of victory, saying that a great omen would come to proclaim it to all my people. They described that omen and now it has appeared. Look into the sky above you, Commander Wake, and you will see their prophesied sign, based upon five thousand years of studying the celestial heavens."

Hiep Hoa pointed up at a forty-five-degree angle to the northeast, toward the coast. "The omen is over the exact area where the French will arrive with their notorious weaponry. It is a rare alignment of the stars . . ."

There was a period of confusion in the translation of the stars' names, which Khuyen couldn't interpret. Petrusky walked over and assisted, putting the emperor's words into English. "The alignment of the stars of the Pleiades, Hyades of Taurus, Saturn, Mars, and over there, now Jupiter is coming into view. They form a line in the sky, a line which has not occurred in many years. The line points down to where the French will die. I believe Mars is the symbol of your classical god of war, it is not? For us it symbolizes fire."

I studied the sky to the northeast. Yes, there was indeed an unusual configuration of those stars in the sky—they were pointing down, or up, from where the French would begin the battle, and Mars was the classical Greek god of war. But that anyone in a position of national authority in a modern day and age would pay any attention to such hocus-pocus was beyond my comprehension. I had not a clue as to what to say to his bizarre logic. Then it struck me—Hiep Hoa's title. The emperor was considered to be a celestial son of heaven. No wonder he was so attentive to his astrologers.

Hiep Hoa took my silent contemplation as a sign of defeat and started in again, railing against European reliance upon technology, French decadence in behavior and culture—which I found highly ironic coming from a man who had hundreds of concubines—and general Western arrogance about their place in the world. He stopped, pleased with himself and his trouncing of my argument.

It was frustrating. He still had no conception of what the French could do in battle, or the bloodbath his men would face. Then I got an idea.

This encounter with the emperor was late at night in the middle of August, the time of the year for the annual showers of Perseids—a meteor display featuring hundreds of "shooting stars." All naval officers were familiar with it. Above us the meteors were just beginning for the night, coming in from the north and northeast.

"Your Majesty, an omen in the sky will not stop the French. The French warships will rain horror down upon your soldiers. It will be incessant death, the likes of which you and your soldiers have never seen."

I waved my hand across the sky.

"Do you see the meteors, Your Majesty? The stars shooting across the sky? That is the omen of what the French rockets will look like. In addition to the rockets, there will be huge guns hurtling explosive projectiles that are three times bigger than the biggest of your old-fashioned guns. And those French engineers who built your forts years ago? They know where all the weaknesses are and have passed that knowledge to the attackers. This is eighteen-eighty-three, Your Majesty. The age of stone walls is over. They provide nothing more than a false sense of security."

I shook my head in genuine pity for the poor souls in Hiep Hoa's army. The thought of what was about to happen was sickening.

"Now I have done my duty, sir. I have warned you of what will happen and any more talk is merely redundant. The decision, and the lives of your people, is your responsibility, sir."

Just at that moment a flaming line zoomed across the entire sky. In seconds, four more streaked through the night. To the south, thunder rumbled from a summer storm. Hiep Hoa regarded me curiously as my last words were interpreted. His haughtiness dimmed somewhat. Maybe I'd gotten through. No one spoke for several tense seconds.

Then the emperor abruptly turned around and walked away, calling out testily to Khuyen, who told us his remarks. "It is late now and I am tired. The Americans have spoken words that have the sound of truth, and I think with honor as a guide. I want to resume my conversation with them tomorrow. They will stay under my personal protection in the Can Thanh Residence guest house. Make it so, Mandarin Nguyen Khuyen."

Then he was gone.

A general sigh of relief went through our group. My legs felt rubbery and I looked for a place to sit. There was none. Strom and Petrusky congratulated me. Rork raised an eyebrow and shook his head.

Khuyen, who'd been staring at me, finally spoke. "That was extraordinary, Commander Wake. Emperor Hiep Hoa respects and likes you. No one speaks to the emperor like that and lives."

He ushered us toward a path, saying, "I will have your belongings delivered here. I must repeat, Commander, Chief Minister Strom, this is an extraordinary event—no foreigner has ever stayed within the Can Thanh Residence. Perhaps we *will* be successful and avert this disaster."

Strom slapped me on the back. "Nicely done, Peter. Though I feared the old boy was going to have a fit there for a while. I must say, you really do seem to tumble into the most irregular situations, don't you?"

I was about to come up with a witty repartee when a gunshot rang out. It came from the direction of the main Cam Chanh Palace, behind us. We all spun around in reaction, except for Rork, who had been following me.

My friend fell to the ground.

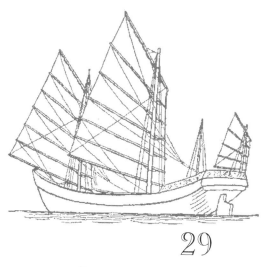

29

Nguoi chet co tinh
cach dang qui trong!

Tuesday, 14 August 1883
Inside the Forbidden Purple City
Hué, Annam
Empire of Viet Nam

Several things happened at once. Rork rolled over and fired his Colt twice at some bushes fifty feet away, Petrusky pointed toward a figure running from the bushes toward the main palace, and Khuyen called out for help from the guards in the area. Bui knelt down and helped Rork—who was clutching his left forearm and swearing in Gaelic so I knew it wasn't a mortal wound—and I, revolver drawn and enraged beyond description, ran after the fleeing form into the torch-lit gardens.

Fortunately I was in full dress uniform and the responding guards didn't try to arrest or shoot me, but I was already well behind the gunman, whose form was only a dark fleeting mass against the shadowy bushes up ahead of me. I saw the form stop, then erupt into a double flash—he was shooting at me from sixty or seventy feet. I knew that was a long enough range in the dark to ensure inaccuracy among most pistol shooters, so I dodged to the right and kept on going.

A soldier ran up to me from a side path, rifle leveled at my gut. I stopped and pointed at the man running off, then gestured for his weapon, a new Gras. The soldier hesitated, confused as to who I was—that was his mistake. There was no time to waste so before he knew it, the rifle was in my hands and at the point-shoulder position.

Even in dim light, fifty yards is no challenge with a decent rifle. And I had the good luck to have the perpetrator run across the front of a line of lanterns, silhouetting him perfectly. The soldier was yelling something, calling for a sergeant, I presume, but it only took seconds to bring the muzzle sight on target, allow for his speed, let out a breath, and ease the trigger back.

I handed the rifle back to him and said thank you in Vietnamese—*cam on*—then trotted over to where the gunman had dropped out of my view. I found him crawling under the bushes, barely holding the pistol with one hand and gripping his chest tightly with the other. It was who I suspected, but now his face was transfigured from a smiling urbane conversationalist into a snarling mask of fear and rage. He looked up at me and gasped for air, blood spewing from his mouth with every breath. The round had gone into his chest and he was pumping out fast, but still struggling to escape.

I kicked the revolver out of his hands, then picked it up from the ground near him and examined it. An eleven-millimeter St. Etienne French army model—the equivalent of an American forty-five caliber. Rork was lucky. If that round had hit his chest, he would be the one dying. Or it could've been me. There was no doubt I was the intended victim.

The soldier came running up and gaped down at the writhing body. Other soldiers arrived, agitated, leveling their rifles at me, then the body, not knowing what to do. The man on the ground was going to lose consciousness in seconds, die in minutes, and I needed to know the reason behind his actions.

"*Why,* Maurice? We were no threat to France or to you."

I leaned down close, so I could hear his answer. The voice was distant, blood slurring the words. "Lose . . . everything . . . it took us . . . so long . . . *to build* . . ."

"You were wrong. Did Commissioner Harmand know?"

The eyes were opaque, the life leaving them, but he grunted with effort and moaned, "Harmand is . . ."

It was his last breath.

The crowd of soldiers opened up for a nervous subaltern, who apparently told all but two to go off and scour the gardens for more threats. No one arrested me, but I didn't even try to leave, for Khuyen and my group were arriving.

Khuyen was panicked, his usual indifferent manner gone. His voice shook as he said, "I just told the emperor what happened, Commander. The royal physicians will be here momentarily to treat Mr. Rork. You will have very intense protection tonight."

Khuyen made a slight bow, then continued. "The emperor is angry that the sanctity of the royal grounds within the Forbidden Purple City has been violated and that a personal guest has been assaulted. The emperor has given orders for the arrest of Courcy and Brière—if they can be found. Ruff and Pavrie are gone. It seems that most of the French left the city after the reception and are heading south to Tourane, where their fleet arrived this afternoon. Messengers from that place reached the emperor moments ago. They report the French warships are readying themselves to attack Hué."

"It's all unfolding now. Just as I feared," sighed Petrusky, and I remembered his words on the Mekong—had it really been three months since then? So much had happened. But my main concern was Rork. It was an arm wound, but a nasty one.

"How bad is it, Sean?"

"In an' out through meat, no bone. I'll live."

I was still worried about that wound. "I think he was aiming for me, Sean."

"Aye, probably so. Me left arm was stretched out reachin' for you when the round hit. Oh, quit the anxious looks, sir. 'Tis nothin', though methinks a decent drink *would* be a proper repayment for this, not to mention the medicinal value."

"I'll buy you two."

Rork looked at Blundell's body. "Aye, center mass, single round—good shot, sir. Better than that bugger's wing job on me—bad shootin' by Monsieur Froggie."

He pulled his left arm close against his body, grimacing from a sudden bolt of pain. "But I'll be a sinner in heaven if it don't hurt like bloody flaming *hell*." He spit on the body. "An' may that slimy friggin' sonovabitch fester in his rottin' grave in this swamp o' a country." He grunted through another wave of pain. "Sweet Mary, mother o' God, but I'm gettin' far too old for this sort o' thing."

That was followed by a string of graphic Irish curses upon the family, friends, future descendants, and colleagues of Blundell, and the French nation in general. It went on for several minutes.

"*Perceptions*, gentlemen," said Petrusky, wagging his head in reflection. "Blundell acted on his perception of what you Americans are doing here. It was a false perception, of course, but that didn't stop him from his desperate act. Just as it won't stop the war about to be unleashed."

Some ancient men in robes fluttered up carrying valises and rattan boxes. Khuyen explained they were the royal doctors. He glanced around nervously and suggested we all retire to the guest house of the emperor's residence for some rest.

Rork growled in Gaelic when the doctor touched his wound, then turned to me. "I could *really* use a dram o' decent rum right about now, sir."

I looked at Khuyen, who shook his head. "We only have the emperor's preferences here—rice and fruit wines and liquors. There is no rum. I am sorry, Mr. Rork."

"What about the French champagne and wine from the reception?" I asked.

"They took the remainder with them."

My friend looked skyward and moaned.

"No bloody rum. Gawd, how I hate this backward bloody country . . ."

Hiep Hoa showed up in our room at sunrise unannounced. Khuyen was with him. A physician entered behind them and went to Rork in his bed across the room from mine. The emperor appeared relaxed; the gaunt mandarin looked exhausted as he translated.

"Did my physicians alleviate the pain and begin the healing of your wound, Mr. Rork?"

Rork sat up. "Aye, sir. That they did. The pain went away after that opium, an' the girls here did a fancy job o' massagin' me achin' arm an' shoulder in just the right places."

He cocked an eye up at a beautiful girl clad in a blue *ao dai* that was holding a damp cloth to his forehead. Two of the royal concubines had been by his bed all night. The physician gently unwrapped the dressing. I could easily tell that the opium had done its work on Rork, who cast a roguish grin at the doctor, who in turn ignored him.

"Never had me own concubine, sir. Could get right used to this, I could. Wait till the lads hear o' this."

"Very good. It pleases me my guest is feeling better," said the emperor. He then turned to me and asked, "Do you still maintain your position of last night, Commander Wake—that my country is too weak to defend herself?"

"Well, ah, sir," I stammered out. "Nothing has changed, so yes, I do."

"I saw last night you wear the famous medal of the French. Perhaps you have an affiliation with them that colors your judgment?"

"No, Your Majesty. I base my judgment on the *facts*."

"But you omitted one thing last night. An important factor that many times decides battles. I was surprised when you did not mention it."

"Sir?"

"The fighting spirit of the men. My soldiers have it. They are fighting for their homeland. They are fighting for—"

Rork screamed out in pain. The doctor had probed his wound. He probed again and Rork gasped, manfully trying to stifle a scream. It came out as a low, moaning howl.

"Sorry 'bout that, sir," growled Rork. "Caught me a bit unawares, he did."

The doctor clucked, held the arm and sprinkled some powder on it, mumbling to himself. The emperor said something in a stern tone and the two concubines fled the room as Khuyen, Hiep Hoa, and I went to Rork's side. Moments later Mr. Bui, Strom, and Professor Petrusky joined us around the bed.

The doctor put the bandage back over Rork's arm, but I didn't like the way my friend's face was contorted in pain. It was far beyond what that wound would produce, especially while doped with opium. I reached across and pulled the dressing away. All of us flinched back at the sight—Rork's swollen skin between the wrist and elbow was black and yellow directly around the bullet hole, fading to dull red farther away. The redness extended above the elbow. Foul-smelling yellow-green pus oozed from the wound.

As a bosun's mate who's seen and done everything, Rork doesn't outwardly show fear often, but it flashed across his face then. He and I both knew what it meant. The wound was infected. If he didn't get advanced medical care within twenty-four hours, it would turn into the worst-case scenario.

Gangrene and amputation. Or death.

The doctor clucked crossly this time and swatted my hand, pulling the bandage back over the wound and chanting to Rork. Pulling out more powder, he mixed it with some leaves in his hand and sprinkled it over the arm, on the outside of the bandage. I looked at Petrusky, who slowly nodded in agreement with my thoughts. This was some sort of shamanism, not medicine. Suddenly, all the political and military posturing took second place—I didn't care who won the battle of Hué or how many died during it. Rork needed real help now.

"Your Majesty, I need to take my man to the French naval surgeons for immediate treatment of that wound. Professor Petrusky, Bosun Rork, Chief Minister Strom, and I need your royal authority for an urgent passage to Tourane. *Right now.*"

To his credit, and my eternal appreciation, Hiep Hoa didn't hesitate. He calmly issued orders to some underlings outside the room, then returned. In minutes, Khuyen reported that a procession would be assembled within the hour to take us to the French naval rendezvous at Tourane.

Then the emperor pulled me aside, with Khuyen close by, interpreting.

"Because of this new development, Commander, you will be with the French during the battle. I want you to know something in your heart as you watch us fight. It is the factor you have overlooked. I was about to bring it up when your man was stricken with pain."

I wasn't concerned about any of them anymore, but I still needed their help so I said, "Yes, sir?"

"Remember when I told you about how we beat the French in Tonking recently? We won the battle, but we lost many men in that victory. Many patriots who were defending their land, their people. You are an honorable warrior and will understand that. You will also understand that this is why we will prevail in the upcoming battle—our memory of those patriots will give us strength. We will fight for *them . . .*"

The emperor reached out and gripped my arms, those narrowed black eyes like molten onyx mere inches from mine, the tense mouth passionately hissing out the words. *"Nguoi chet co tinh cach dang qui trong . . ."*

Khuyen, almost in tears, whispered it reverently in English.

". . . the honored dead."

Then Emperor Hiep Hoa did something remarkable. He hugged me. Straightening up, he said his next words slowly, Khuyen's voice echoing the emotion in them.

"Commander Peter Wake, of the United States of America, your gaze is clear, your voice is strong, and it is obvious to me that you have no hidden motives. As an experienced warrior, you have told me the truth in order to save the lives of my people. I thank you for that, even though I cannot follow your advice. Things have evolved too far to stop now."

Hiep Hoa's eyes were sad as he added something else. He nodded slowly while Khuyen translated it. "Commander, I wish you to go forth with good fortune, my friend."

The emperor let go of me and walked out of the room, leaving me standing there dumbfounded. Without a further word, Khuyen bowed his head and followed his emperor.

That was my last sight of either man.

30

Les Morts Honorés

After a tense journey by wagon through a countryside of glowering faces peering at us from within thatched huts, we arrived at Tourane at sunrise the next day, the sixteenth of August. Climbing aboard the flagship of the French fleet, *Bayard*—a state-of-the-art, steel-armored monster newly completed the year before—Strom went to see Admiral Courbet while Petrusky and I stayed with Rork, who was at once taken to the sick bay. His wound had gotten worse and the opium wasn't mitigating the pain anymore.

One look and the doctor ordered it thoroughly cleaned out in a very painful procedure called debriding. I held Rork's hand, locking my eyes onto his eyes and trying not to cringe as they scraped away the inside of the infected hole, which was now five times its original size. Like the Vietnamese doctors' opium, the French laudanum didn't alleviate the pain much, but Rork never screamed out or crushed my fingers as he could have done.

Next came the detailed examination. The surgeon, humming as he probed and peered, took forever. When it finally came, his conclusion was not good. Gently, he told us gangrene had already started and the poison it generated was spreading into Rork's system. The arm would have to come off. He would try to save the elbow.

Rork just swallowed hard and nodded, saying, "Please get on with it, then."

An hour later my friend was given much more laudanum and strapped down. His eyes stayed on mine until the drug took over, stupefying him mercifully. I held his head and good arm in case he should awaken and be frightened. Professor Petrusky stood there during the entire procedure, his hand on my shoulder while he quietly murmured prayers.

The surgeon was as tender as he could be, mainly for my benefit, I think, since Rork was out of it. Two other naval surgeons were standing by to assist, but the procedure was relatively simple—scalpel away the skin and muscle, carefully cut the veins and suture them, saw the bone, and sew the flap back over the stump, with a small tube of India rubber to drain the wound. I wondered if it was India rubber from a plantation owned by one of Blundell's cohorts.

Rork was left with a six-inch stump below the elbow, which the doctor wrapped in clean gauze, padding it into a large ball. I couldn't help crying. It was so damnably unfair. Sean Rork had survived the famine in Ireland, the Civil War, various bandits and renegades in sundry hellholes of the world, and thirty years at sea, all to have some greedy delusional fool in Indo-China hit him with a bullet meant for me.

When Rork came to afterward, he groped at the ball of gauze, but kept his thoughts quiet. I asked if he was in pain and he nodded. I brought him rum—the French had some aboard— and he took it without comment. Other than that, he stared at the deck beams overhead.

The doctor told me later that Rork's reaction was normal, that he would get used to the amputation. He also said that infection was still a possibility because he had tried to leave enough for a workable stump. We would know in forty-eight hours.

The next day my friend spoke to me. I was expecting bitter hopelessness, but what I heard was pure Sean Rork.

"Bloody friggin' ironic, ain't it, Peter? Some daft Frenchie bastard wings me arm in this Godforsaken arse o' the world, an' another o' his kind saves me life."

"Yeah, I was thinking that too," I lied.

"An' no wonder the Froggie bastards always lost to the Limeys—did you get a swill o' that sorry stuff they call rum? Piss water. Couldn't put the stuffin' in a man with a gallon o' it. Explains their bleedin' history, don't it?"

He held his left arm up, the bandage reddish-black with dried blood. "But that medico did all right. I've seen worse jobs. An he said the ship's carpenter's makin' me a wooden forearm. Gonna have a screw base in it, with different attachments. Just screw one o' the little buggers in according to me frame o' mind at the time. For drinkin'—one'll be a rubber hand with fingers in a fist to wrap round a bottle o' tankard. For workin' there'll be a bosun's marlin spike, an' maybe I'll get another one with a hook, like a pirate in them books you read."

I tried to show good spirits. "Yeah, he told me, Sean. The rubber hand will be painted flesh-color and put on over the spike. Nice of them to do all that. Hey, you'll look pretty fearsome with that hook get-up. Instant weapon when you take off the hand."

"Aye, that marlin spike'll be damned useful in a fight."

He reached out with his right hand for mine, gripping it strongly.

"Hey there, Peter Wake, 'tis no one's fault 'cept that sonovabitch Blundell, an' he won't be causin' no more troubles for nobody. So lose your gloomy manner, me friend. I may have left me *hand* in the Orient, but damned if I'll leave me life here."

He'd read my mind. I had been ruminating the what-ifs of

my decisions while on the mission. If I hadn't gotten sidetracked to the meeting with Hiep Hoa, Rork would be fine. And even worse, the meeting hadn't even produced tangible results. There'd still be a battle.

Then he frowned and added, "Though me life's considerably less *tolerable* without any decent friggin' rum."

I changed tacks. "All right, Sean Rork. Since you insist—I'll be gay as hell. And do my best to find you some decent rum. Hmm . . . maybe the French admiral's private stash?"

"Now that's the spirit, laddie. Afore ya know it, we'll be bound for home to that island o' ours in Florida. Those wankers in Washington owe us some leave time after this Oriental cock-up."

We'd been anchored off the mouth of the Perfume River for a day, the fleet preparing for the battle. Blundell's co-conspirators, who escaped imperial arrest, along with Harmand and his diplomatic staff, were aboard the flagship, but I hadn't seen them. Even Strom, a senior diplomat, hadn't seen them. We Americans were aboard only out of international naval courtesy as a result of Rork's need for sophisticated medical attention. Otherwise, we were barely tolerated by the French staff officers, several of whom pointedly exchanged whispers about me when passing by or eating meals.

A dozen warships were in sight, not all of them French. The German, British, Spanish, and Dutch had ships there. No American warship was around—I'd been told the nearest was at Hong Kong—or we would've been among our own on a U.S. deck.

I stood at parade rest in the admiral's great cabin aboard *Bayard,* waiting to be addressed by the man himself. I noted a copy of the U.S. Naval Institute's January 1883 *Proceedings* magazine on his desk, opened to the articles about the British bombardment of Alexandria the previous November. My Royal Navy friend Jacky Fisher had written me of his participation in the battle and I'd read that copy of the *Proceedings* while still in Washington. It dawned on me the French were about to emulate the British operation—a methodical preparation of the battlefield with gunfire to obliterate resistance, followed by landings on the beach.

Rear Admiral Amédée Courbet appeared less than happy when he finally deigned to look up at me. He was about to launch an attack against a fortified enemy that outnumbered his landing party ten to one—and he had Americans in his midst who were known to be sympathetic with the other side.

Courbet was about a decade beyond me in age, but looked even older. Tall, thin, and serious, he was an engineering graduate of the esteemed École Polytechnique of France, and known as one of the smartest senior officers in the French Navy. But at first sight, he was certainly not an imposing figure. Balding hair was combed forward in the classic Napoleonic style of eighty years before. Below the hairline were droopy eyes, a small slit for a mouth, and a jaw line unadorned with hair except for long, narrow sideburns. He looked to me like some dreary academician. A tired, humorless one.

I appreciated it when the admiral kept his comments in French basic enough that I could mentally transform them into English. He also knew a little English, and we were able to communicate in a jumble of the two languages.

"I am informed that your man is doing better, yes?"

"Yes, sir. Bosun Rork is doing much better. We are extremely grateful for the skilled medical assistance."

His brow furrowed momentarily at my attempt at his language, then got to what was really on his mind, "Very good, Commander. Now, I understand you were with the enemy ashore just days ago. What is the disposition of their forces?"

He said it nonchalantly, but the question angered me. We both knew that as a neutral professional naval officer, I was prohibited from passing along any intelligence of his enemy I may have gained while in their midst. It was a well-known rule of war and some officers might have considered even the *question* an insult upon their honor. I thought of Hiep Hoa's emotional goodbye inside the Forbidden Purple City, and of the French surgeon's life-saving operation on my friend. Courbet was hoping my gratitude would outweigh my professionalism. Fortunately, there was an easy way out of my dilemma.

"I was not in the area of the coastal forts, sir. I was upriver at the city. Never got a detailed look at those fortifications, either. It was dark when I entered and when I left."

The cold stare never changed as he said, "Hmm. I understand, Commander," in a manner that unmistakably implied the opposite, even in a foreign language.

Remembering my effort with Hiep Hoa, I decided to give it a try with the other side of the conflict. "Admiral, is there some way to avert this battle and save lives?"

His look said it all, but the reply was even more instructive. "No. The enemy has chosen this battle and this war. They did that when they dared to attack French soldiers and sailors in Tonking. They took it beyond any reconciliation when they displayed Commander Rivière's head on a pole in their purple city of decadence in Hué. They will come to regret that barbarous act."

"Admiral, I've been *inside* the Forbidden Purple City. There was no head displayed. I heard that rumor when I came aboard *Bayard,* but it isn't true, sir."

"I have already been informed about your sympathies by Dr. Harmand and his staff, Commander Wake—not to mention your . . . *activities* . . . in Hué—so I have no intention of debating the issue with you. France will not forget Commander Rivière and his brave soldiers and sailors at Tonking . . ."

He paused, then softly said, *"Les morts honorés . . ."*

Good God, I thought, it was the same thing Hiep Hoa had said—both sides were invoking the honored dead. I had no quick reply to that, and Courbet continued with, "And the *world* is watching us here today. You have no doubt noticed Commodore Louis von Blanc of the Imperial German Navy is on station here, with his flagship *Stosch* and three of her consorts. Rear Admiral William Hewitt of the Royal Navy has arrived with *Iron Duke* and several ships. The Spanish have sent a gunboat and the Dutch a frigate. Even the Portuguese are sending a ship to observe. All of them are here to see what Frenchmen will do when their honor is assaulted."

I started to speak but the admiral waved a hand. He wasn't done. Glancing briefly at the scar on my head from the pirate battle, he leveled his eyes at me again.

"You, because of your status as a *Chevalier* of the *Légion d'Honneur,* and your reputation among certain senior officers of the French Navy, will be able to watch our operations from my action station on the bridge, if you wish. Of course, a man of your considerable reputation for action would want to be ashore with the landing party and observe the combat from a *closer* position, I am sure. I will gladly give you that signal honor, one that is not being offered to any other officer from a foreign fleet."

My mind reeled. An exclusive offer to get myself killed in battle? No, thank you—I'd had more than enough mortal danger lately. Quite the contrary, my goal had shifted and it was to get Rork, me, and Strom out of there alive.

"Thank you, sir, for the generous honor. I think I will stay aboard and observe from the command position."

Courbet raised a disapproving eyebrow, then snapped out an order to his staff aide, who disappeared out the door. The admiral glanced back at me, his expression indicating he didn't know why I was still there.

"You are dismissed, Commander."

That was a bit rude, I thought, but then realized he had a lot on his mind. The enemy he faced was not some primitive native tribe in Africa or Oceania. No, the Asians had already humiliated France in Tonking—a dangerous thing for them to get away with in the minds of Europeans—and Courbet was responsible for rectifying that situation. All the world, because of their naval contingents at the battle, would know of his victory, or lack of it, at this place. And after Hué, he would have to go to Hai Phong in Tonking and reassert French dominance, probably fighting all seventy miles upriver to Hanoi. And after *that,* he still had to deal with the new Chinese fleet.

Grateful I didn't have Courbet's responsibilities—or personality—I did my very best about-face and departed his luxurious great cabin for the tiny one, two decks below, I shared with a lieutenant by the name of Louis Viaud. Strom, as a senior diplomat, had his own cabin requisitioned from a senior staff officer down the passageway from Courbet. Petrusky was the unwelcome guest of the petty officers' mess in the orlop.

I'd become friends with my cabin-mate in the short time I'd been aboard. Some of his character assets I truly appreciated. Viaud wasn't a staff officer, he was a secondary-battery gun division officer. He also spoke English, didn't make a face when I spoke my bad version of French, and had a self-deprecating sense of humor.

When I arrived back at the cabin after Courbet's odd interview, my new friend gave me the news—he was to go ashore on day two of the operation. Viaud was not thrilled, saying he wanted to be at his guns during the battle and besides, he thought the insects would ruin his day at the beach. I assured him that he could prevail over some little bugs and that I would be behind him all the way—far behind, as in "on the flagship." He didn't appreciate the pun.

Shortly after the feeble attempt at humor, my comeuppance arrived in the form of an engraved envelope. A steward knocked on the door and handed me *my* orders, signed by Admiral Courbet himself. Apparently, I was wrong when I first thought him humorless. He had a sense of humor all right. A vicious sense of humor.

It seemed that I—and by extension the U.S. Navy—had been given a great honor and designated heretofore as the "Official Neutral Naval Observer of the United States of America at the Battle of Hué." It was a very neat trick, a distinction which I could not refuse, or thus risk dishonoring my service and country. According to international law, neutral observers followed the orders of their host nation, and Courbet's orders were very specific.

All French naval and military officers were commanded to render every type of assistance within their power for me to succeed in the performance of my duties, which would be with the landing party ashore, beginning on day two of the assault, with a certain Lieutenant Viaud as my liaison.

Lieutenant Viaud got a nice laugh out of that.

"Welcome to my war, Peter," he offered, a trifle smugly.

The first day of the battle of Hué was predictable. At two in the afternoon, the fleet anchored in an orderly fashion just off the pass into the lagoon at the mouth of the Perfume River, which was guarded by large forts on either side. At the same instant, every ship hoisted huge French national ensigns, bugles blared, and ships' bands played *La Marseillaise,* the stirring old national anthem that had been recently reinstated.

Ashore, the forts raised their own flags of the Empire of Viet Nam—red Chinese script on a yellow field, surrounded by a blue fringe. The Vietnamese fortifications were situated on long narrow barrier islands—little more than large sandbars, really—that paralleled the mainland and divided the lagoon from the sea. Small fishing villages were near the forts. Other than the villages and a scattering of coconut palms, the islands were bare. The entrance pass was perhaps a quarter-mile wide at most. To an observer ignorant of modern warfare, like Hiep Hoa, the forts would seem to be a robust defense. The French naval officers around me just smiled.

A leisurely Gallic start—they had their wine first—to the cannonading at half past five gradually progressed to a massive bombardment from *Bayard, Atalante, Annamite,* and *Chateau-Rénaud.* The small gunboats *Lynx, Drac,* and *Vipère* darted around close inshore taking pot-shots at any groups of infantry foolish enough to show themselves near the beach. Aboard *Bayard,* gunnery orders were shouted with much enthusiasm and most agreed that shooting practice was never this much fun.

The general bombardment was something to behold and I wondered if Hiep Hoa was doing just that. The point-blank range of less than one mile ensured that every shot was accurately on target. Huge chunks of stone and brick were hurled through the air. Large, reddish-black clouds roiled up from the forts. Soon gray and black smoke covered the islands.

Little peeps of light flashed from the smoke—the emperor's gunners were bravely firing back. Through the tops of the dark bank of cloud could be seen those defiant yellow flags. I wasn't a patriot for the locals by any stretch, but I was glad to see those flags, since Americans like to cheer for the underdogs. These particular underdogs weren't destined to live long, however, for the sight of those banners infuriated the French and they redoubled their efforts.

By eight o'clock they had achieved their goal, from what we could see from the bridge of the flagship in the night. No guns replied from the mounds of rubble anymore. Courbet nodded sourly and ordered his gunners to cease fire. The fortresses were in flames, as were the villages and anything else that was combustible.

As I went below to dinner in the wardroom, I scanned the horizon and registered an odd incongruence around me. To the east, over the South China Sea, a huge amber tropical moon rose, forming a romantic view guaranteed to soften the coldest heart. But if one's eyes strayed to the west along the shore, it was a scene from Dante, the blackness periodically erupting in hellish reds and yellows. Secondary explosions could be seen in glaring white, the detonations incessantly continuing in a rolling growl. I couldn't hear the screaming inside the forts from that distance, but I knew the poor souls were crying in vain for their mothers and Oriental gods to help them.

Pleased with their work, the French officers granted their men rest from battle stations, telling them to make the most of it, for at dawn they would land on the beaches and see for themselves the mettle of the enemy that had butchered their comrades in Hanoi. Sharp bayonets and cutlasses were encouraged, and soon the grim sound of metal scraping on whet stones could be heard on every deck.

Vengeance is a heady scent.

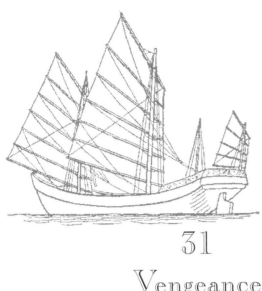

31

Vengeance

Monday, 20 August 1883
Coastal barrier islands near Hué, Annam
Empire of Viet Nam

With a fleeting look of panic, Viaud spun around and motioned for me to get down. Somehow, through sheer ineptitude, we'd ended up on the front line after wandering south across the beach dunes while surveying the enemy's fortress.

Seconds after we burrowed into the sand, a flaming bombette dropped out of the dawn sky and hit the beach behind us, splashing liquefied fire in a small circle. Within a minute it died out, but two more arced through the air and we ducked again. Dozens of them followed, the volley launched by some sort of multiple catapult system from behind the enemy trenches, but none caused any casualties or damage.

It didn't take long for the troops around us to ignore them and continue the advance, mocking the Vietnamese efforts as child's play. Terror forgotten, Viaud grinned over at me and trotted forward like the rest, while I warily tagged along, worried it

327

was some Oriental deception of apparent weakness to lull us from our wits. I knew well the mindset of the men trying to kill us. My new friend Viaud didn't.

When I'd seen him in the pre-daybreak darkness of the bridge that morning, Courbet was obviously displeased, to put it mildly. His planned two-day operation to overwhelm the Vietnamese with the might of the French empire had now dragged into its third day. The main French landing party had only then hit the beach—with their reluctant American observer—at sunrise, far behind schedule. For the preceding two days and nights the warships had bombarded the forts, only to see those yellow flags and the counter-battery fire reappear every time out of the rubble. I learned some new curse words in French in those two days.

No one was predicting an easy time anymore, for Hiep Hoa's imperial troops had proven far braver than I, or the French, had anticipated. In addition, Mother Nature displayed a decidedly anti-French bias, kicking up a surf too high to safely land the fleet's boats. Thus, the carefully orchestrated operation, which had ignored the weather and the enemy as factors to be reckoned with, unraveled in front of the assembled naval observers: the hated Germans, the despised British, and the lowly Spanish.

Anger finally overrode judgment in the end and the order went out to effect the landing anyway. I would've waited another day for the seas to subside. As it was, several boatloads capsized and lost part of the landing force's equipment. Other boats beached away from the intended zone, still others were run up on the sands but then stayed there, unable to launch back out through the waves.

To top it all off, now that we were finally on dry land, mobile Vietnamese field artillery—bought from the French—was harassing the landing party, and their forward picket lines had hindered the French advance. It'd taken hours for the sailors and marines to manhandle their supplies and weaponry through the surf and get set up in attack formations, adding further delay. Seeing the chaos, I thought the French very lucky it was the Vietnamese on the other side. A professional opponent like Robert E. Lee would've had a field day with them, with little effort expended.

At last, around seven-thirty in the morning, with an orange sun rising from the sea behind us, bugles sounded along the line and on our right a mass of blue-jacketed sailors from *Bayard* and *Atalante* rose up and charged the enemy's lines two hundred yards ahead. The French did a creditable job, stopping to fire by volley four times, then rushing together the last fifty yards with bayonets leveled at the shallow trenches inhabited by the Asians.

Viaud and I brought up the rear, but were close enough to feel a Vietnamese volley fly overhead and then see at least a thousand of the enemy stand up as one thick line—triple our number—and exit the trench line. Then they ran away, most without their rifles. It was what I'd suspected. The forward trenches held only general conscript troops armed with single shot muzzle-loaders, not the imperial guards with those Gras rifles. We hadn't met the tough ones yet.

In front of us, the sailors were whooping and hollering as they ran after the fleeing black pajama–clad peasants. The French smelled victory, but to me it still looked too easy. I soon saw why.

A previously unseen artillery battery manned by imperial guards opened up from the right flank, enfilading the attack formation, while in a neat bit of timing the heavier guns in a large fort across the lagoon opened up on us. It was brilliantly done and should've resulted in our massacre, but it didn't. The continuous din of artillery fire and banks of smoke covered the landscape, but no one around Viaud and me fell. After the first sense of dread, the sailors lost their fear and bellowed even louder as they walked briskly over the enemy's positions.

Viaud and I were mystified. Were the Vietnamese firing blanks? He picked up some projectiles that landed in a shallow pond near us and showed them to me. Scrap metal and smoldering wood. The Vietnamese were firing grapeshot. It was composed of anything they could cram in their old barrels, and shot from too far a distance.

Those loads would work at close range, but by the time they reached us, they'd lost their velocity. And their lethality. Just like the shot from the Malay-Chinese pirate that had hit me. I examined an ancient solid shot buried in the sand and still smoking. It was an old round ball, probably fifty years old at least—dangerous back then to a large solid wooden target, but just a nuisance to us now. To me, it symbolized Hiep Hoa's vision of his army of the Empire of Viet Nam. He had modern guns, firing useless ammunition.

The *Vipère* had been loitering close inshore for just such an opportunity and unleashed a broadside at the battery. For five minutes there was a duel back and forth—a foolish move on the part of the Vietnamese, and one they paid for with their lives. Then there was silence. The blue line got up and moved onward, again at the run, kepis bouncing and gear jangling. We followed.

By eight o'clock, the major weight of the French forces ashore was being thrown at the forts on both sides of the entrance pass into the lagoon. The forts over on the mainland side of the lagoon were under bombardment as well, but my primary concern was on the northern side of the pass, where Viaud and I were dodging the odd enemy rifle shot and some stray French shrapnel that flew overhead.

We ran after the sailors as they charged across the last of the trenches. Each ditch crossed revealed piles of writhing bodies that hadn't died yet, as if their brains hadn't gotten the word there was no body left to follow orders. Gore and limbs were strewn around as testaments to the lethality of modern explosive shells. The last ditch in front of the fort had been the target of concentrated fire. It was no longer a ditch, but a field of craters. I recognized the black and dark blue uniforms of Hiep Hoa's imperial guard infantry. Every one of them was dead and I wondered briefly if the soldier whose rifle I used to kill Blundell was among them. I couldn't tell. His own mother wouldn't have recognized him in that pile of bloody meat.

The smell of explosive powder—the French were using that new stuff they bought from the Germans—filled the air. It was so thick I choked on it, and began coughing violently. I tasted it and my clothing reeked of it for days afterward. But compared to Hiep Hoa's men, I had it easy. I stopped estimating the number of dead bodies after two hundred, and the wounded must have numbered in the thousands. There was no medical assistance for them. We did our best to ignore the screams and moved onward. Viaud wasn't grinning anymore.

At the fort the French sailors paused to form lines again, but not for long. They didn't want to give the enemy time to recover from the apocalyptic storm of gunfire hitting the rubble from the ships. Just before the attack on the fort itself, the ships stopped firing and the bugles blared again. The lines of sailors stood as their officers, swords in hand, strode to the front to lead the attack.

That was when the emperor's imperial guards attacked. Rushing out from the ruins of the fortress, they formed a wedge and advanced, firing several parade ground volleys at the French. Then they dashed back inside. It looked good, a brief sally forth to disrupt an attack on their position, but in reality it was all a magnificently played out failure. Only two of our people were hit, neither badly.

I immediately remembered Hiep Hoa's misplaced pride that his soldiers had each fired ten rounds in practice and would carry twenty for battle. My prediction came to pass. The Vietnamese volleys had produced little effect upon the French, and the imperial guards were now probably out of ammunition.

The sailors around me went crazy when they saw the enemy troops withdrawing. Without waiting for orders, they raced after them right into the fortress, shooting and cutting them down without mercy. It was a scene of crazed fury on both sides—the Vietnamese guardsmen that couldn't run away were cornered and fought viciously to the end. Bullets crisscrossed the air, with ricochets pinging off the rubble in strange trajectories. Screams and growls erupted all around me. Viaud and I stayed near the breach in the wall, uncertain where to go. There were no battle lines and the officers in command were still trying to find out where all their men had gone in the frenzied attack. As we stood there, two naval officers lost in a land battle, I noted that the rifle fire was decreasing and said as much to Viaud. He suggested we find the advance headquarters and report in.

I then saw a naval lieutenant that I recognized and was about to ask directions, but stopped. It was Poidlotie, another officer from *Bayard,* his determined face precluding my inquiry as he ran by with a huge tricolor draped around his shoulders. Viaud and I followed him to where a thin spar had been erected in the debris, the original flagpole having been exploded into toothpicks. Poidlotie ran the flag up a halyard on the jury-rigged mast, the weight of the banner in the wind bending the pole. I looked across the pass at the fort to the south. A small blue, white, and red flag was floating over it as well.

The effect was electric upon the men when they gradually noticed their national flags. The shooting stopped and was replaced by an even louder sound—men shouting. A roar went up in waves as each unit got the word and saw the flags. It spread to the ships offshore. In minutes, thousands and thousands of Frenchmen were cheering lustily. From the deck of the *Bayard,* the ship's band struck up a tune and within seconds every man afloat and ashore was singing the *La Marseillaise.*

All right, yes, I will admit it—even to my jaded and melancholy mind it was a stirring sight, the likes of which I had never seen. My career's battles had always been small, intimate, and just as deadly. Even my experiences in the South American war weren't as large-scale and violent as this.

But this was different. It was a *spectacle,* an enormous stage production, the effort of a famous and determined people who had spread an empire around the world, and my pulse raced at the sight and sound. Dismissing the moral aspects of the whole thing from my mind, I grudgingly gave them their due and imagined dour old Courbet on the bridge of his flagship, looking out at his foreign counterparts anchored nearby, smiling at last.

That was when Blundell's revenge upon *me* arrived.

I never saw them, not at first anyway. It was damned stupid of me to have forgotten them. Especially after Viaud's warning a few days earlier when I first came aboard. But I am sorry to say I had forgotten. Caught up in Rork's horrific wound and then the shore battle, I forgot I still had dangerous enemies of my own.

Courcy and Brière, Blundell's co-conspirators, were in the rubble too, waiting for their chance to silence a witness who could yet send them to prison for their scheme against Strom, not to mention the attempt to kill me and my party on the Mekong in Cambodia. The desperados chose their moment well, for even as the French sang their anthem, the sailors began pot-shotting at the Vietnamese trying to swim across the lagoon from the barrier island to the safety of the mainland. Blundell's bastards used that confusion to do some shooting of their own. At me.

Of course, I didn't even realize it. Never even knew they were ashore. Fortunately, Viaud was more alert and pointed them out as they took aim for the third time, then yelled for me to get down just as several rounds sent rock chips zinging into my face. Instantly, the state of affairs became obvious, and I clawed among the pile of stones while they had target practice, scoring a couple of near misses but no hits. One hunk of stone hit near my right eye, scaring the hell out of me for a few seconds until I understood it was just a ricochet. Then it was my turn to shoot and I loosed off some enraged but ineffective shots of my own in their direction. But my friend Viaud was faster and smarter. He had obtained a rifle.

Viaud, not being the object of my enemies' wrath, had taken

the time to set up a firing position about twenty yards to my left. He calmly cranked off four rounds as I was still trying to locate my assailants. The shooting from Courcy and Brière stopped.

"I think I hit them, Peter," called out my friend. "Let us go to see. But be careful."

Careful? Ha, I wanted blood by then. I charged across the rocks, prepared to beat those two to death with Vietnamese rubble, but found two crumpled bodies instead. Viaud stumbled up to me and looked down, then shrugged. "Yes, I did hit them."

Well, I should say. Each of them had a hole in his face. Problem ended. I lowered my revolver and dropped the rock in my left hand.

"Louis, thank you," I said, very sincerely meaning it. "You saved my life. Good shooting, too."

He shrugged again. "It was an easy shot, Peter. No more than fifteen meters, and from their flank. And, of course, it will save the cost of a trial and embarrassment to my country. If there are any more of Blundell's conspirators, they will now know they have no friends in the French Navy."

Viaud looked at me and smiled. "But, my dear friend Peter, *you* do."

Night had fallen. Gunfire from the land artillery and the ships continued sporadically. Our camp was among the smoking ruins of the fort on the mainland at the mouth of the Perfume River. It hadn't taken that long to capture, once the troops crossed the lagoon. Now there was only one major fort left on the river, plus some trench lines, before the French reached the Citadel of Hué, and the Forbidden Purple City inside. Scouts advised there were log barriers across the river and some smaller fortifications at various points, but nothing as elaborate as what had already been captured.

I sat at a campfire, physically and emotionally exhausted.

Poidlotie and Viaud were going over the scenarios of attack on the Citadel, both agreeing it would take several days to go the three miles upriver, get the siege set up, and begin a methodical attack. Behind us, more troops were arriving ashore, including native colonial regiments from French Cochin. Viaud predicted total victory in a week. Poidlotie said four days. Wagers were put down with me as the holder. Disheartened by the day's events, I refused to participate in the conjecture further. I just wanted to get back to the ship and Rork. In the morning I would do just that, even though I had no official permission to leave the battlefield.

I couldn't stand being an official observer anymore—it seemed a sick voyeurism of useless death. And the future promised more of the same as far as I was concerned. For I knew—better than my young colleagues around the fire—that the slaughter would continue and be even worse, far worse, in the crowded confines of Hué. The French would, of course, employ their advantage in artillery and prepare the battlefield ahead of their attack as they had at the coastal forts. The number of enemy dead for the day just ended was now estimated at two thousand, with at least five thousand wounded. I thought those conservative numbers from what I'd seen. Hué would be ten times worse. Unless Hiep Hoa somehow came to his senses and ended it by surrendering.

At ten o'clock, I was spreading my blanket when a messenger came running into camp. He interrupted the officers' prognostications and told Viaud the enemy was sending a parley commission. They were being escorted back from the front lines.

Moments later, I saw a strange sight—a slow procession of Asians, silhouetted against a glowing skyline of burning villages, trudged into our bivouac. There were an unarmed escort of Vietnamese imperial guard soldiers, their eyes sullen and wary; three mandarins walking behind them, clearly frightened; and eight servants carrying a palanquin on their shoulders. It was lowered to the ground near our fire and a terrified face peered out of the side curtains. It was a European. No one in our camp knew him. Except me.

In seconds, the curtain opened completely and Bishop Caspar emerged, to the surprise of my naval colleagues and his diplomatic cohorts. Caspar hugged me, his voice distraught as the words gushed out in English.

"*Peter!* Thank God for His mercy in sending *you* here! We have tried to explain to these French troops that we are on a peace mission, but cannot find an officer who is senior enough to stop this carnage. Please help me get them to stop the bombardment. The emperor wants a ceasefire and will negotiate a peace. I have a senior mandarin inside with me who has orders from Hiep Hoa to end the bloodshed immediately."

I turned to a very perplexed Viaud and told him, "Louis, this is Bishop Caspar of Hué. I know the bishop and trust him completely. Can you get him to the senior commander ashore and help end this insanity as fast as possible?"

"But, of course, Peter."

He ordered a runner to the senior officer at the beachhead and let him know that the enemy was surrendering, then arranged an escort of sailors under Poidlotie's command to take the peace emissaries to the French headquarters.

When the envoys and Poidlotie had left, Viaud sat down on a stump and smiled tiredly. "Well, my friend, we saved many lives just now, but it would appear that I have lost my bet. Ah well, I think it is a fair exchange."

I was too done in to make a witty reply. Instead, I nodded and stretched out on the blanket, trying to shut out those visions in my mind and the sound of the wounded around us in the dark. I concentrated my brain on the morrow. In the morning I would be with my friend Rork and away from this charnel place, trying to arrange transport to Hong Kong or Singapore, or anywhere. Maybe the Brits could give us a ride.

There was nothing else to "observe." The battle of Hué was over. Rivière and the honored dead of Tonking had been avenged.

The next morning I talked to the Brits. They regretted not being able to assist me, for none of their vessels was due to leave for Hong Kong or Singapore. Likewise the Spanish. The Germans initially said no, too. But then Commodore von Blanc, a remarkably friendly man, unlike many of his compatriots I have met, said one of his gunboats was headed to Hong Kong in a week or so and we could go with them. Anything was preferable to staying, so I gratefully accepted. Accordingly, Rork and I embarked aboard the *Wolf* on Friday, August thirty-first, bound on the first leg of our journey home.

But in the meantime, we stayed aboard the *Bayard* and witnessed three significant and poignant events.

The first was on the morning of Saturday, the twenty-fifth. Viaud, Petrusky, Strom, Rork, and I were ashore for a final walk together to stretch our legs. Our team was separating. The professor and Strom were bound for Saigon aboard a French gunboat, Viaud had just received word he and *Bayard* were heading north to Hai Phong in a few days to attack the Chinese Black Flags, and Rork and I would soon be heading east, courtesy of the Imperial German Navy. As odd as it seems, Viaud had arranged for us to have a picnic on the beach, but it was at a relatively nice spot away from the carnage of the past few days.

It was there, while enjoying a relaxing repast of wine and sandwiches, that we all witnessed the signers of the peace treaty emerging from a large tent further up the beach. Harmand represented the French; a mandarin I didn't recognize was the emperor's signatory. They were surrounded by their various minions, and everyone looked somber. Viaud walked over, spoke to a French Marine captain, and returned to us.

"Annam and Tonking are now full French Protectorates," he said without emotion. "The empire has two new colonies."

My French friend seemed sad. Petrusky turned away and looked out to sea. The only reply from anyone of us was when Strom said, "Good luck, Louis. I think you'll need it."

The rest of the picnic was a quiet one. We faced away from the land and looked out to sea. No one spoke of Viet Nam.

The second event was an unexpected sequel to the treaty. In the early afternoon of the next day, after Sunday divine services were held on *Bayard's* main deck, a rumble could be heard, not definitive but faint, like the wheels of a gun carriage three decks down. It lasted about five minutes. It wasn't gunfire, nor was it thunder from a storm. The direction was indistinct, but it wasn't from the land. It appeared to come from the south, across the sea.

Two days later, the Dutch ship confirmed what some had guessed—telegraphs ashore sent word that a thousand miles away down in the Dutch East Indies, a giant volcano that had been threatening to erupt had finally done so. They said it had been on an island and that the entire island had exploded. Thousands of people, natives and Dutch alike, were dead. The Hollander warship weighed anchor and headed south.

The third event was as melancholy as the others. The evening before Rork's and my departure, the half-moon rose in the east as usual, but this time it was an ominous hazy blue. It stayed a sad cerulean throughout its transit across the sky. I wondered if it was a preface for what was coming with China or postscript for what had happened with Viet Nam. There was much speculation about the event among the French officers.

When we awoke on the thirty-first and looked at the sky, it was hazed over totally, not from fog or cloud, but something darker, more sinister. The pall hung over Southeast Asia like a funeral veil for weeks. When Rork and I took our leave from Asia later, it was still there.

The scientists of the world have subsequently explained that the blue moon and months of hazy skies were from the explosion of that volcano at a place now infamous—Krakatoa. But at the time, I couldn't help wondering how Hiep Hoa's astrologers explained it.

Probably as a death knell for their way of life.

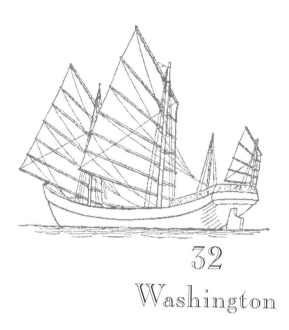

32
Washington

Rork and I had been back in Washington for three days when we were both summoned to the office of Secretary of the Navy William Chandler. Rork, the man who laughed off those Malay pirates in the Gulf of Siam, was as nervous as I'd ever seen him. Because of my rank and work, I'd reported to the secretary's office many times before, but mere bosun's mates never entered the rarified atmosphere of Cabinet-level leadership.

It was a huge room, ornate as ever, but the atmosphere turned out to be even more rarified than we'd imagined. Five minutes after our arrival, the man from the house next door, accompanied by two French diplomats and an Asian man, entered the room. Rork's jaw dropped as his hand was pumped.

"I am sorry for your wound, Bosun Rork," President Chester Alan Arthur intoned while studying the rubber left hand. I remember thinking that he'd really be impressed if he knew about the vicious-looking marlin spike underneath that hand.

Then the president lightened his words. "But you appear to have adjusted well. I sincerely hope you will stay in the navy. We need good men like you."

My friend looked down at his fake appendage and stammered out, "Aye, sir, me arm's jes' fine. Them Froggie surgeons were good. Thank ye, sir. Uncle Sam's navy's been me home for a long time, an' I'm much obliged ta stay in."

President Arthur nodded. "Good, Rork. From what I hear, you're still twice as good as any man with two natural hands. Say, I understand you've got plans to construct a new home down in Florida?"

That brought a grin to Rork. "Aye, that we do, sir. The commander an' me'll be buildin' it this winter down on Patricio Island."

"Well I'd like to hear all about that, but we've got some work to do right now and I'll need to introduce my guests to do it. Mr. Secretary, Commander Wake, Bosun Rork, these two gentlemen are Monsieurs Fontaine and Costel from the French embassy, which represents the foreign affairs of Cambodia, and this is Mr. Thimh, the personal emissary of the King of Cambodia. He came all this way to meet me and say hello, but mainly to present something to Lieutenant Commander Wake and Boatswain's Mate Rork."

Chandler showed no astonishment, but Rork and I did. The president laughed.

"Yes, I thought you'd be surprised. It seems that King Norodom sent Mr. Thimh as a special envoy to convey a token of his appreciation for the service you both rendered His Majesty. I had the honor to meet Mr. Thimh yesterday." He bowed to the Cambodian and said, "Mr. Thimh, I thank you for your efforts and you may proceed with your duties."

Rork and I came to attention as I remembered that day of the pirate battle, when I declined an imperial Cambodian naval commission. What had Norodom sent? I noticed that Secretary

Chandler and the president were amused but the Frenchmen were solemn. Did they know about the Blundell business?

Thimh stepped forward and spoke in reasonably good English.

"Lieutenant Commander Peter Wake. Boatswain's Mate Sean Rork. I come here today on behalf of, and by the personal order of, His Majesty King Norodom of Cambodia. The purpose is to present to you with the Royal Order of Cambodia."

Thimh produced two small teak boxes, inlaid with a golden elephant standing in front of the royal palace. Opening the first, Thimh held up a medal for all to see. It was slightly similar in shape to a French Legion of Honor, but green and blue with red ribbon. He pinned it on my chest, did likewise for Rork, then announced, "His Majesty wishes it to be known, by one and by all, that Peter Wake and Sean Rork shall forever have a friend in the form of the King of Cambodia, for their brave and selfless service, which brings great credit upon themselves, their navy, and their country."

Thimh stopped abruptly and leaned forward so the others could not hear. To Rork and me, he whispered, "You both will always have His Majesty as a firm friend. His Majesty wants you both to always keep in communication and to never hesitate to ask for anything. His Majesty owes you both his life and his kingdom."

The whole thing was simply extraordinary—and pure Norodom. Here we were, in the presence of my own president and secretary of the navy, not to mention the French foreign ministry diplomats, and Norodom had the audacity to make sure his man whispered a personal message they couldn't hear.

I replied for both of us. "Mr. Thimh, *awkun.*"

My effort at Cambodian worked. Thimh smiled, and I knew he would let Norodom know my "thank you" was in their language.

"And please convey to His Majesty the profound appreciation of both Bosun Rork and myself, for this most honored of awards, one that comes from the heart of a man we both respect and admire."

There were more words from the others in the room, typically inane utterances of the international diplomatic types, but it didn't take long. Five minutes later the foreigners were gone.

President Arthur shook Rork's hand again. "Good luck, then, Rork, and thank you again for your work over in the Far East. And congratulations on the medal. You both deserve it. You're a good man and I wish you well."

Rork took his cue to leave. The rascal winked at me on the way out. Oh, I knew *that* look. Within the hour, his cronies at the tavern down by the Navy Yard would be hearing a lively rendition of Rork's award ceremony with a medal from his old pal, the king of Cambodia, plus the conversation with his new pal, the president of the United States. Well, that's what he usually would've done, but it turned out that in this case I predicted erroneously.

Once Rork had departed, the president sat down with a sigh. He looked bone tired, having been through a lot in the past few years. Large-framed, with serious eyes that could light up with mirth when he relaxed, President Arthur also shared a sad bond with me, one that we'd discussed at an earlier meeting. He'd lost his wife a year, almost to the day, before my Linda died.

Nell Herndon Arthur was the daughter of a naval officer and favorite niece of the famous Matthew Fontaine Maury, the naval officer and world-renowned ocean scientist, commonly known as the "Pathfinder of the Seas." That distinction lost its luster during the war. Maury ran the naval observatory in Washington before the fighting, but, like so many others, he stayed loyal to his state of Virginia and joined the rebels. His reputation never recovered.

His daughter, poor Nell Arthur, wife of the man nobody thought would be president, died of pneumonia twenty months before her husband became president, by way of his chief's assassination. I'd always felt sorry for President Arthur.

The president turned to me. "Well, that was a pleasant inter-lude in my day, but now back to work. I've read your report and now I have some questions, Commander. Ready?"

"Yes, sir."

Anger tinged his words. "What happened to the other Frenchmen who misled my envoy, Beauregard Strom?"

Chester Arthur, veteran of New York's political wars, was a man who knew when to pick his battles. If he decided to fight for something, he'd go all the way. My evaluation of what had hap-pened with Blundell would color his decision on whether to pick one now with the French.

"We don't know the whole story, sir, but probably nothing. It was all quietly swept under the rug to avoid humiliation to Jules Ferry's government in Paris and Harmand's mission in Indo-China, and also to avoid enraging the American government. I still think Harmand wasn't in on it.

"Mr. Strom told me that Harmand was irate when he found out what had happened once we all arrived at the French flagship and they spoke at length. So I do not think it was sanctioned by anyone in authority, but we'll never know who all was involved peripherally. It probably went beyond Blundell, Courcy, and Brière, but of course, they're dead and not talking. Lieutenant Viaud—he's in my report, sir—told me that he heard that Courcy and Brière were declared insane from the stress of battle and the matter was considered closed—he never had any official scrutiny of his shooting those two men. The public will never know of this affair."

Arthur nodded. "Good, I don't want it out in the press either. All right, so we don't have a problem with the French on that score."

He glanced at Chandler. "We've got enough disagreement with France about that canal in Panama, and we don't need any more problems, do we, Bill?"

The president returned his gaze to me, with a quick glimpse at the medal. "Now, this Norodom fellow, I read your description about what happened out there, and about the Phu Kwak Island matter. But I want your *personal* assessment of him. What sort of fellow is he?"

"Shrewd, sir. Decent in heart, decadent in taste, knowledgeable of European culture, but above all, politically very shrewd. I think he will last a long time on the throne, albeit as a puppet of the French. He was able to continue power upon his return to Phnom Penh. The expected coup had not yet begun when he arrived back at the palace."

"And, obviously, he has become your good friend?"

"Yes, sir. We keep in correspondence, though he never told me about the medal."

"Any reason at all for us to be involved over there in Cambodia?"

"Absolutely none, sir. Your refusal of his offer regarding Phu Kwak was right on target."

"Very good, Commander. Just as I had thought. And now for that newest emperor over in Hué—I forgot his name. Never can remember these confounded Oriental names. I want your assessment of him."

"Emperor Hiep Hoa, sir, sixth of the Nguyen Dynasty. Intelligent, educated in the classic Confucian culture, but unlike Norodom, he is ignorant of Western ways. He was never groomed to be emperor and didn't have the interaction with foreigners that others had in the imperial household, but I do think he's sincerely devoted to his empire, which isn't much anymore. Not decadent either, which is unusual for that part of the world. But unfortunately, he is under the sway of the mandarins. They are anti-French in particular and anti-Western generally."

"So how long will *he* last?"

"Hard for me to say, sir, but the odds aren't in his favor to last long. He alienated the mandarins by surrendering to the French, and I've read that he's alienating the French by not implementing their changes as rapidly as they want. I give him a year, at the most."

"And did this Hiep Hoa become a friend of yours too?"

"In a way, yes, sir, I think he did. Not a good friend like Norodom, but a friend."

Arthur's eyebrows went up at that. "You have collected quite a menagerie of acquaintances around the world, haven't you, Commander?"

Hmm. That was a loaded question. Washington egos were very fragile.

"Nature of my work, sir."

"Yes, well, is there any good reason for us to be involved in *that* country, or colony, or whatever the hell it is now?"

"Officially it's become a protectorate, sir. But actually, it's a *de facto* colony. In the near future they'll make that official. Other than some cable-laying companies that might be interested in contracting for rubber from that area, there's absolutely nothing political, military, or economic that I can see to draw us to that entire area either. There's a lot of turmoil there we don't need. I recommend we stay out of it."

The president's famous double chin wobbled in accord. "I agree. What about these Germans? They are spreading everywhere. What's their relationship to that particular region?"

I was very concerned about the Germans and glad he asked. "They have colonies now among the Pacific islands, one in China, and some in East Africa, sir. Very confident, some are arrogant. I think they'd like to have a coaling station, at the very least, near Singapore to support their new trade routes, but the Brits, Dutch, and French already have the Southeast Asia pretty much sewn up. And they're watching the Germans like hawks, which I think is a wise idea."

A conversation over dinner aboard the *Stosch* came to my mind. "Commodore von Blanc, commander of their Asiatic squadron, was quite candid with me one evening, sir. He said Bismarck is the real power, not the Kaiser, and has persuaded their version of a parliament to fund a global empire of colonies and a modern navy to support it. Said they wanted their own 'place in the sun,' like the other European powers. Made it sound like a point of national prestige, sir. At one point, he joked that even the American hemisphere had room for some Teutonic energy and efficiency. I didn't much like the sound of that."

The president's face tightened.

"Yes . . . I don't either. We know they've been courting the Venezuelans and Mexicans with bank loans. And as you saw for yourself two years ago, Commander, they are quite established in Argentina and Chile. A German empire around the world—who would've thought of that just fifteen years ago?"

"Yes, sir, they're on the move, no doubt about that."

"Did you hear anything from them about Samoa, Commander?"

Samoa? I hadn't heard anything about the Samoan Islands from anyone. The Brits were paramount in that area of the Pacific. Was the U.S. government eyeing them for a naval station? Was Germany looking to get a colony there? With a cagey look on his face, Secretary Chandler craned forward to hear my answer.

"No, sir. Nothing about Samoa," I replied.

The president smiled at Chandler and nodded. "Good. Now tell me about what you predict will happen in Asia in the near future with our dear friends, the French."

That was simple. "War with China, sir."

"How so?"

I pointed to a map of Southeast Asia on the table beside us. "The peace treaty signed in Hué only extended to Emperor Hiep Hoa's forces within the Annam and Tonking parts of the empire of Viet Nam. It did not extend to the Chinese and Black Flag armies in Tonking massed along the Chinese border. The French will attack them in Tonking to drive them out, which won't be easy, and I am sure the French will attack the Chinese fleet to remove it as a threat. I don't know where for sure, but probably at their base at Foochow. The Chinese fleet is modern, sir, and represents a threat to all the Europeans in Asia. By the way, much of it was built by the Germans."

"And who will win that naval battle?" asked Chandler.

"The French, sir, as long as they stay out of ramming and boarding range, where the Chinese can swarm aboard them." The mob at Cai Be came to mind and I felt my heart pound. That had been close. Too close. "Admiral Courbet will pound them from a distance, then move in for the kill."

There was a knock at the door and a clerical assistant announced the entrance of Admiral Porter, my boss. Porter strode in, said good morning to the secretary and the president, nodded to me, then sat in a chair. I noticed that, as usual, he didn't wait to be asked. Such are the benefits of seniority and, in Porter's case, an irascible temperament. I'd long earlier realized that most politicians were afraid of the admiral. He'd outlasted scores of them.

"Did I miss anything important yet?" asked Porter.

"No, just another foreign bauble for Lieutenant Commander Wake, along with his impressions of the Asian situation," replied Chandler. Porter eyed the medal and shook his head with a chuckle.

"Good, then I'm here in time for the main event in question."

The president looked at his watch, then stood. "Hmm, I see I'm late for a group of the Republican Farmers Association of Indiana, gentlemen. Is there anything else, Lieutenant Commander Wake, that's not in your report already?"

"No, sir."

"Very good." He turned to Secretary Chandler and Admiral Porter. "Then let's complete our next duty, shall w,e gentlemen?"

They all stood, which made me pop up. I prepared to go, but Porter put a hand up.

"Where are you going? You're not dismissed yet, Lieutenant Commander."

Why were they all emphasizing my rank? Common custom was to omit the prefix "lieutenant" when addressing lieutenant commanders.

Secretary Chandler laughed. "He's running away, Mr. President!"

President Arthur grinned, then said, "Don't run off just yet, Peter. Remember when you were asked to do this sort of naval intelligence work two years ago?"

This didn't sound good. I wondered if I was in some kind of trouble. But if I was, why were they smiling?

"Yes, sir."

"You were told then that you'd never get the kind of recognition regular line naval officers get. No ship commands, no press communiqués, no Congressional supporters. Your work would be *quiet* and unsung. A different kind of honorable service."

That was all true. I remembered the conversation well. "Yes, sir."

"But you were also told that you would have the appreciation of a few senior people, people who would know of your work. And that you would eventually see some promotion, so that you could still have a professional career."

"Ah, yes, sir. I remember that part too."

One of the president's beefy hands shook mine, placing two items in my palm. They were silver oak leaf insignia. At the same time, Admiral Porter said, "By the authority of the Secretary of the Navy and the President of the United States of America, I am honored to hereby congratulate you, Peter Wake, on your promotion to full commander."

He removed the gold lieutenant commander oak leaves in my epaulettes and replaced them with the silver ones of a full commander. I was stunned.

An Irish accent chimed in from behind me. Rork hadn't gone to the tavern after all, at least not yet. He came to attention in the doorway and saluted.

"'Tis a fine, fine thing, an' nary a day too soon, sirs. Congratulations from the lower deck, Commander. You deserve it. May I have the honor of being the first to salute you?"

The president beckoned to him. "Rork, you old sea dog, get

in here and take part in the commander's glory."

I regarded him dubiously. "Rork? You knew all along?"

"Of course he knew!" growled Porter as Chandler poured an amber liquid into several glasses on a sideboard. "These old bosuns know every damn thing that goes on in the navy. Have a drink, son. You too, Rork. Mr. President, some rum? Those farmers can wait a little longer."

And that was how I got promoted to the Navy's equivalent of an Army lieutenant colonel, after nine long years as a lieutenant commander. No public ceremony, but one hell of a private one.

And at the end of it, just as we were about to leave, Chandler pulled Rork and me aside to let us know our assignments were going to change a bit in the future.

"Men, I want you to not wear the foreign decorations while in Washington. Incites too much Congressional curiosity into your work, which can lead to political problems. As of this coming January, you won't be in Washington too much anyway. You'll still be on special duty status to the Bureau of Navigation, but not with Mason at Naval Intelligence. You'll be reporting to Admiral Porter and me, but effective this coming February you'll only come into naval headquarters occasionally. That island of yours in Florida will be your main station when not on assignment. Understood? You will work out of the public glare."

Rork said nothing, but I could tell he was concerned at this unusual state of affairs. I asked for us both, "This will be in writing, sir?"

Chandler huffed back, "No, Commander. And some of your most important work from now on will not be in writing either. But rest assured, it will be *very* important work."

Chandler wasn't jesting. From that moment on, my career changed. Dramatically.

33

The Trunk

Monday, 3 December 1883
Office of Naval Intelligence
Naval Headquarters
Washington, D.C.

On a cold, blustery day, a gift to commemorate my journey to tropical Indo-China arrived at my office—an item not requested or imagined. It was an enormous trunk. My office mates were unable to contain their curiosity when it arrived at headquarters.

No one had ever seen such a thing. It was capable of holding a good hundred and fifty pounds of cargo. Two men were required to lift it when empty. Many sailors' chests have some sort of decoration, but this had far beyond that, the fanciest I'd known, with intricate scrollwork on the iron framing straps and some beautiful wood patterns in the corners and around the latch. When Rork studied it later, he said the wood was a special type of mahogany, with rosewood and ebony for the inlays, all of it lacquered to a fine gloss.

With uncharacteristic awe, he pronounced it "the finest work o' the art me eyes have e'er seen, worthy o' display in the palace o' the blessed Pope, hisself."

A large yellow dragon, with gilt-accented claws and fangs, was painted across the lid, at the tail end of which sat a French steam warship wreathed in gun smoke, presumably Courbet's *Bayard*. At the dragon's other end, where the ferocious fangs were bared, a message to me in bloodred Chinese characters emerged from the mouth.

The timing of the chest's entry into my life was eerie, seemingly a gift from the dead. The day before, I'd read a newspaper snippet about the trunk's sender—a sad epilogue for a sad man.

I've lost the clipping, but remember the gist of it from the *Washington Post*:

Emperor Hiep Hoa, the third potentate of Viet Nam inside of five months, is deceased. Viet Nam is an Oriental land south of China, and a recently acquired colony of France. Dr. Francois Harmand, who runs the foreign affairs of the place, published the French government's regrets and condolences November 27th, instanter, along with official support for the new successor, soon to be named.

I found myself depressed after reading the article, for I knew that, in the Asian way of things, Hiep Hoa had probably been murdered in some despicably gruesome manner. Most likely by someone he trusted.

The chest's shipping receipt reported that it had been sent from Hué in early October, six weeks before the emperor's death. My spirits lifted a bit when I opened the chest and read the personal note scrolled up inside and tied with a golden silk ribbon. It was written in perfect English penmanship for the emperor, probably by Mr. Bui or Mandarin Khuyen.

At the Palace of the Emperor, Sixth Celestial Son of Heaven
Within the Forbidden Purple City

My Dear Peter Wake,
May this missive of thanks find you and your family well, with sat-
isfaction of things past and pleasant anticipation of things planned.

For one evening and a morning this year, you were an unantic-
ipated herald of the future. Filled with false knowledge, I doubted
your wisdom at the time, but you saw what was to come far more
clearly than my own astrologers and learned ones, and were far more
honest to me than the Frenchmen's promises. I never thought you mis-
leading, but unintentionally mistaken. Two thousand one hundred
and forty-seven of my men died, and four thousand four hundred
were wounded, to prove that I was wrong. And you right.

This trunk is my gift to the one man who was honest with me
in my time of travail, and who tried to warn me and save lives. My
hope is that when you look at the artistry of this trunk, you will see
in it the beauty of the land and people of the Empire of Viet Nam,
and know that you will always have a friend here.

Thank you for trying to warn me, Peter. I have learned the les-
son of humility, however late. May you live the life you desire, with
the tranquility of the jasmine flower and the freedom of the sparrow.
And may your man recover from his wound, to know harmonious
contentment.

Nyguen Hiep Hoa

That was an auspicious day, for that afternoon a letter came
in the post from Indo-China. You can picture the increasing
astonishment of my colleagues, none of whom knew precisely
where I'd been or why. The letter was written in the style of an
accomplished linguist, well-versed in calligraphy.

Peter and Sean,
I pray Sean's wound is healing rapidly. Bishops Caspar and Galibert
send their best wishes and sincere thanks for what you did at Hué to

expedite the end of the battle. They have informed their superiors in Europe.

Sadly, my country no longer exists. We still have an emperor, but in name only. The French dominate everything. It is bittersweet for me. Change was needed, but not this kind, and not that way.

I am proud to call you my friends. It was an honor to be with you, and quite an education about the ways of your great nation and people. I have returned to the dull life of an academic, but still have vivid memories of my brief time as a warrior beside my American friends.

God bless you both. May we meet again, in better circumstances. Until then, please keep in correspondence.

Sincerely, from your linguistic friend . . .
P

Messages from two men, so dissimilar, who both wanted the best for their people. One now dead and the other disillusioned. I wondered what would become of Petrusky and feared the worst when I read his letter. I was convinced that he would join some fledgling movement of intellectuals at odds with the occupiers, sure to perish in some magnificent gesture that would end in failure—like those imperial guards at the battle of Hué.

But he didn't become a revolutionary. At least not overtly. Naturally, since the French still dominate his people to this day, I cannot report his personal opinions and actions in recent years. His patriotic concerns have not eased, of course, but the professor seems to have been able to adapt and live his life well, rooted in his faith—ironically, the same faith as the foreigners who rule his land.

We still keep in touch, friends bound by blood shed and death defied. It is a correspondence of great professional, and profound personal, value to me.

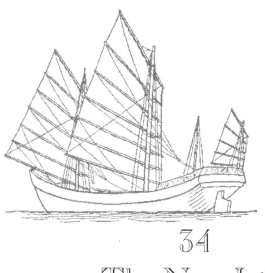

34
The New Life

Sunday, 9 December 1883
Patricio Island
Lower Gulf Coast of Florida

By the time the sun was well past its zenith, and starting to descend rapidly, everyone was totally worn out, none more so than my old friend. The prosthetic appliance (the term U.S. Navy's doctors in Washington called the thing) had been chafing Rork's stump all day, what with the constant strain of lifting and holding, and he'd quietly readjusted the straps and padding several times. But, in spite of my requests, he wouldn't let up in his work.

"Aye, 'tis the least I can do, Peter. You're puttin' most o' the money in this, so I can put in a wee bit o' me own sweat."

We'd been hauling lumber up to the top of the island's ridge—about twenty-five feet above the beach—all day from our sloop, the *Nancy Ann,* and the small barge she'd towed out to the island. Just getting the whole mess to Patricio Island from Punta Gorda had taken two days. Red-heart pine and bald cypress boards are heavy, especially when they're twenty feet long, two inches thick, and a foot wide.

Now we had three piles, right next to the shell, sand, and lime foundation for the house and rainwater cistern. One pile of wood was siding and flooring—those pine and cypress boards. Another pile was of detailed trim pieces for windows and doors— that one my fourteen-year-old son Sean brought up by himself. The last stack consisted of the heavy eight-by-eight-inch framing members. The house's frame would be erected in the morning, or at least we'd *start* putting it up. With any luck, and a lot of hard work, I figured we'd have Christmas dinner under some sort of a roof.

Rork and I were on two months of accumulated leave. By February second we had to be back in Washington for a briefing on our next assignment—an assessment of the French canal effort in Panama, where things were apparently not going well. Washington was worried about that, and just how far Paris would go to ensure success.

Up on the hill, I saw Rork massaging his arm, probably from another phantom pain or itch. It was time for a break, and besides, the sun was pretty low in the west, a point upon which several in my little hired crew had commented already. So I went over to the sloop and broached the rum cask, announcing to the men on the hilltop, "The rum locker's open. Come and get some, boys. Then we'll eat."

"About time! I'm damned near dead," said Charlie.

"Yeah, I thought this big dumb Irish maniac was gonna flog us there for a while," muttered Kip as he eyed Rork, then threw a clump of dirt at him in jest.

"Sailors, geesh . . ." was all that Brian could get out as he stumbled down the slope.

Rork came down to me and added his opinion. "Aye, an' these landlubbin', lobster-skinned boyos ain't no good for a day o' real man's work. Yard dogs is what they are, all right. No doubt about *that!* But let's give 'em some rum jes' the same, Peter. 'Tis the Christian thing to do an' all."

Rork summed it up pretty well. Brian, Kip, and Charlie were friends of mine. We met during the war, when they'd been draftees in the army from Ohio and Wisconsin, sent down to Fort Taylor at Key West in 1864. They settled in Florida after the war, ostensibly preferring it to the winters up north, though I suspected there may have been unresolved legal matters at home. Rumors had it that the boys had several wives each. Reputedly, Kip had been with several *other* men's wives down in the Keys. He denied it, but I suspected that was why they weren't in Key West.

Unskilled at much of anything else, the trio was a traveling troubadour show billed as The Yard Dogs, the old Southern swamp term for alligators. Usually, when not in jail for excessive revelry, they worked in taverns on the Florida west coast and in Key West, but now they were in between engagements and needed some money, so I contracted with them to help build the house.

That may have been a mistake—as Rork commented halfway through the day. "This detail will take a wee bit o' time, sir. These lads are jes' not at their best with *physical* labor."

My son interrupted my contemplation of that fact by piping up from the end of the line of men. "Hey, can I have some rum, too? I worked like everybody else."

Rork cocked his head toward the boy, whom we call "young Sean" to distinguish between the two, and gave me that sly grin of his. The three musicians gravely nodded their heads in accordance, and I immediately deduced a conspiracy among the crew.

I gave in. "All right, young Sean, you may have a sipper— just enough to wet your *upper* lip. But for God's sake don't you dare tell your sister Useppa, or she'll think me the Devil himself."

"Thanks, Dad," came the reply from my son, who then whispered a little too loudly to Brian. "She's a temperance missionary, you know."

Brian shook his head sadly. "Yeah, I heard that, Sean. Sorry."

Rork put a hand, his best one, on my son's shoulder. "Aye,

you earned a wee tot today, lad. An' you'll be in the navy soon enough as a commissioned officer an' *gentleman,* so you ought to know that taste. You'll see it on liberty ashore enough, an' will have to deal with it in your crew. Just don't grow too fond o' it, your ownself. It's ruined many a good man, it has."

"Yeah, like us," said Kip. "So don't slow up the line, Rork, ya Gaelic ogre."

Rork belly laughed and wagged his marlin spike stub at Kip like a cutlass. "Ah! Me point exactly, lad. Like me dear friend Kip, who twangs a mean gitjo, though he's had a bad day here under *naval* discipline."

After we all got our cups filled—or in young Sean's case, slightly filled—we trudged up the hill and sat on folding chairs in front of the foundation. Around us were our tents, supplies, and cooking fire. Fat grouper and mangrove snapper were slow roasting, the greens pan frying with bacon, and it wouldn't be long until supper was ready.

The grove of gumbo limbo trees, their red bark peeling and green, fernlike leaves already starting to fall in south Florida's version of winter, lent a soft touch to the scene. A salt-tanged gentle nor'east breeze brushed us with the light scent of the jasmine and papaya and bananas that grew wild on the island. In the west, past Mondongo Island, the orange sun was descending over Lacosta Island. A conch shell sounded its wail from Palmetto Island, then one from the Cuban fishermen at Useppa, and another from the settlers at Bokeelia to the east—the end-of-day signal among the islanders that all was well.

I leaned back in the camp chair and drank it all in—a fantasy, the likes of which my naval co-workers up north at headquarters could only dream. My island. My home. My son and friends. It was a good place to be in life. In a few days, my daughter Useppa was due to arrive for Christmas, up from her mission station in Key West. We'd all be together again, as a family. Closing my eyes for a moment and shutting out worries, I felt Linda's soothing presence, which was no wonder, for her ashes were scattered on Useppa Island, my daughter's namesake a mile to the south.

These islands held so many memories. It felt right to be back, and I was deeply thankful for Rork and me having lived through hell on the other side of the world, a place so very different from this. The sun was down now. My fellows were gathering around the cooking fire, Charlie handing out plates piled with steaming food. Kip and Brian were singing a ballad. Something about a Cajun girl living in Florida. Rork was laughing with them.

I stayed where I was, mesmerized by the colossal thing we'd carried up the hill like some ancient family relic. I sat there, consumed by all it represented, and the haunting visions it evoked. Hiep Hoa wanted the trunk to bring me pleasant memories, but the scenes that kept floating through my mind weren't what he had intended—Whangtai's cold-eyed opium mercenaries swarming aboard the *Tonle Queen* that night on the river, Petrusky's furtive lessons on the foredeck about who was who in Indo-China, Norodom desperately fighting the Malay-Chinese pirates, and later, each of us inexorably dying of thirst and hunger on an endless glassy sea. Memories of An's soft warmth at the dance on Condore Island and the sad guilt I later felt for enjoying it—still felt when remembering it. Then, pleading for Hiep Hoa not to fight the French, knowing that he would anyway, and that thousands would perish for nothing.

I closed my eyes against the sight of the emperor's dragon on the trunk, but that only made it worse. In my mind I saw Rork fall wounded, over and over. His contorted face kept flashing in my mind, a stark horrible tableau in long-drawn-out motion, like one of those magic-lantern picture shows that are all the rage among the swells these days. I saw Blundell running away in the night through the garden, felt the cold pleasure of lining him up on the rifle's sight, then gently easing the trigger back until I felt the recoil. Then, Rork lying there, eyes locked on mine, before they sawed off his arm. And the whole damnable thing ended with that nauseating memory of my grand finale in Asia—walking through that ghastly field of gore after the horrific battle at Hué.

My son had been pestering me to tell him about our journey, particularly after the trunk arrived. Of course, I wouldn't give him any of the confidential information about our mission, but I found myself not wanting to even tell him about much of the non-secret parts. For some unfathomable reason, I didn't know how to camouflage the descriptions for polite conversation anymore. How could I nicely describe the stupid waste of human life at Hué, the gruesome mutilations of modern total war? Of watching my dearest friend, and my son's godfather, lose his arm because of a ludicrous misperception on the part of a greedy predator? Was I losing my self-confidence, my inner strength?

As the others reveled around the fire, I admitted to myself the real reason for my reticence—I didn't want to chance it that young Sean would see his father's emotions exposed. I worried that he might possibly perceive those insidious doubts about my profession that had plagued me for twenty years, since I first saw combat on the misnamed Peace River, not so far from where we all were sitting. Especially about my work now, which easily morphed from one shadowy form of justification to another. Or even deniability, according to the whims of the cologned elite in Washington. I knew the genuine explanation for my melancholia—cowardice of letting my son see the real me. Recognizing it didn't make it any less disturbing.

The music was louder now and my eyes opened to quite a scene. Having wolfed down his dinner, Kip was back in high spirits, leading the singing with Brian alongside, banging a Jamaican rhumba box in rhythm, while the others joined in on the chorus of "What do you do with a drunken sailor?"

Joviality all around, except for me. Hell, if only I could shake my depressed state of mind.

Rork came over with two plates balanced on his good arm and collapsed in the chair next to me, propping his boots up on the trunk's dragon. He handed me a plate of grouper.

"What's the matter, Peter? Here ya are, lord o' all you survey, an' ya look sadder than an Ulsterman lost in Derry."

Never could hide anything from him—he knew my moody ways too well.

"Thinking about all we went though over there. This trunk just brings it all back to me."

Rork sighed loudly, like he was blowing out bad memories. "Aye, it's been one hellova bloody damned year, but the thing's almost o'er now. A new year's a-comin' an' we got work to do yet, me ol' friend." His serious face lightened into a cunning leer. "Aye, an' them Panama girls, they *do* love us sailors, don't they just? So cheer the hell up, Commander."

All the girls of the world loved Rork, and he loved them. I thought of that servant girl at the hospital in Mytho and hoped he hadn't loved her too much. I really didn't need the Church tracking us down for *that* indiscretion.

"My son's been on me to tell him about our journey, like I usually do. But this time I can't, Sean. Not yet, anyway. You know, in two years he'll be at the academy; in six he'll be a naval officer and facing these same things. He'll find out soon enough for himself what it's like."

Young Sean was singing loud now in company with Kip—"Shave his belly with a rusty razor—that's what you do with a drunken sailor!"—and I questioned if he'd had more than just a sipper.

I was about to get up and check on my son's cup when Rork gently laid his spike on my arm and leaned over, his voice low. "Still, maybe someday . . . when he's a bit older . . . you should tell him everything that happened. Might help the lad later as an officer, to learn from what you've done an' seen. The *real* story—not some pub room yarn full o' drink from the likes o' me. No, Peter, you owe him the truth, from one man to another. One *naval officer* to another."

"Yeah, I suppose I do."

He shifted his gaze from me back to the dragon glinting in the firelight.

"An' someday, the boyo'll probably need a good trunk, too—once he gets up in rank, o' course. This one here'd do quite nicely. Me thinks it'll serve him better than you, anyway."

I decided right then that I *would* pass along what I'd learned over the years—usually the hard way—to my son. In addition, the trunk would be a tangible token of my work in the East for young Sean. But for him, Hiep Hoa's wish could come true—it would be a thing of beauty, not a reminder of brutality.

"Rork, you irrepressible rogue, damned if you aren't right on all accounts. All right, I'm *officially* cheered the hell up. Thank you."

He clinked his cup to mine. "A toast then, to this island—to our new life here in this wee bit o' paradise."

"To our new life here on the island, Sean. May we build this house well."

Warming to the task, Rork proposed yet another. "Aye! *Onward* an' *upward,* for us both, come what may . . ."

Not to be outdone, I echoed it, with an addendum. "Onward and upward, for us both—and for young Sean too."

"Damn right, for the lad too."

A moment later, I quietly slipped over to the fire and checked my son's cup as his voice rose to a moon emerging from the trees over on Pine Island. The cup was empty. Brian caught me looking and shook his head with a mellow smile. Young Sean wasn't drunk on the rum at all; he was intoxicated on camaraderie, after a tough day's work.

I understood that completely.

Postscript

26th day of June, 1890
Graduation Day
Ensign Sean Wake, U.S.N.
United States Naval Academy
Annapolis, Maryland USNA Class of 1890

To my dear son Sean,
Frequently over the years, my best endeavors have been Sean Rork's ideas initially. So it was with this narration as well. Then and there, in the firelight of that tropical Florida evening six and a half years ago, I made the resolution to someday write down the story of what had happened to us in the Orient. Rork, as usual, was right. I did owe the truth to you, my son.

With this well-deserved graduation you are a naval officer now, like your father, and I've fulfilled that pledge to myself. My wish is that this tale assists you in your career, and that you grow to love the Navy and the sea as much as I have over the years. It's not an easy life, especially on a family, but it can be a good one.

And now that you've read the story I think you'll understand why I never answered some of those questions you asked about my work and about that big old trunk.

Emperor Hiep Hoa's trunk is yours now. Let it serve you well.

With a father's love and pride,

and best wishes for the kind of exciting life only a U. S. Navy man can know . . .

Peter Wake

Commander, United States Navy

Office of Naval Intelligence

Special Assignment Section

Naval Headquarters

Washington, D.C.

Chapter Endnotes
for this Novel

For the reader's interest, the following is historical evidence I've uncovered related to Wake's tale of adventure in French Indochina. I have also provided some background from the previous novels in the Honor Series.

Chapter Two—Memories
Peter Wake's great love affair and marriage to Linda is described in the first six novels: *At the Edge of Honor, Point of Honor, Honorable Mention, A Dishonorable Few, An Affair of Honor,* and *A Different Kind of Honor.* Her tragic death is recounted in the novel preceding this one, *A Different Kind of Honor.*

The lunar eclipse that Wake saw is documented in history—an unusual celestial event visible for only an hour and a half in that part of the world on 22 April 1883.

Chapter Three—Under Way
Throughout his eventful career, Wake met unique individuals in various corners of the world who later proved to be crucial in times of peril. Was it by luck or ingenious design? He never let on, and frequently his descriptions of them are so sketchy, possibly from a security point of view, that I can't confirm their existence by independent research. Professor Petruski, whose name Wake misspelled with a 'y,' is an exception. He is referred to in J. Thomson's memoir of travel in Indochina written in the 1870s, a few years before Wake met the noted Asian linguist.

Chapter Five—Friends of Friends
The Society of Foreign Missions of Paris still exists. Over the last four centuries it sent members all over the French empire, particularly in Indochina. They endured countless persecutions and massacres, and gradually their congregations became an influen-

tial force in the Vietnamese culture in the twentieth century. The Sisters of Providence of Portieux are still in Cambodia and, among their many good works, run a home for disabled children.

For the intimate details about Wake's intriguing relationship with the Jesuits, read *An Affair of Honor*, where they helped him get out of some ticklish spots in Europe. Then read *A Different Kind of Honor*, where he was almost killed repaying the debt in South America.

Chapter Six—The Lessons of Tu Duc

Wake was receiving accurate political advice that night on the steamer's foredeck. Modern Vietnamese historians like Nguyen Phuc Vinh Ba and Ton That Binh share a similar view of the imperial court at Hué and the turbulent events leading up to 1883, a very significant year in Vietnamese history.

Chapter Eight—Façades

Garnier d'Abain and Whangtai were very real. D'Abain arrived in Phnom Penh in 1874 and became the royal opium general. He wrote all about his start in the business, and Whangtai, in *Scribner's Monthly Magazine* that year.

The debate about using India rubber versus gutta percha for submarine telegraph cables raged for years in magazines such as *The Living Age* and *Manufacturer and Builder*. Fortunes were at stake. Gutta percha won out in the end and the Brits in Southeast Asia made millions.

Chapter Nine—A Poisonous Stew

I've discovered references from this time period in Southeast Asia that confirm the existence of McCarthy, the Irish surveyor; Dupuis, the French trader; and Heard, the American merchant. Dupuis was the most feared by far, having cheated death several times. Heard, like d'Abain, was a writer. He published an article about Indochina in an 1886 issue of *The Century Magazine*. He ended up as the U.S. ambassador to Korea from 1890 to 1894.

Chapter Ten—Home

Patricio Island still exists in Pine Island Sound. An uninhabited wildlife refuge today, the remnants of a settler's cistern remain on the central ridge, under a forest of gumbo limbo trees.

It seems that Wake had *Lutin's* designation wrong. She was still commissioned in the French Navy while he was aboard her, but frequently "loaned" to King Norodom. It wasn't until 1897 that she was officially transferred and became the king's permanent royal yacht.

Chapter Eleven—Phnom Penh

The Royal Palaces still exist and are magnificent. I went there to research this book and found them just as Wake describes them. Unfortunately, the Grand Hotel, at the corner of Lagrandière and Rue Jeanneau, did not survive the horrific Khmer Rouge years in the 1970s.

Wake's friend George Dewey is none other than the future hero of the battle of Manila Bay in 1898. Dewey, known in the navy as an active and intelligent officer, was two years older than Wake and an 1858 graduate of the naval academy. This man, who almost died of typhoid in 1882, went on to become a four-star Admiral of the U.S. Navy and one of the first naval officers warning of an eventual war with Germany.

Chapter Twelve—Norodom

Resident Superior Foures directly ran the external—and indirectly much of the internal—operations of the Cambodian government from 1881 until 1885, the year of a bloody failed revolution. Bishop Courdier served in Cambodia for forty-eight years, as a young priest in 1847 until his death in 1895.

Most of the current *stupas* at the palaces are replacements for the originals and were built in the early twentieth century. There are *stupas* for both Ang Duong and his son Norodom I, who was one of the longest reigning monarchs in the world—from 1860 until 1904.

Bokator is still practiced in Cambodia. I briefly watched a match with some extremely enthusiastic fans in a dusty village along the Mekong.

In an effort to experience what Wake did, while on the Mekong River I drank cobra liquor and can testify that it is very dangerous stuff, indeed.

Chapter Thirteen—The Mission

I've found historical references to King Norodom attempting to bring the Spanish into Indochina to offset the French influence, but none naming Wake's fellow passenger Altamonte. By that point in history, however, the Spanish Empire had too many other problems to deal with and Norodom never got them to invest politically or economically.

President Chester Arthur, who became president when President Garfield was assassinated, was a former Collector of the Port of New York City. Because of that background, he was a man of world vision and understood the necessity for a strong navy and the bases it would require. Negotiations for naval base and/or coal depot leasing rights were under way at many locations in the world.

The Mekong in late spring is at it lowest level due to lack of rain. To this day, larger vessels (including the riverboat I was aboard to research this novel) frequently have to stop transits in April and May until the monsoon arrives with sufficient rain to raise the river levels again. By the end of monsoon season in the fall, the river level usually rises in excess of thirty feet.

Chapter Fourteen—The Coast

The krait is an extremely poisonous snake that was later commonly called by Western soldiers a "two step." That is the number of steps you *might* be able to take after a bite before you are disabled or dead.

Chapter Fifteen—Phu Kwak

I have used the spelling from the Westerners' maps of that period. For hundreds of years it was known as a pirate haven and designated on maps as such. Today the island is spelled "Phu Quoc" and is part of Vietnam. It is famous for pepper farms in the interior and beautiful tourist beaches on the west side—one of the few places in Vietnam where tourists can watch a sunset over the sea.

There was a ferocious woman pirate who roamed the South China Sea in the early 1800s named Cheng I Sao (Wake misspelled it), based out of Canton, China. Head of a huge organization of renegades, she retired in 1810 after settling up with the Chinese government and ensuring that most of her thousands of pirates would be granted amnesty. Cheng married, had a son (name unknown), and later died in 1844 at the age of sixty-nine, a wealthy woman who ran gambling houses. Was Shu her granddaughter? We'll probably never know.

Chapter Sixteen—Chaos

There is debate about the first use and original composition of Greek fire. Earliest mention is with the Byzantine Greeks in 670 A.D., who used it extensively to repel Muslim invaders. The Chinese have records of its use back to 917 A.D. Wake had a good idea—rice husks burn very hot and are used as fuel in brick kilns in Southeast Asia, palm oil would provide an adhesive, and high-proof rum would act as an accelerant.

Chapter Seventeen—Drifting

There is well-documented oceanic evidence that supports Wake's story about drifting out of the Gulf of Thailand and around the parrot's beak of the south cape of Vietnam. The currents in the Gulf of Thailand and the South China Sea change annually according to the monsoon seasons and average one knot. In May and June, they are changing into the Southwest Monsoon and switch from moving northward to moving southward in the Gulf of Thailand. At the same time, on the Vietnamese coastline of the

South China Sea, they change from moving southward to moving northeastward.

Chapter Eighteen—Dugong
The dugong is the Asian relative of the West Indian manatee, which the native peoples of the Florida/Caribbean region used as a food source for centuries. Wake and Rork saw them in Florida during the Civil War and would have immediately recognized a dugong as a manatee. In Florida, they are a beloved endangered species that has had noted success in regrowing their population.

Chapter Nineteen—Puolo Condore
The modern name for Puolo Condore Island is Con Dao. During the French colonial years it was known as Con Son and was a notorious prison for Vietnamese political prisoners, a sort of Indochinese version of France's Devil's Island off French Guiana. That function continued into the post-colonial governments. The current Communist rulers of Vietnam say they shut down the prison and are trying to attract tourists to the island where prisoners used to slave away.

There are indeed references in Raphael Semmes' account (*Cruise of the Alabama and Sumter*) to then-ensign Bizot on Condore Island in 1863 when the Confederates stopped there, but I could find no mention of Bizot after that. Condore was, and still is, a seldom-visited place.

It is known that Norodom I was in Saigon several times during this period; however, we have only Wake's account of the king's excursion to Phu Kwak and his near death at the hands of the woman pirate Shu.

Chapter Twenty—Necessities of the Service
USS *Juniata* was well known in the navy for her mechanical breakdowns. Commissioned in 1862, she served thirty months in wartime service—thirteen of which were at naval yards being repaired. After the war, her bad luck continued—*Juniata* spent

from 1876 to 1882 being extensively repaired again. Naval records show information regarding her transit, under Dewey's command, between Singapore and Hong Kong, but nothing is documented relating to Wake's mission.

Chapter Twenty-One—First-Class to Binh Thuan
Maloney was a well-known man in Key West and there are many accounts of his work as a lawyer there. Patricio Island and the whole area around Fort Myers, Florida, was part of Monroe County, the seat of which was in distant Key West, until 1887. In that year, the area became Lee County, named to honor the Confederate general who had died seventeen years earlier. It is still Lee County.

As ominous clouds of war gathered over Southeast Asia in 1883, the United States hoped the situation could be de-escalated. The Chinese viewed American policies as the most neutral and beneficial to China of all the foreigners in Asia. Therefore, John Russell Young, the U.S. envoy to China, was asked by China to mediate the crisis in Tonking between China and France. Young tried quite diligently, but neither side was willing to compromise after Rivière's death. Large-scale war loomed in the near future with both sides rushing reinforcements to the region. No one was able to stop it.

Chapter Twenty-Two—A Damned Skawly Place
At that point, Wake was above 10 degrees north latitude and in the typhoon belt. As a general rule, they strike the coasts of southern China and northern Vietnam in the summer, and southern Vietnam in the fall. In a study by the City University of Madrid, it was found that typhoon activity in the 1880s and 1890s more than doubled from the previous decades. There is a typhoon on record in July of 1883 that came through the Philippines and roared westward to the Gulf of Tonking—Wake was lucky to be on the southern fringe of it, under the lee of the land. His trick of determining the center of a tropical revolving storm relative to

one's position still works. I used it in a cyclone in the Indian Ocean while researching this book.

Durian fruit is highly prized in Indochina and widely known there as "the king of fruits." However beloved it is, the stench of ripe durian can be detected for some distance, hence its common name among Westerners—"stinky fruit." From my experience on the Mekong River, I can personally attest to that and certainly understand how Rork was desperate enough to consider mutiny.

Kam Ranh was the original spelling of Cam Ranh Bay, which became a famous U.S. Navy and Air Force base in the 1960s. Many American veterans of Vietnam will remember first arriving in-country at Cam Ranh Bay for their twelve-month tour of duty. But Americans weren't the first to use it as a naval base. Twenty-one years after Wake's visit, the Imperial Russian Navy used it as a rendezvous en route around the world to their demise at the Battle of Tsushima in 1905. The Imperial Japanese Navy used it to stage their invasion of Malaysia in 1942. And from 1979 to 2002 it was a Soviet, then Russian, naval base—the largest outside Russia. The Vietnamese now call it Cam Lâm.

Kwang Ngai, known by Vietnamese as Quáng Ngāi, is about five miles up a small river from the coast. About halfway to Kwang Ngai along that river lies a village with a heartbreaking history—My Lai.

Wake's information about Duc Duc's reign was correct—he lasted only three days, from the 19th to the 21st of July, 1883. There was a dispute over how Tu Duc's will was read, and how it decreed Duc Duc as successor, along with general concern about his debauchery overwhelming his ability to govern. Duc Duc was immediately thrown in prison on several charges, the most serious of which was having sex with Tu Duc's senior concubine, Hoc Phi. He was intentionally starved, dying after four weeks on August 20, 1883, and was buried in a commoner's grave. In 1889, his son ascended the throne and built a large mausoleum for Duc Duc, officially restoring his father's ironic royal title of "Master of Honor and Dignity."

Chapter Twenty-Three—The Poet-Warrior

The beach to which Wake and the others swam became famous in the 1960s as China Beach, a rest and relaxation place for thousands of American GIs over the years. It is a tourist beach to this day.

The rifles Hung was smuggling were probably Remington Lee bolt-action model 1879, 11mm types, one of the first with a box magazine, since it is known that the Chinese imperial army bought four thousand of them six months later, in 1884, with which to fight the French. Rork would've known that rifle well—the U.S. Navy used 1,300 of them in the 1880s.

Touran was the colonial French name for the cape, bay, and town—captured by their forces in 1858. The world has known it for the last fifty years as Da Nang—the huge American Marine and Air Force base in the 1960s and 1970s.

Mandarin Nguyen Khuyen, raised near Hanoi, was known as one of the most brilliant of the mandarins and served the imperial court in various functions from 1871 until 1885, when he resigned after becoming gradually more disenchanted with the court.

Chapter Twenty-Four—The Forbidden Purple City

Hundreds of concubines and eunuchs lived within the Forbidden Purple City. Concubines were of nine ranks, kept in seclusion, and only allowed outside the inner walls when guarded by royal eunuchs. They never traveled beyond the outer walls of the Citadel. Many eunuchs and concubines became very powerful and quite rich, but lived lives of semi-imprisonment within the walls of the Forbidden Purple City.

Bishop Caspar served Annam from 1864 to 1907. He was made bishop just three years prior to Wake's arrival. He died at Hué in 1917.

Bui Vien is a celebrated figure in Vietnamese history. He was a Western-educated reformer who tried to modernize and liberalize the rule of the imperial court, and was the first emissary of the empire to the United States. In 1873–75, he visited Washington, D.C. and met with President Grant, requesting closer relations with America. However cordial the visit was, it resulted in no substantive agreements. Some historians refute the importance of Bui Vien's visit, or even that it occurred. The Vietnamese, however, still proudly invoke the name of Bui Vien when speaking of their early history with America.

Regrettably, the Forbidden Purple City is largely unknown today, having been destroyed when the Communists bombed it in 1947 and later occupied it in January 1968. Some areas have been restored, however, and I spent several days exploring the ruins. Fascinating today—it must have been truly amazing when Wake was there. The Cam Chanh Palace still exists, an exquisite place. The Citadel's outer walls and fortresses have been restored and are as impressive as Wake's descriptions. One can understand how the emperors thought themselves secure from attack.

Chapter Twenty-Six—The Gong
Auguste Pavrie comes down through history as a very tough individual. Beyond what Wake reports, Pavrie was subsequently involved in starting the Franco-Siamese War of 1893, which gained Laos for France. He also was a writer, like so many of the men Wake met in Indochina, and published his memoirs—*Mission Pavrie: Indochine 1879–1895*—twenty years later at the turn of the century.

Jules Ruff was yet another remarkable man. He went to Indochina at age twenty, and by the time he met Wake was one of the most influential colonials in the region. When he returned to France in 1900, he was given the award of the Legion of Honor with the ranking of commander.

Francois-Jules Harmand was a French naval surgeon, natural scientist, and diplomat. He was the man more responsible than any other for France's consolidation of power over Vietnam, Cambodia, and Laos. He also served in senior French diplomatic posts in Siam and, subsequent to meeting Wake, in India and

Japan. Many of the prominent of France were personal friends. Quite a man of the world, in 1891 he was involved in tumultuous events in Chile, and again four years later in China and Japan. During Wake's career to 1907, he will come across Harmand several times.

Champeaux's diplomatic career continued, but not for long. In 1887, he was made Resident Superior in Cambodia, where he dealt directly with King Norodom I, who had been forced by the French to sign away sovereignty. Champeaux left Cambodia in 1889 and returned to France, where he died at Marseille the same year.

Rheinart was quite the colonial administrator. He was appointed Chargé d'Affaires of Annam-Tonking three separate times in the 1870s to early 1880s, and the Resident Superior of Vietnam twice in the mid to late 1880s. He died at age sixty-two in 1902.

Chapter Twenty-Seven—No Recourse and No Escape
While researching this project at the Citadel in Hué, I checked the paneled walls of the Cam Chanh Palace for hidden doors but could not find the one Wake refers to in this story. The side building where they met in the cabinet office still exists, as do remnants of the emperor's private palace, the Can Thanh Residence.

Chapter Twenty-Eight—Stone Walls
There is documentation of the unusual celestial alignment Hiep Hoa showed Wake that night, and of the Perseid meteor shower, which occurs annually. Also, the Chinese symbolism of Mars is well known.

Chapter Twenty-Nine—Nguoi chet co tinh cach dang qui trong
Infection and gangrene killed tens of thousands of men during the Civil War who would've survived the initial wound if it had been kept clean. Soldiers and sailors dreaded serious infection, for they knew the only option after that was amputation.

Chapter Thirty—Les Morts Honorés
Admiral Courbet served in Asia for years. His friend and mentor was Admiral Depetit-Thouars, who saved Wake's life at Lima, Peru, in 1881 (described in *A Different Kind of Honor*). At the Battle of Foochow in 1884, Courbet's warships destroyed the Chinese fleet, about half of which was modern and very capable. Still on station in 1885, he died two days after peace was finally signed between China and France. Three ships of the French Navy have since been named after Admiral Courbet. The latest is a frigate, commissioned in 1997.

Lieutenant Louis Marie Julien Viaud had a busy naval career (much of it in the Middle and Far East) that lasted from the mid-1870s until his retirement as a captain in 1910. As impressive as his naval life was, most of France still remembers him by his *nom de plume* of Pierre Loti—one of the premier French novelists of the latter nineteenth century, with forty-two works to his credit. By the time Wake met him in 1883, he already had published five books. He died in 1923.

Chapter Thirty-One—Vengeance
The Harmand Treaty ended Viet Nam's last semblance of independence. Hiep Hoa was deposed on November 28, 1883, and subsequently poisoned and beaten to death by the imperial guard.

Krakatoa had been rumbling for months and was expected to erupt—but no one thought it would explode as it did, causing catastrophic damages locally and influencing world weather for years. "Blue moons" were seen off and on around the world for months after the Krakatoa explosion.

Chapter Thirty-Two—Washington
Norodom's award to Wake—the Royal Order of Cambodia—was initiated in 1864 by Norodom to recognize significant military and civil contributions to the Kingdom of Cambodia. The French later appropriated it as a colonial medal of the empire.

Acknowledgments

This novel was a fascinating project for me. After five months of initial research, I embarked upon a three-month journey, steaming across the Pacific from California to Vietnam. Once there, I ascended the Mekong and Tonle Rivers into central Cambodia, and later spent time at the Perfume River by the ancient imperial capital city of Hué, in Vietnam. I must confess that Indo-China, that mystical land of alluring tranquility and cold barbarity, managed to get deep into my soul. After the trek came another eight months of writing, with continued examinations of historical accounts. Along the way of this grand adventure many people in various countries helped me. Here are some of them.

I am frequently asked about my investigations into the historical events of my novels. On this project, among the most important authors who have my appreciation are these writers and works from around the world—Ambassador Julio A. Jeldres, personal advisor to the King of Cambodia, who wrote *The Royal House of Cambodia*, the definitive work in English on that subject. Michael Buckley's very informative *Vietnam, Cambodia and Laos Handbook* was my guide during journeys on the Mekong, Tonle, and Perfume Rivers. Milton E. Osborne's *The French Presence in Cochinchina and Cambodia—Rule and Response 1850–1905*, and Nicola Cooper's *France in Indochina—Colonial Encounters*, were invaluable for understanding the nineteenth-century history of that area. Ton That Binh's *Life in the Forbidden Purple City* and Nguyen Phuc Vinh Ba's *Stories of the Nguyen Dynasty's Kings* were important sources on the secretive lives of the Vietnamese emperors. Dean Meyers's translation of the original 1872 *The French in Indochina* was insightful to the French mindset leading up to the events of 1883. The eyewitness account of the 1883 attack on Hué written by French naval officer Lieutenant Louis Viaud—known to history by his *nom de plume* as the famous novelist Pierre Loti—was crucial in understanding the French attitude and the hour-by-hour mechanics of the battle. It was translated into English by William Marchant for the June 1898 issue of *The Living Age* magazine. Garnier d'Abain's

1875 description of running the opium concession in Cambodia for *Scribner's Magazine* shed light on that odd topic. Dr. Lewis Chere's *The Diplomacy of the Sino-French War (1883–1885)* explained the diplomatic intrigue in the region. The University of Michigan furnished their reprint of J. Thomson's 1875 memoir, *Ten Years' Travels, Adventures, and Residences Abroad*, an absorbing contemporary view of Indochina and her peoples. Cornell University, as usual, provided outstanding nineteenth-century media views on Asia and the domestic American issues. Monsoon weather and ocean current information was obtained from Stephen Davies and Elaine Morgan's first-rate *Cruising Guide to Southeast Asia, Volume I*.

Frank Emory Bunts' memoirs, *Letters from the Asiatic Station 1881–1883*, provided an insider's look at the life of American naval officers on that far-flung post. Mark Russell Shulman's *Navalism and the Emergence of American Sea Power 1882–1893* is an excellent reference for this intriguing period of naval history. Kelly Erlinger's staff at the U.S. Naval Institute managed to arrange a copy of the January 1883 *Proceedings* report, which contained reports of the Royal Navy's attack on Egypt in 1882. Stephen Roberts' compilation of Theodore Ropp's 1937 *Development of a Modern Navy—French Naval Policy 1871–1904* provided understanding of the French national and naval thinking of the time. Terrell D. Gottschall's *By Order of the Kaiser—Otto von Diederichs and the Rise of the Imperial German Navy 1865–1902* illuminated the German naval presence in Southeast Asia. *The Chinese Steam Navy—1862–1945*, by Richard Wright, supplied the information about China's newly acquired warships in the 1880s. And, of course, many thanks to Randy Briggs and the Pine Island Library staff for obtaining hard-to-get reference works.

But my research includes more than reading th ousands of pages of narrative. I also do "eyeball recon," where I make the voyages, go to the places, and meet the cultures that are in my novels. I am quite fortunate that my global network of reference sources in various fields so often point me in the right direction to find the juicy tidbits of history. In this sort of endeavor, good contacts along the way are critical, not just for research, but for safety.

In Washington, Lonnie Hovey, former White House historical preservationist, has assisted greatly on nineteenth-century Washingtonian topics, as has Jan Herman, historian of the original Naval Observatory. Michael Woodgerd also assisted with historical forays in that imposing city.

In Southeast Asia, Captain Marco San Giacomo, master of the beautiful *Silver Cloud,* took me through two cyclones in the Indian Ocean, the island maze of Indonesia, the remarkable Straits of Malacca, and across the South China Sea to Vietnam so I could start my research trek for this book. The Silver Sea liners are wonderful ways to get around in the world. *Grazie, amico.* Once in Saigon, Hang Tan and Tuan managed to get me seventy-five kilometers across the Mekong Delta to the riverboat at Cai Be on time, barely. *Rat thích!*

There I met with Captain Nguyen Van Bay and Purser Neville Joseph, of the Irrawaddy Flotilla Company's riverboat *Tonle Pandaw,* aboard which I ascended the legendary River of the Nine Dragons—the Mekong—into central Cambodia. My sincerest thanks—*cám on, awkun, chesutimbali*—to them and the entire Vietnamese, Cambodian, and Burmese crew for an incredible journey. The Irrawaddy Flotilla Company has been a renowned part of Indochina since 1865. If you want a memorable experience, steam up the Mekong, Irrawaddy, or Chindwin Rivers aboard one of their vessels.

In Cai Be, Vinh Long, and many villages on the lower Mekong, Mr. Bui Van Hau was a wonderful source of information about river life in the Delta. Hau is one of those persuasive kind of fellows—while explaining the culture of the Delta people, he got me inebriated on cobra wine and afterward managed to drape a giant python around my neck. *Chúc ban may man!*

Upriver, in Phnom Penh, Cambodia, the lovely Ms. Kang Naroam guided me through the spellbinding world of the Royal Palaces, explaining with patience the myriad symbolism of that beautiful site, which means so much to so many in that part of the world. Also in the capital, Mrs. Vishu Shiva has my thanks for showing me around the national museum's extraordinary collection of ancient Cambodiana. *Suh-awt nah. Awkun.*

On the upper Mekong River, deep inside Cambodia, Mr. Kim Boral helped me understand the very complicated history of the Angkorian and Khmer empires, as well as village life on the great stream, much of which hasn't changed for centuries. *Knyom bon troe lop mohk vanh.*

At Siem Reap and Angkor Wat, Mr. Ieng Por Heng, historian, musician, and philosopher, was my guide for three incredible days among the ruins of that amazing civilization. He brought the complicated culture of the Angkorians, which still influences Cambodia, to life for me.

In the imperial city of Hué, Vietnam, and out among villages along the Perfume River, Mr. Hhom Kim Long became my assistant, diligently getting me to various locales I never would've found on my own. *Cám on.*

The extraordinary celestial events in this novel were brought to my attention by my dearest friend, noted amateur astronomer Nancy Glickman. Her research has illuminated similar incidents in my previous novels, to the considerable delight of Peter Wake fans. No matter what the historical locale and year, she always rises to the challenge and amazes me with her discoveries.

Thanks go to June Cussen and Helena Berg for excising my literary gremlins over the years; to the novelists of the Parrot Hillian Writers Circle, Roothee Gabay and Kaydian Wehrle, for their constant support; and to Randy Wayne White for the Vietnamese linguistic help, sage professional advice, and some really decent rum on the porch.

All in all, I am not only blessed to be able to work at something I love, but to do so for the very best audience an author could hope for—my loyal readers around the world, who spread the word with such enthusiasm and make me feel so appreciated. Thank you all so very much.

Onward and upward!
Bob Macomber

Other Books in the Honor Series:

At the Edge of Honor by Robert N. Macomber. This nationally acclaimed naval Civil War novel, the first in the Honor series of naval fiction, takes the reader into the steamy world of Key West and the Caribbean in 1863 and introduces Peter Wake, the reluctant New England volunteer officer who finds himself battling the enemy on the coasts of Florida, sinister intrigue in Spanish Havana and the British Bahamas, and social taboos in Key West when he falls in love with the daughter of a Confederate zealot. (hb, pb)

Point of Honor by Robert N. Macomber. Winner of the Florida Historical Society's 2003 Patrick Smith Award for Best Florida Fiction. In this second book in the Honor series, it is 1864 and Lt. Peter Wake, United States Navy, assisted by his indomitable Irish bosun, Sean Rork, commands the naval schooner *St. James*. He searches for army deserters in the Dry Tortugas, finds an old nemesis during a standoff with the French Navy on the coast of mexico, starts a drunken tavern riot in Key West, and confronts incompetent Federal army officers during an invasion of upper Florida. (hb, pb)

Honorable Mention by Robert N. Macomber. This third book in the Honor series of naval fiction covers the tumultuous end of the Civil War in Florida and the Caribbean. Lt. Peter Wake is now in command of the steamer USS *Hunt,* and quicly plunges into action, chasing a strange vessel during a tropical storm off Cuba, confronting death to liberate an escaping slave ship, and coming face to face with the enemy's most powerful ocean warship in Havana's harbor. Finally, when he tracks down a colony of former Confederates in Puerto Rico, Wake becomes involved in a deadly twist of irony. (hb)

A Dishonorable Few by Robert N. Macomber. Fourth in the Honor series of naval fiction, this historical thriller takes the reader from the Caribbean to the halls of power in Washington, D.C. It is 1869 and the United States is painfully recovering from the Civil War. Lt. Peter Wake heads to turbulent Central America to deal with a former American naval officer turned renegade mercenary. As the action unfolds in

Colombia and Panama, Wake realizes that his most dangerous adversary may be a man on his own ship, forcing Wake to make a decision that will lead to his court-martial in Washington when the mission has finally ended. (hb)

An Affair of Honor by Robert N. Macomber. In this fifth novel in the Honor series, it's December 1873 and Lt. Peter Wake is the executive officer of the USS *Omaha* on patrol in the West Indies. Lonely for his family, he is looking forward to his return to Pensacola—but fate has other plans. He runs afoul of the Royal Navy in Antigua, then he's suddenly sent off on staff assignment to Europe, where he finds himself running for his life after getting embroiled in a Spanish civil war and gets caught up in diplomatic intrigue. The real test comes when he and Sean Rork are sent on a no-win mission in northern Africa. Not the least of his troubles is Madame Catherine Faber de Champlain, wife of a French diplomat; her many charms involve Wake in an affair of honor. (hb)

A Different Kind of Honor by Robert N. Macomber. In this sixth novel in the Honor series, it's 1879 and Lt. Cmdr. Peter Wake, U.S.N., is on assignment as the American naval observer to the War of the Pacific along the west coast of South America. During this mission Wake will witness history's first battle between ocean-going ironclads, ride the world's first deep-diving submarine, face his first machine guns in combat, and run for his life in the Catacombs of the Dead in Lima. (hb)

Other Fiction:

Black Creek: The Taking of Florida by Paul Varnes. This novel is set in the midst of the historical upheaval caused by the Seminole Wars. White settlers Isaac and his son, Isaac Jr., serve as scouts in the Second Seminole War—one of the bloodiest, costliest, and least successful wars in American history. Isaac Jr. is torn between his loyalty to his family and white neighbors, on the one hand, and his unique understanding and appreciation of the Indian way of life, on the other. The characters in *Black Creek* are based on the author's family members a generation before those he used for his first novel, *Confederate Money,* set in Florida during the Civil War. (hb)

Confederate Money by Paul Varnes. Two young men from Florida set out on an adventure during the Civil War to exchange $25,000 in Confederate dollars for silver that will hold its value if the Union wins. Training to be physicians, they get mixed up in some of the war's bloodiest battles, including the largest battle fought in Florida, at Olustee. Along the way, they meet historical characters like Generals Grant and Lee, tangle with criminals, become heroes, and fall in love. (hb)

A Land Remembered by Patrick D. Smith. This well-loved, best-selling novel tells the story of three generations of MacIveys, a Florida family battling the hardships of the frontier, and how they rise from a dirt-poor Cracker life to the wealth and standing of real estate tycoons. (hb, pb)

Nobody's Hero by Frank Laumer. In December of 1835, eight officers and one hundred men of the U.S. Army under the command of Brevet Major Francis Langhorne Dade set out from Fort Brooke at Tampa Bay, Florida, to march north a hundred miles to reinforce Fort King (present-day Ocala). On the sixth day, halfway to their destination, they were attacked by Seminole Indians. Only three wounded soldiers survived what came to be known as Dade's Massacre. Only two of those men managed to struggle fifty miles back to Fort Brooke. One of them, wounded in shoulder and hip, a bullet in one lung, was Pvt. Ransom Clark. This is the story of his incredible journey. (hb)

For God, Gold and Glory: De Soto's Journey to the Heart of La Florida by E.H. Haines. Between 1539 and 1543 Hernando de Soto led an army of six hundred armored men on a desperate journey of almost four thousand miles through the wilds of *La Florida*, facing the problem of hostile natives, inadequate supplies, and the harsh elements, as they left a path of destruction in their search for gold and glory in the name of God. Told from the point of view of de Soto's private secretary, this is a riveting account of the tragic expedition. It's a tale of adventure and survival, of undying faith, unconquerable friendship, and the dark aspects of human nature that greed and power brought to the depths of the unexplored New World. (hb)

For a complete catalog, write to Pineapple Press, P.O. Box 3889, Sarasota, Florida 34230-3889, or call (800) 746-3275. Or visit our website at www.pineapplepress.com.